PRINCE RUPERT

PRINCE RUPERT
Admiral and General-at-Sea

FRANK KITSON

CONSTABLE · LONDON

First published in Great Britain 1998
by Constable and Company Limited
3 The Lanchesters, 162 Fulham Palace Road
London W6 9ER
Copyright © Frank Kitson 1998
The right of Frank Kitson to be identified
as the author of this work has been asserted by him
in accordance with the Copyright, Designs and Patents Act 1988
ISBN 0 09 475800 X
Typeset in Sabon by
Rowland Phototypesetting Limited
Bury St Edmunds, Suffolk
Printed and bound in Great Britain by
St Edmundsbury Press Limited
Bury St Edmunds, Suffolk

A CIP catalogue record for this book
is available from the British Library

TO ELIZABETH

In recognition of thirty-five years
of constant love and support

ACKNOWLEDGEMENTS

I wish to record the immense debt of gratitude that I owe to Richard Ollard for reading my manuscript, chapter by chapter, and for the invaluable advice and support that he has provided throughout the time that I have been writing this book. I fully appreciate my good fortune in having had such a great historian of the seventeenth century with a detailed knowledge of naval affairs to monitor my work. Needless to say, I remain responsible for any conclusions expressed in the book. I would like to express my great appreciation and thanks to Charles Frewer for lending me a mass of documents relating to Prince Rupert which he has collected over many years and for copies of a number of pictures and portraits, some of which appear as illustrations in the book. I would also like to express my gratitude to David Davies, himself the author of an important study of the Restoration navy, for his kindness in providing me with a copy of a most useful paper on the political background to the period.

CONTENTS

LIST OF ILLUSTRATIONS

Between pages 160 and 161

Charles II as a youth. Artist unknown (*by courtesy of the National Portrait Gallery, London*)

The Constant Reformation. By Van de Velde, 1649 (*National Maritime Museum*)

Prince Rupert. By Bouidon, 1654 (*Brunswick Collection*)

Michiel Adrianszoon de Ruyter. By Hendrik Berckman (*National Maritime Museum, Greenwich, London*)

Admiral Sir Thomas Allin. By Sir Godfrey Kneller (*National Maritime Museum, Greenwich, London*)

James Duke of York and Albany. By Sir Peter Lely, *c.*1665 (*by courtesy of The Royal Collection, Her Majesty Queen Elizabeth II*)

Prince Rupert of the Rhine and Duke of Cumberland. By Sir Peter Lely from the Flagmen of Lowestoft series, 1666 (*The Royal Collection, Her Majesty Queen Elizabeth II*)

George Monck, first Duke of Albemarle. By Sir Peter Lely from the Flagmen of Lowestoft series, 1666 (*National Maritime Museum, Greenwich, London*)

Mrs Margaret Hughes. Artist Unknown (*The Hulton Getty Picture Library*)

Sir Robert Holmes. By Sir Peter Lely (*National Maritime Museum, Greenwich, London*)

Battle of the Texel, August 1673; the junction of the Red and Blue squadrons, late afternoon. By Van de Velde the Elder (*National Maritime Museum, Greenwich, London*)

Prince Rupert, a late portrait. By Samuel Cooper (*National Maritime Museum, Greenwich, London*)

LIST OF MAPS

PREFACE

In the second half of the seventeenth century, battle fleets were larger and battles more fiercely contested than is usually realised today. For example, the fleet that Prince Rupert and the Duke of Albemarle commanded against the Dutch in 1666 consisted of over eighty ships of the line manned by 22,000 men – that is to say nearly two and a half times as many men as were in the Royalist army at Naseby. In the first of the two large battles fought in 1666, the number of casualties suffered by both sides, including prisoners, exceeded the entire strength of the Royalist army at Naseby. In the second battle Rupert, with eighty-nine ships of the line, defeated de Ruyter with eighty-eight, inflicting 7,000 casualties on him for the loss of only 350 in his own fleet. By comparison Nelson at Trafalgar commanded twenty-seven ships of the line manned by around 17,000 men when he destroyed the Franco-Spanish fleet of thirty-three ships.

Rupert in 1666 was a few months younger than Nelson was at Trafalgar. Had he been killed in the second of these two battles, he would probably have been remembered as one of the greatest of England's fighting admirals, but fate decreed that he should survive to command the fleet again in 1673, in an unpopular war with an unreliable ally. This time de Ruyter, with an inferior fleet, frustrated Rupert's attempts to fight a decisive battle in the open seas until August. When at last Rupert brought about such an engagement, his French squadron left him in the lurch at a critical moment so that the campaign ended in acrimonious recrimination rather than victory. As a result Rupert, who had performed with good sense and gallantry throughout, and who had preserved his fleet in the face of many disappointments and perils, is remembered, if at all, as a competent if rather cautious admiral. Nothing could be further from the truth.

This book takes up the story of Prince Rupert from the point when his career as an army officer came to an end in 1647. It is therefore a sequel to *Prince Rupert: Portrait of A Soldier* and its purpose is to examine his work as an admiral, then sometimes known as a general-at-sea.

When Rupert first took charge of the Royalist fleet at the end of 1648, the Commonwealth government was firmly established in England. For the next four and a half years he kept the Royalist flag flying in the approaches to the Channel, the Mediterranean, the Atlantic and the Caribbean, with no base, harried by Parliamentary commanders such as Blake, Ayscue and Penn and subjected to the violence of the elements as well as the enemy. It was a tremendous achievement and an illustration of endurance and courage of epic proportions, even though it did little to advance the Royalist cause at the time.

After the Restoration Rupert returned to England, where until his death twenty-two years later he played a prominent role in the country as a first cousin of King Charles II. Throughout this time he was a member of the government and a leading figure in the business of exploring and exploiting recently discovered territories in Africa and Canada. At times during the second and third Dutch Wars he was, as mentioned, commander-in-chief of the fleet and took part in some of the most heavily contested battles in naval history. After the resignation of the Duke of York as Lord High Admiral in 1673, Rupert became First Lord of the commission set up to carry on the work of the Admiralty, a post that he held for the next six years.

Although much has been written about the Dutch Wars and the navy of the period, and although Rupert's activities are naturally mentioned in this context, no attempt has been made to carry out a systematic analysis of his ability as an admiral. Most of Rupert's biographers have covered his naval life only in outline as an addendum to his short but brilliant career as commander of the King's armies in the first Civil War. It is therefore desirable that an attempt be made to fill this gap.

In his private life Rupert was active in the field of science and art and was an early member of the Royal Society. His passion for country sports never left him, hunting with hounds and shooting being woven into the fabric of his being. He did not marry but was never short of feminine company. After the Restoration he had two long-term attachments, each of which produced a child on whom he lavished care and affection.

As with my earlier book about Prince Rupert, I do not claim to have unearthed any startling new material; equally, I have not attempted to justify with a reference every statement made. But when I have written something that could be regarded as controversial, I have indicated where the facts on which I based it came from. The bibliography is merely a list of the books and papers mentioned in the references and is not designed as a comprehensive reading list.

1

1648

At THE START of the year 1648 Prince Rupert was twenty-eight years old and living at the court of the exiled Queen Henrietta Maria on the outskirts of Paris. He was immensely tall and powerful, and he was recovering well from a bullet wound to the head that he had received four months earlier when fighting with the French army against Spain along the borders of the Spanish Netherlands. In addition to this injury he was still getting over the strains and stresses of the English Civil War, during which time he had driven himself to the limits of his endurance. In the past ten years he had changed from being a graceful youth into a hard, lean and handsome man. He had learned to control his violent temper to a limited extent, and he was even prepared to listen to other people's views with more sympathy than had formerly been the case. All the same he was a person more likely to inspire respect than affection.

By his exploits in the Civil War Rupert had won the admiration and devotion of many of his former officers, some of whom were now in exile on the Continent, while others were back at home in England resentful of their conquerors and dreaming of former glories and of better days to come. Rupert's own fame was such that to this day it overshadows his many later achievements.

But he had not won such laurels without making enemies among those Royalists who were either jealous of his success or who found the strength of his personality and the speed at which he worked unnerving, or who disagreed fundamentally with his ideas. Some of these people were now at St-Germain, where the hothouse atmosphere of the court encouraged the growth of factions. The interplay of these groups combined with the jealousies and frustration of exile must have weighed more heavily on Rupert than the memory of his past successes.

There was also a pressing need for him to find work so that he could support himself and his immediate followers. Although few soldiers in Europe had a reputation higher than his own, there were difficulties about his employment. On being released from his long imprisonment in 1641, he had sworn never again to take up arms against the Emperor, which restricted the circumstances in which he could be employed by France. The fact that he was a Calvinist also limited the commands likely to be offered him by Spain or by the Emperor himself. Above all, his commitment to his uncle, King Charles I, meant that he did not want to get too involved elsewhere in case an opportunity for renewing the struggle with the English Parliament presented itself.

In the event Rupert did not have long to wait for employment, but when it came he found himself fighting at sea rather than on land. It is not necessary to discuss events nation by nation in order to understand the background against which Rupert's career as an admiral unfolded during the remaining thirty-five years of his life, but a short description of the situation that existed in 1648, particularly in France, the United Provinces and England, will avoid later distraction. And one of the most significant ways in which Europe was developing was that sea power was becoming important to an increasing number of countries. A brief survey of the maritime scene will therefore also be necessary.

The Thirty Years War started in 1618 as a dispute between the new Habsburg Emperor Ferdinand II, who was also King of Bohemia, and the Bohemian people, who decided that they would prefer to have Rupert's father, the Elector of the Palatinate, as their king. The dispute spread into a general conflagration between the Roman Catholic and the Protestant states of the Empire, with outside countries making contributions designed to forward their own interests. The most dramatic of these incursions was that of the Swedish King Gustavus Adolphus, who set himself up as the Protestant champion and at one time almost forced the Emperor to his knees, but the pressure eased when Gustavus was killed and the Emperor subsequently regained much of the ground that had been lost. Throughout this long period of strife the main losers were the people of the many small states involved, who were subjected to famine and pestilence in the wake of the warring armies. One of the worst affected was the Palatinate itself, which lost nine out of ten of its population.

But amid disaster there were some who gained; of these the greatest was France. At the start of the conflict France was in a state of turmoil from which it was rescued by Cardinal Richelieu, who virtually ruled the country on behalf of King Louis XIII from 1624. His first task was to establish and maintain stability at home, but he was always conscious of the fact that the country was hemmed in on its eastern flank mainly by the Empire and on its northern and southern flank by the Habsburg King of Spain, who also held some of the provinces along France's eastern border. Richelieu's second concern was therefore to extend France's eastern border towards the Rhine and the northern border into the Spanish Netherlands (an area which is now occupied by Belgium, Luxemburg and parts of northern France). The first of these objectives mainly involved gaining concessions in return for help given first to one ruler and then to another: in particular, France used its influence to support the Protestant Gustavus Adolphus at one stage and the Roman Catholic Elector of Bavaria at another. The second involved weakening the power of Spain and attacking its possessions in the Spanish Netherlands, sometimes in conjunction with the Protestant United Provinces (the present Netherlands), which had themselves broken away from the Spanish Netherlands during the last quarter of the previous century.

In addition to these two main strands of policy, Richelieu realised that France would need to become a great sea power in order to safeguard its growing foreign trade, to weaken Spain and to guard itself against its traditional enemy, England.[1] But building up an effective navy with all its support would take a long time and a vast amount of money. Although Richelieu and his successors stuck doggedly to the achievement of this aim, it was many years before their foresight and energy bore fruit.

When Richelieu died in 1642, followed shortly afterwards by the death of Louis XIII, his policy was, in its essentials, continued by Cardinal Mazarin and Louis's widow, Anne of Austria, who was regent for the five-year-old Louis XIV. Anne of Austria was sister to Philip IV of Spain, another sister being married to Ferdinand III, who had succeeded his father as Emperor in 1637. Cardinal Mazarin was an Italian. It is worth recording that the Empress had used her influence to secure the release of Prince Rupert from captivity in 1641 and that Anne of Austria provided him with employment in the French army in 1646.

France's hostility towards Spain had an important bearing on the future of the United Provinces in that it finally removed the possibility of Spain regaining control over them. Spain was not strong enough in the Spanish Netherlands to launch a major attack in the north while defending itself in the south against France, but it continued to harass the United Provinces when it could, especially as the United Provinces' control over the Schelde Estuary meant that much of the wealth that had formerly come to Antwerp was passing through Dutch and even English ports.

Power in the United Provinces was shared between the Stadt-holder, who was a prince of the House of Orange Nassau, and the Grand Pensionary, who was the leading politician in the States General, a body composed of representatives of the seven provinces. Throughout the Thirty Years War three Stadtholders in succession held unchallenged power. The first of the three was Prince Maurice of Nassau, son of William the Silent, founder of the republic. He was followed at his death by his brother, Prince Frederick Henry, who was in turn followed at his death just before the end of the war by his son Prince William, whose wife was the daughter of King Charles I of England.

The United Provinces owed their existence at least partly to the support they had received from England in the early days of their existence. Although during the reign of James I, when he was pursuing a policy of peace with Spain, this support was less open than it had been during the reign of Queen Elizabeth, it remained important and a significant part of the Stadtholder's military strength derived from English and Scottish regiments stationed in the United Provinces. But as the danger from Spain receded, the United Provinces, in particular the maritime prov-inces of Holland and Zealand, greatly extended their seafaring activities around the coasts of Western Europe[2] and in more distant parts of the world, such as India, Ceylon and South-east Asia, where their East India Company gained a near monopoly of trade by the establishment of trading posts and colonies. The United Provinces also traded with the New World through their West India Company, though with no monopoly in this area. In all of this they inevitably competed with English interests, a fact that was aggravated by competition in the North Sea fishing grounds.

A certain irritation therefore crept into relations between the United Provinces and its greatest benefactor and ally, England. Indeed, on two occasions – in 1630 and again in 1634 – Charles I entered into negotiation with Spain in an attempt to carve up the United Provinces between them,[3] despite the fact that as recently as 1625 the Dutch had provided warships to fight with the British fleet in its attack on Cadiz. Although these negotiations came to nothing, King Charles constantly harried the Dutch at sea, demanding salutes from their ships and levies for fishing in English and Scottish waters.

In summary it may be said that the basic conditions brought about by the Thirty Years War which would influence events to the end of Rupert's life were all in place by 1648, although it would have taken a far-sighted person to discern them. The weakening of Spain gave the Dutch a short-term advantage at sea that led to hostility with England, but in the long term the rise of France, filling the power vacuum left by the Habsburgs, produced a threat that brought them together again in defence of their interests and, in the case of the Dutch, of their territory. Prince Rupert himself played a leading part in the conflict between the English and the Dutch and an even greater part in alerting England to the growing threat from France. This at one time caused him to give some support to those opposing the government, thus causing a future historian to hail him as the first Whig!

In England itself the Thirty Years War made less impact than it did on the Continent. When Charles I succeeded his father in 1625, England's pro-Spanish policy was replaced briefly by friendship with France and the mounting of the expedition against Cadiz. It was at this time that King Charles married the French King's sister, Henrietta Maria. But this was soon followed by expeditions to help French Protestants against their own King, which in turn gave way to a period when external military involvement was ruled out by the King's need to economise while he ruled without Parliament between 1629 and 1640. Although the King's dispute with his other kingdom of Scotland ultimately obliged him to recall Parliament, it did not enable him to exert any more influence on European affairs. On the contrary, the dispute led directly to the outbreak of the Civil War in England in the summer of 1642.

The causes of this war and the land operations in which Prince Rupert played such an active part and which mainly determined its outcome have no place in this book. Suffice it to say that by the middle of 1646 Parliament was completely victorious, the King having surrendered himself to the Scottish army and the Prince of Wales having fled to France. A brief account of the naval operations that took place is given below, but before turning to them it is necessary to look briefly at the ships that sailed the oceans at this time.

Originally, warships were designed to run alongside enemy warships so that soldiers on board could engage in battle with swords, spears and arrows as if they were on land. Such ships carried large castles fore and aft from which archers could fire down into the ranks of those waiting on the decks of the enemy ships. The advent of gunpowder resulted in the mounting of small brass guns designed for defence and to cause casualties to the enemy as the ships of each side closed with one another. But in the first half of the sixteenth century the English devised the idea of an artillery duel to damage and if possible to sink the enemy ships as an alternative to boarding them. To do this they mounted in their ships a number of much heavier guns, including some of the newly developed iron guns. King Philip II of Spain was impressed by the power of the English guns used in Drake's attack on Cadiz in 1587 and hastily collected together as many as he could to arm the ships with which he was preparing to invade England the following year. The different conclusions drawn from the progress of the Spanish Armada by England and by the United Provinces governed the way in which warship design developed during the next half-century.

In the Armada's progress up the Channel the English were careful to keep their distance from the Spanish ships, being wary of their very heavy guns. Only after the Armada had been broken up by fireships at Calais were the English prepared to isolate individual Spanish ships and tackle them with superior numbers. Even then none was sunk directly by fire, although many were damaged severely. In practice the English need not have been so cautious, as the Spanish guns were badly mounted and some even blew up because of faulty design or workmanship. None the less the conclusion drawn in England was that warships should be armed with even larger and more powerful guns.

The Dutch, on the other hand, took the view that as neither side had managed to defeat the other with heavy guns, the best results would be gained by reducing the weight of guns carried in order to get greater speed. They planned to carry only enough guns to cripple their opponents by damaging masts and sails so that they could draw alongside and board in the old-fashioned way.[4] To get better speed the Dutch abandoned the tradition of building ships in three parts with bulkheads between each, replacing them with decks that ran the whole length of the ship, although there would still be one or more extra decks in the forecastle and poop. Their ships became longer in relation to their width, and the ships sailed better as a result. During the first half of the seventeenth century ships built in this way were described as being frigate built. Size was not then the criterion, although later, when all warships were being constructed in this way, only the smaller ones were described as frigates.

In working out how to increase the number and weight of guns in a ship the English independently came to the conclusion that the continuous deck from stem to stern was needed, if only to be rid of the joints that were likely to suffer damage from the recoil effect of a broadside. Too many heavy guns on upper decks might also destabilise the ship in heavy weather, so the height of both the poop and the forecastle was reduced.[5] These decisions were taken in time to affect the design of ships built from 1618 onwards, and most of the English ships operating in 1648 were built either around then, or in the second half of the 1630s.

At the start of the Civil War in 1642 the English navy consisted of twenty-six powerful warships, later known as ships of the first, second and third rates, together with nine more of the fourth, fifth and sixth rates. Although, technically, rating, when it was introduced in 1653, would refer to the captain's pay, this itself depended on the size of the crew, which in turn depended largely on the number of guns carried.[6] Rating was therefore more relevant as a measure of a ship's armament than of her captain's pay, and it is in this context that the term is generally used. In 1648 ships of the first rate had three gun-decks and those of the third and fourth rates had two. Second-rate ships, such as the *Constant Reformation*, were somewhere in between, having two full gun-decks and additional guns in the waist and on the quarterdeck, which virtually turned them into three-deckers.[7] Some lightly armed ships with two or one gun-decks were also built for scouting and escort work; these were the fifth- and sixth-rate ships.

In the same way that an army had many different sizes of artillery pieces, so a ship had many different guns. These ranged from the cannon firing a forty-two-pound shot, through demi-cannon (thirty-two pounds), culverin (eighteen pounds) and demi-culverin (nine pounds), to the saker (six pounds). The mix of guns in a ship also varied greatly and often included some brass pieces which, being more expensive, were often reserved for flagships. For example, one second-rate ship carried twenty-two cannon, twenty-six culverins and twenty-four demi-culverins, while another carried twenty-two demi-cannon, twenty-eight culverins and sixteen demi-culverins. There seemed to be no fixed pattern of armament for any rate of ship, which took on board whatever was available. The number and size of guns increased steadily during the first half of the seventeenth century. The size of a ship's company also varied greatly, from about 500 or more in a first-rate ship to about 175 in a fourth-rate ship.[8]

In addition to guns and men, warships had to carry spare sails and spars, ammunition for the guns and enough food and drink to keep the ship at sea for weeks at a time. This meant that every inch of space on board was valuable. In particular, living room for the sailors was cramped, with perhaps 300 men eating and sleeping on two gun-decks where the headroom seldom exceeded five and a half feet; the need to keep the overall height of the hull down in the interests of stability precluded more headroom being provided. Warrant-officers, such as the master's mate, boatswain, surgeon, etc., had to have more room and the few officers still more, all of which increased over-crowding on the gun-decks.

Life was therefore very different in a warship from that experienced in a merchant vessel, which required fewer sailors because there were few, if any, guns to man. Sometimes a mer-chantman sailing through an area infested with pirates or priva-teers would carry more guns, but the crew would never be large enough to keep the guns in action for long. Usually a broadside would be fired as a deterrent, but reloading more than a few weapons was seldom attempted. None the less the larger mer-chant ships were mostly constructed in such a way that guns could be carried, and they were therefore capable of being converted to warships at short notice. In times of emergency this was the quickest way of expanding the fleet.

Navigation in the middle of the seventeenth century was still a relatively unsophisticated procedure, although arrangements to distinguish magnetic from true north introduced in the 1630s constituted a considerable advance. Basically, calculations were made either by astral observation, as in the days of antiquity, or by relating the course shown on the compass to the ship's speed worked out by the use of a log line and a sandglass. This could be supplemented in shallow water by establishing depth by means of a lead line and comparing it with a chart, if one existed, and by taking compass bearings on landmarks if in sight of land. The main difficulties arose from the lack of reliable charts and from the inaccuracy of sandglasses as timekeepers. Other timepieces then in existence were virtually useless at sea because of instability and humidity. The advent of the chronometer, which revolutionised navigation, was still nearly a century into the future.

In summary it can be said that life at sea was hard and perilous to a degree seldom experienced ashore, but great progress had been made in ship design, gunnery and navigation in the sixty years that had elapsed since the launching of the Spanish Armada. In all of these advances England had been well to the fore, as would shortly be demonstrated in the Dutch Wars. It is now necessary to look at the history of the English navy of the 1630s and 1640s.

The English navy of the 1630s had, as described, some good, modern ships commanded by competent officers, but the shortage of money caused by the King's having ruled for so long without Parliament meant that the men's pay was often in arrears and the ships themselves inadequately victualled and equipped. The resulting discontent, added to the fact that many naval officers were Presbyterians, meant that when the break between King and Parliament came in 1642 the fleet followed the Lord High Admiral, the Earl of Northumberland, and his deputy, the Earl of Warwick, into the Parliamentary camp. At this time members of both houses of Parliament were claiming to be the King's loyal supporters, anxious only to free him from his evil councillors and to get him to govern in conjunction with them. This was certainly the way in which most naval officers regarded the situation.

Before the outbreak of war the navy's job had been to secure the country and its shipping from attacks by foreigners. Now two further tasks were added. The first was to prevent Royalist supporters overseas from getting supplies of arms and warlike stores into the country; the second was to prevent the garrisons of Parliament-held ports, such as Hull and Plymouth, from being overrun by Royalists. It was immediately clear that the fleet, which had been designed to carry out only the first task, was too small to undertake the extra commitments arising from the Civil War. The only way to increase its capability quickly was to requisition and arm merchant ships. Warwick set about this task at once and twenty-four were soon operational.

During the next few months a number of actions took place at sea which reduced the supplies getting through to the Royalists but which failed to cut the supply line altogether. The most celebrated incident concerned the efforts made by Warwick's vice-admiral, William Batten, to prevent the Queen from getting herself and a convoy of arms from Holland to England. At her first attempt she and her escort of Dutch ships were forced back by a storm, but in February 1643 she reached the English coast at Bridlington Bay in Yorkshire, where she was fired on by Batten's ships as she disembarked.

When Prince Rupert captured Bristol in July 1643 he not only made himself master of the second city in the kingdom but also took possession of the shipping in the port, which included one small warship and eight large armed merchant ships together with numerous smaller vessels. Sir John Pennington, who was appointed admiral of the Royalist fleet, soon added a further ten armed merchantmen to them, after which he continued to make further ships ready for war. This greatly complicated Warwick's problems.

Another complication from Warwick's point of view arose in September 1643, when the King's representative in Ireland, the Earl of Ormonde, patched up a truce with the Kilkenny Confederacy, which exercised broad control over most of the Irish rebels. This reduced the military commitment in Ireland, enabling Ormonde to dispatch a number of regiments to England to join the Royalist army. Warwick was now faced with the problem of intercepting these troops as they crossed the Irish Sea.

By the end of 1643 a rapid building programme had increased the number of small warships available to Warwick, but by the same token the Royalists had got hold of more small craft and transports to move the men from Ireland. Warwick was obliged to split his fleet into a number of squadrons to carry out his varied commitments – a squadron to support operations along the south coast, for instance, a large squadron to intercept troops from Ireland, a squadron in the region of the Thames Estuary and one in the north-east to interfere with movement to and from the Royalist-controlled ports of the area. In accordance with the custom of the times, each of these squadrons would have its own admiral, vice-admiral and rear-admiral in the same way as each little army had its own general, lieutenant-general of horse and major-general of foot.

In passing, it is worth noticing that the term admiral referred to the appointment and did not denote rank in the present sense of the word. Admirals were usually colonels, majors or captains, and when their names were used they would be referred to as such (unless they were peers or knights). The term admiral, vice-admiral or rear-admiral was also used to refer to an admiral's flagship. Captain was the basic rank of command and was usually held by those commanding a troop of horse, a company of foot or a ship.

Early in 1644 when the Scots, allied to Parliament, invaded England, the Royalists lost control of the ports in the north-east. This allowed Warwick, whom Parliament had by now appointed Lord High Admiral, to redirect the ships that had been employed in this area. In the late summer of 1644 he was concerned mainly with supporting the advance of the Earl of Essex's army into Cornwall. When the King's army, following close behind, bottled up Essex around Lostwithiel, the fleet was its only hope. But contrary winds kept it away and the Parliamentary army had to surrender.

By the end of 1644 Parliament had largely recovered and in 1645 went from strength to strength, first destroying the King's main army at Naseby in June and then recapturing Bristol in September. The only ports of any consequence still left in Royalist hands were Chester and Falmouth, both of which fell in 1646.

Warwick and his fleet had played an important part in Parliament's victory, but Warwick himself had by this time been obliged to resign as Lord High Admiral as a result of the self-denying ordinance. Instead, he became the chairman of a Parliamentary commission set up to execute the office of the Lord High Admiral, which greatly reduced his influence in the fleet, now commanded by William Batten.

Although during the Civil War there had been no significant battles at sea, Parliamentary ships had been involved in a surprising variety of operations. They had mounted some small blockades in order to prevent particular ships or groups of ships from leaving port, as for example the watch Batten kept on Scheveningen in January 1643, when the Queen was trying to get to England, and again on Falmouth in July 1644, when she was trying to escape to France. In both cases she got through, as also did the Prince of Wales when he escaped to the Isles of Scilly in March 1646. Parliament's ships had been more successful at ensuring the security of Plymouth, which they saved from capture both by supplying the population with food and by breaking up attacks mounted from across the Tamar Estuary. They also saved Lyme in 1644 and Weymouth in 1645. They had mixed success in supporting Parliamentary commanders in the field, having a good record in the British Channel and South Wales and also in carrying a body of horse out of the besieged city of Hull in the summer of 1643, thereby enabling it to fight elsewhere. The navy failed in a much more important operation designed to support the advance of Essex's army in Cornwall in August 1644.

But however the balance sheet is totted up, there can be no doubt that the navy and its commanders had gained a great deal of experience with particular reference to the logistic problems involved in operating fleets. This would stand England in good stead over the next twenty-five years, when so much of its fighting would be carried on at sea.

The chain of events following the end of the Civil War in 1646 which turned the King's best general, Prince Rupert, into an admiral was highly complex. The King himself had been moved from pillar to post since leaving Oxford to join the Scottish army at Newark in April 1646. Although the Scots had treated him with all due ceremony and respect, they had kept him secluded from his friends while they tried to reach an agreement with him designed to promote their interests in Scotland and England. In January 1647 they finally came to the conclusion that they would gain no lasting advantage from any such arrangement and handed him over to the English Parliament in exchange for money owed them for their keep in England. Parliament moved the King to Holmby House near Northampton, where he was allowed freedom to hunt and receive friends but otherwise treated him in much the same way.

By the middle of 1647 Parliament was in dispute with its army over its plans to disband units without proper pay settlements and without passing an act of indemnity for actions carried out in the Civil War. These issues were bedevilled by the wider differences that existed between the dominant Presbyterian faction in Parliament and the Independents, who mainly influenced the army. The matter was complicated by the fact that an extreme faction among the Independents in the army was making it difficult for the moderate Independents to reach agreement with Parliament. In order to strengthen their hand, an officer of this militant group forcibly removed the King from the custody of Parliament in early June and took him to army headquarters at Newmarket. The army then moved on London, housing the King at Hampton Court shortly afterwards.

The army allowed the King much more freedom than had the Scots or Parliament, and he was soon joined by two Royalists from France, Sir John Berkeley and John Ashburnham, and by Prince Rupert's close friend Will Legge, who as well as being a gallant soldier was one of the King's Gentlemen of the Bedchamber. The King was also permitted to visit the three of his children held by Parliament and to receive visits from his cousin and friend, the Duke of Richmond.

During this period the generals, usually Cromwell and Ireton, entered into discussions with the King in an attempt to get him to approve the proposals that the army wanted to put before Parliament. The army's quarrel with Parliament over disbandments and the act of indemnity had now turned into a major disagreement about the way in which the country should be governed. Both sides needed the King's agreement as neither yet contemplated doing away with the monarchy.

Although the King appeared to get on well with Cromwell and Ireton on a personal basis, he was not prepared to endorse their proposals which in any case were opposed by a significant faction in the army itself. This faction wanted a far more radical form of government than that favoured by Parliament or the generals, and in discussion with the King Cromwell told him that his rooms for manoeuvre was being boxed in by these extremists, who were hostile to both King and Parliament. Eventually, the King, alarmed by the increasing militancy of the radical faction, escaped from Hampton Court in November. Sir Philip Warwick, one of the King's attendants at the time, suggested that the escape was engineered and connived at by Cromwell himself as a means of undoing the King when he realised that the King would not back the army against Parliament.[9]

While the King was in hiding, Ashburnham unwisely arranged for him to put himself under the protection of the governor of the Isle of Wight whereon the governor kept him as close a prisoner in Carisbrooke Castle as he had formerly been at Hampton Court. The governor did, however, allow some of his principal advisers from the Civil War days, such as the Marquis of Hertford, to join him so as to speed up and facilitate future negotiations. The King for his part reopened negotiations with the Scots who, like the King, were becoming frightened by the increasing militancy of the Independents in Parliament and in the army. They were therefore prepared to offer the King a better deal than they had done when he was their prisoner ten months earlier. This time the dominant faction in Scotland, led by the Duke of Hamilton and known as Engagers to distinguish them from Argyll's more extreme Covenanters, undertook to send an army to restore him to his rights providing that he would agree to establish the Presbyterian Church in England for a trial period of three years. It was also suggested that, if the safety of the Prince of Wales could be guaranteed, he should go to Scotland to help unite the country behind Hamilton and his friends.

At the same time as these arrangements were being made, the situation started to improve in Ireland. Sixteen forty-six had been a bad year because the confederates repudiated the treaty that had been negotiated by the Earl of Ormonde to prolong the wartime truce. They did this under the influence of the papal nuncio, who had persuaded them that they could now get better concessions for Roman Catholics from the King than those they had negotiated with Ormonde, because the King's condition had further deteriorated. But the effect of this ill-judged move was, first, to alarm the Irish Protestants and those Roman Catholics loyal to the King and, second, to cause Cardinal Mazarin to withdraw France's offer of help against Parliament's army.

Ormonde, who was no longer strong enough to contain the rebels, had nowhere to turn for help and reluctantly handed Dublin over to Parliament as the only authority capable of preserving the country from another appalling massacre.

But circumstances change fast in Ireland, and in 1647 the confederates who had repudiated the treaty were ousted from the leadership by those who felt that only an alliance with the Royalists could save them from being overrun by Parliamentary forces. Even some of Parliament's own supporters, such as Lord Inchiquin in Munster, were worried by the direction that events were taking in London and opened negotiations with Ormonde. Early in 1648 Ormonde himself appeared at St-Germain, followed shortly afterwards by representatives of the Confederacy, with an offer to raise an army to recover Ireland for the King. Like the Scots, they suggested that the Prince of Wales should return with them to Ireland to lead the army.

Early in 1648 it became clear that a favourable situation from the Royalists' point of view was developing in England as well as in Scotland and Ireland. The first resistance to the authority of Parliament occurred in South Wales, where troops failed to disband when ordered to do so. They took possession of a number of strongpoints and, joined by local people, outnumbered a small force sent by Fairfax, the Parliamentary commander-in-chief, to enforce the disbandment. They then declared for the King.

At the same time riots and demonstrations took place in London, Cheshire, Lancashire and North Wales. In April Sir Marmaduke Langdale, who had made a name for himself in the Civil War as the commander of the Northern Horse, captured Berwick, and shortly afterwards Sir Philip Musgrave took Carlisle. But these uprisings, together with one in Norwich at the end of April, were uncoordinated and did not yet constitute a serious threat to Parliament's power. Only the outbreak in South Wales constituted an uprising, and at the end of the month Fairfax dispatched Cromwell with a relatively small detachment of the New Model Army to restore the situation.

At the end of April the fifteen-year-old Duke of York, who was one of the King's three children held by Parliament, escaped from St James's Palace dressed as a girl. Early in May, guided by Colonel Bampfield, who had engineered his escape, he arrived at

The Hague, where he was taken in by his sister and her husband, the Prince of Orange.

Meanwhile, discontent was rife in the fleet. In August 1647 Batten, who was a Presbyterian, had been relieved of his command because it was correctly thought that he was unreliable from the army's point of view. A few months later he was replaced by an army colonel called Rainsborough, a republican and a man sympathetic to the Levellers, who was also the leader of the extreme militant faction in the army. It may be that one of the reasons for this appointment was to get him away from the army so that Fairfax and Cromwell could more easily gain control of the dissident faction, but in fact he was a far greater danger in the fleet, where most of the captains were moderate Presbyterians and opposed to the Independents, whether moderate or extreme. Rainsborough, who had at least commanded a warship in the early stages of the Civil War, was a tall, eloquent but thoroughly objectionable man. He was soon at loggerheads with his captains, who finally refused to obey him and put him ashore. Faced with the danger of the fleet deserting to the Royalists, Parliament reinstated Warwick as Lord High Admiral, but when he arrived in the Downs just south of the Thames Estuary the sailors refused to accept him. Summoning Batten to his assistance, he went to Portsmouth to try to gain control of the squadron there, which he succeeded in doing, but meanwhile on 10 June ten ships lying in the Downs sailed for Helvoetsluys in Holland. For the most part the warrant-officers rather than the commissioned officers instigated this move, and all but three of the captains left their ships before they sailed.[10]

By this time further uprisings had occurred, in Kent and Essex, which Fairfax was trying to put down. As a result it was decided that the Prince of Wales should definitely not go to Ireland but that he should move to The Hague, where he would be best placed to exploit events in England or Scotland. Ormonde was sent back to Ireland to make a treaty with the confederates.

At this time St-Germain, on the outskirts of Paris, where Queen Henrietta Maria held her court, was full of English Royalists who had fled the country at the end of the first Civil War. In addition to the Queen and Prince Rupert, the Prince of Wales was there together with a host of disgruntled exiles such as

Lords Wilmot, Percy, Gerard, Culpepper and Digby. Other leading Royalists such as Hopton were in Rouen, whereas Hyde, who had declined to accompany the Prince of Wales to France the previous year, was still in Jersey where the Prince had spent some months after leaving the Isles of Scilly.

While still at Hampton Court, the King had written to Prince Rupert to say how much he valued his past services and to assure him that he would look after him better than any but his own children. He also wrote that he would take the first available opportunity to employ him or have him about his person. He concluded by saying that he had only just heard about his wound and that he was glad of his recovery from it. With the return of his strength, Rupert himself had resumed his favourite occupation of hunting, which he interspersed with the social life of the exiled court and the nearby court of France.

Rupert also endeavoured to settle accounts left over from the Civil War with Lord Digby, who as the King's Secretary of State during the war had so greatly wronged him. He challenged him to a duel, but in this he was thwarted by Henrietta Maria and the Prince of Wales, who arrested the contestants as they were about to fight and demanded that they should patch up their quarrel. This they did to such good effect that shortly afterwards Digby defended Prince Rupert's honour in a duel with Wilmot. A few months later Rupert fought Lord Percy, whom he suspected of denigrating his honour, but thereafter lost interest in avenging past wrongs, which was just as well since developments in England were about to recall him to a wider stage than the environs of Paris.

On 29 June 1648 the Prince of Wales left St-Germain for Calais, going from there by ship to The Hague accompanied by Prince Rupert and the old Earl of Brentford who, as Lord Forth, had been the Royalist Lord General in the early years of the Civil War before Rupert took over from him. With them went Culpepper, Hopton and Wilmot. A message was sent to Edward Hyde in Jersey to join the Prince of Wales as soon as possible.

Soon after their arrival, the young Duke of York was sent to visit the ships in port at Helvoetsluys, where he found that the crews were enthusiastic in their support of the King. It was quickly decided that the Prince of Wales should take command of these ships and put to sea with Lord Willoughby of Parham as his vice-admiral. On the face of it Lord Willoughby of Parham was a strange choice for the post of vice-admiral, especially as he had no previous naval experience. During the Civil War he had been one of the founders of the Eastern Association and had fought for Parliament without much distinction until Cromwell, who was then one of his subordinates, engineered his dismissal. As a moderate Presbyterian he had, like Batten, incurred the distrust of the Independents in Parliament and had been imprisoned briefly in 1647, after which he had removed himself to Holland. He owed his position as vice-admiral to the Duke of York who had, before the Prince of Wales's arrival, placed him in command of the squadron. Despite his lack of experience, someone had to look after the ships and, as a Presbyterian nobleman who had formerly fought for Parliament, he seemed a good person to gain the support of those who, like himself, had switched their allegiance. He did not retain his position for long.

2

FROM GENERAL TO ADMIRAL

ON HIS ARRIVAL at The Hague Prince Rupert was joined by his younger brother, Prince Maurice, and together with a number of courtiers they accompanied Prince Charles on board the *Satisfaction*, a lightly armed but modern vessel that Charles had chosen as his flagship. By this time Royalist officers had been appointed to command most of the ships that had arrived without their captains and to fill other vacant officer posts. The Duke of York was left behind, much to his disgust, to ensure that there would be at least one royal prince for the Royalists to rally around should the Prince of Wales be killed or captured during the ensuing operations. The fleet, now twelve strong, sailed on 17 July 1648.

It is clear from contemporary accounts that, from the time he left St-Germain, Rupert was in excellent spirits. And this was fortunate for Prince Charles, as no one else in his entourage had such a firm grasp of the strategic and political factors governing the way in which events were developing in England. Although Rupert had no direct experience of sea warfare, he had during the Civil War been closely involved in directing the operations of the Royalist ships, particularly those transporting soldiers from Ireland. This would have given him an insight into the problems of providing them with secure ports and of replenishing them with food, powder and stores such as timber, rope and canvas. He would also have had plenty of opportunity for assessing the way in which naval squadrons affected the development of military operations, with particular reference to his own campaigns in Cheshire and Lancashire in 1644 and in the south-west in 1645.

As the little fleet headed out to sea, the Prince of Wales, at that time a great admirer of his cousin, would certainly have depended more on Prince Rupert than on his vice-admiral, but he would also have to listen to the advice of plenty of other people. Of these, Lords Wilmot and Percy were almost automatically hostile to Rupert, while Lord Culpepper, whose temper was uncertain, was sometimes incapable of controlling himself when confronted by the clarity and certainty of Rupert's opinions. On the other hand the seventy-five-year-old Earl of Brentford could be relied on to support Rupert, as could Lord Hopton. The Royalist Attorney-General, Sir Edward Herbert, was another of Rupert's supporters.

The situation that existed when the fleet left port was by no means hopeless from the Royalist point of view. One week earlier the Duke of Hamilton had marched south from Carlisle with an army of 10,000 foot and 4,000 horse. Cromwell, who finally extinguished the revolt in South Wales on 11 July, was moving north to meet him with a much weaker but better-trained force. Fairfax, who had suppressed most of the disturbances in Kent and around London, had a large part of his army tied down besieging the Royalists in Colchester. If the Royalist fleet could throw its weight behind either the Scots or the Royalist forces in the south, it might manage to influence the outcome of events decisively.

The first thing that the Prince of Wales did was to issue a manifesto laying down the purpose of his operations. This was stated as being to help promote the agreement that the Scots had made with the King: to restore the King to his rights; to maintain the freedom and privileges of Parliament; to abolish many taxes by disbanding the army; and to obtain a general act of indemnity. These measures were well calculated to appeal to moderate men throughout the country.

The first destination of the fleet was Yarmouth, where the Prince of Wales hoped to persuade the town to declare for the King as a first step towards spreading the uprising throughout Norfolk and Suffolk. But although there was much sympathy for the Royalist cause, there were Parliamentary troops in the town and, with Fairfax and a large part of the army outside Colchester, it was too dangerous for the civic authorities to commit themselves to such a course. The fleet therefore moved to the Downs off the coast of Kent, from where it would at least be well placed to keep the Parliamentary squadron at Portsmouth from joining Warwick's ships in the Thames.

The Royalists, with twelve ships carrying 199 guns, were much too strong to be attacked by the Portsmouth squadron of nine ships carrying 185 guns. On paper the Thames squadron of nine ships carrying over 300 guns was strong enough to attack the Royalists,[1] but it was unlikely to do so as some of the crews were on the point of mutiny. On 10 August Batten joined the Prince's fleet. He had left the Thames in mid-July when he felt that he was in danger of arrest for stirring up disaffection within the Parliamentary navy. Sailing with Captain Jordan in a privateer jointly owned by himself and the Earl of Warwick, he had missed the Royalists in Holland and off Yarmouth before finally meeting them in the Downs. The Prince of Wales made him welcome, knighted him and made him his rear-admiral, but from the start Rupert had reservations about his conversion to the Royalist cause.

In naval terms Batten was by far the most important defector to the King's cause. Aged forty-seven, he was a professional who had served in both merchantmen and warships before becoming Surveyor of the Navy in 1638. As a moderate Presbyterian he would be strongly in favour of an accommodation being reached between the King and Parliament at the expense of the Independents and the army. As Warwick's vice-admiral and friend throughout the Civil War, he would tend to favour moves to attract further naval defections rather than battles with his former colleagues.

It was now necessary for the Royalists to decide on a course of action designed to promote the aims put forward in the manifesto. Four possible plans were considered.

The first, which was backed by Batten, was that the fleet should sail to the Firth of Forth to support the operations of Hamilton's army. This course would also enable the Prince of Wales to become involved in events there, as envisaged in the plan agreed by the King with the Scots. The disadvantage was that the Scots were moving down the west coast from Carlisle and would not be greatly helped by the fleet. Also, this plan would remove the Prince of Wales from the main area of the revolt against Parliament around London.

The next plan was that the fleet should attempt to help the Royalists in Colchester. This would have been favoured by courtiers such as Wilmot and Percy who had friends within the besieged town, but it was deemed impractical because the batteries covering the seaward approaches to the town were firmly in Fairfax's hands.

The third plan, favoured by the captain as being the one most likely to gain the approval of the sailors, was a direct attack on the Thames squadron. This would have been risky in view of the defences covering the anchorage at Chatham, where the squadron lay, but would have had great impact on events had it succeeded in capturing some of the enemy ships or causing them to defect to the Prince.

A fourth plan, allegedly proposed by Prince Rupert, was to sail first to the Isle of Wight and land a force to rescue the King. With the King on board, the fleet would then sail up the Thames. While part of the army was with Fairfax at Colchester and part with Cromwell heading north to intercept the Scots, it might be possible for the King, supported as he was to a considerable extent by the city of London, to come to an agreement with Parliament. It was felt that the Thames squadron would not oppose the King in person, especially as the declaration of principles put out by the sailors at the time that Rainsborough was put ashore contained the demand that 'the King's Majesty, with all expedition, be admitted in safety and honour to treat with both houses of Parliament' and, second, 'that the army now under the command of Lord Fairfax be forthwith disbanded, their arrears being paid them'. But this plan had several drawbacks. First, the King might be killed during the rescue from the Isle of Wight. Second, Warwick had by now replaced a number of officers in order to ensure the loyalty of his fleet to Parliament, so a battle with the Thames squadron could not be ruled out. Third, Fairfax could get back easily from Colchester with enough troops to coerce Parliament during the time that it was negotiating with the King; and no speedy agreement was likely to be reached judging by past experience. On balance it does not seem that this plan would have had a great chance of success. Furthermore, there is no firm evidence that Rupert proposed it or even supported it.

At the end of the discussion, it was decided that the fleet should, for the time being, stay based in the Downs, from where it could capture prizes that would if nothing else provide money with which to pay the seamen and buy supplies. The fleet could also try to relieve Royalist garrisons still holding out in the castles at Deal and Sandown which Fairfax had not had time to reduce before moving north into Essex.

In the event, although men were landed to relieve these castles, they failed to defeat the besiegers. The fleet had better fortune in capturing prizes in the mouth of the Thames but in

doing so inevitably alienated some Royalist support in the city
of London, where the losses were felt financially. For political
reasons the Prince of Wales, as a result of negotiations carried
out by Batten and Jordan, released the prizes in return for a
cash sum that the city sent him, but this annoyed the seamen
who felt that they were losing prize money that rightly belonged
to them.

On the same day that Batten joined the fleet the Scottish Earl
of Lauderdale arrived on board the *Satisfaction* to persuade the
Prince of Wales to accompany him to Scotland. Hamilton's
enemies in Scotland, led by Argyll, were working to undermine
the agreement with the King, and without the presence of the
Prince Lauderdale feared that the Scottish army might be forced
to withdraw from England. The Prince himself was anxious to
go, because he longed to lead the army in person, but certain
conditions imposed by the Scots about his visit had not been
agreed. These conditions were about the people he could take
with him and the way in which he should worship.

With regard to the first condition, the Scots were adamant
that he should not be accompanied by Digby, which the Prince
was happy to concede; they were also determined that he should
not bring Prince Rupert or Prince Maurice with him. About
this latter point Lauderdale reported back to the Scots that
Rupert's powers over the Prince were so absolute that he would
accompany him even if the whole of the Prince's council voted
against it, and indeed Charles personally struck out the offend-
ing condition with his own hand. Rupert himself provided the
solution by agreeing that he and his brother would not go to
Scotland providing that the condition was not put in writing.
Over the coming weeks Lauderdale became so impressed by
Rupert's conduct and good sense that he wrote to the Scots
saying that Rupert's coming to Scotland would after all be of
great advantage.[2] By then the whole situation had altered, but
Rupert had gained the good opinion of a man with whom he
would work closely in government after the Restoration.

More troublesome was the Scottish insistence that Prince
Charles should adopt the Presbyterian form of worship while in
Scotland. As the King had already agreed that the Presbyterian
religion should be adopted in England for a trial period of three
years if he were restored to his throne by the Scottish army,
this condition seemed reasonable, but it had been opposed by
most of the Prince's council because of the adverse effect it

might have on Royalist support in England. Prince Charles, however, signed the agreement with Lauderdale despite the reservations of some of his councillors.

As a result of this agreement Prince Charles became anxious to get back to Holland from where he could take ship to Scotland. By the third week in August Colchester had fallen, as had Deal Castle, and the fleet was running short of supplies. Soon afterwards, a strong rumour reached the fleet to the effect that Hamilton's army had suffered a setback at the hands of Cromwell. On 26 August a council of war was held, where it was decided that the fleet should return to Helvoetsluys to replenish, a decision that was strongly resented by the sailors themselves.

It would seem that by this time the Prince of Wales and his retinue had transferred from the *Satisfaction* to Rainsborough's former flagship, the larger and more powerful *Constant Reformation*. A crisis now developed in this ship as some of the sailors decided to throw Lauderdale and Culpepper overboard: they evidently believed that these two were primarily responsible for Prince Charles's decision to return to Holland. The situation was saved by the Prince himself who confronted the mutineers and persuaded them of the necessity of returning there to replenish the fleet.

The route back lay first north into the mouth of the Thames, thence east-north-east across the North Sea to Helvoetsluys. It is difficult to work out exactly what happened next, but most accounts suggest that, after the recent unpleasantness, Culpepper had moved to another ship and that this ship suddenly set off into the Thames, where it met a small vessel with news that Warwick and the powerful Thames squadron were sailing down the river towards the Royalist fleet. At this news the sailors expressed a determination to fight regardless of the need to replenish.

On 29 August Warwick's fleet came in sight and the Prince of Wales sent a message to him asking him to remove the standard that he flew as Lord High Admiral and surrender his fleet in return for a general amnesty. Warwick held a council of war which recommended that he refuse the Prince's terms but avoid fighting until joined by the Portsmouth squadron. But by this time the Royalists were bent on fighting and started to manoeuvre to get to windward of Warwick's ships.

By the following afternoon it looked as if a battle was imminent as a stiff breeze was carrying the Royalist ships straight down on their enemy. Prince Charles was apparently in a state of high excitement, waving a pistol above his head, while Batten tried to get him to go below to a safe part of the ship. In a story allegedly told by the Prince himself when King many years later, a frightened Batten was holding a large white napkin under his chin to mop up the sweat that was pouring from him. Prince Rupert, who was walking the deck with Prince Charles, claimed that the napkin was to be used to betray them all to Warwick, although by what means is not clear. At any rate Rupert is supposed to have told the Prince that at the first sign of trouble he would personally shoot Batten. In the event this proved unnecessary, as the wind dropped at the critical moment and the fleets drifted apart and had to anchor for fear of running aground.

Next morning the wind still made it impossible to engage Warwick's ships, and by now the last of the rations were gone. The sailors were therefore persuaded that there was no alternative but to sail for Holland – which they did, Warwick's ships following at a discreet distance. As it got dark, information was received that the Portsmouth squadron was moving past them into the mouth of the Thames; some time later Prince Rupert, being on deck, was told by the ship's master that a light was in sight. Assuming that it came from the Portsmouth fleet, Rupert advised the master to steer towards the other ships. As the master altered course, Batten noticed what was happening and told Prince Charles that the ships were only colliers and persuaded him to continue towards Holland. It turned out that the ships were indeed the Portsmouth squadron and had the Royalists closed with them they might either have persuaded them to join them or alternatively they might have destroyed them. But it was a gamble because in a night engagement anything might happen, including the possibility of the Royalist ships being taken in the rear by Warwick while fighting the Portsmouth squadron.

On 3 September the Royalist fleet came to anchor off Goree, where it replenished its supplies. The Prince of Wales, Prince Rupert and many of the Prince's councillors and courtiers, including Sir William Batten, immediately set off for The Hague, where they received confirmation of the fact that Cromwell had defeated the Duke of Hamilton and the Scottish army at Preston on 17 August.

From Lauderdale's point of view this made it all the more

important that Prince Charles should go immediately into Scotland to try to keep the country behind Hamilton's party and thereby thwart Argyll, who aimed to take control of the country: Hamilton himself had been captured by Cromwell. But virtually all the Prince's council, considering such a course too risky, urged him not to go; this time the Prince agreed with them. The decision proved correct, as Argyll, with some help from Cromwell, swiftly re-established himself. Hamilton, who had been sent to London, was executed some months later.

Meanwhile, in the absence of the Prince of Wales the Royalist fleet was becoming restive. Willoughby, who was still with the fleet, had no desire for further service, and Batten also refused to go back to the ships because the seamen blamed him for the loss of prize money that they would have received had the vessels captured in the Thames Estuary not been returned. It has been suggested[3] that Rupert was instrumental in stirring up trouble for Batten among the seamen because he wanted the command for himself, but this would have been totally contrary to his character: throughout his life he abhorred intrigue of any sort. Furthermore, as Hyde later wrote in his *History of the Great Rebellion*, 'There was in truth nobody to whom the charge of the fleet could be committed but Prince Rupert ... The seamen were too much broke loose from all kind of order to be reduced by a commander of an ordinary rank.' The Prince of Wales therefore asked Prince Rupert to take the ships in hand and secure them against defection.

On 19 September the Earl of Warwick appeared off Goree with the ships that had been with him in the Thames, together with the Portsmouth squadron. Next day both fleets followed each other into the harbour at Helvoetsluys, the Royalists anchoring at the top of the harbour while Warwick's fleet anchored below them nearer to the open sea. Exactly when Rupert returned to the Royalist fleet is not known, but it must have been towards the end of September or in early October.[4]

Some days later Warwick tried to capture the *Convertine*, the second-largest ship in the Royalist fleet and the one anchored nearest to Warwick's ships. His idea was to float one of his small vessels down on to her and capture her with a boarding party. Somehow Rupert got wind of this and concealed a number of men armed with swords and pikes by lying them on the deck where they could not be seen: his aim was to overpower the boarding party and capture the Parliamentary ship. Unfortunately, a Parliamentary look-out stationed up the mast saw the Royalist ambush just in time and the enemy ship dropped away. Shortly afterwards, the Dutch sent a squadron of ships under the command of van Tromp to Helvoetsluys to separate the two fleets and prevent overt hostilities. Thereafter such confrontation as there was took place ashore, especially in the numerous taverns dotted around the town.

For the next six weeks Warwick tried to persuade the crews of the Royalist ships to desert, offering them an amnesty should they do so, while Rupert strived to retain their loyalty, which he could do only by paying the men and providing them with supplies. Very soon Warwick sent one of his senior officers to Rupert to ask whether he might be allowed to address the sailors. Rupert said that he could do so in his hearing but that if he said anything amiss he would throw him over the side. Rupert evidently did not like what he heard but instead of carrying out his threat he merely held the officer in custody until being asked to release him by the Dutch authorities, who objected to the use of force or coercion inside their harbour.

During October Rupert had some of his ships partially unrigged to prevent pilfering and for the purpose of repair and maintenance. At the same time, backed by the Prince of Wales's council at The Hague, he was using all his energy and skill to raise money and build up supplies, as he had formerly learned to do when keeping his armies in the field during the Civil War. His problem this time was, however, different to the extent that, being in a foreign land, he had no power of coercion and had to rely on the goodwill of his contacts in the United Provinces and the sale of prizes taken by Royalist privateers. But such was his persistence and the force of his personality that he kept most of his men from deserting.

Nevertheless the men in some of the ships were still wavering in their loyalty, and matters came to a head when Rupert sent to the *Antelope* for a party of skilled men to come on board the *Constant Reformation* to help re-rig the ship. On being told that the men had refused to obey because of a dispute about victuals, Rupert, with ten of the military officers who were with him in the fleet, went on board the *Antelope*, where he repeated the order himself to a group of surly-looking men who had surrounded him on deck. At this point one of the ringleaders moved towards Rupert in a menacing way, calling on others for support, whereupon Rupert picked him up bodily and held

him over the side of the ship, saying that he would drop him in
if the men did not instantly do what they were told. (Clarendon
maintains that he did throw one or two overboard to drown,
but it seems more likely that the threat was sufficient.) At any
rate, Rupert had no more trouble from the men.

For the most part the sailors had little natural affinity with
the Royalist officers, who were steadily increasing their hold on
the fleet, but they were beginning to respond to the strength of
Rupert's leadership. If he could once get the ships to sea with
the prospect of action and prize money, he had little doubt that
the men would play their part with zest.

During this time Rupert had been acting on behalf of the
Prince of Wales, who was still officially admiral. But it was
clear that Prince Charles would not be available to command
the fleet in person, and it was therefore necessary to appoint a
new admiral. The Duke of York was one possibility, having
been proclaimed Lord High Admiral designate when he was
only five years old; the Earl of Northumberland was to hold
the post until the Duke was old enough to exercise it himself.
But the Duke was only fifteen and had no experience of warfare.
Another contender was Henry Jermyn, the Queen's chamberlain
and loyal supporter throughout the Civil War, but he had no
experience of war at sea and was in any case with the Queen
at St-Germain. That left Prince Rupert, who was by far the best
man for the job, although like many admirals at the time he
had no direct experience as a commander at sea. Not wishing
to cause friction in the royal family, Rupert suggested that the
Duke of York should hold the office of admiral and that he
should act on his behalf, but the Prince of Wales, realising that
Rupert would need every bit of authority that he could get,
insisted that he should be admiral, and so he was appointed at
the end of October. No doubt some on both sides may have
felt that the appointment of such an uncompromising Royalist
as Rupert would put an end to any chance of an agreement
being reached between the Prince of Wales and moderate Presbyterians such as Warwick, but in practice the speed and
thoroughness with which the army had put down the uprisings
in England and defeated the Scots would soon make moderate
Presbyterians irrelevant.

Early in November van Tromp's squadron was withdrawn
to avoid having to winter in the outer harbour. Almost immediately the ship that Batten owned jointly with Warwick rejoined

the Parliamentary fleet, and soon afterwards Batten and Jordan asked the Prince of Wales for passes to return to England under the terms of Warwick's amnesty. Surprisingly, the Prince let them go. Batten returned to England, where he remained unemployed until the Restoration.

The confrontation between Warwick's ships and those of Prince Rupert now intensified, and a race developed between them to gain possession of the sluice at the top of the harbour which led into an inner harbour at the mouth of a canal. In the event the *Tenth Whelp*, a small and fast ship from Warwick's fleet, arrived at a quay next to the sluice marginally ahead of Prince Rupert in the *Constant Reformation*. On shore by chance was the Royalist Thomas Allin, captain of the *Guinea*, who called to the *Tenth Whelp* to throw him a rope so that he could make her fast. But when the crew did so, he dropped the rope at the critical moment so that as her sails were backed the ship fell away from the quay. As a result the *Constant Reformation* tied up in this strategic position.

Rupert then managed to get seven of his large ships, together with five smaller ones, hauled up through the sluice into the inner harbour, but he lost the *Satisfaction* which grounded in the outer harbour while the operation was in progress. He also lost two merchant ships and a ketch that surrendered to Warwick.[5] Rupert then fortified the inner harbour, laying the *Convertine* across the entrance and raising fortifications and gun emplacements on shore. The Dutch protested vigorously, but Rupert refused to remove them unless the Dutch themselves took on the responsibility for his defence. Violence in the taverns increased, and again Rupert asked the Dutch to intervene. But this situation did not continue for long because, like van Tromp, Warwick could not afford to have his ships stuck in the outer harbour over the winter. Accordingly, he too sailed away on 21 November, leaving Prince Rupert free to use the port as he wished.

Ever since the fleet had returned to Helvoetsluys at the beginning of September a debate had been going on regarding the best way of using it, a discussion that was naturally connected with a decision about the Prince of Wales's own movements. With Scotland ruled out for the moment, there were two possible ways in which the fleet could be deployed. The first was for it to remain based in Holland and to capture prizes, the proceeds of which would not only be able to support the fleet itself but also the impoverished court of the Prince of Wales. The disadvantage of staying in Holland was that doing so would not advance the King's cause to any appreciable extent and would not be popular with the Dutch, who had no wish to provoke the hostility of the victorious English Parliament. The second option was that the fleet should move to Ireland, from where it could still take prizes for the benefit of the exiled Royalists and also support the operations of the Earl of Ormonde. This was the plan accepted by Prince Charles.

But although the defeat of Hamilton's army and party had caused the Prince of Wales to decide to use the fleet in Ireland for the time being, the possibility of action in Scotland at some future date was not discounted. In the autumn of 1648 Montrose, who had been so successful before his defeat in 1645, reappeared on the scene. Having left Scotland in the summer of 1646, he had spent some time trying to get support in northern European countries before turning up at Henrietta Maria's court at St-Germain. Here he got little satisfaction because of the negotiations that were in train between the King and Hamilton, who would have nothing to do with Montrose. In early 1648 Montrose moved to the Imperial court at Vienna, where the Emperor authorised him to raise troops and referred him to his brother, the Archduke Leopold, governor of the Spanish Netherlands. Leopold, who had just suffered defeat at the hands of Condé, was in no position to help, so Montrose established himself in Brussels to await developments.

Once there, he wrote letters to the Prince of Wales, the Duke of York and Prince Rupert in an attempt to interest them in a campaign based once more on the Highlands designed to take advantage of the confusion in Scotland following Hamilton's defeat. Although he did not say so in as many words, his idea was that, if supported by the Royalist fleet, he could overthrow both Argyll and the remains of Hamilton's party and unite the country behind himself.

Initially, he got no response from the Prince of Wales or the Duke of York, who were still negotiating with envoys from the other two parties in Scotland, but he did get answered by Rupert, whom he so greatly admired and who recognised him as by far the best soldier and most honest of the Scottish leaders. They continued to correspond with each other until Rupert eventually took the fleet to sea in January 1649, and they would have met had it been possible. But at the time Montrose was not allowed to come to the Prince of Wales's court and Rupert had no time to visit Brussels. After Rupert sailed, the whole political scene in Scotland changed following the execution of Charles I, an event that genuinely shocked all parties in that country. Montrose was then invited to The Hague, where he stayed from February to the following June. During this time Rupert's mother, Elizabeth of Bohemia, was one of his staunchest supporters, and a suggestion has even been made that he wanted to marry Rupert's sister Louise, although this seems unlikely. His subsequent adventures in the Highlands, his abandonment by Charles II and his execution at the hands of Argyll in 1651 have no place in this story as they all occurred when Rupert was away with the fleet.

While Rupert was at Helvoetsluys he made frequent visits to The Hague, which was only twenty miles away as the crow flies, to take part in the meetings of the council as well as to coordinate support for the ships. In early September Edward Hyde had rejoined the Prince of Wales together with King Charles's old treasurer, Lord Cottington. Hyde's presence brought some much-needed method into the conduct of business, and contrary to his natural instincts he became a strong supporter of Prince Rupert's efforts.[6] But as usual the Royalists found plenty to quarrel about, and on one occasion Culpepper lost his temper and blackguarded one of Rupert's agents in Rupert's presence to such an extent that a duel seemed inevitable. A few years earlier Rupert would have flared up, but on this occasion he behaved in such a calm and dignified way that Culpepper was persuaded eventually to apologise.

At some stage when at The Hague, Rupert must have met his mother, for the first time since he left for England in July 1642. Whether this happened in the week before the fleet sailed in July or whether it happened after it returned in September is impossible to know. During the Civil War Elizabeth maintained links with both sides. On a personal level she still loved the King her brother, but she drew an allowance from Parliament which she could not afford to lose; she also hoped that Parliament would help her eldest son Charles Louis, who was living in London from the middle of 1644, in his attempts to regain the Palatinate. On several occasions, at Charles Louis's instigation, she issued statements dissociating herself from the part that Rupert was playing, which could not have improved relations between them. Two further sources of friction occurred when he was in France. The first was that, much to his mother's fury, he failed to condemn his young brother Philip when he killed a French nobleman who had been paying court to Louise and getting too familiar with Elizabeth herself. The second was that he supported another brother, Edward, when he converted to Catholicism in order to marry a French heiress. But these matters were now in the past and it is clear that any residual resentment was forgotten.

During the autumn of 1648, when the Thirty Years War was finally brought to a close by the signing of the Treaty of Westphalia, Charles Louis was again in London and Rupert's eldest sister Elizabeth was staying in Berlin. Maurice was working with Rupert to get the fleet ready for sea, and Edward and Philip were out of the country. As a result Queen Elizabeth had only three daughters living with her: Louise, the artist, Henrietta and the mischievous eighteen-year-old Sophie, who her mother hoped might marry the Prince of Wales. Prince Charles at this time was deeply attached to Lucy Walters, whom he had met on his arrival at The Hague and who was soon to present him with his first son, later the Duke of Monmouth. Sophie and the Prince spent time together, to the satisfaction of her mother, but both probably realised that the relationship would lead nowhere. Although eventually Sophie mothered an English king, it was not as a result of marrying the Prince of Wales.

Elizabeth, who was now seriously worried about the future of her brother, had unreservedly turned against the English Parliament. Despite her poverty, she pawned more of her fabulous collection of jewels to help Rupert get his ships ready; her faithful friend Lord Craven also provided a sizeable contribution.

Elizabeth's concern for the King was fully justified. The negotiations that the King was carrying on in the Isle of Wight with Parliament were meeting opposition from the army and his guards were becoming menacing. At the end of October the King dispatched Will Legge to Rupert with instructions to send a ship to lie off the Isle of Wight in which he would try to escape. Rupert was to act with the utmost secrecy, not even telling the Prince of Wales. Rupert arranged for a ship commanded by Captain Sayers to rescue the King, but by now the King was too heavily guarded and the attempt failed. This was followed by Pride's Purge, when a regiment in London commanded by Colonel Pride evicted from the House of Commons over forty of the Presbyterian members who favoured an agreement with the King, thereby effectively removing any opposition to the Independents in the army. Soon afterwards, the remaining members, known as the Rump, pushed through a bill forbidding further negotiation with the King. At the end of November the King himself was taken by stages to London and the resolution was made to put him on trial, a decision that caused much consternation at The Hague.

Meanwhile Rupert was pressing ahead with preparations for getting the fleet to sea. To raise more money he decided to lay up the *Antelope* and sell her old-fashioned brass cannon. He also took advantage of the departure of Warwick's squadron to send two of his smaller ships in search of prizes, namely the *Roebuck*, commanded by Captain Marshall, and the *Guinea*, commanded by Captain Allin.

During the final weeks of preparation there was much discussion with the Prince of Wales and his council regarding the exact terms of the commission to be issued to Prince Rupert, with particular reference to the relationship that would exist between himself and the Earl of Ormonde in Ireland. Inevitably, intrigues were already afoot to stir up trouble between them. One of the principal Roman Catholic noblemen in Ireland wrote to beg Rupert to lead the Confederacy, saying that he and his friends were faithful to the King but did not want to follow Ormonde. Troublemakers at The Hague who wrote to warn Ormonde that Rupert was in touch with his enemies were disconcerted to hear that Rupert had passed the letter straight to Ormonde as soon as it had arrived.[7] Luckily, Ormonde, who was one of the noblest and most attractive characters of the day and who disliked intrigue as much as Rupert did himself, had worked in complete harmony with Rupert during the Civil War. When Jermyn wrote to him on behalf of Henrietta Maria to ask him to stay on good terms with Rupert, he replied that he had always worked hard to retain Rupert's good opinion and he felt himself in no danger of losing it, Rupert having always got on well with him both with regard to their business and personally.[8] They remained close associates and firm friends for the rest of Rupert's life.

Eventually it was decided not to go into too much detail regarding Rupert's status in Ireland but to give him all the powers over His Majesty's forces that he had held in former times,[9] i.e. during the latter stages of the Civil War, when he held the chief command under the King. It was also decided that Prince Rupert should have discretion to fly the royal standard, denoting the presence of the Lord High Admiral should he feel it necessary for the achievement of some particular objective.

Early in the New Year both Allin and Marshall returned with valuable prizes that financed the last remaining arrangements. Rupert had used all his powers of leadership and persuasion to retain the sailors in the face of Warwick's blandishments; although many had departed, some had stayed and some new ones had been recruited. None the less his ships were undermanned, especially the three largest. He had also worked himself to the bone to ensure that the ships were properly equipped and victualled. On 21 January 1649 Rupert led his fleet out of Helvoetsluys.

Rupert himself sailed in the *Constant Reformation*. Maurice, his vice-admiral, who as a senior Royalist commander had been his faithful companion throughout the Civil War, sailed in Raleigh's old flagship, the *Convertine*. His rear-admiral was Sir John Mennes, who had long experience as a naval officer up to the start of the Civil War. During the war he first took command of a troop of horse but soon became the general of artillery in Lord Capel's army based in Shrewsbury. Later still, after Capel's replacement by Lord Byron and then Prince Rupert, Mennes became the Royalist leader in North Wales before returning to sea in the closing months of the war. He was therefore an experienced seaman and commander by land and sea as well as being a committed Royalist. He sailed in the *Swallow*. Of all the ships in Rupert's fleet, only the *Swallow* would survive the four-year voyage on which Rupert was now embarked.

As the Dutch coast faded from sight Rupert would doubtless have been aware of the many uncertainties lying ahead and of the sparsity of the resources at his disposal. But he must also have felt a surge of new life as the jealousies and quarrels of the exiled Royalists faded into the distance. From his youth at The Hague and at Leyden, he had wanted to command a fleet, and he had almost achieved this ambition in 1637 when King

Charles had offered him command of an expedition to seize and hold Madagascar. At this time he had spent many hours visiting ships and studying the problems of a maritime operation. He had even been present at the launching of the *Sovereign of the Seas*,* the pride of his uncle's navy and still the most powerful ship in the world. But he had been compelled to abandon Madagascar in order to join his brother's army in its attempt to regain the Palatinate. His subsequent capture and three years' imprisonment constituted the first serious setback of his life. His recent experience at sea with the Prince of Wales must have been frustrating rather than instructive, but he would at least have had first-hand experience of life aboard a warship.

Now that he was the admiral, his quarters would be more commodious than when his cousin Charles was occupying the best cabin. Indeed, on board the *Constant Reformation* everyone's accommodation would have been more comfortable than usual because of the shortage of men. Where normally she would have had a crew of around 300, at this time she carried no more than 120, two-thirds of whom were soldiers. Rupert's own cabin constituted the after part of the upper gun-deck. Below him was the wardroom in which the ship's officers lived together with the gentlemen volunteers who accompanied Rupert. Above him in the cabin under the quarterdeck was the ship's captain. The *Constant Reformation* was one of the largest English ships then in commission, as the first-raters such as the *Sovereign of the Seas* were laid up for lack of men and to save expense; she was 106 feet long and, with 52 guns on board, probably weighed about 700 tons.

The full significance of undermanning in the days of sail needs to be understood. A ship could not fight unless she could be manoeuvred, and therefore enough seamen had to be available to handle the ship: the rougher the weather, the more men were needed, especially if the pumps had to be worked. At the same time the ship could not fight unless some at least of the guns were manned. The firing sequence required a gun to be loaded, run out so that the muzzle stuck out beyond the side of the

* Like so many ships at the time, this one often changed its name. It started as *Sovereign of the Seas* in the reign of Charles I, became *Sovereign* during the interregnum and even for a time *Commonwealth*, then *Royal Sovereign* at the Restoration, though frequently abbreviated to *Sovereign*.

ship, and then sponged out and reloaded after the recoil from firing had brought the muzzle back inside again. The number of gunners required to do this varied between three and five men per gun, according to the size of the gun. For the *Constant Reformation* to fight properly would have required about 100 seamen to handle the ship and about 200 to man the guns and bring up powder from the magazines. With the numbers carried on the voyage to Ireland, even if the manning of the sails were cut to the minimum, no more than about fifty to sixty men would have been left to work the guns. Had she been obliged to fight, the best that could have been done would have been to load and run out all the guns on one side of the ship in advance, so that one broadside could be fired like a merchant-man facing privateers or pirates. After this the few available gun crews would only have been able to keep about fifteen guns in action. In other words, the ship would have had little chance of survival if faced with a properly manned opponent.

It was not unusual in the seventeenth century for the admiral to have two captains in his flagship, one to act as his chief of staff and one to act as captain of the ship. Throughout the voyage Captain Fearnes was Rupert's chief of staff, often referred to as his flag captain. Initially, the officer designated as captain of the *Constant Reformation* was Richard Feilding, who had commanded a tercia (brigade) at Edgehill but who had been court-martialled for surrendering Reading a few months later. Condemned to death, he was saved only by the direct intercession of Rupert, after which he spent the rest of the war fighting bravely as a volunteer. But Feilding died of fever after about a year at sea and was succeeded by Captain Kettleby, a professional sea officer.

To the modern mind appointing a soldier to command a ship seems strange but in the seventeenth century the practice was not unusual. In any case the commissioned officers, consisting of the captain and one or two lieutenants, were not directly concerned with sailing and navigating the ship, which were the jobs of the master and his mates. Senior warrant-officers looked after other functions of running the ship, that is to say the gunner, who managed the guns and the ship's magazine, the boatswain, who looked after the masts, spars and rigging, and the carpenter, who was responsible for the maintenance and repair of the ship's structure. These people were in effect the executive officers of the ship. Other warrant-officers filled the non-executive posts of surgeon, chaplain and purser. All of these people were men of standing in the community and had to possess some education in order to carry out their functions. For instance, the gunner, in addition to knowing how to handle the guns efficiently and safely, had to have the mathematical ability to calculate distances and angles of elevation aided by various tables and instruments. He also had to have an intimate knowledge of seamanship in order to call out instructions to the helmsman which would bring the ship on to a sufficiently even keel to enable the guns to be fired at the critical moment.

In addition to Feilding, the *Swallow*'s Captain Chester was a former soldier who had fought in the Marquess of Newcastle's northern army during the Civil War. Other captains, such as Allin of the *Guinea* (sometimes referred to by the Royalists as the *Charles*) and Jeffries of the *Thomas*, were sea officers. Marshall of the *Roebuck* had been the ship's gunner and had been responsible for carrying her over to the Royalists.

Among the former army officers serving as volunteers was an officer called Billingsley and the young Robert Holmes, who had spent the war as an officer in Prince Maurice's regiment of horse and then served as Prince Rupert's page in his French campaign. Rupert's personal attendants included his new page, Rivers, the Frenchman Mortaigne, his Master of the Horse throughout the Civil War and in France, and a French surgeon called Choqueux who had treated him when he received his headwound. Colonel Legge, who had returned to the King after delivering his letter to Rupert, joined Rupert in Ireland some time after the King's execution.

Another officer deserving mention was Captain Valentine Pyne, who may or may not have started out as a sea officer but who appears to have been a gunnery expert and who probably sailed as the fleet gunnery officer. After the Restoration he commanded several of the King's ships and finished up as Master Gunner of the Ordnance Board, the body responsible for the administration, supply and effectiveness of guns for both the army and the navy. He is generally considered to be part-author of the narrative *Prince Rupert's Voyage to the West Indies* (reproduced in Warburton, vol. 3, pp. 279–389), on which so much that has been written subsequently relies. Judging from the way in which the narrative was written, he probably sailed in the *Swallow*, becoming one of Rupert's close associates after

Rupert made the *Swallow* his flagship in 1651. He stayed with Rupert for a time after the voyage was over.

Altogether Rupert had with him as he moved across the North Sea in addition to the three flagships three other fighting ships, *Guinea*, *Thomas* and *James*, and two small vessels, a ketch and a hoy, suitable for scouting or moving stores. Two further ships, *Roebuck* and *Blackmoor Lady*, had left Helvoetsluys ahead of the main fleet with orders to seize prizes and rendezvous off the Isles of Scilly. Sailing with the fleet for protection from privateers and pirates were three large Dutch merchantmen.

Rupert did not have to wait long for his first brush with the enemy. On the day after leaving Helvoetsluys he met four ships commanded by Robert Moulton, who as Warwick's flag captain had been sent to talk to Rupert's crews at Helvoetsluys. Unlike most Parliamentary captains, he was a strong supporter of the Independents in the army and was now vice-admiral command-ing the ships kept in commission during the winter to guard the mouth of the Thames and the entry to the English Channel. Rupert's heavily undermanned fleet was in no condition to fight, but with his usual audacity he altered course as if to do so. Moulton, who may have taken the Dutch merchantmen for warships, decided that the odds were too heavily stacked against him and withdrew rapidly under the guns of Dover Castle, where the *Satisfaction* ran aground.

The Royalist fleet continued down the Channel unopposed collecting five prizes as it went. Most of the ships arrived at Kinsale on 26 January, but Rupert in the *Constant Reformation* got separated from the rest of the fleet and arrived at Castle-haven some forty miles west of Kinsale, where he was spotted by William Penn, vice-admiral of Parliament's western squadron. Penn, who was in the thirty-gun *Assurance*, mistook Rupert for an Irish privateer and moved in to attack. He realised his mis-take just in time and withdrew as smartly as Moulton had done. On 31 January the *Constant Reformation* rejoined the remainder of the fleet at Kinsale.

On arrival, Rupert wrote to Ormonde assuring him that he would follow his advice and do his best to provide him with what support he could. Rupert now had to make a plan that would cater for this in conjunction with two other tasks. First, he had to recruit and train the seamen and soldiers whom he needed to turn his fleet into an efficient fighting force, at the same time keeping it supplied with food, water and warlike stores. Second, he had to capture and sell enough prizes not only to pay for this but also to send money to The Hague in order to sustain the exiled court. And all of this had to be done while based on a port that was neither prepared to provide for a sizeable fleet nor protected from attack.

The position in Ireland when Rupert arrived was confused. After leaving the exiled court at St-Germain, Ormonde had reached Kilkenny in late September 1648 with the intention of uniting all those prepared to act together against Parliament. He speedily disbanded the Confederacy and formed a government made up of both Protestants and Roman Catholics, including some members of the Confederacy. The confederate commander O'Neill, who had been a strong supporter of the papal nuncio, declined to join Ormonde and initially remained neutral, as did a number of other local leaders particularly in the far west of the country. On the other hand the Scottish commanders in Ulster, Munro and Stewart, were sympathetic to his new government, and from Munster he was soon joined by Lord Inchiquin, who had recently been supporting Parliament.

Ormonde now felt that the Prince of Wales should come to Ireland to unite the waverers, but it was not until March that Charles heard about the agreements that Ormonde had reached with the confederates and received the invitation. By this time he had become King on the death of his father and was negotiating with the Scots, so that it was not until the end of May, when these negotiations broke down, that he agreed to come to Ireland when arrangements could be made to get him there.

Opposing Ormonde in February 1649 were two small Parliamentary armies, one based in Dublin and the other in Ulster. Both were commanded by veteran professional officers: Jones in Dublin and Monck in Ulster. At sea, Parliament's small western squadron was designed to keep links open between England and its armies in Dublin and Ulster while doing what it could to control Irish privateers. At this time a number of Irish ships operated out of the Munster ports on behalf of Ormonde's government, but they sailed individually or in small groups and do not seem to have been organised as a fleet. Soon after Ormonde's arrival, Monck's forces captured Munro and

Stewart, thereby gaining control of Belfast and Londonderry.

In addition to the internal position in the country, Rupert had to take into consideration the threat from Parliament's naval forces when making his plan. It is unlikely that he would have had much information about them, because the government was in the process of reorganising the whole system of naval direction and administration in the aftermath of the King's trial and execution, news of which did not reach Kinsale until 12 February. What Rupert would have known was that the three ships of Penn's western squadron, despite having recently captured three Irish ships off Land's End, would not be able to interfere to any appreciable extent with his plans to seize prizes. At the same time he must have realised that ultimately Parliament had the resources to concentrate a superior force against him should it wish to do so.

It might be thought that the correct course for Rupert and Ormonde to pursue would be to concentrate on taking Dublin, using Rupert's fleet together with all available Irish ships to support land operations and to block attempts to reinforce or resupply Jones from England. If Dublin could be captured swiftly, it might be possible to secure the whole country and consolidate it as a bastion of Royalism beyond the power of Parliament to overthrow. Had Rupert's fleet been influential in bringing this about – and it is certainly what Ormonde would have liked him to do – it would have constituted a greater achievement than the sum total of its activities over the next four years.

But a campaign of this sort was well beyond the powers of the combined forces of Rupert and Ormonde in the early part of the year. In particular, such a plan could have worked only if the various forces supporting Ormonde could be concentrated quickly and if the rear of his army could be secured against Monck in Ulster and possible interference from O'Neill. In this connection Rupert wrote to O'Neill and other uncommitted leaders soon after he arrived in Ireland[10] in an attempt to gain their allegiance to the King but with little success, as can be seen from the correspondence that subsequently passed between him and Ormonde.[11] But even if he had been successful in this respect, Rupert's fleet could not have played its part until brought up to strength and provided with the necessary logistical backing. A period of preparation was therefore needed during which Ormonde and Rupert would have to operate separately before such an ambitious project could be undertaken.

Rupert's first act was to arrange for the sale of the prizes taken in the Channel and to use the money to pay his men and get as many ships as possible ready for sea. Throughout the coming years manpower would be a constant struggle, and Rupert was often obliged to render some ships inactive in order to keep others in fighting order. In some cases less seaworthy ships might be sold and prizes converted to replace them. Guns, like crews, would be moved between the ships to keep those at sea in fighting trim. For the moment men were taken from the *Constant Reformation* and *Convertine* while these ships were refitted.

When arranging sorties in search of further prizes Rupert could count on harbours with resupply facilities in the Channel Islands and the Isles of Scilly, both of which were held for the King, as well as along the south coast of Ireland, and this greatly increased his ability to interrupt English merchant shipping. News of the King's execution was greeted with horror by all European countries, which meant that Spain and Portugal as well as France would be likely to offer support to Royalist ships. Indeed, Rupert wrote to the King of Portugal on 13 March asking for various privileges to be granted to his ships in Portuguese ports and received a reply, dated 18 May, in which most of his requests were granted.[12]

Communications between Rupert and King Charles II at The Hague were clearly difficult, as can be seen from a letter written by Hyde on 28 February. In this Hyde complains that the court has heard no news of Rupert since his departure from Helvoetsluys and none from Ormonde since 2 October.

The arrival of this letter, together with a new commission formally appointing him admiral and lieutenant-general of the King's naval forces, prompted him to issue a strongly worded declaration in which he deplored the bloody and inhumane murder of his uncle and stated his determination to take vengeance on 'the arch-traitors pretending the name of Parliament who maintain perpetual sessions of blood-thirstiness and massacre at Westminster'. Rupert continued by saying that he never desired the supreme naval post and would have been satisfied with an inferior place which would have enabled him to punish such traitors and rebels. He was clearly still very upset about his uncle's death, which is hardly surprising considering the close bonds that existed between them through the tumults and dangers of the Civil War, despite the difficulties that beset their relationship after the fall of Bristol in 1645.

By the middle of March Rupert was able to send a squadron of four ships under Mennes to make contact with the Royalists in the Scillies and to capture prizes. They returned after about three weeks complete with five prizes. One of these was taken into the fleet as the *Scott* and armed with thirty guns. The rest were sold at Kinsale. In addition to Rupert's captures, other prizes were being taken by Irish ships and by privateers operating out of ports in the Spanish Netherlands and France. All of this caused alarm in Whitehall but was done at the expense of helping Ormonde, who had on 8 March asked Rupert to attack enemy ships at Londonderry which were preventing his forces from taking that place and who on 23 March again asked for naval support to complete the blockade of Dublin.[13]

With the death of the King the pretence of a monarchy in which the King was temporarily estranged from Parliament was abandoned in favour of the idea of a commonwealth in which executive power was exercised by a council of state. This was presided over by John Bradshaw, a barrister from Cheshire, who had also presided over the court that had tried and condemned Charles I. In addition to a number of the leading Independents in Parliament, the council included the commander-in-chief, Fairfax, and his lieutenant-general, Cromwell.

At this time Parliament's Navy Committee, hitherto concerned mainly with finance, had its powers extended and its membership enlarged to include a number of leading republicans, including Cromwell and Ireton. In the middle of February three army colonels, Popham, Blake and Deane, were appointed to exercise joint command of the fleet that was being prepared for the summer. A few days later Warwick was dismissed from the post of Lord High Admiral, and the colonels were appointed as admirals and generals of the fleet now at sea. In the middle of March a small Admiralty committee of the council of state was set up to exercise the Lord High Admiral's administrative duties.[14]

The council of state was now faced with a number of problems concerning the navy. First, it had to ensure the loyalty of its officers to prevent a repetition of the previous year's desertions to the Royalists. This involved a continuation of the process whereby moderate Presbyterians were replaced by Independents sympathetic to what was left of the House of Commons, known to history as the Rump, the House of Lords having been abolished. Second, the fleet had to be strengthened in the face of European hostility so as to be in a position to defend the country from a possible invasion and to support army operations designed to remove Royalist influence in Ireland, Scotland, the Isles of Scilly and the Channel Islands. Finally and most immediately, it had to cope with the problem of Rupert's blocking the western end of the Channel while European-based privateers brought shipping to a standstill in the Channel itself.

News of the Royalist capture of five ships south of the Scillies in the middle of March reached London on the twenty-fourth and galvanised the council of state into action. Popham was ordered to the Downs, thereby releasing Moulton, who had been reappointed as vice-admiral to the generals-at-sea, to sail to Plymouth with his squadron. Popham remained in the Downs until 16 April and then sailed with three more warships and an armed merchantman, joining Moulton north of the Scillies on 20 April. By this time Blake and Deane had hoisted their flag at Tilbury and were assembling as many ships as they could. At about this time, too, Sir George Ayscue was appointed admiral of the Irish Seas with William Penn as his vice-admiral.

Meanwhile, on 9 April Rupert had sent four more ships to take additional officers and soldiers to the Isles of Scilly and to cruise for further prizes. With them went a letter from Rupert to the governor, Sir John Grenville, commending the officers he was sending and indicating his intention to move the fleet there if the worst came to the worst in Ireland.[15] One of the ships also landed letters in France from Rupert to the Royalist court.

Unfortunately, on this occasion two of the Royalist ships, which had become separated in fog, were met by Moulton's squadron on the way back to Kinsale, and the *Guinea* and the *Thomas* were captured. The *James* and the *Roebuck* returned to Kinsale with a prize. These losses evidently gave rise to disaffection in the Royalist fleet, with some officers blaming Allin

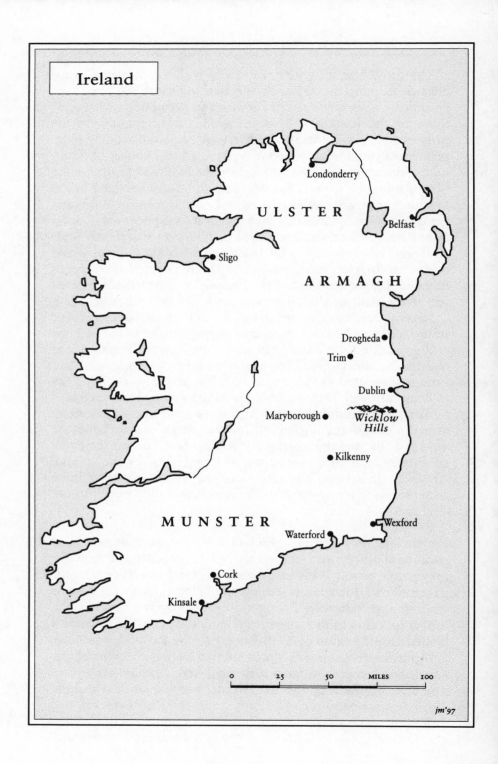

Ireland

ULSTER

ARMAGH

MUNSTER

- Londonderry
- Belfast
- Sligo
- Drogheda
- Trim
- Dublin
- Maryborough
- *Wicklow Hills*
- Kilkenny
- Wexford
- Waterford
- Cork
- Kinsale

0   25   50   MILES   100

jm'97

and Jeffries for the loss of their ships, whereas others blamed the officer in command of the squadron, who was either Sir Henry Stradling or Captain Brathwaite of the *James*.[16] In order to minimise the bad effects Rupert played down the whole incident as one of little importance.

In April Ormonde opened his campaign, which was initially successful. In Ulster Enniskillen declared for the King and in May Ormonde's General of Horse, Lord Castlehaven, captured Maryborough, thirty miles north of Kilkenny, which persuaded many of O'Neill's men to support Ormonde. Munro escaped from Parliamentary custody and resumed command of the Scots in Ulster; soon afterwards, in conjunction with Ormonde's troops in Connaught, he captured Sligo. As a result of these Royalist successes Monck abandoned Ulster and fortified himself in Dundalk and Drogheda.[17]

But while the situation was improving on land it was deteriorating rapidly at sea. By mid-May Blake and Deane had arrived at Plymouth with their ships, and immediately afterwards Sir George Ayscue and William Penn took the Irish squadron, consisting of four powerful ships and a ketch, off to Dublin. On 18 May the three generals left Plymouth with ten ships, arriving off Kinsale three days later, where they proceeded to blockade Rupert's fleet. They were later reinforced by two of Ayscue's ships but lost one of their own, which took Popham back to London to report on events. Moulton was left at Plymouth.

It was against this background that Rupert had to respond to a request from Ormonde that he should blockade Dublin; Ormonde also asked for money or prize goods to enable him to pay his men. In his reply, dated 29 May, Rupert made clear that shortage of men and the financial necessity for capturing prizes to support the fleet made both requests impossible.[18] He might have added that the presence of Blake and Deane lying off Kinsale meant that his ships could not even put to sea without fighting a battle.

At about this time Rupert called a council of war to decide whether the Royalist fleet should engage in such a battle. The council concluded that the Parliamentary fleet was too strong to be attacked by Rupert's undermanned ships, but that an attack should be launched as soon as more men could be found and fireships prepared.

At the end of May Blake and Deane were forced by a gale to abandon their watch on Kinsale, but the same gale prevented

Rupert's ships from putting to sea. As soon as the winds abated the enemy returned. Meanwhile, Rupert had fortified the mouth of Kinsale harbour with two batteries of guns and set off to collect more seamen from the southern Irish ports. In this he had considerable success, collecting over 260 by 23 June.

By the end of the month Rupert was ready to attack. As the fleet dropped down Kinsale harbour towards the open sea, another council of war assembled to decide whether battle should be joined, although this was not specifically considered in relation to supporting Ormonde. Contrary to Rupert's wishes, the captains strongly advised against fighting, recommending instead that when suitable weather conditions existed, the best ships should escape through the enemy fleet by night and carry on operations from some other more secure base: by this time they probably knew of the arrangements that Rupert had made with the King of Portugal. *Prince Rupert's Voyage to the West Indies* suggests that Rupert realised that the captains were motivated by self-interest but that he would not overrule the majority for fear of being judged rash should the battle go against him.[19]

It is not likely that Rupert wanted to fight in order to go to Ormonde's assistance. He would certainly have been worried at the thought of being pinned down in Kinsale with a hostile army behind him should Ormonde's operations prove unsuccessful, and he also wanted to be in a position to capture more prizes. This is borne out by a letter that Rupert wrote to Ormonde three weeks later, in which he tells him of his future plan to base himself in Portugal. In this letter he makes the point that with safe harbours and short voyages between the coasts of Spain and France he would be in a good position to cross England's main trade routes, adding that every south and west wind that confined Commonwealth ships to port would bring big prizes into his lap from the south and the east, which was in marked contrast to the position at Kinsale where the same winds that drove his enemy off station also prevented him from leaving port.[20] By this time, too, Ormonde had probably realised that the build-up of enemy naval strength made it impossible for Rupert to do anything useful in the seas off Dublin, and he certainly concurred with Rupert that the first priority was to preserve the fleet.[21]

It is interesting to consider what would have happened to the Royalist fleet had it attacked Blake. Rupert appears to have had, ready for sea and reasonably well manned, nine of his own ships carrying a total of 220 guns. It is also reasonable to assume that he had one or more fireships ready and he might have been able to make use of one or two other ships in Kinsale harbour. It is less easy to know what Blake had, because of the constant movement of vessels between his squadron off Kinsale and Plymouth and the Irish Sea. He probably had seven ships carrying two hundred and thirty-two guns, and he may have had two more carrying an extra seventy-four guns.[22] But numbers were not the only consideration. The crews of Rupert's larger ships would have had little chance to work together and must have included many recruits, whereas Blake's crews had been working together for some months. On the other hand Rupert's major ships should have been in better order than Blake's, having spent most of the past few months refitting while Blake's were battered by weeks at sea. Another consideration was the competence of the senior officers. Neither Rupert nor Blake had ever fought a fleet action, and Blake had been at sea for only three months. In Rupert's favour was the experience of Sir John Mennes, but two at least of his captains were land officers who might have been at a disadvantage compared with their opponents. On balance it is improbable that a battle would have resulted in total victory for either side, the most likely outcome being that each would have sustained damage and casualties and that some at least of the Royalist ships would have broken out.

Although the decision to avoid fighting Blake may have seemed like a setback for Ormonde, who was now with Inchiquin closing up on Dublin, it was not the only one. As he and Inchiquin were preparing to attack Dublin, they heard that the unpredictable O'Neill had patched up a truce with Monck which threatened Ormonde's rear. Ormonde therefore sent Inchiquin with a sizeable detachment to neutralise the threat, which he did with commendable speed in July, capturing Drogheda and Trim. He then moved rapidly and got between Monck in Dundalk and O'Neill. Without being reinforced by O'Neill, Monck had insufficient men to hold Dundalk, which surrendered soon afterwards, Monck returning to England.

While these operations were in progress, two regiments of foot of the New Model Army, together with guns and powder, reached Dublin from England escorted by ships of Ayscue's squadron. It was now known that Cromwell, who had been appointed in March to eradicate all opposition in Ireland, was almost ready to invade with a force of 8,000 foot and 3,000 horse, together with dragoons and artillery.

With this shipload came someone who got a message to Ormonde saying that Cromwell intended to land on the coast of Munster to take advantage of the fact that the defenders of this area were all with Ormonde outside Dublin.[23] At a council of war held by Ormonde on 27 July, the vulnerability of the Munster coast and the danger that the Royalist fleet would be in if Cromwell landed there caused Ormonde to detach a sizeable force to watch the south-east of the country. When he attacked Dublin in early August his depleted force was repulsed by the recently reinforced garrison, with heavy loss. Three weeks later Cromwell's army crossed the Irish Sea, protected once more by the fleet, and landed at the mouth of the Liffey. With such a large force of highly trained men at his disposal it was clear that the King's cause in Ireland could not long survive.

The effectiveness and brutality of Cromwell's subsequent campaign are well known. In the short term the campaign squared the account for the Irish massacre of Protestants that had taken place in 1641; it resulted in the total subjugation of the native Irish, and it eradicated all Royalist influence from the country until the monarchy was restored eleven years later. In the long term it is often regarded as being a major cause of the alienation that is supposed to exist between England and Ireland.

Having taken the decision not to fight, Rupert was faced with the problem of continuing to pay his crews and to keep his ships supplied. A difficulty in this respect arose from the fact that the blockade that made it virtually impossible for Rupert's ships to put to sea and capture prizes also made it difficult for overseas merchants to get to Kinsale to buy the contents of prizes already taken.[24] Once again Rupert had to redistribute some of the men to the smaller ships and pay off others whom he could not employ for the time being.

One of the ships he made ready for sea in this way was a very fast vessel provided by his Irish allies, which was given the task of breaking through the blockade to take letters from

Rupert and the Irish leaders to the King. Colonel Legge went with her to give the King a first-hand account of the situation. Unfortunately, she was captured by two of Blake's ships early in July and Legge became a prisoner, as he had done on several previous occasions in the Civil War. The *Blackmoor Lady* was more successful in evading the blockading squadron, managing to leave Kinsale early in July, to take a prize that she delivered to Cherbourg and return to Rupert unscathed.

Rupert's fleet remained shut up in Kinsale harbour for two months after Cromwell's arrival in Dublin, during which time its only influence on events was to tie down the Commonwealth ships that were keeping it there. It is, however, worth recording the development of Cromwell's campaign because it influenced the future deployment of Rupert's fleet.

Although in August 1649 Ormonde's forces outnumbered Cromwell's, they consisted of many different detachments commanded by men who were often antagonistic to each other, and whose only bond was their dislike of the English Puritans. At the top end of the scale were a few regiments of English Royalists left over from the Civil War and the remains of the old Irish army that Ormonde used to command from Dublin, which was largely officered by Protestants. Some of the other detachments consisted of regularly organised regiments, but many of the others were little better than guerrillas. The whole army was spread over a large area, from the Wicklow Hills to the south of Dublin in a huge arc to the sea north of Drogheda. It was impossible to hold this force concentrated for more than a few days because it had to live off the land in the absence of proper logistic backing. Ormonde himself was at Trim, some twenty-two miles north-west of Dublin.

Cromwell, not wishing to become involved in a guerrilla war in the bogs and valleys of central Ireland, decided to attack Drogheda, which would open up a route into Ulster and remove an enemy strongpoint that would otherwise threaten his rear when he started to move west or south. Ormonde, anticipating this, reinforced Drogheda. Cromwell took some time to move his army and siege guns into position and then took Drogheda by storm on 12 September. Cromwell also ordered all Roman Catholic priests in the town to be killed, and the town itself was given over to the soldiers to sack. Estimates of the number killed vary, the most likely being about 3,500, of whom around 3,100 were soldiers and the rest civilians. Cromwell's idea was to set an example of severity to encourage swift compliance with his orders. After taking Drogheda, Cromwell detached Venables with two regiments of foot and two or three troops of horse north into Ulster and then returned briefly to Dublin. His next objective was Wexford to the south. Making use of a squadron of twenty-nine ships commanded by Deane to transport his guns, he invested the town between 2 and 11 October and thereafter took it by storm, treating the garrison and the town itself as he had done at Drogheda. New Ross followed on 16 October. Cromwell then halted to consolidate before moving into the centre of Ireland. Venables was also successful in the north, establishing himself firmly in Belfast and Armagh.

Cromwell's advance down the Irish coast must have given Rupert cause for concern and in fact he was in some personal danger, as subsequently transpired. While Cromwell was investing Wexford, Ormonde's governor of Cork asked Rupert to join him for a day's hunting. Rupert was unable to go and was asked again shortly afterwards. By now Rupert was getting suspicious; it transpired that there was a plot to capture him, after which Cork would be handed over to Parliament. When Rupert failed to turn up on the second occasion the governor handed the town over on 16 October. By this time Rupert had taken over the fort at Kinsale from the Irish to prevent its being betrayed to the enemy, but the young officer whom he placed in charge then tried to do so. Fortunately, his plan was discovered and he and his fellow conspirators were hanged.

The strain on the Commonwealth navy resulting from Cromwell's operations had by now begun to tell on Blake's blockading force, which was reduced to five ships. In mid-October they were forced to withdraw to Milford Haven as a result of bad weather, and by the time they got back at the end of the month Rupert was gone. He had in fact sailed with seven of his best ships on 20 October, leaving the *James* and the *Roebuck* at Kinsale, where they fell into enemy hands the following month.

Meanwhile, the King, who had left The Hague for Ireland at the end of June 1649, spent some time in Paris and St-Germain before arriving in Jersey at the end of September. He narrowly missed being captured by a strong Commonwealth squadron commanded by Popham, because it arrived too soon and departed before Charles got there. On reaching Jersey he heard of the disasters that had befallen the Royalist cause in Ireland and realised that his move to that country would have to be delayed indefinitely. He therefore stayed in Jersey until February 1650, conducting negotiations with the Scots which led to his arrival in Edinburgh the following June.

Rupert's performance during the months that he spent in Ireland is not easy to assess, especially as there are no clear-cut pictures of him at work as there are in the Civil War battles or at the time when the Royalist fleet closed with Warwick's ships at the mouth of the Thames. Nor is it possible to get much idea of his personal feelings, or of his reaction to events other than the declaration that he issued after King Charles I was put to death. During the period when the *Constant Reformation* was being refitted, he may occasionally have gone to sea in another vessel, but it is likely that for most of the time he was based ashore. Apart from the account of the council of war held as the fleet dropped down Kinsale harbour and of the days spent collecting recruits from the Munster ports, it is difficult to know where Rupert was at any particular moment. Nothing is recorded of his movements except for a brief mention in a letter received at Queen Henrietta Maria's court that he had in May been helping with the army around Cork.

It is clear that Rupert was in close touch with Ormonde by letter and that he also had some contact with other commanders in the country, but there is no evidence that he actually met Ormonde. During the Civil War Rupert had been renowned for his energy, thinking nothing of riding great distances to coordinate the actions of the different parts of the Royalist forces, and his vigour in preparing the fleet for sea in 1648 showed that this energy was undiminished. But it would seem that he had become more sensitive to the authority of other Royalist leaders than he would have been six or seven years earlier. In particular, he had no wish to jeopardise Ormonde's position, which would almost certainly have happened had Rupert appeared in person with the army, as some at least of Ormonde's commanders would have wanted to follow him. Rupert was a far more able operational commander than Ormonde, who incidentally missed the chance of disrupting Cromwell's army while it was investing Drogheda, but Ormonde, as head of one of the ancient Norman-Irish families and a former commander of the army in Ireland, had a lifetime's experience of conjuring up alliances from the various factions and knew instinctively what each could be expected to achieve: he was also better placed to raise money from the King's supporters. Furthermore, although Rupert had been invested with a loosely worded authority over all Royalist forces, Ormonde was the King's Lord-Lieutenant in Ireland. It is easy to feel that Rupert should have taken firmer control of the campaign, but it is unlikely that he would have saved Ireland for the King and he might well have lost the fleet in the process.

His handling of his ships is easier to assess. The fleet that sailed from Kinsale in October 1649 consisted of the same number of ships as had left Helvoetsluys nine months earlier, but they were better and stronger ships, better manned and better found. In addition, Rupert had been able to reinforce Grenville in the Isles of Scilly and send significant sums of money to the King from the sale of the prizes captured. More important in the long term, Rupert had gained valuable experience in the business of getting ships to sea and keeping them there in all sorts of circumstances, which is one of the basic elements of naval strategy. In years to come Rupert's experience in this field would prove useful.

But although at Helvoetsluys and Kinsale Rupert had gained experience of fitting out ships and directing naval operations, he spent little time at sea. He had therefore virtually no opportunity to manoeuvre the fleet under sail, an activity that depended on an understanding of seamanship, or of controlling it at sea, which depended on communications. It could be said that he had completed the change from general to admiral and that during the next three and a half years he would learn the fundamentals of his new trade in a very hard school.

3

FROM PORTUGAL TO THE
WEST INDIES

Rupert's fleet, when it left Kinsale, consisted of the three flagships together with the *Scott* (30 guns), *Mary* (24), *Black-moor Lady* (18) and *Black Knight* (14). Where the *Mary* and the *Black Knight* came from is not known, but they may have been renamed prizes like the *Scott* or they may have been provided by the Irish. From Kinsale the fleet headed off across the Bay of Biscay towards Portugal but got separated by the storm that had enabled it to put to sea. Some days later all the ships met up again at a rendezvous to the west of Finisterre and then started to cruise around in search of prizes. Soon they were again separated by a further bout of bad weather.

Rupert in the *Constant Reformation* together with Mennes in the *Swallow* now found and chased a ship that they failed to catch, but the hunt took them well downwind of the next rendezvous. They spent two days beating back and then sighted a squadron of seven ships which turned out to be the rest of their fleet together with two prizes, a ship taken by Maurice and another from Newfoundland full of fish taken by Marshall. Next day the fleet met two good ships out from London together with a ketch. Three of the small fast vessels chased them and fought them for some hours before the flagships caught up, after which the two big ships surrendered. The ketch escaped.

After making some necessary repairs to the prizes, Rupert took his considerably enhanced fleet towards Lisbon, sending off in advance to discover what sort of a reception he would get. While waiting for an answer, Rupert himself captured a large English ship that was taking a Portuguese cargo from Brazil to Lisbon. On receiving a favourable answer to his enquiry he took his whole fleet into the mouth of the Tagus, where he sold three of the prizes, taking the other two into his fleet as the *Second Charles* (40) and the *Henry* (36). He also bought a Dutch ship that became the *Black Prince* (30). In order to find the guns and crews for these new ships, *Blackmoor Lady* was sold and the *Convertine* laid up. The exact date of his arrival in the Tagus is doubtful, but it was probably towards the end of November 1649.

Rupert's fleet remained based in the Tagus until mid-October 1650, that is to say about six weeks longer than the time spent at Kinsale. As at Kinsale, there was an initial period when his ships had access to the open sea, after which they were block-aded by Blake for seven months, including some weeks when they shared the lower reaches of the river with the Common-wealth fleet intent on their destruction in much the same way as they had shared the outer harbour at Helvoetsluys with War-wick's fleet in 1648. But circumstances in Portugal caused the Portuguese government to exert different pressures on Rupert from those that he had experienced at Kinsale or Helvoetsluys.

Until 1581 Portugal had been an independent country, but at this time the royal line died out and the throne was claimed by Philip II of Spain, a cousin of the dead King. Sixty years later, when war between Spain and France was weakening the Spanish hold on Portugal, Spanish rule was challenged by John, Duke of Braganza, who also had a claim to the Portuguese throne. In December 1641 this man was adopted as King John IV by the Cortes, Portugal's Parliament, and recognised as such by England and France. France and the United Provinces sent assistance to Portugal in its struggle to remain independent of Spain, but within a few years commercial rivalry led to war between Portugal and the Dutch.

It was against this background that King John IV, who was expecting the Stuarts to be restored to the English throne, extended a welcome to Prince Rupert and his ships. Some of his ministers, including his principal adviser the Count de Miro, were unhappy with this policy, fearing the effect that the enmity of the English Commonwealth might have on Portugal's vulner-able overseas trade. The first problem that arose soon after Rupert arrived resulted from the fact that the large ship that Rupert had captured was carrying a Portuguese cargo from Brazil to Lisbon and his right to sell it was challenged. Next there was opposition to Rupert's intention to send Prince Maurice to sea to capture further English ships and sell the contents in Lisbon, on the grounds that this would further annoy the Commonwealth government. Finally, exception was taken to Rupert's insistence that all foreign ships entering or leaving the Tagus should salute his flag. All of these issues involved lengthy letters being written to him by the Portuguese Secretary of State which he left unanswered and largely ignored, although Maurice did not set out on his cruise to take prizes as planned.[1]

Clearly Rupert could not have taken so high-handed a line had he not been assured of King John's support. Soon after his fleet arrived, the King permitted him to move it further upriver into Oeiras Bay and to take his prizes to Lisbon for disposal. Furthermore, both Rupert and Maurice regularly visited the King at Lisbon and took a full part in the social life of the court. They also spent much time getting to know the local gentry by hunting with them and by moving around among them without the guards and escorts that normally accompanied royalty in the Iberian Peninsula, thereby demonstrating an unaccustomed and welcome informality and trust. Later, as English naval and diplomatic pressure strengthened de Miro's hand, Rupert and Maurice successfully urged the clergy to use their influence with the people to back the King in his support of the Royalists. The Church took the line that it would bring dishonour on the Crown and the country to abandon them to English rebels.

The letter that Rupert wrote to Ormonde in July explaining how he would operate from Portugal was intercepted by enemy troops in Ireland and so never reached its intended destination, but neither did its contents get relayed to the generals-at-sea, who were divided in their opinion as to whether Rupert would base himself in the Isles of Scilly or make for the Iberian Peninsula. At this time Deane was ill and it was left to Popham and Blake to recommend a plan to the council of state. It soon became clear that Rupert had gone to Portugal and it was decided that Blake should pursue him. On 17 January he received orders from the council to scatter and destroy all the ships of Rupert's fleet and any others adhering to them. If foreign ships were to support Rupert, they were to be attacked as well, and Blake was given power to requisition whatever merchantmen he might need. Blake assembled a fleet at

Portsmouth consisting of eleven fighting ships, two fireships and two ketches; they sailed on 1 March and anchored at the mouth of the Tagus in Cascais Bay ten days later. With this fleet came Henry Vane's brother Charles to act as envoy of the Commonwealth government to the King of Portugal.

Blake immediately sent Vane with a letter to the King saying that he was sure that the King would not mind him sailing up the river to exterminate the pirates, as he described Rupert's fleet, and added that he hoped he might be allowed to use Portuguese ports freely. Next day, without waiting for a reply, his fleet headed off upriver but was fired at by the two forts on either side of the entrance. At this time the wind dropped and Blake found himself in a vulnerable position. A messenger from the King now appeared saying that the forts had fired without orders but that Blake had been to blame for trying to enter the river uninvited. Blake took his fleet back to Cascais Bay and a few days later Vane negotiated an agreement under which, with written permission, his fleet might come as far as Oeiras Bay in the event of stormy weather, but that if it did it was not to attack Rupert and that to avoid trouble the crews were to stay on board except when collecting water and supplies. Blake almost immediately took advantage of bad weather to move his ships into Oeiras Bay, where they anchored some two miles downstream of Rupert's ships which were protected by the guns of the Tower of Belém.[2]

Although subjected to considerable pressure from Vane and those members of his government who wished to be rid of the Royalists, the King, influenced by his wife and the clergy, continued to favour Rupert. Early in April he ruled that no additional English ships should be allowed to reinforce Blake, which weakened his position when Rupert was himself reinforced by two French warships a few days later.

In the middle of the same month, according to the writer of *Prince Rupert's Voyage to the West Indies*, Blake planned to have Rupert and Maurice killed while they were out hunting. An ambush was laid by a party of sailors allegedly ashore to collect water, but the plot was discovered and the ambush party was obliged to make 'use of their legs instead of their arms: some going to their long home while others by a willing and forced mistake went aboard our fleet instead of their own'. Blake's version was that one of his peaceful watering parties was subjected to an unprovoked attack by Rupert. Soon afterwards,

Rupert responded by devising and making a firebomb out of a keg filled with inflammable material, which he tried to get on board the flagship of Blake's vice-admiral, Robert Moulton. This ruse also failed because the sailor, disguised as a Portuguese boatman, who was trying to deliver the bomb gave himself away by swearing in English at the critical moment. Vane tried to persuade the King that Rupert's action constituted an act of war and that Blake should therefore be allowed to attack Rupert's fleet, but the King did not agree.

A further period of armed neutrality followed until, in the second half of May, Blake took his ships to sea in an attempt to lure Rupert out of the river. While there, he attacked and captured nine English merchantmen hired by the Portuguese, which were leaving Lisbon for Brazil in company with a number of Portuguese ships. At the end of the month Blake was reinforced by Popham with a further four warships together with four requisitioned merchantmen. With this reinforcement came further instructions from the council of state ordering the destruction of Rupert's fleet wherever it might be found and adding that if obstructed by King John they could attack his trade.[3]

Popham and Blake now wrote to the King demanding that he should hand Rupert's ships over to them, in which case they undertook to release the ships on hire to Portugal that they had captured. Vane did not wait to deliver this message but escaped in disguise so as to avoid being taken into custody by the infuriated King, who vented his anger by seizing a number of ships belonging to English merchants in Lisbon together with some individuals known to support the Commonwealth. No longer was Blake's fleet permitted to enter the Tagus or to collect water from the mainland, a serious matter since the water storage capacity of a ship was much less in terms of days of consumption than the food storage capacity. Blake's ships originally had been victualled for six months, and as additional supplies brought out by Popham were found to be bad it would soon be necessary to send groups of ships off in succession to find further supplies.

So far, Rupert had played his hand well, having built up enough support with the King, clergy and local gentry to offset the influence of de Miro and the business community while keeping his fleet safe from Blake under the shelter of the Portuguese forts. At the same time he had goaded Blake into action that had alienated the Portuguese to such an extent that the Commonwealth fleet was committed to mounting a blockade from the open sea with no friendly port nearer than Cadiz. He had tied down a Commonwealth fleet of over twenty ships, with all the expense involved, sent to prevent him raiding their commerce, which he could resume doing as soon as a storm forced Blake off station. This at any rate was the gloomy assessment made by Popham in a letter to his wife.[4]

But there were two main weaknesses in Rupert's position. First, although the prizes that he had already taken had been sold for enough to keep his men paid and fed for the time being, eventually he would need more and could not stay indefinitely protected by the Portuguese. Second, the Portuguese struggle with Spain and their dependence on imports from their overseas possessions, which were vulnerable to the Commonwealth's navy, meant that they could not endure the hostility of England for long. Rupert might himself need support from Portugal after leaving the Tagus and it was important that he should not overstay his welcome.

Meanwhile, the Commonwealth government, which had been steadily increasing its naval strength, opened hostilities with France at sea and kept up the pressure on Portugal by interfering with their fishing fleet. Towards the end of June King John, anxious to be rid of the Royalists if he could do so with enough honour to satisfy his subjects, offered to cover Rupert's departure by interposing his own fleet between Rupert and Blake for long enough for Rupert's ships to make their escape. At this time Blake's strength was depleted because eight of his ships had gone to Cadiz for supplies.

In the early days of July there was a build-up of Portuguese naval strength in Oeiras Bay as a fleet of thirteen warships assembled, together with a number of small craft and fireships: opinions differ as to exact numbers. Rupert's own fleet, including the two French ships that had joined him in April, amounted to a further ten ships, so that he and his Portuguese allies had twenty-three ships against the ten warships plus three armed merchantmen and the nine recently captured ships of the Brazil fleet immediately available to Blake and Popham.

But although numerically the allies were well placed, Blake

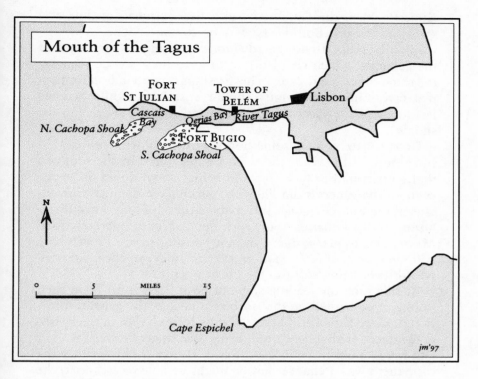

Mouth of the Tagus

FORT
ST JULIAN

TOWER OF
BELÉM

Lisbon

Cascais
Bay

Oeiras Bay

River Tagus

N. Cachopa Shoal

FORT BUGIO

S. Cachopa Shoal

N

MILES

0   5   15

Cape Espichel

jm'97

and Popham could at any moment be reinforced by the return of the squadron that had gone to Cadiz. Furthermore, King John did not want a full-scale battle which, if successful, would totally alienate the Commonwealth and, if a failure, would gravely affect his own position. The allies therefore intended to avoid battle if possible. Their plan was for the Portuguese and French ships to interpose themselves between Rupert and Blake during the day and then after dark to show extra lights, thereby luring Blake's ships towards them on the assumption that Rupert was with them. Meanwhile, Rupert's ships with all lights extinguished would slip away under cover of darkness.[5]

On the morning of 26 July, with the wind from the east-south-east, the allies decided to act. At this time the Commonwealth fleet was at anchor in Cascais Bay. Because the Portuguese ships, commanded by an ancient admiral, had difficulty in getting to sea, Rupert, with the larger of the French ships (40 guns) leading his line, found himself heading down the river in front of them. With the French ship were four fireships ready to take advantage of any opportunity that might present itself. At the sight of

[75]

Rupert's ships the Commonwealth fleet weighed anchor and sailed out to sea. Both fleets were on the port tack.

Initially, Rupert had the advantage of being to windward of the generals, which enabled him to keep his distance while at the same time able to launch his fireships downwind on to them if a favourable opportunity should arise: this would become less likely as the fleets got further away from the shore and the shoals.

Unfortunately, after some hours with the Portuguese still in the mouth of the river, the wind swung round to the south so that Rupert had to tack to avoid being blown down on to the enemy. The generals did likewise, which gave them the advantage of the weather gauge and enabled their leading ships, *Resolution* (68), *Phoenix* (36) and the captured merchantman *Mayflower*, to get within a distant gunshot of the French ship and the *Constant Reformation*, the remainder of the Commonwealth fleet being still too far off to open fire.

At this time the leading ships of both fleets must have been sailing close-hauled on the starboard tack in the general direction of Cape Espichel. There was now little chance of the Portuguese, faced with a headwind, being able to get between Rupert and the Commonwealth fleet, but if Rupert could weather the cape there was a chance that he might be able to escape to the south in the dark.

For some hours there was a desultory exchange of fire at long range, which did little damage, after which in the late afternoon Rupert, realising that he would not be able to clear Cape Espichel, changed course again so that he was heading back towards the mouth of the Tagus and his Portuguese allies. According to Commonwealth accounts, Rupert did this by bearing away, that is to say by going in an anticlockwise direction, whereas the Royalists maintain that he tacked, i.e. moved clockwise away from the land, which he might have been obliged to do if, for example, the water was too shallow to permit his getting any closer inshore. If true, this would have brought him nearer to the enemy, which would make sense of a Portuguese report to the effect that the *Constant Reformation* received some hits and the *Resolution* lost her foremast.

There is no doubt that if the Commonwealth fleet, which included some new and powerful ships, could have closed right up at any time during the day it could have done serious damage. This was particularly true of the heavily armed generals' flagship, the *Resolution* (formerly *Royal Prince*), one of the two first-rate ships in the Commonwealth navy at that time and which had been built as recently as 1641. But according to Popham's report, 'shots passed between us and the Frenchman, but we could never get within shot of Rupert, do what we could'.[6] Although not literally true, this was a notable tribute to the tactics employed in Rupert's fleet.

As it got dark Rupert took advantage of the fact that his ships needed less water under their keels than the *Resolution* to give the enemy the slip. He anchored his fleet in six fathoms of water up against the North Cachopa Shoal covered by the forts. The Commonwealth fleet came on as far as the South Cachopa Shoal but, rather than risk anchoring where the ships might be blown on to the shoal or dragged by the current into the mouth of the river, pulled back to the open sea.

Early next morning the enemy made as if to return towards Cascais Bay but found the whole of the allied fleet heading in that direction, where they soon anchored, covered by the guns of the forts. There was only a light east wind, which meant that the allies were unlikely to put to sea again for the time being. This gave the Commonwealth ships no option but to return to the open sea.

King John then arrived on a visit, but there was no further action that day. During the coming night the *Assurance*, one of the ships belonging to the squadron that had been sent to Cadiz, came close enough to keep the allies under observation. In doing so she gave an indication that the Commonwealth fleet might have been restored to its full strength. In fact, this was not yet the case, as the *Assurance* had returned in advance of the rest of the squadron.

Next morning Rupert made a further attempt to get away under cover of the Portuguese ships. The allies headed out towards the Commonwealth fleet but, when threatened, retired under the guns of the forts. The enemy followed them, but when they got too close to the forts or shoals they moved back out to sea, followed by the allies. The trouble was that the Portuguese did not want a full-scale battle for the reasons already mentioned, and the generals could not afford one until the Cadiz squadron returned. On the other hand the Portuguese hoped to bring about a situation that would enable Rupert's ships to make good their escape while Blake and Popham were determined to contain him even if it meant becoming involved in some limited fighting. In the event there was no fighting and Rupert was unable to get away. Late in the afternoon the wind again turned to the south and soon afterwards seven or eight ships were sighted out to sea. Expecting these to be the Cadiz squadron, as indeed they were, Rupert returned the allied fleet to the safe anchorage at Cascais Bay.

The generals now felt strong enough to take on the whole of the allied fleet, but next day a brisk easterly wind prevented them from launching an attack. Rupert equally realised that there was no longer a chance of getting away, so the whole of the allied fleet returned to Oeiras Bay.

During the previous four days, little damage was done but Rupert had not achieved his objective of getting his ships away from Portugal. This was due above all else to the inefficiency of the Portuguese admiral, who was dismissed soon after the return to Oeiras Bay. But the operations had afforded Rupert his first opportunity of commanding a sizeable fleet in action, thereby giving him practical experience of several problems that would recur in his life on a much larger scale, such as the intricacies of working with allies at sea.

Rupert himself must have enjoyed the experience immensely and it is easy to imagine him standing on the quarterdeck of the *Constant Reformation* as she headed out to sea, watching the Commonwealth fleet across the waves and cursing the inability of the Portuguese to get their ships out of the river in time. Standing with him would have been his flag captain, Fearnes, the captain of the ship, Kettleby, and probably the master. These would have been the people who would have become aware of the changes of direction and intensity of the wind and who would have advised Rupert on the options available to him in terms of bearing away or of tacking, or possibly of releasing a fireship. Their advice would have enabled him to foil the best efforts of Popham and Blake to pin him down on the first day, and it would have been their skill that enabled him to make good use of the shoals and forts to throw off the enemy that evening. But throughout the period it was Rupert who never lost sight of his ultimate aim, which was to preserve his fleet intact in order to capture prizes for the good of the Royalist cause.

On land during the Civil War Rupert had shown himself to be a fine tactician, which derived from his having a detailed knowledge of the capability of his men and their weapons, equipment and horses combined with an eye for the country and a wonderful sense of timing. Over the past year he had been gaining a similar knowledge of the men, ships and guns that made up his fleet. This he now had to combine with an understanding of seamanship in order to become as good a tactician by sea as he had formerly been on land. Seamanship consisted of an intricate combination of measures for the working of the sails and the trimming of the ship in order to get the maximum value out of every shift of wind, weather, current and tide. It involved the use of blocks and tackles and capstans to haul ropes and to move heavy objects such as guns, ships' boats and anchors. This was something that would inevitably appeal to Rupert, whose great delight was in finding out how things worked. Clearly, he must have had much to learn, but the operations off Portugal indicate that he had grasped the connection between seamanship and tactics that was indispensable to operational success at sea.

There is no reference in any of the reports of the operation to another important tactical requirement, that is to say to the system of communications used within the allied fleet. At the time this aspect of command remained in a primitive state, a few simple orders being sent by changing the position in which the standards and ensigns of the flagship were flown, or by altering the way in which a particular sail was set or by the firing of a gun. It would take the experience of the first Dutch War, still three years into the future, to produce the first systematic attempts to relate signals to tactics, a subject in which Rupert would become closely involved in years to come.

Soon after the allies returned to Oeiras Bay, the generals were subjected to pressure from the council of state to reduce the size of the fleet blockading Rupert. This came about mainly because operations in Scotland, following the arrival there of Charles II in June, led to an increasing naval commitment.

Some weeks earlier Cromwell, who had almost finished defeating the Royalist forces in Ireland, had been withdrawn to England, leaving others to complete the subjugation of the Irish by imposing the new Land Act. On his return he found the army under Fairfax preparing for a campaign in Scotland: Cromwell was required to resume his position as lieutenant-general. But Fairfax, not wanting to fight his old allies, resigned, and on 15 June 1650 Cromwell was appointed Lord General in his place. Soon afterwards, he moved north with 16,000 men. With the army went Colonel Monck, soon to command the land-based artillery.

David Leslie, who was in effect commanding the Scottish army, built lines of defence to cover Edinburgh and repulsed Cromwell's attempt to force them on 29 July, an operation that was going on at the same time as Rupert and the Portuguese were sparring with Popham and Blake. Cromwell's subsequent attempt to get around the flank of Leslie's position put a heavy demand on naval support.

It was at this time that Popham and Blake were told to release some of their fleet. As a result, on 3 September, Popham with eight ships, including the *Resolution*, sailed to Cadiz to replenish before setting off for England. Blake, now flying his flag in the *George* (56 guns), was left with nine ships to watch Rupert. On the day that Popham sailed, Cromwell beat Leslie at Dunbar. Four days later Rupert again tried to break out.

Attempting to unravel the many contradictory accounts of the events that took place off the coast of Portugal over the ensuing weeks has proved a major problem to several eminent historians.[7] The incident that most directly involved Rupert was a brush that took place on 7 September when he was once more briefly in action with Blake. At some stage that morning the Royalist fleet, together with Portuguese and French ships, put to sea. They had thirty-six ships between them. It was a foggy day, but they briefly sighted Blake at 11 a.m. before his ships disappeared into the mist.

At 4 p.m. Rupert, in the *Constant Reformation*, was leading the allied fleet and was evidently some distance to windward of the main body. Suddenly, out of the fog dead ahead appeared Blake's flagship, the *George*, sailing directly towards him on the opposite tack, followed by the *Phoenix* (36) and the *Expedition* (36). According to Blake's account, he wanted to get to windward of the *Constant Reformation* but was unable to do so because of the direction of the wind, which indicates that it was coming across Rupert's quarter and on to Blake's bow. On being told by his master that he could not weather Rupert, Blake gave orders to keep straight on, which would result in a collision unless Rupert gave way. Rupert could not afford to become entangled with the *George* as he would immediately be attacked by the two ships following Blake, which would inevitably arrive before the leading units of his own fleet. Clearly, the allied ships were not only downwind of him but some distance away, as there is no mention of their having opened fire when the engagement took place. Rupert therefore gave way, passing downwind of Blake with whom he exchanged a broadside, subsequently receiving broadsides from the *Phoenix* and *Expedition* as well.

The ensuing chaos is easily imagined, with smoke from the enemy guns blown down on to the *Constant Reformation*, whose fore-topmast was shot away in the fight. The *Constant Reformation* sailed downwind until she joined the allied fleet. Blake headed out to sea in search of the rest of his ships. The Royalists, not wishing to set off on a long cruise with a damaged flagship, returned to port in company with the rest of the allied fleet.

In all of this there is no record of the direction of the wind, which makes it impossible to work out where either side was or where they were going when the encounter took place. It is therefore difficult to comment on the tactics employed by either side, except to express surprise that the *Constant Reformation* should have been sailing unsupported by any other ship at the moment when the *George* loomed up out of the fog. There may well have been a good reason for this, and it was certainly bad luck that Blake should have appeared exactly where he did, since he could not have arranged it. But there is no obvious reason why Rupert should have detached himself from his main body in the way described.

The most that can be said is that the day's operations must have provided both Rupert and Blake with additional experience of war at sea. It would be interesting to know whether these two great men caught a glimpse of each other as their ships passed amid the roar of the broadsides, the smoke and the fog. They would never see each other again, as Blake died at sea of fever in his cabin on board the *George* in 1657, three years before Rupert returned to England following the Restoration. It was perhaps as well that he did die in his moment of glory. Although a great admiral, he was an uncompromising republican and Puritan who would have found it difficult to fit into the Restoration navy in the way that Monck, Montagu and Penn did when the time arrived.

*   *   *

A week later Blake intercepted a fleet of twenty-three ships returning to Portugal from Brazil which he scattered, sinking one and capturing seven others. Five more were captured later, probably by Popham's ships, which were at that time returning to England having replenished at Cadiz. Only nine of the Portuguese ships reached safety. This was a serious blow to the Portuguese economy, which relied heavily on its trade with Brazil, and the King sent his fleet to sea to drive off Blake. He also asked Rupert to reinforce it, which Rupert did on 16 September, but his ships got separated from the Portuguese and he returned to port.

King John was now more than ever anxious to get rid of Rupert, whose presence had caused so much damage to Portugal. Luckily, circumstances were now favourable for him to escape as Blake was obliged to take his ships to Cadiz to sell the prizes he had taken and to get further supplies of water. He was still there on 12 October 1650 when Rupert's ships, having been refitted and resupplied by the Portuguese, finally sailed down the Tagus to the open sea.

At this time Rupert's fleet consisted of six ships: *Constant Reformation* (52 guns), with Captains Fearnes and Kettleby; *Swallow* (40), Captain Chester; *Black Prince* (40), Captain Goulding; *Second Charles* (40), Captain Marshall; *Henry* (30), Captain Burley; and *Mary* (24), Sir John Mucknell, who had been the captain of a Royalist privateer working out of West Country ports during the Civil War. Of these ships only *Constant Reformation* and *Swallow* had started life as warships. *Black Prince* had been bought at Lisbon; *Second Charles*, *Henry* and *Mary* were converted prizes.

In terms of officers, Mennes parted from the fleet at Lisbon and was not replaced as rear-admiral and Feilding had died. Allin, who had been captured the previous year off the Isles of Scilly, managed to escape and make his way back, reaching Rupert at Lisbon in March. Popham, who had captured Allin, maintained that he was regarded by the Royalists as 'one of the principal hinges upon which all their sea business moves'.[8] At the time of his return, all the ships had captains so he was held as a supernumerary until a ship could be found for him.

Apart from his surgeon Choqueux, who had been sent with a letter to King Charles, most of Rupert's personal entourage, such as Mortaigne, Rivers, Holmes, Pyne and Billingsley, were still with him, probably split between the two flagships. The total number of all ranks in the fleet is not known for certain. In a letter to the King written when he arrived in Portugal, he reported that he had 1,200, and although some would have deserted at Lisbon and some been lost through sickness, he would have recruited others so that probably he would have been left with as many as he had had when he arrived.[9] At any rate numbers would not be a problem until he had to start manning prizes.

This soon happened. On leaving the Tagus Rupert headed out into the Atlantic for about 100 miles where he found three English merchantmen on 14 October. In some way he persuaded them that the *Constant Reformation* was Blake's flagship and that *Black Prince* was the *Assurance*, and in this way he captured two of them without a fight. The *Second Charles* was less fortunate with the third ship and chased her over the horizon. Rupert waited a whole day for her return, during which time he put a crew into the larger of the prizes and burned the smaller one, having transferred her cargo into his ships.

Rupert now brought his ships into the Mediterranean, passing through the Strait of Gibraltar on 18 or 19 October and casting anchor off the African coast in Tétouan Bay. It must have been at about this time that the writer of *Prince Rupert's Voyage to the West Indies*, having explained that Portugal had made an agreement with the Commonwealth not to give shelter to the fleet, penned the poignant passage: 'so that now misfortune being no novelty to us, we plough the sea for a subsistence, and, being destitute of a port, we take the confines of the Mediterranean Sea for our harbour; poverty and despair being companions and revenge our guide.'[10] It is difficult to know why the writer of this passage was so gloomy as the fleet, having left Lisbon only a week earlier, must have been well supplied and in good condition at the time.

Two days later, with no news of the *Second Charles*, Rupert sailed to Málaga on the coast of Spain having on the way exchanged shots with an English vessel that he could not capture because she was too closely protected by the Spanish fort at Estepona. In the anchorage at Málaga were a number of English merchantmen that Rupert wanted to capture.

Rupert's plan was that the *Henry* should sail into Málaga pretending to be the merchant ship *Roebuck*, which she had been before her conversion, and anchor where she could cut off the English ships should they try to escape. The rest of the fleet would attack under cover of darkness. Unfortunately, some disaffected seamen from the *Henry* got away in a boat unnoticed by the officers and warned the merchant ships which immediately retreated up the harbour.

Next day Rupert sailed to the small port of Vélez-Málaga, some twenty miles to the east, where other English merchant ships were anchored. On 24 October Rupert took his fleet into that port, but the merchantmen had already asked for Spanish protection and the governor begged Rupert not to take any action until he heard from Madrid. But Rupert, who was becoming increasingly exasperated by the obstruction of the Spanish authorities, did not wait to have the matter resolved by diplomacy. Instead, he burned two of the merchantmen (or possibly they burned themselves to avoid being taken) and then moved off along the coast.

Two days later, at Motril, Rupert found more English ships, which he destroyed. Shortly afterwards, he was rejoined by Marshall in the *Second Charles* who had been involved in various adventures. On the night of 19 October, while outside the Strait of Gibraltar in company with a friendly French warship, he narrowly escaped destruction by Blake's fleet, the French vessel being captured. Marshall then passed through the Strait and took a good ship called the *William and John* after a lengthy action in Tétouan Bay, putting on board a prize crew under Captain Allin, who had evidently been sailing in the *Second Charles*.

On 28 October Blake, who had returned to Cadiz with his French prize, heard that some of Rupert's ships had been seen at Málaga. He set off immediately in pursuit. He reached Málaga two days later, where he heard that Rupert was at Alicante. He sailed on without a moment's delay.

By this time Rupert's fleet had again become fragmented. *Constant Reformation* and *Swallow* were chasing a merchantman south towards Africa. *Second Charles*, with the prize taken by Rupert in the Atlantic and the *William and John*, was heading towards the coast of Spain to get the *William and John* repaired. On the way they were joined by *Black Prince* and *Mary*. Soon afterwards, these five ships set off to chase eighteen merchantmen which subsequently turned out to be Dutch and therefore not fair game.

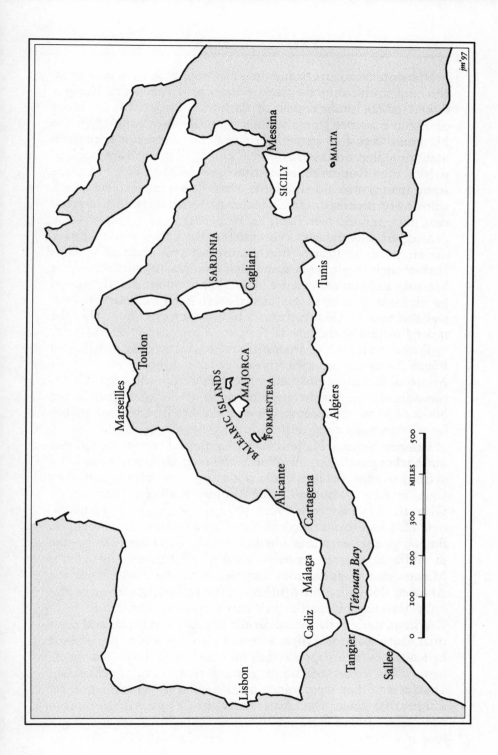

Marseilles
Toulon
SARDINIA
Cagliari
Messina
SICILY
•MALTA
Tunis
Algiers
BALEARIC ISLANDS
MAJORCA
FORMENTERA
Alicante
Cartagena
Málaga
Cadiz
Lisbon
Tangier
Sallee
Tétouan Bay

jm'97

0   100   200   300   500
MILES

The ship that Rupert and Maurice was chasing was a large and well-armed merchantman of 400 tons called the *Marmaduke*. Although they caught up with her before dark, the onset of night prevented any serious fighting. Next morning the *Marmaduke* put up strong resistance and it was not until midday, after her captain had been killed, that she surrendered. By this time they were in sight of the African coast. The three ships then sailed north to the next fleet rendezvous, which was at Formentera in the Balearic Islands, where they arrived on 4 November.

Meanwhile, early on 3 November Blake's ships came up with the *Henry* and captured her because her crew refused to fight against such heavy odds. Later that day the Royalist ships that had been chasing the Dutch sighted Blake, who promptly chased them. Blake's faster ships quickly overhauled the *Black Prince*, and the *Second Charles* turned back to support her. This the other Royalist ships were not prepared to do and fled to Cartagena followed by the *Second Charles* which could not defend *Black Prince* on her own. *Black Prince* did, however, beat off the advanced units of Blake's fleet but could not reach Cartagena during the night. Next morning, as she was again being overhauled by the enemy, she was beached and burned by her crew to escape capture.

Later in the day Blake reached Cartagena, where he entered the harbour and anchored near the four Royalist ships. The Spanish authorities asked him not to take any action until they could receive instructions from Madrid, but before these could arrive the Royalists tried to escape during the night of 6 November. But the escape failed as the ships ran ashore, whereupon the wind got up and dashed them to pieces so that by the morning they were all totally wrecked. Blake then sent a letter to the Spanish authorities claiming that the contents of the wrecked ships were the property of the English government and on 9 November set off to look for Rupert and Maurice.

When Rupert arrived at Formentera with Maurice and their prize there was naturally no sign of his other ships. But Rupert had no reason to suppose that they had been destroyed, so he merely left a message under a stone marked by a white flag appointing a further rendezvous at Cagliari in Sardinia and set sail for that place. Soon afterwards, the *Constant Reformation* became separated from the other two ships in a storm and got blown down to Sicily, where she stayed at Messina to repair the damage. Maurice, with the prize, somehow weathered the storm and sailed to Toulon, where he arrived, greatly worried about his brother's fate, on 25 November.

Meanwhile, Blake, who knew of the Formentera rendezvous from papers captured with the *Henry*, arrived there only to find Rupert gone. Although he found the paper under the stone appointing the next rendezvous, he did not continue the pursuit, returning to Cartagena via Majorca and Alicante. At one of these places he received a letter from the council of state ordering him to return home with most of his ships and saying that Penn was being sent out to command those remaining in southern seas. Blake sailed for Cadiz, where he refitted and replenished on his way home.[11]

Rupert left Messina around the middle of December and joined Maurice in Toulon. The Royalist account of their reunion makes it very clear how greatly the two princes had missed each other, describing their embraces and saying that Maurice had not even been ashore from the time of his arrival because of his grief at the thought that Rupert might have been lost at sea. For his part there is no doubt that Rupert loved this brother, who had shared so much with him in their early years and during the Civil War, above all people on earth.

Although Rupert and Maurice had good cause for rejoicing over their reunion, they had little else to celebrate. In the two months that had elapsed since leaving Portugal they had taken a number of prizes, all of which they had lost except for the one that Maurice had brought to Toulon with him. In addition, they had lost all of their own ships with the exception of the *Constant Reformation* and the *Swallow*.

It is difficult to apportion the blame for these misfortunes between Rupert and his captains, but with hindsight it would seem that Rupert's failure to realise how closely he was being followed by Blake was one of the main causes of the disaster. It has been suggested that Rupert believed that Blake's fleet had returned to England after visiting Cadiz,[12] but even if he had thought this initially he must have realised his mistake as soon as he met up with the *Second Charles*. Having done so, he could with due consideration of wind and tide have worked out that Blake might arrive at short notice. Although the mere sighting of the *Second Charles* outside the Strait would not necessarily convey to Blake the fact that Rupert had passed into the Mediterranean, Rupert should have recognised the possibility that he would draw this conclusion, in which case it was dangerous for him to pursue the *Marmaduke* towards Africa, thereby depriving his weaker ships of the protection of the two flagships.

Another cause of Rupert's misfortunes was the fact that Spain favoured Blake, not only because of its hostility to Portugal and France, which had been helping Rupert, but also because the Commonwealth had become too strong at sea to be trifled with. In the last resort this strength meant that the Commonwealth could always maintain a superior force in any area where Rupert was capable of causing serious damage to its interests. Before leaving the subject of Rupert's misfortunes it is necessary to add that on balance Blake had outperformed his opponent in the very areas in which Rupert himself had been pre-eminent on land, that is to say in deduction, speed of decision and execution.

In terms of the Royalist cause as a whole, Rupert's misfortunes did not rate highly. In Scotland King Charles and his unfriendly government took refuge together in Perth following the defeat at Dunbar, while Cromwell secured strategic centres in the south of the country. In the United Provinces William of Orange, Stadtholder and husband of Charles's sister Mary, suddenly died in November, as a result of which the Grand Pensionary, who was far less sympathetic to the Stuarts than William had been, became the most powerful man in the land. In France the second stage of the Civil War, sometimes known as the War of the Princes, was in full swing. Toulon was in an area that supported Condé against Anne of Austria and Mazarin, who were still running the country on behalf of the young King.

Despite his setbacks, Rupert went to work to rectify the situation. One of the first things to be done was to establish responsibility for the loss of the *Henry* and for the abandonment of the *Black Prince*, with a view to restoring the authority and reputations of those officers who had done well and disposing of those who were to blame. By January all of the captains and some of the crews had made their way to Toulon from Cartagena and an inquiry was set in train.

So far as the *Henry* was concerned, most felt that Burley was at fault with particular reference to Blake's getting details of the fleet rendezvous at Formentera: they considered that he had been too friendly with Blake after being captured. Burley claimed that his men had mutinied and that he had been power-less. Rupert banished him from the fleet with a recommendation that he should never again be employed by the King.

When the *Black Prince* was overhauled by Blake's leading ships, Marshall in the *Second Charles* had sailed to her support expecting that Allin in her prize would back him. But Allin, together with the *Mary* and the other prize, fled to Cartagena. Allin reckoned that the important thing was to save the prizes, and Goulding of the *Black Prince* felt that he could have coped with Blake's lightly armed ships by himself, but Marshall made such a strong case against Allin, accusing him of cowardice, that it was generally felt he would be condemned to death by the court set to try him. Much to everyone's relief and probably with some inside help, Allin escaped and made his way to Jersey. Although Rupert arranged for him to be expelled from that place, he harboured no long-term grudge against him and befriended him after the Restoration.

The authorities at Toulon were immensely respectful and friendly towards the princes on a personal level, but there was initially considerable difficulty about selling the cargo of the prize and getting certain items necessary for refitting the ships, such as a new mast for the *Swallow*. One of Rupert's greatest problems was the replacement of the guns, which he had so carefully moved from ship to ship over the past two years. After a time Rupert managed to make contact with the Duke of Vendôme, who was Admiral of France (Grand Master of Navigation), and he provided a licence to furnish the Royalist fleet with whatever was necessary, including twenty-five guns.

With this backing Rupert repaired and refitted the prize, which he renamed *Revenge of Whitehall*. He also bought another vessel, which he named the *Honest Seaman*. While this was going on he was joined from Marseilles by an English ship commanded by Captain Craven, which he renamed the *Loyal Subject*. All these arrangements took some months to complete, but by the end of April he once again had a fleet of five ships.

It is recorded that there was no shortage of seamen, but even with the extra guns authorised by Vendôme and allowing for the fact that some guns must have been aboard the new ships when they were acquired, there must have been a considerable shortage in the fleet as a whole. Another difficulty that became important later on was that Rupert ran up some heavy debts in order to buy what he needed.

It may be that the French had afforded Rupert their assistance on the understanding that he would concentrate his activities against the Spanish with whom they were at war, as opposed to the English whom they were starting to placate.[13] Rupert would have needed little persuasion to attack Spanish shipping. In addition to the obstruction that his fleet had met earlier and the help that the Spanish had afforded to Blake, both he and his men were incensed at the way in which the crews of the ships stranded at Cartagena had been treated, many having been pressed into the Spanish army as they made their way to Toulon. But it is inconceivable that Rupert would have consented to any let-up in his hostility towards the shipping of the English Commonwealth. His actions on leaving Toulon make it clear that he had every intention of continuing with his appointed mission of taking all prizes consistent with the Royalist interest.

More important, Rupert had now become convinced that European waters were too dangerous for his depleted strength, which left two practical options open to him. First, to make for the West Indies, where there was still support for the Royalists in the English possessions of St Kitts, Nevis, Antigua, Montserrat and Barbados. This was particularly so in Barbados, where Lord Willoughby of Parham had been sent as governor after he left the fleet in 1648. Here Rupert might find a secure port from which to intercept and capture ships trading with Europe. Furthermore, he would be able to coordinate the defence of Royalist interests in these islands against interference by the Commonwealth. In fact the council of state had already decided that Ayscue, with a squadron of ships, should be sent to secure these places for the Commonwealth, but it is unlikely that Rupert knew of this when he was at Toulon and it would be many months before Ayscue was ready to sail.

The second option was to comb the Atlantic for prizes, selling them and their cargoes in Madeira, the Azores or the Cape Verde Islands where fresh supplies could also be obtained. Merchants in each of these Portuguese archipelagos might be expected to trade with Rupert on a commercial basis, but whether extra help would be forthcoming would depend on the attitude of the governors of the various islands concerned and on the direction they received from Lisbon. Of these archipelagos the Azores were the best placed for him to intercept shipping coming from the West Indies and the American Colonies. Madeira and the Cape Verde Islands were well placed for intercepting shipping from Brazil or the East Indies. The Azores and to a lesser extent Madeira afforded good opportunities for the sale of prize cargoes and the supply of grain, but ports and anchorages in the Azores were dangerous in bad weather. The Cape Verde Islands, though poorer in commercial terms, provided safe anchorages, meat and water. In terms of distance and the prevailing winds they also offered the best staging-post for an Atlantic crossing to Barbados.

In choosing between these two options Rupert would have had to bear in mind the problem of maintaining the hulls of his ships. The hulls of wooden ships attracted great quantities of weed which reduced the ship's speed unless it was scraped off at regular intervals. They were also vulnerable to attack from two varieties of shipworm which could cause the planks to crumble and rot if not regularly treated. In the middle of the seventeenth century these two problems were dealt with by scraping off the weed and smearing the ship's bottom with a mixture of fish oil, resin from pine trees and sulphur, known as white stuff. Alternatively, a mixture of tallow and soap could be used. Attending to these two problems caused a considerable amount of planning and expense in home waters, where ships were based on ports with docking facilities. Without such facilities ships had to be hauled up on a beach safe from the weather and enemy action and chocked up with timbers before being scraped and treated. This time-consuming business was known as careening.

The immediate problem was to avoid Penn, whose fleet of eight ships was too strong to be taken on by Rupert alone. Penn, on the other hand, was not strong enough to tackle Rupert and the French together, and he therefore had to keep his distance from Toulon. For some time Rupert had been dropping hints that he intended to sail to the eastern Mediterranean in the hope that Penn, who was then at Majorca, would get to hear of it. This seems to have worked, as Penn moved to Sardinia on 5 May. Two days later Rupert's ships, now best described as a squadron rather than a fleet, sailed. Initially they headed

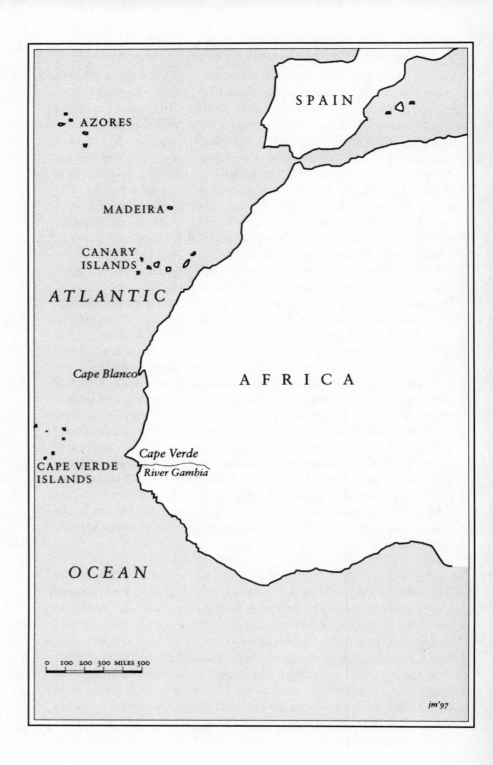

SPAIN

AZORES

MADEIRA

CANARY
ISLANDS

ATLANTIC

AFRICA

Cape Blanco

Cape Verde
River Gambia

CAPE VERDE
ISLANDS

OCEAN

0   100   200   300   MILES   500

jm'97

[92]

east to continue the deception, but when out of sight of land they turned south until off the African coast, after which they turned west towards the Strait of Gibraltar. It is not known exactly when they passed into the Atlantic, but Penn did not even discover that they had left Toulon until 25 May, and it was not until 29 July, when he was in Sicily, that he realised that Rupert had left the Mediterranean. He himself did not reach Gibraltar until 9 September, after which he spent some weeks guarding the Strait to ensure that Rupert did not return.

On 5 June 1651 Rupert captured a merchantman which the Royalists decided was a Genoese ship heading for a Spanish port: doubt has been cast on both these assumptions. Three days later, between Cadiz and Cape St Vincent, he captured a Spanish ship returning from the West Indies. Then with his two prizes he headed off to Madeira, where he got a friendly reception and sold as much of the cargoes as he could, together with the Spanish ship. Captain Goulding, formerly of the *Black Prince*, was put in command of the other ship, the *St Michael the Archangel*. The squadron left Madeira on 1 July.

Rupert now wanted to sail for the Cape Verde Islands, but there was resistance from some of the officers and seamen who guessed that his real goal was Barbados. A council of war was therefore called on 7 July[14] at which Goulding backed Rupert while the rest voted to go to the Azores to sell the rest of the prize cargoes. They emphasised the advantages of the Azores as a base for intercepting further prizes. Rupert's flag captain Fearnes backed Rupert in principle but expressed doubts as to whether the *Constant Reformation*, which was leaking badly, was in any state to reach the Cape Verde Islands. In view of this, Rupert decided to go along with the majority. On 25 July they reached St Michael, a large island in the south-east corner of the Azores archipelago where the two princes were warmly welcomed by the Portuguese governor.

For the next two months Rupert's squadron moved between St Michael and the island of Terceira some seventy-four miles to the north-west. At that time Terceira was the centre of wealth, commerce and agricultural production in the Azores as well as being the political and military capital,[15] so that it was to this island that he had to go to arrange for the needs of his squadron to be met. On his way to Terceira Rupert captured another Spanish ship returning from the West Indies. On the return trip Rupert's ships ran into a gale that caused the *Constant*

Reformation to leak badly. On reaching the anchorage, every effort was made to patch the ship up, but despite sending a diver to scan the ship's bottom, the exact source of the leak could not be found. At about this time *St Michael the Archangel* deserted and sailed to England with thirteen guns on board.

By now Rupert had officially made known his desire to go to the West Indies, a plan objected to by many of the officers and seamen, as he well knew. He also knew that he could not embark on such a venture without a considerable body of support, so on 13 September he called on the senior officers of the squadron to send him their views in writing as to where the ships should best be employed. This time Chester of the *Swallow* was in favour of returning to the mouth of the English Channel, but the remainder recommended a move to the south *en route* for the West Indies, their aim being to preserve their ships in less stormy seas than those found in the North Atlantic and to take prizes.

Unfortunately, this decision was reached too late to prevent a disaster greater than the losses suffered at Cartagena. On 26 September, when the squadron was at Terceira, a violent storm arose which blew the ships out to sea, where they had to run before the wind. For three days the strength of the tempest increased and the seas rose ever higher. Battered by the waves, the *Constant Reformation*'s leaks got worse. The crew worked with all their might at the pumps, and large quantities of raw meat were pressed into gaps in the planking where the water was coming in. The largest of the ship's boats, a pinnace that was being towed behind the ship, broke lose and sank. Early in the morning of 30 September the flagship's condition worsened when the forward end of one of the underwater planks was torn away from the ship so that water poured in and the pumps could no longer hold their own. By midday, the guns having been thrown overboard to lighten the ship, it became apparent that all was lost.

Most of the ships of the squadron had been scattered by the storm, but the *Swallow* and the *Honest Seaman* were still close at hand. Marshall in the *Honest Seaman*, at great risk to his ship, came close alongside the *Constant Reformation* in an attempt to rescue some of the crew, but they were so determined to live or die together that none would leave. The two ships were soon thrust apart by the force of the sea and the opportunity was lost. Then Rupert, who was easily distinguishable amid the spray by reason of his great height, indicated that he wanted the *Swallow* to come near enough for him to give his final instructions to his brother. Maurice ordered his captain to close up to the *Constant Reformation* so that he could go aboard, but Chester was not prepared to risk his ship as Marshall had done, and although the two princes came close enough to shout they could not hear each other against the roaring of the storm.

It was now the turn of the *Constant Reformation*'s officers to try to get Rupert out of the sinking ship. It was Rupert's duty to shift his flag to another ship if this could be done, his own being no longer capable of performing the office of a flagship. There was still a small ship's boat on board the *Constant Reformation*, described as a yawl, which might with luck get him to one of the other vessels. Rupert, however, refused to leave, saying that 'as they had run all fortunes formerly with him, so he was resolved upon this last pinch not to forsake them'. But together with his page and six others, he was either forced or persuaded to get into the boat; eyewitness accounts differ on this point. As the seamen let the boat down into the sea, they desired him to remember that they died his true and faithful servants.[16]

Shortly afterwards, Rupert arrived on board the *Honest Seaman* and immediately set about trying to save as many of the *Constant Reformation*'s crew as he could. His first action was to send the boat back with instructions to bring off as many as could be fitted in, naming particularly his flag captain Fearnes and other members of his personal staff such as Mortaigne and Billingsley. By this means Fearnes was taken to the *Swallow*, but Mortaigne and Billingsley insisted on remaining. Judging by the fact that Pitts and Holmes survived, it is likely that they came off with Fearnes unless they had been in the yawl with Rupert. At any rate the boat sank after one trip and no one else escaped.

Rupert and Marshall then took the *Honest Seaman* up to the *Constant Reformation* but could not get near enough to take off any of the crew. Aboard the *Swallow* Chester, backed by his officers, continued to defy Prince Maurice's efforts to assist in the rescue. They even refused to lower their own small boat for fear of losing it. As it got dark two blazing torches were erected on the *Constant Reformation*'s poop so that the other ships could see where she was. At about 9 p.m. these lights went out as the ship disappeared beneath the waves, carrying with her 333 of Rupert's best men, including some of his closest associates.

Next day, the wind having abated, Maurice got his brother on board the *Swallow*. They were by now 225 miles south-south-west of Terceira, far out into the Atlantic, and it was not until 19 October 1651 that the two ships were able to beat their way back to the Azores in search of the remains of the squadron.

By this time the Royalist cause was in a very bad way. Early in September King Charles and his Scottish army had been brought to battle at Worcester by Cromwell and totally destroyed. Scotland itself was held by Monck with an army of 6,000, while the King was left a fugitive in England, hunted by the New Model Army. After a series of dramatic wanderings he and Lord Wilmot reached the south coast, from where they were carried across the Channel to France, arriving on 16 October. The Commonwealth government and its army, funded by the most severe taxation ever endured by the English, now held Ireland and Scotland, as well as England, in a grip of iron.

Nurtured by these same taxes, the Commonwealth navy was able to eliminate smaller areas of Royalist influence. In April Blake had captured the Isles of Scilly, and he was even now closing in on Jersey; it fell to him on 22 October. Ayscue, who had sailed from Plymouth at the beginning of August, reached Barbados on the same day that the King arrived in France, but the island proved a tough nut to crack and did not finally surrender until 11 January 1652. Had Rupert been able to take his squadron there after leaving Toulon, he might have been able to save it for the Crown, for a time at least, but there was now nothing worth while for Royalists to do anywhere other than wait for better days.

As the *Swallow* and *Honest Seaman* sailed painfully back to the Azores, Rupert would not have known of these disasters, but his own situation was bleak enough. From a personal point of view the shock must have been considerable. He had lost most of the people who had been closest to him since he took over the fleet three years earlier, including some who had been with him for many years before that. Mortaigne, for example, had accompanied him to England in 1642 and had been close to him throughout the Civil War, riding at his side in all the great cavalry charges, including the one at Newark where he certainly saved Rupert's life. Later, though wounded himself, he helped Rupert rescue Holmes from some Spaniards who had shot him down in a skirmish. It is of course impossible to know which individuals Rupert would have missed most, but throughout his life he spent much time with quite humble people from whom he learned how things worked. During the voyage he would doubtless have talked at length to a number of the warrant-officers about navigation and how the sails and rigging functioned and the problems of gunnery at sea, and he may have become personally attached to some of them. After living in her for three years, Rupert might even have had some feeling for the *Constant Reformation*, and he would inevitably have felt the loss of his possessions, weapons and clothes.

From a professional point of view the loss to Rupert was even more serious because the *Constant Reformation*, though old, was the only Royalist ship capable of taking on major units in the Commonwealth navy. Her broadside could keep small and fast enemy vessels at bay, or she could force the surrender of a powerful prize that had been overhauled by lightly armed ships of his own squadron. Her presence outside a neutral port added considerable weight to his negotiating power, and to cap it all she had in her hold all the most valuable items of the captured cargoes that could be sold profitably only in Europe. Another cause of concern must have been uncertainty over the fate of the *Revenge of Whitehall*, the *Loyal Subject* and the recently captured prize.

Rupert had experienced large-scale disasters before, but with the exception of a short period of depression after his defeat at Marston Moor, he had never shown the slightest signs of distress. But this time he does seem to have lost his usual sparkle, and it is recorded that for some days he left affairs in the hands of his brother, spending most of his time in his cabin. This arrangement continued as a matter of policy when they reached the Azores on 19 October, because the brothers did not want the Portuguese to know of the *Constant Reformation*'s loss: with Rupert out of sight the Portuguese would think that the ship was elsewhere.

The first island they reached was Fayal, some seventy miles to the west of Terceira. Here they found the *Revenge* and the prize but also discovered that the *Loyal Subject* had been wrecked on the rocks at the height of the storm, albeit with little loss of life. Over the next few days two relatively minor incidents served to arouse the hostility of the governor of Fayal and of the neighbouring island of Pico as a result of which a number of Rupert's officers were imprisoned. This obliged Rupert to emerge from his self-imposed seclusion, to hoist the royal standard and to call on the governor. The shock of his appearance, his fearsome reputation and imposing presence, coupled with the threat of a letter to his friend King John, soon had the desired effect. All prisoners were released and every assistance was forthcoming with regard to revictualling and the disposal of the prize.

At the end of October Rupert visited Terceira, capturing a small English vessel on the return trip. On 21 November they sailed to the island of St Michael, where Rupert once more sought the opinions of his senior officers as to the future employment of the ships. This time all were in favour of the West Indies, except for Chester who asked to quit. His constant opposition, combined with his inadequate performance during the storm, made it a pleasure to accede to this request. The squadron finally left the Azores on 7 December 1651.

It was essential for the three remaining ships to be careened before attempting to cross the Atlantic. A natural harbour was known to exist on the African shore at Cape Blanco (on the present-day border between Mauritania and the Western Sahara), where they arrived on 30 December. Fortunately, a Dutch ship was there and the captain put Rupert in touch with a small Dutch settlement about twelve miles away, which was able to provide the timber needed for chocking up the ships and for making the necessary repairs.

While these were going on, Rupert tried to make contact with some of the nomadic inhabitants of the area in order to barter goods for meat. This he failed to do because of their suspicion and fear of strangers. In the course of a number of encounters he lost two men and gained a small child, abandoned during a skirmish, who stayed with him for the remainder of the voyage and indeed for some time thereafter.

By the last week of January Rupert had transferred the cargo of his latest prize to the Dutch ship with instructions that it should be delivered to King Charles in France. He also sent letters to the King and to Hyde giving an account of recent events and asking specifically that the money gained by the sale of the prize cargo should be used to pay the debts incurred on the King's behalf at Toulon.[17] On 26 January the squadron sailed for the Cape Verde Islands. By now Prince Rupert had taken over the *Swallow* and Prince Maurice had shifted into the *Revenge*.

Unlike the islands in the Azores archipelago, which are spread over a distance of 350 miles from the north-west to the south-east, the Cape Verde archipelago, 300 miles off the African mainland, is fairly compact. It is shaped like the head of an arrow pointing at Africa and consists of ten main islands. Of these St Vincent in the north had the best harbour, whereas Santiago in the south had the best facilities for providing ships with what they needed in the way of food, drink and stores. On 1 February Rupert's squadron arrived at Boa Vista island, the tip of the arrowhead, where he heard that Ayscue had already been in the West Indies for some time. The next two weeks were taken up with obtaining water and goats' meat, after which the squadron sailed to Santiago, chasing two English ships on the way without capturing them.

When Rupert called on the governor he found him friendly and helpful. He told Rupert that English ships were trading from the mouth of the River Gambia and lent him two pilots to help him navigate the river. Leaving Santiago on 21 February, Rupert reached the Gambia, where the two Portuguese pilots promptly ran both the *Swallow* and the *Revenge* aground, although not so badly that they could not be got off. On the northern bank of the river Rupert found a fort and a ship belonging to the Duchy of Courland. Acting on information provided by the Courlanders and with the ship's master as pilot, Rupert found and captured a small English ship called the *John*. Captain Holmes was given command of the prize. On board was an African interpreter called Captain Jaques.

Next day the squadron captured a Spanish ship of ten guns. About fifteen miles upstream they chased another small English vessel that escaped up a tributary. Next morning Prince Maurice followed and found a large English ship of 400 tons carrying 29 guns called the *Friendship*, which surrendered after a short battle; he also captured the smaller ship, called the *Supply*. These welcome additions allowed Rupert to reorganise the

squadron. Prince Maurice and Captain Price moved into the
Friendship, which was renamed the *Defiance*. Marshall took
over the *Revenge*, Clarke was made captain of the *Honest Seaman*, and the captain of Rupert's guard was given the *Supply*.
The small Spanish ship, which was deemed unseaworthy, was
given to the Courlanders as a reward for their assistance.

While this reorganisation was going on and the squadron was
collecting water, some ships' boats explored upstream to a large
flat and well-populated island about 150 miles from the coast
where a number of Portuguese were living. Here the officers
found evidence of various wild animals, such as elephants, lions
(referred to as tigers), leopards and monkeys, and even heard
tales of unicorns. They were also told that the river continued
for a further 150 miles and that somewhere a mine existed
consisting of a large and solid rock of gold which would amply
repay the cost of finding it. The people on the island made a
living by trading ivory, wax, hides and ambergris for cloth, iron
bars, beads, coral, crystal, amber, brass and strong liquor. The
officers also brought back information about the natives and
their customs, and Rupert himself made contact with the
brother of the local king who came on board the *Swallow* and
told him more about the ways of the local people and their
laws.[18] Rupert would doubtless have liked to go up river to see
these wonders for himself but, being anxious to reach the West
Indies before the summer storms set in, could not afford the
time.

In the middle of March Rupert and his enlarged squadron
left the river and sailed north along the coast towards Cape
Verde, his aim being to pick up a favourable wind from that
place which would take him back to the Cape Verde Islands.
Just short of Cape Verde itself, probably about fifteen miles
south of the present port of Dakar, Rupert anchored off a native
village to assemble his ships. While there, one of the seamen of
the *Defiance* who had formerly lived in the place went ashore
to visit his people and was prevented from returning.

Rupert set off with Holmes in the *Supply* to recover this man
and when nearing the shore sent a boat to find a place at which
to disembark. The boat overturned in the surf, and as the seamen struggled ashore they were surrounded by hostile Africans.
Rupert then sent Holmes in another boat to rescue them, but
this boat also capsized so that Holmes and his men were in as
much danger as the others. Luckily, Captain Jaques, a native

of the area who had recently been released by Rupert, appeared and rescued the men, whom he took to his house. Rupert sent a third boat to collect them; the boat reached the shore safely and took the men on board while Holmes with one man went to collect Captain Jaques in the mistaken belief that Rupert wanted to see him. While they were gone, a pinnace from the *Defiance* captured a native canoe, shooting dead an African in the process. The shooting was seen from the shore and resulted in the infuriated Africans taking Holmes and his escort prisoner.

Captain Jaques now tried to negotiate the release of the prisoners in return for the canoe. After a time Rupert went close inshore in a ship's boat to take a hand in the talks, telling all his ships to man their boats with armed men who should join him off the surf if he called for them. He also ordered that the canoe should be released on his signal.

Terms were eventually agreed, but when the canoe was released the treacherous natives let only one prisoner go, keeping Holmes. They then ran down the beach firing arrows at Rupert, whose boat's crew returned the fire. The Africans plunged into the surf and started swimming out towards the boat, diving under the water as the crew fired. Rupert's intention was to lead a rescue party ashore as soon as reinforcements arrived, but before they did so he was hit by an arrow which sank in deep above his left breast. Immediately, he took a knife and cut it out himself.

As always, Rupert had no intention of abandoning one of his men regardless of the danger. By this time reinforcements had arrived, and despite his wounds Rupert was preparing to plunge into the surf when once again Captain Jaques saved the day. In the confusion on the beach he assembled a few of his friends and grabbed Holmes, whom he took to a deserted spot from where he was rescued by a boat from the *Defiance*.

When Rupert saw what had happened he broke off the action. The only loss of the day was the *Supply* which, being manned largely by people from settlements along the coast, took the opportunity afforded by the fighting to overcome their captors and sail away. Rupert sent word to Captain Jaques that he would pick him up from a nearby settlement and reward him for his good work, but with many expressions of gratitude he said that he wished to stay with his people.[19]

On 29 March the Royalist squadron set off from the African

coast, arriving a week later in the Cape Verdes at the island of Mayo, next to Santiago. Here they found two English ships, one of which – the *Sarah*, of eighteen guns – was quickly captured by Rupert. In chasing the other the squadron got split up so that the *Defiance* and *Honest Seaman* finished up at Santiago, while *Swallow* with the other ships returned to Mayo, the *Revenge* being in a separate anchorage to the rest.

While there, two English vessels of around 250 tons anchored close to the *Revenge*, which promptly captured them. Rupert sent the prizes to Maurice at Santiago escorted by Holmes in the *John* and set off for the island of Sal, some sixty miles to the north, with the *Revenge* in search of further prizes. On the way, when the two ships were out of sight of each other at night, some prisoners in the *Revenge* overcame the crew, depleted by manning prizes, and took the ship. They then sailed for England with their prisoners, including Marshall who had served Rupert so well. Marshall evidently made his peace with the authorities, as he was given command of a Commonwealth ship shortly afterwards, later being discharged for 'political unreliability'. After various adventures, early in May Rupert reached Santiago where he found the rest of the squadron.

The seizing of the *Revenge* had been organised by William Coxon, who had been mate of the *Supply* when she was captured. When the *Revenge* arrived back in Plymouth he wrote a report to the council of state in which he vilified the Royalists in extravagant language, quoting Rupert as having said that providing he might but ruin and destroy the English interest he cared not whether he got a farthing more while he lived.[20] It is interesting to find the intensity of his feeling against Rupert reflected by Blake, who told the council that he would have accounted it his greatest outward happiness to have secured the total destruction of that piratical crew, and by Penn, who called on the Lord to forgive the bloody wretch (Rupert) and convert him if he belongeth to him, or if His Holiness please, suddenly to destroy him.[21] Rupert had inspired the same sort of frenzy against himself in the Civil War among people who had not met him, a frenzy that changed to respect and even admiration when his detractors met him face to face.

On 9 May 1652 Rupert's squadron, consisting of the *Swallow*, *Defiance*, *Honest Seaman*, *John*, *Sarah* and one of the prizes taken at Mayo, finally set sail for the West Indies. But he was too late, as Ayscue had already subdued opposition to the Commonwealth in all English possessions there and was now on his way home.

On the crossing to the West Indies the squadron got off course as a result of chasing a ship that eluded them, after which the *Swallow* developed an alarming leak. Eventually, all of the ships except for the prize arrived at a deserted spot on the west coast of St Lucia on 29 May. Having replenished their water and mended the *Swallow*'s leak, they moved on to the French island of Martinique, where they were well received by the governor. It was at this point that Rupert learned of Ayscue's success and of his departure. Although realising that he was too late to influence the situation on land, Rupert resolved to make his way around the islands in search of prizes, which is what he did for the next three months before the next major disaster struck him.

During this time he sailed steadily north from island to island, taking one prize at Montserrat and another from under the guns of the fort at Nevis, where his secretary, Pitts, was killed. By the end of June, having got rid of some of the prize cargoes at St Kitts, he took his ships into a small harbour now known as Rupert's Bay, in the Virgin Islands. From there the *Sarah* was sent to nearby Santa Cruz to get water and found the ship that had got lost during the voyage from Africa. Being fearful of attack from the Spanish in Puerto Rico, whom he thought might have heard of his arrival from deserters, Rupert fortified the harbour, after which he thoroughly refitted the *Swallow*, *Defiance*, *Honest Seaman* – now commanded by Craven – and the recently recovered prize. The remaining ships were burned. On 29 August he again put to sea.

On this occasion he sailed for some distance to the north, presumably searching for prizes. On 13 September, almost a year after losing the *Constant Reformation*, the squadron was hit by a northerly hurricane. Visibility was soon reduced to no more than the length of the ship as a result of the drenching rain and the spray whipping off the colossal waves. Men were unable to stand on deck because of the tearing wind. The ships of the squadron were scattered, never to be seen again by Rupert. For a time the *Swallow* was blown in a southerly direction under one new and strong sail on her mainmast until this split and got blown away. The ship was then at the mercy of

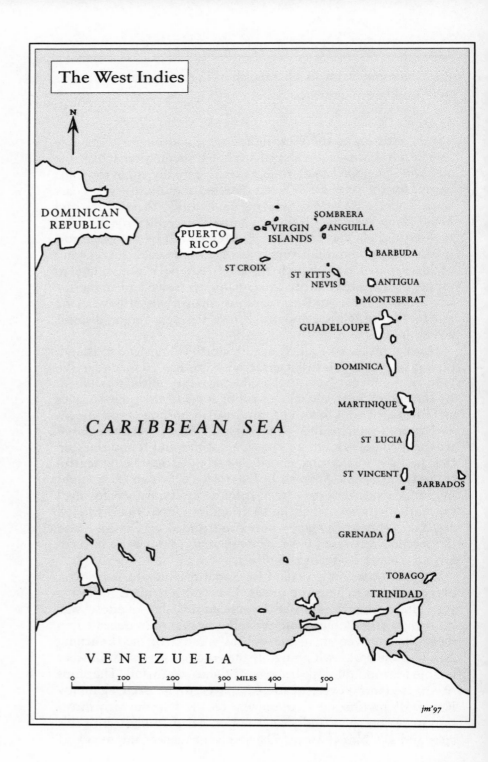

The West Indies

N

DOMINICAN
REPUBLIC

PUERTO
RICO

VIRGIN
ISLANDS

SOMBRERA

ANGUILLA

ST CROIX

BARBUDA

ST KITTS
NEVIS

ANTIGUA

MONTSERRAT

GUADELOUPE

DOMINICA

MARTINIQUE

CARIBBEAN SEA

ST LUCIA

ST VINCENT

BARBADOS

GRENADA

TOBAGO

TRINIDAD

VENEZUELA

0   100   200   300 MILES 400   500

jm'97

the wind and sea, crashing from the crests into the troughs and back again until enough sail was set on the stump of the mizzenmast to get her under way once more. And so it continued for four days and nights without any let-up in the wind, which at some stage veered round to the east.

No one can be sure where the *Swallow* went during these days except that in the middle of one night, she passed within two miles of Sombrero and next morning almost ran on to a narrow ledge of rock. On 17 September Rupert managed to bring the ship to anchor off an uninhabited stretch of coast that turned out to be St Anns in the Virgin Islands. But the storm was still raging, and it took the release of a seaman held in irons for a sexual offence, who was an exceptionally good pilot, to get the ship into a sheltered anchorage. Only seamanship of a very high order aided by divine providence or sheer good luck could have brought the *Swallow* and her crew through such a battering. Next day, the storm having abated, Rupert took her to the harbour where the squadron had spent July and August.

Although this harbour was sheltered and safe, it had proved difficult to get food there to such an extent that, before leaving at the end of August, all ranks in the squadron, including Rupert and his brother, were on very reduced rations. By 25 September the food situation was again becoming critical, and Rupert was forced to leave in search of supplies. This time he sailed southeast along the islands until on 5 October, with starvation looming ever closer, he captured a small English ship off Montserrat. After an abortive chase of a Spanish ship, on 10 October he anchored at Guadeloupe where he was able to buy what he needed. To his distress there was no news of his missing ships, but he did hear that England was now at war with the Dutch. He also heard that there were some English merchant ships at Antigua which he decided to capture if he could.

Arriving there on 30 October, Rupert found two good ships anchored under the shelter of the fort. With commendable daring he sent Holmes with fifty men ashore to attack the fort. When he did so the defenders made off, so Rupert was able to capture the ships. He then returned to Guadeloupe, and on 11 October, after a spirited chase, captured another English ship. While at Guadeloupe he heard a report that Prince Maurice had reached safety at the island of Tortuga off the north coast of Hispaniola.

It is difficult to know whether he believed this, but with four prizes to man he was very short-handed and setting off into such unfriendly seas would have been the height of folly. He did, however, take his ships north along the islands searching for news or prizes until he reached his old harbour in the Virgin Islands once more on 5 December. Rupert was now ill from some tropical disease and very worried that he had received no reliable news of his brother or of his other ships. Although he must have been intensely reluctant to leave the West Indies before discovering what had become of them, it seemed that no more could be achieved with his depleted crews and that the time had come to return to Europe before losing the last four prizes. On 12 December Rupert, with his five ships, put to sea.

Mercifully, the return voyage was relatively uneventful, although any hope that he might have had of a friendly reception in the Azores was disappointed when he was shot at by the forts at Fayal when he reached there on 16 January 1653 and later at St Michael when he tried to go ashore. Portugal was now firmly allied to the Commonwealth regime in England and could give no assistance to Rupert. None the less, although it is not recorded it seems likely that he anchored in some deserted spot to take on fresh water.

Rupert now headed for France but could not resist the chance of capturing a ship that he sighted off Cape Finisterre. But in this he was unlucky, and on 4 March 1653 he entered the mouth of the Loire and anchored off St-Nazaire with his four prizes, four years and a few weeks after leaving Helvoetsluys. Even then his troubles were not over as the pilot who was taking the *Swallow* up the river to the port of Pamboeuf ran her aground. By his seamanship in getting all the guns hauled first to one side and then to the other, he got her off and took her to her final berth. Then at last he went ashore.

During those years the Royalist fleet had achieved relatively little. It did not influence the outcome of operations in Ireland or succeed in sinking or capturing any Commonwealth warships either there or off Portugal. Equally, it failed to coordinate or prolong the defence of Royalist interests in the West Indies. Of the forty to fifty sizeable prizes taken, many had to be kept to replace ships captured by the enemy, or otherwise lost, and much of the money raised from the sale of the remainder and of the cargoes was used to pay the seamen or to buy the food and supplies needed to keep the fleet at sea.

On the credit side, some of the proceeds were used to sustain the exiled court at a time when the King desperately needed every penny he could get. Some were used to strengthen the defence of the Isles of Scilly and some may even have reached Ormonde after the fleet arrived in Portugal. Rupert's ships also kept the Royalist flag flying for a time after it had been lowered in England, Scotland, Ireland, the Channel Islands and the West Indies. They also obliged the Commonwealth government to incur expense and effort in safeguarding the country's trade. Above all, the voyage stands as a memorial of what can be endured by a band of resolute men struggling in a few ancient and battered sailing-ships over a period of several years against the combined assaults of a powerful enemy and the elemental power of the seas.

Needless to say none of this could have happened without the impetus of Rupert's driving will. Although not initially an experienced seaman, his courage and powers of leadership were widely known and admired before the fleet ever left port. Throughout the long years at sea and the numerous blows rained on him by outrageous fortune, he never failed to stand by his men and in this they trusted him implicitly. They followed him because they recognised him as being worthy of their respect, not because they were flogged, keelhauled or hanged into obedience. The sight of this magnificent regal being treading the decks, subjected to the same privations and discomforts as themselves, inspired confidence and even affection. Many, including some of the officers and warrant-officers, became uneasy from time to time as to where they might be taken next, and they muttered and intrigued in an attempt to influence his decisions. But whenever a crisis arose they stood by him in the most touching way, as when the crew of the *Constant Reformation* insisted on saving him as their ship went down, begging him meanwhile to remember that they died his true and faithful servants. And these seamen were not disciplined members of a regular armed force, like the Royal Navy of later years, but a collection of individuals of many races, colours and creeds, recruited from the various ports and harbours visited by the ships and supplemented by the crews of the prizes taken.

From a personal point of view Rupert had gained a lot. In the first place he now knew exactly what ships needed if they were to be kept at sea in fighting trim. He had experienced at first hand the problems of getting hold of masts, spars, canvas, rope, food and drink, and, having bargained his way from the United provinces to the West Indies, he knew what it all cost and could tell at once when he was being cheated. He also knew of the physical problems involved in maintaining ships above and below the water-line and of the time it all took. During his time at sea he had learned much of seamanship and navigation and was as confident in handling a ship as any of his captains. In Portugal he even had some limited experience of handling a sizeable fleet in the presence of the enemy, which would at least give him an understanding of the problems involved and enable him to discuss them sensibly with those who had more knowledge than himself. In short, he had served a lengthy and exacting apprenticeship as an admiral which would stand him and England in good stead in the testing years ahead.

But he had paid a great price for all this in personal terms. While the fleet was at sea he kept going despite the physical privations, frustrations and disasters that he experienced, even remaining outwardly cheerful in the face of the loss of his brother and of his physical ailments. But once ashore he could carry on no longer, and for some time he lay at Nantes desperately sick from internal bleeding and fever. In a week or two he was on his feet, although his iron constitution was never quite the same again. It took him much longer to get over the death of his brother Maurice.

4

LENGTHY INTERLUDE

As soon as the news of Rupert's return to France reached the
court of Charles II in Paris, warm letters of welcome were sent
by the King himself and by Lord Jermyn on behalf of Queen
Henrietta Maria: also by Hyde begging Rupert to look after his
health and the safety of the ships and goods that he had with
him.

When Rupert was sufficiently recovered to travel, he left
Nantes in a coach provided by King Louis escorted by his first
Gentleman of the Bedchamber, arriving in Paris in early April.
But he was not yet well and as late as 25 April remained confined
to his apartment in the Palais Royal. It is probable that at this
time Rupert, who took a close interest in herbal cures for
wounds, particularly burns, treated himself with a medicine that
he had devised for curing soldiers of the bloody flux. Years later
this prescription came into the hands of the philosopher John
Locke, who was employed as physician by Rupert's friend, the
Earl of Shaftesbury. Locke noted that Rupert had tried out this
particular medicine on himself.[1] Soon afterwards, Rupert cured
Jermyn of a fever with another of his own concoctions, as a
result of which he gained a reputation for meddling in the black
arts.

Rupert's health gradually returned and by May he was joining
in the life of the court. The split between the old Royalists, who
had been with the King at The Hague, and the Queen Mother's
followers was less in evidence now that they were all in Paris.
Charles had recently formed a policy committee to advise him,
consisting of members of each group, notably Hyde, Ormonde
and Inchiquin on the one hand and Jermyn, Wilmot and the Earl
of Norwich on the other. It was hoped that Rupert's presence as
a third force would help balance the other two parties. He was
given the prestigious appointment of Master of the Horse that

he had held under King Charles I, and his friend Sir Edward
Herbert was admitted to the council and made Lord Keeper of
the Seals. Charles I's two old Secretaries of State, Digby and
Nicholas, had not been given their jobs back, although the
former, now Earl of Bristol on the death of his father, had
returned to court and had been appointed to the Privy Council;
Nicholas, who considered himself too infirm to travel, was still
at The Hague. To all intents and purposes Hyde, who kept in
close touch with Nicholas, acted as Secretary of State.[2]

At this time Rupert was reported as being withdrawn and
silent – very different from his former self. But if Rupert seemed
altered he must have found many of his old associates equally
changed. Charles in particular, although warm and affectionate
to his cousin, was now unmistakably King. The humiliations
heaped on him during the year he spent as nominal ruler of the
Scots, followed by the campaign that ended so disastrously at
the Battle of Worcester, had at least provided him with hard
experience of handling people. Although still badgered by his
mother and the various factions at court, he was becoming
accustomed to making his own decisions and getting his own
way. He was already developing the habit of persuading one
group that he agreed with its ideas while assuring another of
his agreement with its contrary opinions, thereby avoiding confrontation at the price of confusion. Although harbouring strong
resentment against those who opposed him, he was learning
how to appear friendly towards them until it was safe to dispose
of them.

The Duke of York, who had grown to manhood during
Rupert's absence, bore little resemblance to his brother. James
possessed many of Rupert's own characteristics, such as energy,
honesty, bravery and a dislike of intrigue, but he did not possess
Rupert's acute intelligence, and he also lacked any semblance
of political common sense. In the previous April (1652) he had
broken away from his brother's impoverished court and joined
the French King's army under Turenne as a volunteer. In this
capacity he had taken part in the lengthy campaign fought
against Condé and his Spanish allies, as a result of which Turenne was able to restore King Louis XIV and his mother to
Paris and push the rebels back towards the Spanish Netherlands.
James returned to Paris at the end of the campaign a month
before Rupert reached France. He would rejoin Turenne for
three further campaigns before leaving the country in 1656. In

these campaigns he rose to the rank of lieutenant-general and gained an enviable reputation as a soldier to say nothing of the pay and allowances which underlined his brother's poverty.

While Turenne was securing France for his King, the first of the three great wars at sea was being fought between England and the United Provinces. On 19 May 1652 the first engagement took place between Blake and Tromp off Dover. This was followed in August by a battle between Ayscue and de Ruyter, consisting of a general mêlée in which thirty-eight English ships charged into a force of thirty Dutch warships accompanied by sixty-odd merchantmen. Another mêlée, known as the Battle of the Kentish Knock, was fought out between Blake and de Witt at the end of September, followed by the Battle of Dungeness at the end of November when Blake suffered a reverse at the hands of Tromp in yet another uncontrollable mêlée.

In the four years from March 1649 that Blake had been a general-at-sea, he had laid the foundations of a navy that could keep the seas and maintain an effective blockade. By his strength of character, persistence and devotion to the officers and men of his fleet, to say nothing of his seamanship and knowledge of gunnery, he had turned the Commonwealth navy into the finest instrument for war at sea that England had yet known. But Blake had not yet developed a tactical doctrine capable of exploiting the navy to the full. In November 1652 Monck was made general-at-sea to fill the gap caused by the death of Popham two years earlier. Although he had no experience of sea warfare, he had been a professional soldier all his life and had written a book on tactics after being captured by Parliamentary forces when fighting for the King in the Civil War. Under his influence the three generals issued a set of fighting instructions designed to impose a degree of control on future battles.

These instructions were tested soon afterwards at the Battle of Portland, which took place two weeks before Rupert reached the mouth of the Loire. In this battle the fleet, divided into three separate squadrons, managed to fight in some sort of a line and won a limited victory, although Blake was seriously wounded. Revised fighting and sailing instructions followed in March.

Monck now reaped the harvest that Blake had so carefully sown, commanding the fleet in two further battles in the summer of 1653 before the war drew to a close. They were both English victories. These battles and the fighting and sailing instructions resulting from them provided the framework within which Restoration admirals such as James and Rupert, backed up by Monck, developed the ideas used in the second and third Dutch Wars.

One further event of importance took place while Rupert was lying sick in his apartments at the Palais Royal. On 20 April 1653 Cromwell, who had become Lord General three years earlier, forcibly evicted the remaining members of the Parliament he was supposed to be serving and set himself up as a military dictator. Eight months later he was accorded the title of Lord Protector.

The problem uppermost in the minds of King Charles's followers in the summer of 1653 was money, there being a constant shortage. This not only restricted activities designed to further the Royalist cause but also reduced the standard of living of most of those present to a greater or lesser extent. The main sources of money available to the King were a subsidy from the French government, contributions from English Royalists and income from privateers licensed by him. Under these circumstances great expectations were placed on the disposal of the prizes brought in by Rupert.

On leaving Nantes, Rupert had put Robert Holmes in charge of the disposal of the remaining ships and their cargoes, a task that would tax his energy and competence to the full. It involved moving cargoes and guarding them while in transit; maintaining the ships, guns and rigging until they could be sold; hiring manpower to do that part of the work that could not be handled by the crews; and paying off the crews when their work was done. In addition, Holmes would have to deal with local officials concerned with the movement of ships and goods and with the merchants who would buy them. He also had the difficult task of passing on Rupert's instructions to the captains of the ships and ensuring that they were obeyed. He had a particularly difficult relationship with Fearnes.[3]

For some months Rupert remained at Paris with his cousins; he also spent time with his brother Edward, who was still living there. It is recorded that one evening in June he was swimming in the Seine to get cool when he got cramp and sank. He was saved by one of the 'blackamoors' he had picked up in Africa, who reached him just in time, grabbing him by his hair and dragging him to the surface. Two of these Africans and the child who had attached himself to him at Cape Blanco were now part of Rupert's entourage and a subject of general interest in Paris.

In June Captain Craven arrived in Nantes. When the fleet had become dispersed following the great storm in September of the previous year, Craven had managed to get the *Honest Seaman*, greatly damaged, to an island two weeks later. After making what repairs he could, he reached Hispaniola but the *Honest Seaman* was soon afterwards run ashore and wrecked in a further storm. Rupert was doubtless relieved to find that Craven and his crew were safe, but news of Maurice was what he so desperately needed.

At some stage during the summer Rupert returned to Nantes to supervise the disposal of the assets, which was complicated by the fact that Cromwell was claiming them for England. By this time Mazarin had realised that France would have to ally itself with England and that this would necessitate the departure of Charles II and his court. In fact, Charles was sick of France and only too anxious to leave, but he needed money for his journey. Mazarin, hoping that it could be supplied by the sale of the ships and their cargoes, frustrated Cromwell's attempts to grab them.

It is not clear whether Rupert went back and forth between Paris and Nantes or whether he spent the whole of the autumn and early part of the winter there, but he was certainly there when the King wrote to him in November[4] with authority to sell the guns of the *Swallow*. He was still there in the middle of December when the King wrote a further letter urging Rupert to conclude his business and return as soon as possible. In this letter he specifically mentions that he wants to discuss the timing and destination of his move from France.[5]

By January Rupert was back in Paris, where he became embroiled in an attempt by those hostile to Edward Hyde to displace him from his position as the King's principal adviser. Ever since Charles had returned to France after the Battle of Worcester, plans had been considered for further Royalist uprisings to take place in Scotland and in England. The King's advisers had mixed feelings regarding these plans, but gradually one group, led by Hyde and backed by Wilmot, Percy and unusually by Ormonde and Inchiquin, tended to oppose them, whereas Rupert's friends, consisting of Gerrard and Herbert together with a number of lesser men, supported them. Latterly, Queen Henrietta Maria and Jermyn backed this group, which thought that Rupert should lead the Scottish uprising.

Hyde's opposition to these plans was based on his understanding of the best way for getting the King restored and was not directly related to his dislike of Rupert as a person. In the roots of his being he felt that if the King could demonstrate an unfailing respect for the ancient laws of the country and for Parliament and if he could convince the people of his adherence to the Church of England his subjects would sooner or later want him back. He was opposed to all plans for a forcible return aided by French or Spanish Catholics or by Scottish Presbyterians.

None the less Hyde and Rupert did dislike each other, being poles apart in most respects. Hyde at forty-four was, by his own admission, over-fat. He was also sedentary and so gouty that he could not even sit on a horse for most of the time. He was separated from his family to whom he was devoted and, when not working, his greatest pleasure was conversing with high-minded and intelligent friends over a bottle of wine. He was a man of ideas, discussion, persuasion and letters. To those outside his intimate circle he seemed stuffy, fussy and pompous. By contrast, Rupert at thirty-four was a man of action, whose natural inclination was to attack those he saw as the King's enemies wherever they could be found, using whatever resources he could lay his hands on. He was strong and athletic, with a passion for hunting; distant rather than pompous, direct in his speech and aggressive towards those who crossed him. Their common loyalty to the King and their complete integrity were not enough to bridge the gap.

At the end of the year, some of those who regarded themselves as Rupert's followers got the King's former secretary, Robert Long, to accuse Hyde of being involved in a treasonable conspiracy with Cromwell on the basis of information provided by Sir Richard Grenville. The case came before the Privy Council in January 1654, but the allegations were patently absurd and the King said so, drawing an unfavourable comparison between Hyde and Long to the latter's disadvantage. Herbert challenged this, asserting that Long was as good a gentleman as Hyde, at which point Rupert turned on Herbert, saying that the King was not referring to their breeding but to the fact that Hyde was honest and Long dishonest.[6]

This dispute hardly improved the standing of Rupert's friends in the King's eyes, and worse was to follow. There were at this time two main groups of Royalist conspirators in England, one the recently formed Sealed Knot, in contact with Hyde through Nicholas at The Hague, and the other dealing direct with Herbert and Lord Gerard in Paris. In February 1654 Gerard produced a Major Henshaw, who claimed that he could arrange for Cromwell to be killed. Rupert took him to the King, who at first approved the idea, but then disowned him on hearing that he was a double agent.

By this time the King and Hyde were becoming frustrated at not getting as much as they had hoped from the sale of the ships and cargoes of Rupert's squadron. As Rupert had already explained, much of the valuable stuff had gone down with the *Constant Reformation* and he had used most of the money from the sales to pay off the sailors and to settle outstanding costs. All that remained was the money that could be got from the sale of the *Swallow*'s guns. Rupert thought that some at least of this should be used to pay the debts raised at Toulon at the end of 1650, which he had asked the King to pay from the proceeds of the prizes sent from Cape Blanco early in 1651.

In February Hyde got the King to ask Rupert for an exact account of all transactions in writing. Nothing could have been better calculated to anger Rupert. His mother had spent a great sum getting the fleet to sea in the first place, and he had himself throughout the voyage remitted his share of the prize money to the King. Inevitably, he regarded this request as a slur on his honesty and in a heated exchange refused to provide any figures beyond those already sent from Nantes. Rupert, who well realised that Hyde was responsible, must have been experiencing the annoyance frequently felt by those who, having endured privation, danger and loss on a massive scale, find themselves plagued by a bureaucrat safely removed from the perils of conflict. Hyde's own sacrifices, real but trivial by comparison, would hardly have impressed Rupert even if he had known of them. Rupert was thoroughly disgruntled. At about this time he told the King that he intended to leave the court in the summer in order to visit the Palatinate.

In March, when it looked as if money would become available from the sale of the guns, Rupert gave the King some outline accounts for his own use but asked him not to show them to Hyde; needless to say, the King did. Rupert also claimed half the money for himself, which the King refused to give him despite the fact that Lord Hatton had some months earlier calculated that the King owed Rupert £1,700 – considerably more than half the value of the guns. The King further upset Rupert by refusing to pay the Toulon debts, and relations between them became strained.[7]

Matters were not improved when in April a further attempt to kill Cromwell, organised by Gerard's cousin John, misfired. John was caught and executed, and documents appearing to incriminate the King were found on him. A number of other Royalists in England were also captured and executed, including some members of the Sealed Knot.[8] Although Rupert had not been personally involved, Lord Gerard was one of his friends and some of the King's annoyance rubbed off on him. The King's anger arose from the fact that the job had been bungled and himself compromised, not because he objected to Cromwell's being killed. Neither he, nor Rupert, nor indeed Hyde[9] were opposed to that. From their standpoint Cromwell had put himself beyond the pale by playing a leading role in the quasi-judicial murder of Charles I, and their view was shared not only by most Royalists but also by many who had supported Parliament in the Civil War. To such people Cromwell was the devil incarnate who had to be destroyed.

Fundamentally, the irritation that was building up between Rupert and the King arose from the fact that, once the business connected with the paying off of the fleet and the disposal of the cargoes was complete, Rupert did not have enough to do. His character was totally unsuited to idleness in a court full of scheming and squabbling exiles. He filled his days with hunting and at the same time became involved in a number of liaisons with ladies of the French court, who were attracted to him as much by his heroic reputation as by his handsome appearance.

Such liaisons were themselves not without risk. One day in March Rupert was returning to his quarters in the Palais Royal after hunting, accompanied only by Holmes, when two horsemen came galloping down the street behind him. The street being narrow, Rupert pulled over to let them pass. As they did so they drew their pistols, turned and fired at him, both missing. Rupert drew his pistols and fired, killing one and mortally wounding the other. At that moment a third man attacked

Rupert, presumably with his sword because when he saw that he was likely to be killed he called out to say that he was the Count de Mongiron, who was the husband of one of Rupert's lady friends. Rupert, surprised that his attentions should have sparked off an assassination attempt rather than a duel, said that he found it hard to believe, but he let him go none the less.

On 11 June 1654, having resigned his position as Master of the Horse a week earlier, Rupert left Paris for Heidelberg with twenty-six followers, including the African child and his two blackamoors. By this time the friction that had arisen between himself and the King had partially evaporated, a fact borne out by a letter that Charles wrote to Rupert's mother saying that he hoped to see Rupert again before long and that they would then meet with more kindness and a better understanding, since he loved his cousin very much and was confident of his future friendship. Accounts of the rift between them, most of which have been coloured by Hyde's letters and subsequent writings, have probably been exaggerated. At any rate the cousins were soon on excellent terms again. Three weeks after Rupert left Paris the King moved to Spa *en route* for Cologne, where he would be based for the next eighteen months.

During the year and three months since Rupert's return from the sea, the King's cause had suffered a series of blows arising largely from the fact that Cromwell, with his instinctive hostility to Spain, had drawn France into alliance with England and then ended the war with the United Provinces by a treaty signed in April 1654. A condition of these arrangements was that King Charles would not be allowed sanctuary in either of these countries. These developments would ultimately oblige the King to turn to Spain, but as a first step he had negotiated from the Empire his refuge in Cologne and some financial support which, welcome as it was, did little to relieve his underlying shortage of money.

One result of the King's move to Cologne was to eliminate the influence of the Queen and her followers, who remained in Paris. Herbert also resigned his post as Lord Keeper of the Seals when the King left France, but Nicholas, a firm supporter of Rupert, joined the court at Spa and resumed his duties as Secretary of State.

The same circumstances that caused the King to act as he did obliged Rupert to be without serious employment for the next six years, before emerging as a leading figure in Restoration England. During this time he took no part in maritime affairs so that it is unnecessary to follow his doings in great detail. On the other hand his daily activities, the relationships and contacts that he made and the tastes that he acquired and developed had enough effect on his future personality to warrant recording them, at least in outline. It is ironic that during the years when he was in his prime he should have been obliged to remain largely inactive. But he had taken a great deal out of himself during the Civil War and while commanding the Royalist fleet, and it was perhaps fortunate that he should have been forced to rest for a few years before undertaking the labours and hazards of the second and third Dutch Wars.

Under the terms of the treaty that ended the Thirty Years War, Charles Louis was reinstated as Elector of the Palatinate, but the Upper Palatinate was retained by Bavaria. Charles Louis quickly took up his residence at Heidelberg but declined to allow his mother to return to her dower house or to provide her with money for her continued existence at The Hague. He had some excuse for his meanness as the Palatinate was destitute and greatly denuded of population, so that every penny was needed for its recovery. But under the laws of the Empire he was required to provide for the subsistence of his younger brothers, now reduced to Rupert and Edward by the deaths of Philip in 1650 while fighting for France against Spain and Maurice lost at sea. In an attempt to meet this obligation he had offered Rupert and Edward 2,500 thalers per annum (approximately £375) for five years, rising to 4,000 (£600) thereafter, which they had accepted. In addition, Rupert hoped for a grant of land within the Electorate which would provide him with additional income and a base. This was important to him, as without it he would be unable to arrange a marriage with a lady of royal blood.

Although Charles Louis had not liked Rupert when they were children and had been at cross-purposes with him during the Civil War, he did his best to make him welcome when he arrived at Heidelberg with his strange band of followers early in July 1654. He met him outside the walls and together they rode to the castle through crowds curious to see their sovereign's famous brother and his exotic entourage. Here Rupert found two of his sisters: Elizabeth, whom he had not seen since his departure for England in 1642, and Sophie, whom he had not seen since 1648. Charles Louis had agreed to maintain them at Heidelberg to reduce his mother's expenses. Of all her children only Louise remained with her at The Hague, Henrietta having died in 1651 soon after her marriage to the brother of the Prince of Transylvania.

While at Heidelberg Rupert heard a rumour that Prince Maurice was alive, having been captured by Algerian pirates while returning from the Caribbean. This led to a flurry of correspondence and enquiries in France and Turkey, but Rupert, who longed for the news to be true, none the less continued to believe that his brother had died at the time of the storm.

After a few weeks Rupert left Heidelberg to visit the Emperor in Vienna with a view to recovering 100,000 thalers (£15,000) allocated to him as compensation for the loss to the family of the Upper Palatinate. He left Captain Pyne, who had come with him from Paris, to survey the land that Charles Louis had tentatively agreed to give him at Langessel.

Rupert arrived in Vienna in September and was warmly welcomed by Emperor Ferdinand III, who had taken such a liking to him after his release from prison in 1641. But when Rupert tried to get the money from the Imperial treasury delays inevitably ensued and obstacles were thrown in his path. During these negotiations Rupert was greatly assisted by the Spanish ambassador, who not only housed him but also explained how things worked in Vienna. Eventually, the Emperor agreed to negotiate with Rupert direct, and it soon became apparent that the trouble was the inability of the Imperial treasury to pay out such a large sum of money all at once. As a result Rupert accepted an offer of a down payment of 18,000 thalers (£2,700), followed by 15,000 thalers (£2,250) for two years and thereafter 10,000 thalers (£1,500) per year plus interest on the unpaid amount.[10] This, together with the money from Charles Louis, plus the arrears of pay finally handed over to him for his service with the French army in 1647, provided Rupert with enough money to maintain his household for the immediate future, although he would need a considerably increased income to maintain his position as a prince of the Empire in the long term.

While these negotiations were going on, Rupert was also

negotiating with the Emperor on behalf of King Charles, who was considering visiting Vienna. This idea found no favour with the Emperor, who did, however, supply Charles with some extra money. At the end of November 1654 Rupert left Vienna and set off for Heidelberg via the Upper Palatinate, now part of Bavaria, where he was well received by the local dignitaries. He reached Heidelberg in mid-December but left again in the New Year to visit King Charles at Cologne, after which he went to stay for some weeks with his mother at The Hague, the first time that he had seen her since his return from sea. He then returned to Heidelberg.

At about this time Rupert was asked by the ruler of Modena, a small state in northern Italy, to raise an army and take command of it for the purpose of defending the country against the Papal States, which he claimed were about to attack him. Rupert needed paid employment, so he agreed and set about raising troops in France and Germany, Charles Louis obligingly allowing them to be stationed in the Palatinate. But difficulties soon arose. First, the French refused to allow their men to be commanded by anyone other than the Duke of Modena in person, who took the opportunity of saying that he would lead the force with Rupert subordinate to him, despite the contract signed in April 1655 giving the command to Rupert. Next, it turned out that the Duke's real purpose was not to defend his country from the Papal States but to take Milan from the Spaniards. Furthermore, King Charles asked Rupert to abandon the enterprise as he wanted him to be available for his own service: plans for an uprising in Scotland were again being made. In view of the Duke's breach of contract and deception, Rupert felt justified in withdrawing from the enterprise in July, although Mazarin, who supported the Duke, blamed Rupert for letting him down and Charles Louis got into trouble with the Emperor for sheltering troops destined for use against Spain. This caused some resentment between Rupert and Charles Louis, who felt that his brother should have been quicker to discover the Duke's true purpose.

Rupert next went to Cologne to see King Charles, who wanted to talk to him about the intended uprising in Scotland. After this he visited William VI, Landgrave of Hesse-Cassel, who would soon become one of his closest friends; William was also Charles Louis's brother-in-law. He then went to Heidelberg and again to The Hague before returning in October 1655 to the King, who was in Frankfurt to meet the eccentric Queen Christina of Sweden, daughter of Rupert's boyhood hero Gustavus Adolphus. It is clear from a letter written in September by Ormonde to Hyde that Rupert's arrival was eagerly awaited, as he was expected to liven things up at court during a dull period.[11]

What Rupert made of Christina can only be imagined, but he captured her extraordinary appearance in an engraving, now in the British Museum. Charles Louis was also in Frankfurt at this time and Rupert tried to reconcile him with King Charles. But the King's resentment at Charles Louis's conduct during the Civil War and afterwards was too strong and he declined to meet the Elector.

At the end of the month Rupert went to Vienna in a renewed attempt to get the Emperor's support for King Charles. He does not appear to have succeeded, but he stayed there for four months before returning to Heidelberg in February 1656. It was from Heidelberg that he wrote to the King advising him not to go begging to Spain. Although he had heard in Vienna that Spain was trying to make peace with Cromwell, he did not think it likely to come off. If it did come off, Charles would get nothing anyhow, and if it failed Spain could be relied on to approach him.[12]

Rupert was soon proved right on this score, as the King of Spain sent word to his viceroy in the Spanish Netherlands to open negotiations with Charles. The result was an agreement reached in April 1656 by which Spain undertook to provide 6,000 soldiers to help the King regain his throne if English Royalists could take and hold a port where they could land. For his part Charles offered concessions to Roman Catholics, the return of various Spanish possessions and naval assistance against Portugal, once he regained his crown. The main attraction from the Spanish point of view was that a Royalist uprising in England would divert Cromwell from further hostile action towards them.

For the next four years Charles based himself in Bruges and collected together a small army consisting of an English regiment, a Scottish regiment and three Irish regiments. The Duke of York joined him from France in September to take command of this force, but there was no suitable employment for Rupert at the time, as the King wrote and explained in June 1656. None the less Charles was at pains to point out that this implied no lessening of his affection and that should he ever get restored Rupert would have a share of his good fortune.[13]

Rupert seems to have remained at Heidelberg for most of 1656, during which time relations with Charles Louis gradually deteriorated. This must have been in part due to the temperamental incompatibility of the brothers, but certain specific causes of irritation also occurred, one of which is well recorded. Apparently, Rupert fell in love with Louise von Degenfeld, one of the Electress's maids of honour. Rupert bombarded her with notes complaining of her coldness towards him, one of which fell into the hands of Charles Louis's wife who thought it was meant for her. Unlike Louise, the Electress was eager for Rupert's attentions, but when she broached the subject with him she discovered the truth, after which she set about persecuting Louise. In the course of doing so she discovered Louise in bed with her husband, whose mistress she had been for some time. This discovery eventually led to the Elector's marriage being declared null and void in 1658, after which Charles Louis married Louise morganatically and fathered fourteen children by her.

Historians have made much of this incident as marking the breakdown of relations between the brothers, but this is unlikely to have been the main reason since Charles Louis gained from the breakup of an unhappy marriage and Rupert suffered no more than minor embarrassment. Also, such occurrences were not taken seriously in the seventeenth century. By far the major source of friction arose from Charles Louis's reluctance to give Rupert the grant of land that he so badly needed. The trouble was that, to be of use, such land had to provide Rupert with an adequate income, and it was the one thing that Charles Louis could not bear to part with. As a result he either made offers that he withdrew or suggested places that would be virtually useless. In the autumn of 1656 Rupert's anger boiled over and he left Heidelberg to pay a lengthy visit to his friend the Archbishop Elector of Mainz. None the less he had not yet abandoned his intention of basing himself in the Palatinate.

The conflict between the brothers continued throughout 1657. First, Rupert wrote to Charles Louis demanding his rights. Charles Louis offered him one of two places, plus a further 1,000 thalers, with the proviso that Rupert should not come to Heidelberg without his permission. Rupert considered neither place suitable and asked the Emperor to order his brother to make proper provision for him. But in April the

Emperor Ferdinand died and his son Leopold could do nothing until formally elected. Meanwhile, neither he nor any of the Electors were prepared to take Rupert's part in case Charles Louis withdrew his support for Leopold in the forthcoming election.

At this point Rupert's mother intervened, begging him to make one last effort to sort the matter out with his brother. Accordingly, Rupert wrote to Charles Louis saying that he was returning to Heidelberg, whereon Charles Louis retired rapidly to his country house and told Rupert that he should stay away from Heidelberg until summoned. He also told the governor of the castle not to admit him should he arrive. But Rupert would not be put off and arrived soon afterwards at the castle gate. When the governor refused him entrance and showed him Charles Louis's written instruction, Rupert swore a solemn oath in the presence of the assembled company that he would never again set foot in the Palatinate. He then retired to Mainz. At the end of 1657 he moved to Frankfurt, where the Imperial election was due to take place the following year.

Sixteen fifty-seven had been a bad year for Rupert, who had made little progress in his attempt to settle down in the Palatinate. There was still no employment for him in the service of King Charles, who, in the absence of an uprising in Scotland or England, had been restricted to putting his tiny army at the disposal of his new ally in the Spanish Netherlands in their war with France. Spain, while making use of it, was slow in providing financial support, so that Charles's followers were poorer than ever. A further misfortune struck the family in December of 1657 when Rupert's sister Louise, who had secretly converted to the Roman Catholic faith, slipped away from her mother at The Hague for a convent in France.

Rupert stayed in or around Frankfurt until Leopold was elected and subsequently crowned Emperor in August 1658. He then made his complaint against Charles Louis. Although Leopold was favourably disposed towards Rupert, he was not prepared to threaten Charles Louis with sanctions but merely asked him to carry out his obligations. With nothing to lose, Charles Louis ignored him. Leopold did, however, invite Rupert to Vienna with an undertaking to employ him when a suitable appointment could be found. Rupert accordingly moved to the Imperial capital, although it was not until the end of the following year that he received employment.

In the interval Rupert visited The Hague to see his mother and almost certainly spent some time with William of Hesse-Cassel, but he was once more getting short of money and his entourage was greatly reduced. Captain Pyne was with him until the summer of 1658 but probably left soon afterwards as the King asked for his return. The black boy had been given away to the Elector of Brandenburg and the two adult blackamoors had killed each other in a fight. It is unlikely that Rupert had with him more than one or two gentlemen attendants, together with some indoor servants, grooms and his huntsman.

Apart from quarrelling with Charles Louis, Rupert did nothing of importance to the historian during the four-year period from the start of 1656 to the end of 1659. He moved between Mainz, Heidelberg and Hesse-Cassel, all of which were within a short distance of each other even by seventeenth-century standards. He made longer trips to The Hague and to Vienna, but even so he must have had a lot of time on his hands and it is clear that he used much of it working as a scientist and artist, developing interests that he had formed as a young man. Our knowledge of his work at this time arises in part from his correspondence with William of Hesse-Cassel but to a greater extent from demonstrations given in England in the years following the Restoration.

In terms of science and art Rupert's interests were wide and overlapped to such an extent that it is difficult to describe them in terms of today's disciplines. From his earliest days he showed an aptitude for art, but he put his drawing ability to work largely in the context of his military interests, especially with regard to fortification. At the same time he developed a knowledge of mechanics largely as a result of his study of gunnery, both in terms of ballistics and in the business of moving heavy weights, and this extended into the field of chemistry with regard to the making and improvement of gunpowder. His concern for the cure of wounds and disease combined his interest in chemistry with an understanding of the use of animal products and herbs. In all of this Rupert's activities were severely practical, and he spent as much time working with his hands as thinking. For him library, studio, laboratory and forge were harnessed together in his many projects.[14]

Rupert's inventive labours during the period include the

making of a quadrant for measuring altitude at sea and the design of a machine for raising water. He was also working on the production of high-quality gunpowder with vastly improved explosive power, which he demonstrated in England soon after the Restoration.

But the work for which Rupert is most famous today was his development of the engraving process known as mezzotint. Both Rupert and a colonel in the household of Elector William of Hesse-Cassel called von Siegen had been interested in various forms of engraving for a number of years and had both in their own way developed systems that produced an end product that was not unlike the pictures later achieved by mezzotint. But these pictures came from starting with a light background and darkening parts as required. Rupert's achievement was the discovery of a way of treating a metal plate so that it produced a very fine grained black surface which could then be scraped as required to lighten parts of the picture according to the design. Not only did he discover the system but he also thought up and made the tools needed to make it work. This system, which he explained as he went along to William of Hesse-Cassel, he demonstrated to John Evelyn in England after the Restoration on 21 February and 13 March 1661, as recounted by Evelyn in his famous diary.

It is necessary to add that, although no one doubted that Rupert was responsible for the invention of this process during his lifetime, a claim was made seventy-five years after his death that it was von Siegen who had invented it and that Rupert had done no more than develop the tools that made it possible and introduce it into England. Some modern scholars accept this theory, including some of Rupert's biographers, while others have continued to attribute the invention to Rupert. Morrah, who gives a detailed account of the controversy,[15] concludes that Rupert was the originator of the idea as well as the developer of the process and it is difficult to quarrel with his reasoning. Nevertheless a degree of doubt remains.

In November of 1659 Rupert was appointed by the Emperor to the post of lieutenant-field marshal and in December he made his way to Mecklenburg where a detachment of the Imperial army, together with troops of the Elector of Brandenburg, was engaged in a war with Swedish forces. Some have expressed surprise at the thought of the Calvinist Rupert fighting against the Swedes, traditional supporters of his family, on behalf of the Roman Catholic Emperor, but Charles X of Sweden, who had succeeded Queen Christina to the throne, was no Protestant champion like his uncle Augustus Adolphus but an aggressor whose actions since the end of the Thirty Years War had damaged many of the Protestant states of the Empire, together with Denmark and Poland. By his victories over Denmark he was able to exact tolls on all shipping entering the Baltic, and by holding key points near the mouth of most of the main rivers of northern Europe he was able to do the same for ships entering and leaving them. He had thus become a menace to many nations trading into the Baltic as well as to the peoples he had overrun.

At the time Rupert arrived, Charles X had just crossed back into Sweden to get money from his Parliament for an attack on Denmark's possessions in what is now Norway; while there he died suddenly, probably from exhaustion. This took the steam out of the campaign, and soon afterwards the regents appointed to look after Charles's four-year-old successor put out feelers that resulted in the Peace of Olva in May 1660. Although Rupert had won a victory at Wismar the previous month, he must have been delighted that the war was over as events in England had caused a total reversal of King Charles's fortunes.

The death of Cromwell in September 1658 had led to a period of ever-increasing chaos in England which was only resolved when, after a certain amount of secret negotiation, Parliament invited the King to return to the throne. Although Charles had been watching events with great interest for some time, his Restoration happened very suddenly. Once he knew that he was to be restored, Charles sent immediately for Rupert, who was unable to leave his post until the fighting ended. As soon as this happened he obtained leave from the Emperor and set off for The Hague where Charles was to join the fleet that would carry him to England. But when he arrived on 29 May, he found that the King had sailed six days earlier. While staying with his mother at The Hague he heard that his sister Sophie, now married to Ernest-Augustus of Brunswick-Luneburg, had given birth in Hanover to her first child, George Louis, later to become King George I of England.

Although on leave, Rupert had not yet relinquished his command so he returned to his men and sent to the Emperor to ask to be discharged from his appointment. Before his discharge

arrived he was again stricken by a recurrence of the fever
that he had picked up during his time at sea. As a result he
was unable to leave his headquarters at Rostock until the
second half of August. On doing so he returned in a leisurely
fashion to The Hague, crossing soon afterwards to England.
On 28 September 1660 Rupert returned to the royal palace at
Whitehall.

5

ENGLAND ONCE MORE

WHEN RUPERT ARRIVED in England he did not know how he would be received. Inevitably, the attitude of people in general would be governed by the reputation he had gained in the Civil War, and although he would have been confident of an enthusiastic welcome from those who had fought in the Royalist army, he was concerned about the effect that the torrent of abusive propaganda poured out by the Parliamentary press would have had on the rest of the population. To counter this he had for some time been working on an account of events designed to put the record straight. In the event, finding no resentment from his former enemies, he abandoned the project.

But he still had to assess the opportunities that would be open to him in England before deciding whether to remain permanently or to return to his nomadic life as a Prince of the Empire. In order to understand the factors governing this decision, it is necessary to examine briefly the way in which the Restoration had come about and the situation that existed at the end of 1660.

Having turned out the Rump in 1653, Cromwell tried various means of getting a Parliament that would do his bidding: he did not hanker after absolute power so long as he could share it with people who thought as he did on major issues. But his efforts were of limited success, and in 1655 he divided the country into eleven districts, each under a major-general, so that the army controlled important issues such as the raising of money to support his wars. In September 1658 he died. Domestically, he had imposed crushing taxation and a mass of petty restrictions on the people, but abroad he extended the country's influence, acquired territory such as

Jamaica and Dunkirk and made the name of England feared.

Cromwell was succeeded as Protector by his son Richard, but a struggle ensued between the current Parliament and the army as a result of which the Protectorate collapsed in April 1659 and the Commonwealth was restored, consisting once more of a council of state and the Rump. In the summer there were a number of Royalist uprisings swiftly put down by Lambert, who then took his army to London where he proceeded to threaten Parliament. England was becoming ever more chaotic and the people longed for relief. In the depths of the country and in the city of London the hope was being expressed that the King might soon enjoy his own again.

Away to the north General Monck was commanding 7,000 men of the New Model Army whose task was to prevent an upsurge of Royalism in Scotland. For some time he had been urged to bring his army south in order to impose a semblance of control over the squabbling factions. On 1 January 1660 he crossed the Tweed and headed for London. When Lambert brought troops to oppose Monck his forces melted away. On 3 February Monck reached London.

From the time of his arrival Monck kept everyone guessing as to his ultimate aim. The first intimation of his intentions came when he recalled to Parliament those members who had been thrown out in Pride's Purge of November 1648. By doing so he restored a sizeable number of moderate Presbyterians, many of whom had in 1648 been in favour of a negotiated settlement with Charles I. After the experiences of the last eleven years they could reasonably be expected to support a restoration of the monarchy on the right terms. When it assembled at the end of February, Parliament made Monck commander-in-chief of the army and appointed him and Edward Montagu generals-at-sea.

Next to Monck, Montagu played the most important part in the restoration. Born in 1625, he was a cousin of the Earl of Manchester for whom he raised a regiment of foot in the Eastern Association Army in 1643. With this regiment he fought at both Marston Moor and Naseby and was present with Fairfax and Cromwell when Rupert surrendered Bristol. After the end of the first Civil War he withdrew from public life, but during the early days of the Protectorate he was a commissioner for the Treasury. In 1656 he was made joint general-at-sea with Blake. Although not involved in their capture, he escorted home the prizes from the Spanish Plate Fleet in 1657. Next year, Blake having died, he commanded the fleet that was supporting a detachment of English soldiers helping the French to capture Dunkirk from the Spanish. In 1659 he took the fleet on a diplomatic venture to the sound in an attempt to compose the quarrel between Denmark and Sweden: the same contest that Rupert became involved in during the early months of 1660. While there he was secretly contacted by the King, to whom he replied agreeing to favour his cause should the opportunity arise.

In March 1660 the King made contact with Monck through two of Monck's cousins, Grenville and Morrice. Grenville soon returned to the King with an encouraging message, and on 30 March the King moved to Breda in the United Provinces. It was from here on 4 April that he issued the famous Declaration drafted by Hyde, Ormonde and Nicholas. In it the King offered a general amnesty to all except the regicides, that is to say those people who had actually signed his father's death-warrant. He also suggested that all important matters should be submitted to a new Parliament that Monck had already called for the end of April. The King sent Monck a commission as commander-in-chief and in order to increase his future influence gave him the right to choose one of the two Secretaries of State.

From this time events moved smoothly. The King and his party were carried by Montagu and the fleet to Dover, where they were met by Monck who in turn escorted them to London. In the end, as Hyde had predicted, Charles II was restored to his throne because this was the unmistakable wish of the English people. Had he been restored by a Royalist uprising backed by Scottish, French or Spanish arms, his situation would have been very different and far less secure, since the country would have been divided into victors and vanquished. As it was, for a time at least, everybody was his friend.

Once returned to his palace in Whitehall the King had to set about restructuring the whole edifice of government and administration. He already had a new Parliament in which the old Royalists and Presbyterians far outnumbered Cromwell's Independents. In a very general sense his government took over where that of his father had ceased at the start of 1642. Laws that had received the royal assent before that time, including those that had been introduced in 1641 to limit the King's powers, stood. Arrangements made subsequently were open to question. So far as the executive was concerned, the council of state was replaced by a Privy Council that built up to a strength of forty by 1664.[1] This number was made up of roughly equal numbers of Royalists and the original Parliamentary leaders, together with four of Cromwell's men including Monck, now Duke of Albemarle, and Montagu, now Earl of Sandwich. Very broadly the Privy Council was the government.

The most important posts were also split between the factions in a way designed to reward those who had done most to help the King back to his throne. In some cases there were also grants of land to produce income that supplemented the salary of the job. Hyde was Lord Chancellor and the most powerful member of the government after the King. Nicholas kept his job as one of the Secretaries of State and William Morrice, newly knighted, became the other on Albemarle's (Monck's) recommendation. The Duke of York, who had for so long been Lord High Admiral without a fleet, now found himself in charge of the most powerful navy in Europe with Sandwich (Montagu) as vice-admiral. Albemarle, as well as being captain-general of the army, became Master of the Horse. Ormonde, now a duke, was Lord Steward and the Parliamentary Earl of Manchester Lord Chamberlain. The Royalist Earl of Southampton became the Lord Treasurer while Ashley-Cooper, who had over the years embraced every shade of opinion, became Chancellor of the Exchequer. Two of the old Parliamentary magnates, Northumberland and Robartes, became respectively Lord High Constable and Lord Privy Seal. The new occupants of these offices had numerous lesser posts to distribute and various opportunities for making money.

The government of Scotland and Ireland also had to be considered. As in Charles I's time, Scotland had its own Convention and Council resident in the country with its Secretary of State living in London. This was Lauderdale. Albemarle was made Lord-Lieutenant of Ireland but remained in England, leaving the running of the country to three Lord Justices.

Over this great edifice the King ruled supreme. In modern parlance he occupied the post of Prime Minister as well as sovereign. The inner circle of the government was the Foreign Affairs Committee of the Privy Council,[2] which later became the Cabinet. Initially, it consisted of Hyde and the two Secretaries of

State together with Albemarle, Ormonde and Southampton. The King's brothers were also members of this committee.

It can be seen that by the time Rupert arrived in London in October, a carefully balanced structure of appointments had been allocated in which recently prominent Royalists were balanced by moderate Parliamentarians. Old Royalists who had lost everything in the Civil War and who had been living quietly in straitened circumstances ever since had done less well, although the King tried to throw lesser jobs in their way when he could. With all of the best jobs allocated, opportunities for Rupert in the immediate future seemed limited, although in the diplomatic field his web of contacts in Europe might prove useful. Another consideration was that Rupert, although discharged from his command in Mecklenburg, still held a commission from the Emperor and could not accept office from the King of England until he had formally terminated it.

Despite these limitations, the King made Rupert welcome, giving him a pension of £4,000 a year, which was a large sum considering the calls that were being made on his bounty. Only Albemarle got more. The King also provided Rupert with apartments in the royal palace at Whitehall.

Undoubtedly the mainspring of Rupert's influence lay in the closeness of his family ties with the King. At the time of the Restoration Charles had two brothers, but three weeks before Rupert arrived in the country the young Duke of Gloucester died of smallpox. Six weeks later Charles's sister Mary paid a visit from The Hague in an attempt to persuade Charles to use his influence on the Dutch to get her ten-year-old son William reinstated as Stadtholder.

During the summer it was discovered that Hyde's daughter Anne, a former maid of honour to Princess Mary, was pregnant by the Duke of York. It furthermore transpired that the Duke of York had undertaken to marry her, which caused certain misgivings, particularly to Princess Mary, who objected to her maid of honour becoming her sister-in-law, and to Queen Henrietta Maria, who had always been at loggerheads with Hyde and who had no wish to have Anne as her daughter-in-law. Hyde himself was concerned that it would complicate his relationship with his sovereign. However, the Duke of York was adamant, the King agreed and the two were married secretly on 3 September. Queen Henrietta Maria arrived in late October with Charles's sixteen-year-old sister Henrietta Anne, known as Minette, to try to break up the marriage, but being unable to do so was reconciled to Hyde, who took on the thankless task of looking after her affairs in England and finding ways of settling her debts. In October the newly wed couple had a son who died within six months. By Christmas the whole business was widely known, Anne was recognised as Duchess of York and Hyde had been made Earl of Clarendon as befitted the father-in-law to the heir to the throne.

In December Princess Mary died of smallpox, and in January the Queen and Minette returned to France. This meant that Rupert became the King's closest adult relation in England after the Duke of York. For the rest of his life he took a full part in all the concerns of the royal family, and the King, who enjoyed many of the same sporting and intellectual pursuits as Rupert, was only too pleased to have near him a close relation whom he knew would be totally loyal to his person however much he might differ from time to time over matters of policy.

For a few months after his arrival in England, Rupert was well occupied with renewing old acquaintances and settling in. As Duke of Cumberland, he took his seat in the House of Lords and attended regularly, being made a member of all the House's standing committees.

Many of the main actors in the Civil War had died in the intervening years, including some, like Goring, Rochester (Wilmot) and Percy, whom Rupert would not have been likely to miss, and others, such as his great friend the Duke of Richmond, whom he was doubtless sorry not to see again. When Richmond died in 1655 it was widely assumed that Rupert would marry the Duchess, but nothing came of this. It is likely that in the nine years between the time that Rupert left England and the time that the Duke died, their feelings for each other had burned low, and it seems probable that the Duchess had decided to look for someone who would give her more attention than Rupert would ever have the time or inclination to do. This at any rate was the view expressed by Rupert's sister Louise some years later.[3] In the event the Duchess married Thomas Howard, brother of the Earl of Carlisle, in 1664.

Rupert's first opportunity to be of assistance to the King arose out of a tussle that took place between Spain and Portugal for an English alliance. At the Restoration the King was favourably disposed towards Spain, whose guest he had been in the last years of his exile. He quickly ended the state of war that still existed between England and Spain but was unable to agree Spanish terms for an alliance because these included the handing back of Dunkirk and Jamaica, which would be hopelessly unpopular at home. Meanwhile, the Portuguese, frightened that Spain, reinforced by England, would be able to re-subjugate their country, set to work to become England's ally. The King of Portugal, son of Rupert's friend King John IV, therefore proposed that his sister should marry Charles, offering such a dowry as to make it hard for him to refuse. In return he asked for an alliance and for some soldiers to stiffen Portuguese defences against Spain. Spain, hearing of these negotiations, said that they would buy back Dunkirk and Jamaica for a good price instead of demanding their return, and offered an even larger dowry to Charles if he would marry the daughter of the Duke of Parma (they having no suitable princess of their own, as the Infanta had married Louis XIV a few months earlier). They later said that the dowry could be attached to a Protestant princess from Denmark or Saxony if Charles did not want a Roman Catholic.

Both these offers were magnificent, especially the Spanish one that gave Charles a wider choice of wives, but there were doubts regarding Spain's ability to find the dowry, in addition to which the Portuguese had spent vast sums bribing the members of the Privy Council, which Spain had failed to do. Another factor that weighed heavily with the King was that Queen Henrietta Maria had arranged for a marriage between Minette and King Louis XIV's brother, the Duke of Orleans, as a result of which Louis was prepared to offer help to Charles, including the transport and maintenance of the English troops that were needed by Portugal, if he would accept the Portuguese offer rather than the Spanish one. In April the King decided to opt for the Portuguese marriage.[4]

One of the disadvantages of the decision was that it would be unpopular with the other branch of the Habsburg family, that is to say with Emperor Leopold. Knowing that Rupert would at some stage have to visit Leopold in order to terminate his contract with him, the King asked him to combine this with a mission designed to placate the Emperor with regard to the Portuguese marriage. Rupert would have the additional problem of explaining why Minette had suddenly married the Duke of Orleans despite the fact that unofficial negotiations had been going on for some time for her to marry the Emperor. As Rupert had himself been involved in these negotiations when he was in Vienna, it is probable that he was upset by the change of plan. Certainly, marriage to the Emperor would have been far better and more pleasant from Minette's point of view than being married to her first cousin, the homosexual Duke of Orleans. But from the point of view of King Charles, his sister would be more use at the French court where she had grown up than she would be in Vienna.

Rupert left London in April 1661 and returned in November. His activities during this time are recalled clearly in a series of fourteen letters that he wrote to Will Legge, who acted as his agent in London.[5] The crossing from England to the United Provinces was rough, but although in his own words 'he made an offering to Neptune' he quickly recovered: it is interesting to discover that he suffered from seasickness. At The Hague he found his mother dejected because he could not tell her when she might expect to be invited to England. Since his own return, Rupert had been prompting the King to invite his mother back, but Charles, not wanting to be burdened with the expense, had done nothing about it. Rupert asked Legge to mention it to Clarendon (Hyde).

From The Hague Rupert made his way to Cleves. In both places he reported that the main topic of interest was the mobilisation of troops to repel a Turkish threat into Hungary, but he also mentioned a renewed threat from Sweden. Rupert then made this way to Mainz, where he heard that his mother had left The Hague. It later transpired that in the absence of an invitation from the King, Lord Craven had moved her at his own expense and accommodated her in his house in Drury Lane.

Rupert arrived in Vienna in June and gave a letter from King Charles to the Emperor. On a personal level he was made welcome by Leopold and his family and remained on excellent terms with them throughout his stay, but his official reception was cool. At this time there was a move to have him made General of the Horse for the expected campaign against the Turks, but this was opposed by some on account of his religion and in any case it is by no means clear that Rupert wanted it.

In a letter from Vienna he described an interview that he had had with the retired Spanish ambassador, who laid the blame for the failure of the Spanish marriage proposal on Clarendon and Ormonde. He maintained that these two had deliberately sent Spain's chief ally at court, Bristol, on a fool's errand to Parma when a dog with a letter tied to its collar would have done just as well. Bristol was certainly very angry about the Portuguese marriage and later tried to have Clarendon impeached for his part in arranging it.

Rupert stayed in Vienna until mid-September trying to winkle money out of the Treasury, owed to him under the Treaty of Munster. He became furious on hearing that Charles Louis had written to warn the Emperor that the King of England was passing information about Austria's war preparations, obtained from Rupert, to the Turks, but no one in Vienna took it seriously. He was saddened by the death of one of his favourite hounds that he had brought across Europe to hunt buck with the Emperor: he recorded that he would have preferred to lose his best horse. Soon afterwards, having taken formal leave of the Emperor, he returned to England via Frankfurt and Cassel, where his sister Elizabeth was staying. She later became abbess of the Lutheran convent at Herford; although she and Rupert corresponded until she died in 1680, he never saw her again.

It is difficult to assess the usefulness of Rupert's mission to Vienna. Although the Emperor's ministers were displeased by the Portuguese marriage, it is doubtful whether they were greatly bothered by it, as their main concern was with the threats posed by the Ottoman Empire and Sweden. Certainly, there was a special relationship between the Austrian and Spanish Habsburgs, but in practical terms the Imperial interest was that France should not get such a foothold in northern Italy as to be able to interrupt movement between Spain and Germany, because this was the route taken by Spanish troops moving to defend the Spanish Netherlands against France. Defence of the Spanish Netherlands was important to Leopold because the region acted as a buffer between France and Imperial possessions astride the lower Rhine. The threat from France was serious, as Louis XIV's marriage settlement gave him the right to compensate himself in the Spanish Netherlands if Spain failed to pay the full dowry of 500,000 crowns, which she could never afford to do. Against such a background it is difficult to feel that the Portuguese marriage or Rupert's mission counted for much, although he may have calmed down some of the irritation felt in Vienna.

In January 1662 the King awarded a charter to a new company called the Company of Royal Adventurers Trading into Africa, which would have exclusive trading rights from Sallee to the Cape of Good Hope. That he did so was largely due to Rupert[6] who on first coming to England in September 1660 had worked on the Duke of York to send an expedition to look for the gold that he had heard about when he visited the River Gambia in 1652. Already two English companies were involved in opening up trade in the area: the Company of Adventurers of London Trading to Guinea and Benin, founded in 1618, and the Company of Merchants Trading to Guinea, founded in 1630. In response to Rupert's prompting, Robert Holmes was given command of a squadron of three ships with which he sailed in January 1661 to investigate the possibilities of finding gold and extending trade. It was the information that Holmes brought back that persuaded the King to award the charter. In addition to the King and the Duke of York, Rupert was a shareholder and an active participant in this company up to 1672, when it was superseded by a new Royal African Company. Other shareholders included Albemarle, Bennet, Berkeley, Jermyn and, reluctantly, Sandwich.

In February 1662 Rupert's life was interrupted by the death of his mother, who had a few weeks earlier moved out of Lord Craven's house into one rented from the Earl of Leicester. After her long exile at The Hague she had been granted all too short a time in the land of her youth but had received much attention from her nephew the King and from Rupert after his return from Vienna. Having been so badly let down by Charles Louis, she got her own back by making him her residuary legatee and then leaving everything to Rupert except for certain specific items to other members of her family. Rupert took full advantage of the occasion to annoy his brother, but in doing so succeeded in upsetting his other brother Edward. The resulting accusations, counter-accusations and arbitration continued for eight years before all outstanding problems were settled. Unfortunately, Prince Edward, who had hitherto been Rupert's friend and supporter, died a year after his mother while family relations were still strained.

[137]

On 28 April 1662 Rupert was once more admitted to the Privy Council and its Foreign Affairs Committee, but it was not until the end of the following year that he was appointed to the Admiralty Committee.[7] In July Ormonde left London for Ireland to take up once more the appointment of Lord-Lieutenant, and in October Sir Edward Nicholas was replaced as Secretary of State by Sir Henry Bennet. In 1653 Charles II had obliged the Duke of York, much against his will, to take Bennet as his secretary, after which whenever the King's wishes conflicted with those of his brother, Bennet used his influence on the King's behalf. When the Duke of York moved to Bruges in 1656 Bennet was sent as ambassador to Spain.

In May Rupert accompanied the King and the Duke of York to greet the new Queen, Catherine of Braganza, when she arrived at Portsmouth. In July Rupert again accompanied the King when he sailed to France to collect Queen Henrietta Maria, who had decided to come to England. On this occasion a storm arose and Rupert was credited with saving the royal yacht by his superb seamanship. The party returned to England the following month. With the Queen Mother came the King's eleven-year-old bastard son by Lucy Walters, James Crofts, soon to be created Duke of Monmouth.

In October Rupert was appointed to another Privy Council committee set up to administer Tangier, which had come under English sovereignty as part of Catherine of Braganza's dowry. It consisted mainly of Privy Councillors but with a leavening of representatives of government departments such as the Navy Board and the Treasury. A base at the entrance to the Mediterranean would enable English ships to interfere with Spanish or Dutch trade with their overseas possessions. Ships based there would also be able to protect English merchantmen from attack by enemies or pirates in the Mediterranean itself and along the coast of West Africa. In the event of war with France or Spain, English ships based at Tangier would be able to hinder the concentration of enemy ships in Mediterranean ports with those based along the Atlantic coast. In other words Tangier's significance was mainly strategic.

Despite its potential, Tangier was beset by problems, notably the fact that a large military garrison was required to protect it from raids by local tribesmen and also that the harbour was inadequate for the protection of ships in bad weather, which necessitated the building of a long and expensive mole. It does not appear from the records that Rupert took much interest in administering Tangier, and Pepys, who was a member of the committee, later recorded that all he did was laugh or swear from time to time. But it is likely that Rupert's interest was confined to the operational use made of Tangier rather than its administration, and this would be discussed either in the Foreign Affairs or Admiralty Committee.

Basically, Rupert was too impatient to prolong meetings which he regarded as being of little significance by taking part in discussion, although he sometimes attended to get an idea of the way in which business was being done. On more important occasions, as at some of the meetings of the Foreign Affairs Committee, he expressed himself fully and forcibly.

In December 1662 Rupert was made a member of the recently formed Royal Society. Seven months earlier he had gone as a guest of John Evelyn to watch an experiment carried out under the Society's auspices on the effect of a vacuum on a man's arm. Over the coming years a number of his own inventions and experiments were demonstrated to the Society, although he himself seldom attended in person.

By the end of 1662 Rupert, now just forty-three, was well established in England. He was a constant companion of the King and the Duke of York, being often out riding or hunting with them or playing tennis. While involved in public affairs by virtue of his position on the Privy Council and its subcommittees, he had not yet crossed swords with any of his colleagues in government. He was even on pleasant terms with those who had formerly been most strongly opposed to him, such as Queen Henrietta Maria and Clarendon. A book written within the lifetime of people who knew him maintained that his temper was less explosive than formerly and his judgement sounder, which made him easier to employ.[8]

On his return from Vienna he had in addition to his lodgings at Whitehall been given rooms at Windsor Castle where he had set up a forge and laboratory so that he was able to continue with his experiments and inventions. Unusually for Rupert, he even had enough money, which meant that he was no longer obliged to scrape around to pay his followers. For the first time in his life he was living a comfortable and carefree existence.

*   *   *

By 1663 it was clear that rivalry with the Dutch would sooner or later lead to a war which would be fought mainly at sea. In this event Rupert, with his extensive experience of operational command and his knowledge of ships and the sea, could look forward to a command in the fleet. This fact, together with his interest in West Africa and Tangier, must have focused his attention on the navy.

At the time of the Restoration King Charles took over a large number of ships. There were thirty ships of the first, second and third rates, capable of carrying between fifty and a hundred guns, and a further eighty ships of the fourth and fifth rates, capable of carrying between twenty-five and fifty guns. There were also twenty-five smaller vessels sometimes referred to as sixth rates.[9]

But only a small proportion of these ships would be capable of putting to sea without extensive preparation. Most of them were laid up in harbour with their masts and guns removed, manned by a skeleton crew. Each year in peacetime a decision would be made as to how many should be fitted out in order to carry out essential functions and these would, for the most part, be ships of the fourth, fifth and sixth rates.

In the years following the Restoration there were a number of routine tasks such as fishery protection in the North Sea and off Newfoundland, convoy duty for merchantmen going to the Mediterranean, and the odd ship on duty in the Caribbean. In home waters there would be three or four ships held as a reserve in the Downs, together with guardships at Portsmouth and Sheerness. The only sizeable squadron would be the one designed to protect trade in the Mediterranean and on the West African coast, and this might amount to around fifteen ships.[10] From time to time other tasks would arise calling for extra ships to be put into service, as, for example, the squadron that Holmes took to West Africa in early 1661 and the fleet that Sandwich took to Portugal to collect the Queen in 1662. Altogether in the years immediately after the Restoration the total number of ships in service was usually limited to between twenty-five and forty, but even so the navy constituted the greatest single item of government expenditure, amounting to a little over twenty per cent of the total.

The Duke of York as Lord High Admiral was the officer of state (member of the government) responsible for the navy to the King. He was also a member of the Admiralty Committee

of the Privy Council. In addition to advising the government
on how best to use the navy and issuing directives concerning
tactics and discipline, he made all flag-officer appointments and
commissioned the captains and lieutenants of ships in service:
the commissions ran only for the time that the ships remained
in service and ceased as soon as they were laid up. He carried
out this task with the aid of a secretary, William Coventry, and
a few clerks.

Two further bodies were responsible to the Lord High
Admiral: first, the Court of Admiralty, which exercised jurisdic-
tion over maritime matters (in wartime it was chiefly concerned
with prizes); second and far more important, the Navy Board,
which administered the navy and was responsible among other
things for the management of the dockyards, the building and
repair of ships, the recruitment and pay of the seamen and the
appointment of warrant-officers. Over the years Rupert, both
as an admiral-at-sea and when standing in for the Lord High
Admiral, had a close and occasionally stormy relationship with
this latter body, so it is necessary to examine briefly how it
worked.

The Navy Board consisted of four Principal Officers: Treasurer, Comptroller, Surveyor and Clerk of the Acts. In addition,
there were three commissioners, that is to say members of the
board who had no specific duties. At the time of the Restoration
appointments to the Navy Board, as to the Privy Council, were
made with a view to balancing the claims of the various factions
in the country. Thus, a prominent Royalist and former governor
of Jersey, Sir George Carteret, who was also vice-chamberlain
and a member of the Privy Council, was made Treasurer and
de facto chairman of the board. Before the Civil War he had
served at sea as a vice-admiral and on the Navy Board as
Comptroller. Another Royalist, Sir Robert Slingsby, was made
Comptroller, i.e. the officer responsible for auditing all the
accounts: he soon died and was replaced by Sir John Mennes.
The Parliamentary admiral Sir William Batten again became
Surveyor, an appointment that he had held in 1638. He was
responsible for the design, building and repair of the ships and
for supervising work in the dockyards. Sandwich's former secretary and man of business, Samuel Pepys, became Clerk of the
Acts, officially responsible for the secretarial side of the board's
work. However, he extended his knowledge by studying the
functions of his colleagues and the work of affiliated organisa-

tions, such as the Ordnance Board and the victuallers, until his influence spread to cover the whole range of Navy Board business.

Of the three commissioners, one was the veteran Royalist Lord Berkeley of Stratton, another was the Parliamentary admiral Sir William Penn, who had served under Batten in the Civil War and who had then been Blake's vice-admiral before becoming briefly one of Cromwell's generals-at-sea, and the third was Peter Pett of the shipbuilding family, whose membership of the board was directly related to his function as director of Chatham Dockyard, the largest of all the royal dockyards.

From 1662 onwards the Duke of York kept in touch with the Navy Board by having a weekly meeting with the officers and commissioners and by making his secretary, Sir William Coventry, a commissioner of the Navy Board in place of Lord Berkeley. Coventry, who was one of the most consistently competent people to have dealings with the navy at this time, was a born and bred Royalist who had at an early age fought for the King in the Civil War. He became the Duke of York's secretary at the Restoration and was devoted to his interests.

Naturally, at the Restoration the vast majority of the sea officers were men who had formerly been opposed to the King, and it was necessary to identify and weed out those who found themselves unable to support the new regime. It was also necessary to provide openings for Royalist officers in order to establish a political balance in the fleet to match that in the country as a whole, and it was not only politically suspect officers who got moved in order to make room for them. It was the function of the Lord High Admiral to carry out this restructuring, which was one in which the King himself took a close interest.

So far as weeding out unsound Parliamentarians was concerned, the Duke depended for advice largely on the surviving generals-at-sea of the Cromwellian era, Albemarle, Sandwich and Penn. From his own knowledge he could select Royalist replacements, although Prince Rupert doubtless put pressure on him to forward the interests of those who had served with him on his voyages, while the King used the opportunities provided to reward former Royalists whom he had been unable to compensate in other ways. Some of these people had no seagoing experience at all.

Clearly, such a radical reshuffle caused hardship and encouraged the growth of faction among those who came to identify their fortunes with the support of one of the great men who were influencing the Lord High Admiral. It also caused resentment among those long-serving but less-well-backed officers who were replaced for political or personal reasons by less-well-qualified men.

In the first three years after the Restoration the struggle for influence in the navy was essentially between the Duke of York, who started with no knowledge or experience of maritime affairs but who fully intended to exercise the office of Lord High Admiral to the full, and Sandwich, who had a detailed knowledge of the fleet together with limited battle experience at sea and who wanted to retain as much influence as he could. Albemarle and Penn both had greater battle experience than the Duke of York or Sandwich, but Albemarle was occupied with other aspects of government, in particular the reduction and reorganisation of the army, while Penn, who was neither a peer nor a Privy Councillor, occupied too humble a position to be considered for command of the fleet in the event of war in preference to the Duke of York or Sandwich. Other former flag officers such as Ayscue and Lawson were less influential than Penn but were in competition with Royalists such as Allin and Holmes for the command of squadrons.

Although Rupert took no direct part in naval affairs in the first three years after his return, his very existence as a senior member of the royal family and a commander of renown with operational seagoing experience automatically posed a threat to the prospects of Sandwich and even, indirectly, to the Duke of York, whom Rupert was qualified to replace should the need arise. At the very least Rupert's claims for himself and his followers would have to be considered in competition to the claims of people whom the Duke might prefer to satisfy. Furthermore, Rupert's detailed knowledge of the problems of keeping the fleet at sea – from the provision of powder and shot, masts, spars, rope and canvas right down to the price of victuals – could make difficulties for the Navy Board were he to be supervising their efforts as a member of the Admiralty Committee or as the commander of the fleet itself.

All these facts were immediately understood by Sandwich's most ardent supporter, Pepys, who recorded in his diary on the day Rupert arrived in England in 1660, 'Prince Rupert is come to court, but welcome to nobody.'[11] No doubt Pepys's feelings were accentuated by the views of Batten and Penn, his two closest colleagues at the time, although he soon fell out with them. Both of them had run across Rupert in the past to their discomfort.

In all this turmoil the Duke of York, Rupert and Sandwich remained on easy terms with each other, although Pepys, whose survival in the early years of the Restoration depended on Sandwich, took every opportunity to promote his patron's interests, while Coventry gained the support of Penn for the Duke of York to the detriment of Sandwich. At the same time Coventry befriended Pepys, whose mastery of Navy Board business was in marked contrast to the fumbling of Mennes and the corruption of Batten. Coventry and Pepys also had a common interest in keeping Rupert out of contention for as long as possible.

The causes of friction that led to the breakdown of relations between the United Provinces and England were basically the same in the early 1660s as they had been in the days of the Commonwealth. They were numerous and complicated but were well summarised by Albemarle, who on one occasion when he had heard many views expressed said: 'What matters this or that reason? What we want is more of the trade which the Dutch now have.'[12]

This view echoed the feelings of those involved in exploiting the wealth of the East and West Indies, West Africa and North America as well as those trading and fishing in and around Europe. It found a ready following in the city and among many of those at court who were constantly about the King, such as the Duke of York, Bennet, Buckingham and Fitzharding. Most of these people had shares in such companies as the Royal Adventurers Trading into Africa, which was one reason for their desire to fight the Dutch, but trade was not the only reason. The Duke of York, for example, wanted to command the fleet in action and to establish a reputation as a fighting admiral,[13] while Bennet was anti-Dutch for political reasons and drew his support in Parliament from those who wanted war with the Dutch.[14]

Despite the clamour for war, both Clarendon and Southampton were strongly opposed to it at the time.[15] Not only were they uncertain of the outcome and reluctant to burden the Treasury with the expense, but Clarendon felt that it might give an opportunity to those who still opposed the monarchy to destabilise the regime. With these arguments the King agreed, as a result of which Clarendon negotiated a treaty with the Dutch in 1662, which together with the Anglo-Portuguese treaty and treaties signed by the United Provinces with both France and Portugal ensured a short period of peace and consolidation in Western Europe. Only Spain was left out.

Over the next two years further developments took place. Spain's hostility made it desirable for England to become more closely allied to France while commercial pressure caused her to demand trade concessions from the United Provinces. France's terms for a closer alliance proved unacceptable to the King, but some progress was made in getting minor concessions from the Dutch. The King, backed by Clarendon, put more pressure on the Dutch, but with no intention of going to war. But some of the King's councillors, particularly Bennet, were edging in that direction.[16]

Bennet's character is difficult to pin down. He was ambitious and to many of his contemporaries he had an unattractive manner: a mixture of pride and pomposity. He was thought to be able but not quick-witted. Without doubt his success in becoming Secretary of State and in holding the job for twelve years was mainly due to his ability to understand and manage the King, both in his pleasures and in council. By contrast, Clarendon, who suffered increasingly from gout and other ailments and who openly disapproved of the King's flagrant immorality and the dissolute behaviour of many of his companions, tended to hold himself aloof from court, doing as much as possible of his business in his own quarters. As a result the King saw less of him and gave more heed to Bennet and those favouring war.

It is sometimes suggested that Bennet used the younger Privy Councillors such as Fitzharding to sway the King in favour of the war, and no doubt he did so to some extent. But support for the war was not limited to the young, and in any case the King did not pay too much attention to his contemporaries as virtually all the most influential appointments were held by much older men. For example, at the start of 1664 Bennet himself was forty-five and the other Secretary of State, Morrice, was sixty-one. The ages of the most important members of the government were Clarendon, fifty-five, Albemarle, fifty-six, Southampton, fifty-seven, Ormonde, fifty-three, Lauderdale, forty-seven, and Ashley-Cooper, forty-two. Members of the

Privy Council who were still in their thirties were comparatively rare. Apart from the Duke of York, thirty, they included Sandwich, thirty-eight, Buckingham, thirty-five, Carlisle, thirty-four and Fitzharding, thirty-three. In practice it was not the influence of any particular group on the King which brought about the war so much as a series of badly controlled events that gradually pushed him past the point of no return.

At the end of 1663 an important step was taken when, reacting to the promptings of the Company of Royal Adventurers Trading into Africa, the Duke of York commissioned Robert Holmes to return to the Gambia and Cape Coast in the *Jersey* of forty-five guns where he was to pick up the Royal Adventurers' Company ship, the *Katherin*, in order that together they might protect and promote the interests of the Royal Company. He was to maintain the company's right to trade where it pleased on the African coast and to capture, sink or destroy any ships trying to prevent this, with particular reference to the *Golden Lion* and her sister ship the *Christiana*, both in the service of the Dutch West India Company and both of which had been interfering with the business of the Royal Company.[17]

The instructions that the Duke of York gave Holmes for his expedition were capable of being interpreted in a number of ways, but the selection of Holmes as commander ensured that every opportunity would be taken to provoke the Dutch. Holmes reached Madeira on 14 December 1663 and sailed for home on 16 June 1664, having caused such mayhem in the interval as to ensure a major Dutch reaction. In addition to carrying out the direct orders given to him, he had captured a Dutch ship and a fortified depot in the Cape Verde Islands and another fort in Sierra Leone. He then captured a Dutch fort on the Gold Coast and, having been joined by three more of the King's ships, including the *Expedition* commanded by Valentine Pyne, he captured Cape Coast Castle itself. In June he sailed to São Tomé off Angola, a Portuguese possession, where he stayed for a month.

Holmes returned to England via the Cape Verde Islands, where by chance he met some Spaniards who gave him the most authentic account of the fate of Prince Maurice yet to be heard, which he passed on to Prince Rupert when he reached England in the following January. Their story was that at the time of the hurricane that struck Rupert's fleet they were living at St John's, Puerto Rico. They said that during the storm a ship was wrecked off the south coast of the island and some wreckage came ashore. There were no survivors and certainly no prisoners, but among the wreckage were a number of pipestaves marked with Prince Maurice's initials.[18]

Before proceeding with the narrative it is worth taking note of two events that occurred in the first half of 1664 and which would affect Rupert in the future. The first was that the King raised his bastard James Crofts to the peerage as Duke of Monmouth on his reaching the age of sixteen. Not only did he do this, but he announced that Monmouth would take precedence over all peers save only the Duke of York and Prince Rupert. He thus indicated his intention of treating him as a fully fledged member of the royal family.

The second event was that Rupert in his usual discreet way took a mistress. The lady in question was Frances Bard, daughter of Sir Henry Bard, who had been a long-serving member of the Royalist army in the Civil War and the commander of a brigade of foot in the Naseby campaign. During his service he lost an arm but gained an Irish peerage as Viscount Bellamont. The Restoration found him impoverished, and the best that the King could do for him was to send him on a mission to the Shah of Persia, on which he died almost immediately, leaving his wife and four children destitute. Lady Bellamont asked the King for help, and it is likely that Rupert, who always showed concern for his former comrades in arms, took a hand in the business.

Frances, the eldest child, was born in 1646 so she was fourteen when her father died and about eighteen when she went to live with Rupert in 1664. From what little is known of her, she appears as a lively and lovable girl. She was undoubtedly a Roman Catholic, which would not have bothered Rupert: firm as he was in his own Calvinist faith, he never concerned himself with other people's religious beliefs. In later life, when living at the court of Rupert's sister Sophie, Frances claimed that Rupert had married her. Although Sophie loved her dearly, she never believed it. After a further two centuries a bogus marriage certificate was unearthed by a descendant of Frances's sister dated 30 July 1664, but it was totally unconvincing.[19] It was a routine feature of seventeenth-century life for marriages to be alleged where none existed. Thus, King Charles was

alleged to have married Lucy Walters, Henrietta Maria was
alleged to have married Jermyn, and the Queen of Bohemia
Lord Craven, to mention but a few.

By March 1664 news of Holmes's activities started to reach
London and by May both the English and the Dutch govern-
ments were well aware of what was going on. It seemed probable that the Dutch would send a squadron to West Africa to
re-establish their forts and trading posts and exact retribution
on the Royal Company; there was even a possibility that they
would launch a direct attack on English shipping at home. In
either event an English fleet would have to be made ready for
sea.

The growing urgency of the situation can be seen from entries
made by Samuel Pepys in his diary. At the Navy Board's Mon-
day meeting with the Duke of York on 4 April there was a
general discussion about preparing the fleet for war. On 18
May Pepys received a letter from Coventry urging speed with
the preparations as it was thought that a Dutch fleet was at sea.
Five days later the King, with the Duke of York and a sizeable
entourage, went to Chatham to inspect the preparations. On 4
June Pepys met the Duke of York to persuade him that it would
be impossible to man the fleet without recourse to the press. Six
days later the Secretary of State issued the necessary authority.

The question of command had now to be decided, which led
to some strange manoeuvring. The Duke of York desperately
wanted to take the fleet to sea if war came, despite his lack of
experience. Albemarle, with his record of victories in the first
Dutch War, had a better claim to the chief command, but the
King required him to remain in England to look after the security of the kingdom, thus improving the Duke of York's chances.
Someone whose claim to the chief command in war would not
jeopardise the Duke's chances had now to be found to command
the twelve ships that were ready for sea. This could be Sandwich,
but a more junior flag officer would be safer from the Duke's
point of view. Also, the Duke feared that if he offered the
command to Sandwich, Rupert might take umbrage.

The Duke and Coventry decided that the best course would
be to suggest to Sandwich that the command of twelve ships
represented too small a squadron for one of his importance, a
consideration that would apply to Rupert as well. On 29 May

Pepys was deputed to sound Sandwich out. Sandwich, already resentful of the fact that the Duke had not consulted him over the selection of captains for the ships, was even more upset that the Duke had not raised the question of command directly with him. But being a civilised and even-tempered man, he avoided the trap and to the annoyance of the Duke and Coventry expressed his willingness to serve. A month later he was aboard his flagship with a squadron that had grown in size to eighteen ships. Allin was his vice-admiral and Teddiman, a veteran of Commonwealth days, his rear-admiral.

By the end of June 1664 the Dutch were doing their best to persuade the King that they had no desire for war. From their point of view the time was not right, as their herring fleet, on which their country greatly depended, was leaving for the fishing grounds, and a number of economically important East India ships were on their way home. They were therefore careful to avoid any action in home waters that might be construed as hostile. Thus, they did not send a squadron towards West Africa from the United Provinces; instead, on 12 August, they decided to send de Ruyter's squadron from the Mediterranean.

News of this decision must have reached London quickly, as within seven days the Navy Board had been told to get another squadron of twelve ships to sea as soon as possible to follow de Ruyter. By the end of the month Prince Rupert was nominated to command it. One month later the ships were ready, although a number of them were converted merchantmen. On 4 October the King and the Duke of York attended a farewell dinner for Rupert, and in the early hours of the following morning they accompanied him downriver to his flagship, the *Henrietta*. By this time de Ruyter had already left Cadiz, having stocked up for his voyage to West Africa.

It was eleven years and seven months since Rupert had returned to the mouth of the Loire at the end of his epic voyage. He was fit and relaxed and over the past four years had built up a secure position in the inner circle of those trusted by the King, which was essential for anyone aspiring to the chief command of the fleet in war. A century later, when the direction and administration of the navy was properly staffed and formalised, it would become possible to separate the functions of forming national policy from the exercise of command, but while these processes were in their infancy the commander of the fleet had to be someone who was fully acquainted with the King's innermost thinking and someone the King could trust to promote his ideas.

Of the three professional qualifications thought to be needed by an admiral, Rupert possessed two in good measure, namely a knowledge of seamanship and of naval logistics. He was also an artillery expert who understood the scientific and practical problems of producing guns and gunpowder. Only in the matter of fleet tactics did he need more practical experience, and this he seemed well placed to acquire in the near future. Altogether his prospects of becoming as famous a commander at sea as he had once been on land seemed set fair.

But matters did not run as smoothly as he would have wished. His first problem was with his chaplain, specially selected by the Archbishop of Canterbury, who became unhinged by life at sea. Instead of fulfilling his duties, he ran around the ship abusing the captain until Rupert ordered him to his cabin and told him to prepare himself to lead the prayers next morning. He was soon sent ashore, and in a letter to Bennet written on 11 October Rupert reported that the ship without the chaplain was a quiet place. God send us another of a better temper, he added; hitherto we have not troubled Him much with our prayers! Next day, thanks to unfavourable winds, Rupert was still in the Downs, and it was not until a week later that his ships arrived off Portsmouth, where they were to be stocked for the voyage to Africa.

Before Rupert had even left London a decision had been taken to set out another thirty-seven ships for the Duke of York to command. On 16 October, while Rupert was at sea, a meeting of the Foreign Affairs Committee put some radical proposals to the King. These were that Rupert's voyage to West Africa should be held up for the time being and that once a sufficiently powerful fleet was assembled at Spithead, orders should be given to seize all Dutch ships in the Channel which would be held to compensate for any injury that might be done by de Ruyter in West Africa. In addition, Allin who had taken some of Sandwich's ships to replace Lawson's squadron in the Mediterranean, should make peace with Algiers, sail for Tangier and try to seize the Dutch fleet returning from Smyrna. Once at Tangier Allin was to take any Dutch ships wherever he could find them and return to Portsmouth by the end of the year.[20]

At some stage after leaving the Downs Rupert met with an accident. Whether he fell and knocked his head or whether, as has been suggested, some rigging gave way and he was struck by a block is not clear. Rupert himself did not initially think it was serious, but the injury stirred up his old wound. He evidently mentioned it in a letter to Will Legge, who told the Duke of York, as a result of which the Duke sent Choqueux post-haste to Portsmouth. Soon after his arrival Choqueux decided to carry out a minor operation on Rupert's skull, assuring him that he would be up and about within a few days. On 6 November Rupert wrote to the King saying that he had not been able to push forward the preparations for his departure to Africa as fast as he would have liked because Choqueux insisted that he lay up for a few more days but that he would soon be in good shape.

On 9 November the Duke of York arrived at Portsmouth to take the fleet to sea for a cruise in the English Channel once all the ships were ready. Sir William Penn would sail with the Duke as his adviser and chief of staff with the unusual title of captain commander. On 11 November the Duke reorganised the fleet into three squadrons, himself commanding the Red, Rupert the White and Sandwich the Blue. Normally the Red, as the senior squadron, sailed in the centre of the fleet, the White, as next senior, acted as vanguard and the Blue brought up the rear. On 16 November the Duke of York issued new sailing instructions that were substantially the same as those issued by the Commonwealth during the first Dutch War. Two days later he issued new fighting instructions which, though based on the old ones, included some important innovations, notably that when the fleet was ordered to get into line, each ship should take station in accordance with a previously issued order of battle.[21]

On 24 November the *Royal Charles* arrived from the Thames in company with fourteen other vessels and the Duke moved into her. Soon afterwards, the fleet, now forty-one strong, put to sea. The ships were back at Portsmouth after a week, during which time they had sailed to the Channel Islands and along the cost of Brittany.[22] Although no enemy put in an appearance, the cruise provided valuable experience, not least in terms of working out how the function of the Lord High Admiral should be exercised in London when the Lord High Admiral himself was at sea. In this case the Admiralty Committee of the Privy

Council was given the task, which proved a total failure, especially as Coventry was at sea with the Duke.

Rupert, far from having recovered from his injury as Choqueux had predicted, was now very much worse, and when the Duke of York left Portsmouth for London on 4 December he took Rupert with him, leaving Sandwich in command of the fleet. The expedition to West Africa was now finally abandoned, much to Rupert's disappointment as he thought that the warm weather might speed his recovery, but at this time Rupert was reported as being mightily worn away and not likely to live. Fortunately, his constitution came to the rescue and he slowly improved.

By the autumn of 1664 the advantages gained by Holmes in West Africa were fully understood by the people of England, as was the outcome of another expedition under Major Nicholls which had captured New Amsterdam in North America from the Dutch West India Company: the settlement was renamed New York in honour of the Duke. These successes greatly encouraged the mercantile community and even made the King's government temporarily popular with Parliament. This body, elected in 1661, was composed largely of the old Royalist country gentry and was not normally sympathetic to the court. Both the city and Parliament were now anxious for more pressure to be put on the Dutch. The city made two loans of £100,000 each to the King to finance further adventures and then, at the end of November, Parliament voted the enormous sum of £2,500,000 to be raised over three years.[23]

With this encouragement the government ordered that Dutch ships world-wide could be taken to offset English losses at the hands of the Dutch over recent years. As a result of the decisions taken in October, Teddiman had in November captured a Dutch convoy of two warships and twenty merchantmen trading with Bordeaux. Soon afterwards, Allin's squadron, now off Cadiz, fought a convoy of warships and armed merchantmen of the Dutch East India Company, sinking two and capturing three others. These successes helped to offset losses sustained in West Africa, where de Ruyter had recaptured all of the forts and trading posts taken by Holmes except for Cape Coast Castle, and captured or sunk most of the Royal Company ships together with a warship.

In the four months from November 1664 to February 1665 over 100 Dutch prizes were taken by English ships. The King still hoped that the Dutch, conscious of the damage that the English could do to their commerce, would enter into a favourable agreement regarding overseas trade and compensation for losses sustained by English merchants in the past. He even asked Louis XIV to mediate, and he put Holmes in the Tower on his return from West Africa claiming that he had grossly exceeded his instructions. But hostility between England and the United Provinces served the interests of France better than an accord between them, as a result of which King Louis did nothing to alleviate the situation and even used his influence to undermine last-minute attempts made by England to enter into an alliance with the Danes.[24] Meanwhile, the Dutch, conscious of the difficulty that England would have in finding the money necessary for keeping a full-scale war going, refused concessions and even demanded the return of New York. They also went ahead as fast as possible with preparations to get their battle fleet ready for sea. On 4 March 1665 the King declared war, realising that it could no longer be avoided.

6

ADMIRAL OF THE WHITE

IN MARCH 1665 orders went out for the English fleet to assemble
in the Gunfleet, an anchorage situated to the south of Harwich
protected by shoals about twenty-five miles north-north-west
of the Buoy of the Nore. The three squadrons were to be commanded by the Duke of York, Prince Rupert and the Earl of
Sandwich, as in the previous November. Because in 1664 the
Admiralty Committee of the Privy Council had made such a
mess of carrying out the functions of the Lord High Admiral
when the Duke was at sea, the King gave the task to the Duke
of Albemarle on this occasion.

On 23 March the Duke of York and Prince Rupert joined
the fleet; Sandwich arrived on 27 March. The Duke flew his
flag in the *Royal Charles* (82 guns), Rupert in the *Royal James*
(82) and Sandwich in the *Royal Prince* (92) which, as the *Resolution*, had been the flagship of Blake and Popham off Portugal
in 1650. This ship, which had been completely rebuilt in 1663,
was now the most powerful in the fleet in the absence of the
Sovereign, which had not been put into commission.

Although Rupert was much recovered from Choqueux's operation, he was still far from well: one observer described him as
frail. Fortunately from Rupert's point of view, the fleet would
not be ready to put to sea for another five weeks, which gave
further time for recovery. During this period the Duke held a
series of meetings attended by Rupert, Sandwich and Sir William
Penn, the Captain Commander together with the vice- and rear-
admirals of the three squadrons and selected captains; at these
meetings the Duke revised the sailing and fighting instructions
and worked out the order of battle.[1]

The fighting instructions that emerged from these deliberations on 10 April were basically the same as those issued in
November of the previous year, with a number of amendments

and additions. Further Additional Instructions were issued on 18 April and some Supplementary Instructions on 27 April. The reason why so many instructions were needed was that in the absence of modern means of communication, likely situations had to be worked out in advance, together with set responses to them and, when relevant, with a simple signal to trigger off the response. There was no other way in which an admiral could control his fleet once it had set sail other than getting ships to come close enough to shout to them.

In 1665 the signals used were primitive, consisting of a variation of position in the ship where various standards and ensigns were flown. There were also a small number of signal flags that could be hoisted in various places, the meaning of which varied according to where the flag was flown. The firing of a gun was also used on occasions either to call attention to flag or lantern signals or to modify the signals in a pre-arranged fashion. At anchor, where flags might not catch the wind, a sail could be displayed in a certain way to transmit a particular order. At night, lanterns hung in different parts of the rigging could be used in the same way, and pre-arranged orders could be passed by the firing of a gun. Messages could of course be sent between ships by boat, a method that had to be used if a complicated instruction had to be given or if the fleet were too far spread out for the admirals' signals to be seen.[2]

The order of battle dealt with the organisation of the fleet, including the make-up of the three squadrons, each of which was divided into three divisions commanded by the admiral, vice-admiral and rear-admiral of the squadron concerned. There were therefore nine flagships in all, which were naturally the strongest units in the fleet. The order of battle, which laid down where every ship in the fleet should be, placed the weaker ships next to the flagships so that strong and weak units were spread evenly along the line. In each squadron the vice- and rear-admirals were placed near the front and rear of their divisions respectively so that there should be a flagship near each end of the squadron.

The selection of flag officers had been worked out earlier, based for the most part on getting the best-qualified men to fill these important positions regardless of previous political affiliations. Thus, the Duke of York had Sir John Lawson as his vice-admiral and Sir William Berkeley as his rear-admiral. Prince Rupert had the same flag officers as he had been given for the cruise in November of the previous year, that is to say Sir Christopher Myngs as his vice-admiral and Robert Sansum as his rear-admiral. The Earl of Sandwich had Sir George Ayscue as his vice-admiral and Thomas Teddiman as his rear-admiral. With the exception of the twenty-six-year-old Berkeley, who was a personal friend of the Duke and younger brother of the Earl of Falmouth (formerly Lord Fitzharding), all the flag officers were experienced Commonwealth commanders. Rupert, with his liking for professionalism, must have been well satisfied with his two flag officers. Myngs in particular had a great reputation dating from his time in the West Indies following Penn's expedition of 1665. Five years younger than Rupert, he came from a humble background and was much liked by the seamen. Many other officers who had formerly commanded squadrons, such as Allin and Holmes, served as captains of ships, Allin in the *Plymouth* (56), Red Squadron, and Holmes, recently released from the Tower, in the *Revenge* (58), White Squadron.

Before moving on it is worth looking more closely at two points: first, the general concept for handling a fleet in the face of the enemy which can be deduced from the sailing and fighting instructions; second, the general layout of the area in which the fighting would take place.

As mentioned in Chapter 1, warships of the early sixteenth century evolved over a period of 100 years into floating artillery emplacements designed to fire into each other in order to put each other out of action. This was to be achieved by the weight of shot poured into an opponent, which would destroy guns, kill many of the crew, bring down masts and sails and fill the hull with holes along the water-line, thus diverting men from the guns to the pumps. As a rule an enemy ship treated in this way, if she did not sink, which was a relatively rare occurrence, would either be boarded and captured or would drift away from her fellows and fall prey to a fireship or other light units of the enemy's fleet.

Clearly, the best way to exploit this idea would be to fight in line ahead (Additional Instruction No. 1) so that each ship could fire her broadside without finding a friendly ship between herself and the enemy. Only in this way would a fleet be able to make best use of its many heavy guns.

So obvious were the advantages of this arrangement that it

is surprising that it was not formally adopted earlier. Only after the first Dutch War had been going on for some months did Monck, with his fine tactical understanding, draw together the lessons of the earlier battles and distil them into fighting instructions designed to bring the concept into effect:[3] these were issued on 29 March 1653 under the signature of the three generals-at-sea, Blake, Deane and Monck. Of course, there must have been earlier occasions when fleets or squadrons fought in line ahead: if they had not done so, Monck and his advisers such as Penn, the vice-admiral at the time, would not have been able to appreciate the value of this formation. But before these instructions were issued, it was not seen as the natural way to operate. In the early battles of the first Dutch War, for example, the two fleets had tended to sail in among each other in what was known as a general mêlée, firing at targets as they appeared and boarding them when the opportunity arose.

When working out an order of battle for fighting in line ahead it was necessary to keep out of the line ships that were so weak as to make their presence in it a liability. In years to come these lighter units were normally regarded as being ships carrying fewer than thirty-six guns, that is to say ships of the fifth and sixth rates, but in 1665 many of the fifth-rates were still included in the line. Ships excluded from the line sailed on the disengaged flank ready to carry out a variety of useful tasks, such as escorting and launching fireships, or alternatively protecting ships of the line from enemy fireships (Instruction No. 13). Other tasks might include carrying out reconnaissance, taking messages from one part of the fleet to another, or finishing off crippled enemy units that had drifted away from their own line.

It is interesting to notice that the smaller and faster warships were now being described as frigates, despite the fact that all modern warships were 'frigate-built', as described in Chapter 1. But it is not possible to be precise about what people meant by the term at this period, either regarding the way in which ships were rated or rigged, because different individuals used the word in different ways.

One effect of adopting the line ahead as the norm was to enhance the importance of fireships, which saw their heyday at this time when fleets were large, cumbersome and comparatively slow-moving and before guns were equipped with accurate incendiary shells. In the days of the general mêlée, fireships sailed around in the confusion looking for a target to appear in a favourable position, but once the line ahead was adopted they could be launched by the side upwind of the enemy, that is to say the side with the weather gauge, on to an opponent's ship, while being escorted by smaller, friendly ships and covered by the guns of the nearest ships in the line. The fireship herself was a small vessel filled with combustible material and manned by perhaps twenty-five men who set fire to her when within a short distance from the intended victim. The crew would aim to fasten the fireship to the enemy by grapnels and take to the boats, hoping to be picked up as soon as possible by one of their own side. It was a very dangerous business and a scale of rewards was laid down for those crews that succeeded in setting fire to an enemy ship, based on the size of the ship destroyed. Mahan compares the fireship of the seventeenth century with the torpedo cruiser of his own time and judges her to have played a conspicuous part in the battles of the day.[4]

Apart from the launching of fireships, the main advantage of being upwind of the enemy was that it enabled the admiral to decide when to close with the enemy's line, and if his fleet was sailing as nearly into the wind as it could, i.e. close-hauled, the fleet downwind could not close with it. If the fleet with the weather gauge were not sailing close to the wind, as might happen if the configuration of land or shoals made it impossible, its opponents could try, by sailing closer to the wind, to cross its line of advance, thereby gaining the weather gauge for itself. On occasions fleets spent some days manoeuvring in this way in order to start the engagement in the most favourable position. The admiral whose fleet had the weather gauge could also choose the range at which the engagement should take place, and he would have the option of sailing right through the enemy's line if desired, although in doing so he would of course lose the weather gauge.

A disadvantage of holding the weather gauge was that smoke from the guns would blow towards the enemy, thereby making it difficult for the gunners to aim the next shot, whereas the enemy's smoke would be blowing back over their ships away from their targets. Another disadvantage in a stiff breeze was that the lower gun ports might be under water and therefore incapable of being opened, whereas the enemy's lower gun ports would be well clear of the water.[5]

From the point of view of causing maximum damage to the

enemy, the best results would be achieved if both fleets were sailing in the same direction on a parallel course having converged on a diagonal one. This would enable both fleets to shoot at each other for a prolonged period. If they approached head-on, the pass would usually be over before much damage was done. Another important consideration was that in order to maintain the line with a close-order spacing of half a cable's length, i.e. 120 yards, between ships (Additional Instruction No. 4), it was necessary to move slowly, say at three to four knots. This meant that as a rule in battle, ships would take in the lowest and therefore principal sail on each mast, known as courses, and fight under topsails. To do otherwise would result in the line concertina-ing, with ships having to luff up into the wind to avoid running into the ship in front. This happened anyway to some extent.

If the English fleet managed to bring about a battle in accordance with the concept that the Duke's instructions were designed to promote, a favourable outcome against a Dutch fleet consisting of around the same number of smaller and less heavily armed ships would be likely. The problem would be first how to bring the battle about with the fleet suitably deployed and then how to continue it for long enough to achieve a victory. Naturally, neither the Duke of York nor any of the flag officers working with him, all of whom had considerable operational experience, would expect a battle, once joined, to follow a set pattern laid down in advance. They would none the less expect that the instructions would help them to take advantage of the various opportunities that might arise as the fighting developed.

The difficulties of bringing the enemy to battle under such favourable circumstances were considerable. First, the enemy's fleet had to be found where it could be attacked. Second, the English fleet had to deploy into its battle formation, upwind of the enemy if possible, in an area of open sea sufficiently extensive to enable the battle to continue for many hours before the side getting the worst of it retreated behind shoals or into a friendly harbour. Even getting into line ahead from an anchorage or from normal sailing stations was a complicated business.

These difficulties can best be understood if they were looked at in a geographical context. From the Dutch point of view their country's survival depended on trade. Apart from ships sailing to and from the Baltic, this meant that all their merchantmen had to pass either through the English Channel and the Strait of Dover or around the north of Scotland and through the North Sea. One way of bringing the Dutch fleet to battle if it did not want to fight was to catch it moving out to meet an incoming convoy or to escort an outgoing one. In both of these cases, because of the distances involved, the best chance of making contact came at the home end of each run. The same applied if both fleets were looking for each other because they did want to fight.

To understand why this was so it is only necessary to look at the figures. In terms of the Channel, the distance from Dover to Calais is twenty miles, whereas it is 105 miles between Ushant and the Isles of Scilly. Likewise, in the North Sea it is 100 miles between Harwich and the Hook of Holland and 175 miles between Harwich and the Texel, but almost 400 miles from Newcastle to Esbjerg on the coast of Denmark. With these facts in mind it is easy to see why all the major battles in the three Dutch Wars were fought either in the southern part of the North Sea or, in a few cases, in the eastern part of the English Channel.

A few more detailed points are worth bearing in mind. A battle would need to last for at least nine hours if it were to have any chance of being decisive. Large ships with a favourable wind could sail at twelve knots and could therefore get from one side of the North Sea to the other in seven hours in the south of the area, or perhaps eleven hours as far north as the Texel. Thus, if battle were joined half-way between Harwich and the Hook and one side wanted to break it off, they would have only around forty miles to go to reach the shelter of their own shoals which, with a favourable wind, they could do within two and a half hours. It was therefore difficult to prevent the side that was getting the worse of an engagement from escaping before critical damage was done. Finally, operations were greatly dependent on the length of time the fleet could stay at sea without replenishment. Ships fitted out for war in home waters carried the maximum number of guns consistent with their design. This meant that crew levels were higher than in ships sailing to distant destinations, and storage space was thus reduced, which in turn meant that they had to replenish more frequently. Also, a shortage of casks bound with iron hoops resulted in leakage and deterioration of water and beer. Yet another problem was that the process of providing enough food and drink for a large fleet was beyond the competence of the victualling authorities in any one place, so that ships sometimes

Charles II as a youth.
Artist unknown.

The Constant Reformation.
By Van de Velde.

Prince Rupert. By Bouidon, 1654.

Michael Adrianszoon de Ruyter.
By Hendrik Berckman.

James, Duke of York and Albany.
By Sir Peter Lely.

Admiral Sir Thomas Allin.
By Sir Godfrey Kneller.

Prince Rupert of the Rhine and Duke of Cumberland.
A detail from the portrait by Sir Peter Lely from the Flagmen of Lowestoft series, 1666

George Monck, first Duke of Albemarle.
By Sir Peter Lely from the Flagmen of Lowestoft series, 1666.

Mrs Margaret Hughes.
Artist unknown.

Sir Robert Holmes.
By Sir Peter Lely.

Battle of the Texel, August 1673; the junction of Red and Blue Squadrons, late afternoon. By Van de Velde the Elder.

Prince Rupert, a late portrait. By Samuel Cooper.

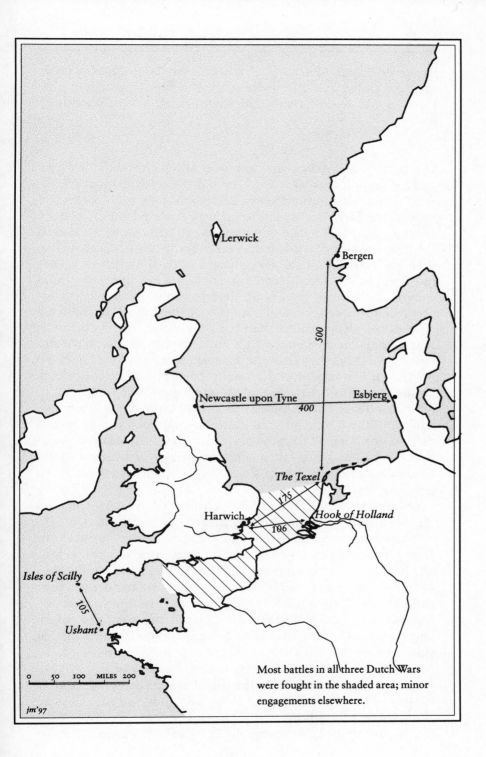

Lerwick

Bergen

500

Newcastle upon Tyne   Esbjerg
                    400

The Texel
                175
Harwich   Hook of Holland
        106

Isles of Scilly

105

Ushant

0   50   100   MILES   200

jm'97

Most battles in all three Dutch Wars
were fought in the shaded area; minor
engagements elsewhere.

had to be dispersed around several ports or anchorages in order to avoid delay. For all these reasons the fleet was seldom able to remain at sea for more than about three weeks, sometimes less.

During the days when the fleet was fitting out and the Duke and his flag officers were working out the fighting instructions, they also discussed the plan of campaign. One such discussion took place early in April when it was reported that a convoy of Dutch East India ships was planning to get back to the United Provinces around Scotland and through the North Sea. At this time the majority of the flag officers were in favour of taking the fleet to the Texel, where it could cut off the East India convoy and oblige the Dutch fleet to come out to fight. But according to a letter written by the Duke of York to the King on 5 April,[6] Rupert disagreed with the others on the grounds that no one knew when the East India convoy would arrive and that it was unlikely that the English would be well enough provisioned to stay on station until they did. Unlike the others, he did not think that the Dutch admiral would come out to fight at a disadvantage unless he had to. Once the English fleet had withdrawn to replenish, he could come out and he would then be in a position to manoeuvre himself into an advantageous position before giving battle. Furthermore, by waiting he might be reinforced by de Ruyter's squadron, which was reported to be on its way home.

On 17 April the Duke of York called a council of war to discuss future plans based on further information that had recently been received. From this it appeared that most of the Dutch fleet was assembling in five squadrons in the anchorage behind the Texel and in the Zuider Zee. These would have been the squadrons commanded by the commander-in-chief, the Earl of Obdam, and by Stellingwerf, Tromp, C. Evertsen and Schram. Another squadron under J. Evertsen, second-in-command to Obdam, was assembling in Zealand, and a further squadron under Kortenaar was nearby in the mouth of the Maas. Once concentrated, the fleet would consist of 103 ships of the line, together with a further thirty smaller vessels including fireships. Altogether it disposed of 4,869 guns and 21,556 men. With three flag officers per squadron, it had no fewer than twenty-one assorted admirals. By comparison, the English fleet had 109 ships of the line, which included twenty-five ships of the fifth rate. There were also twenty-eight smaller vessels, of which eleven were fireships, 4,192 guns and 21,006 men.[7]

Further information indicated that about forty Dutch merchant ships had left La Rochelle to sail around Ireland and Scotland in an attempt to return home and that they had last been seen on 4 April in the Atlantic off the mouth of the Shannon. De Ruyter was not thought to be with these ships.

At the council it was said that the King was anxious that these ships should be intercepted and suggested that this might be done off the coast of Scotland. Other views were that the English fleet should at least put in an appearance off the Dutch coast as an assertion of superiority. Lawson favoured remaining off the English coast, in order to conserve supplies, until the Dutch came out. Sandwich suggested a short cruise off the Dutch coast followed by a withdrawal so as to be ready to put to sea again fully supplied when an opportunity presented itself. Prince Rupert recommended riding at anchor well off the coast of Zealand and sending one party of ten ships to watch Zealand and the Maas Estuary and another to watch the Texel. His idea was that by picking up signs of either group putting to sea it might be possible to intercept and defeat them before they could join forces. But he added that once off the coast they would have to act in accordance with the weather and further intelligence as it was received.

The Duke of York maintained that, although Rupert's plan might be better from the point of view of defeating the enemy fleet, it would leave the way open for the merchant ships coming around Scotland to get into the Zuider Zee. He therefore decided to anchor well out to sea off the Texel and send out scouting parties from there. By this means he hoped to capture the merchantmen or force Obdam out to protect them. The fleet sailed on 21 April and anchored as planned, with the Red Squadron in the centre, Rupert three miles to the north-east of it and Sandwich a similar distance to the south-west.

A few days later the Duke took the fleet near the coast in order to provoke an attack from Obdam, but nothing happened. On 30 April a further council of war was convened which was not attended by Rupert or Ayscue: either the admiral or vice-admiral of each squadron had to remain behind because of the proximity of the enemy. This council again examined the proposal for getting between the two parts of the fleet and dismissed it. It also examined the possibility of launching an attack on the shipping assembled behind the Texel and decided to return to the previous anchorage out to sea while considering it further.

Both Rupert and Sandwich were known to favour an operation of this sort. On 4 May eight Dutch merchant ships were captured, but others, by hugging the Danish coast, got through to the Emms Estuary. A further council on 5 May decided against attacking the enemy anchored behind the Texel because it was felt that ships of the first, second and third rates would draw too much water to get through the channel. Throughout the Dutch Wars the fact that the lighter Dutch ships built for speed drew less water than their English counterparts enabled them to exploit shallow water to avoid fighting at a disadvantage or to outmanoeuvre their opponents. On this occasion, rather than risk the shallows, it was decided to take the fleet back to England to replenish. They sailed for home on 8 May, but owing to contrary winds did not reach England until 14 May.

Thereafter events followed the course predicted by Rupert early in April. Obdam sailed from the Texel on 13 May and joined up with the two squadrons from the south. He then cruised north, capturing twenty-two English merchant ships returning from Hamburg together with their escort, a frigate of thirty-four guns. This was a serious loss because the convoy was carrying masts, spars and other naval stores much needed by the fleet. Not until 29 May was the English fleet ready to renew the contest. On that day it sailed north towards Lowestoft determined to avenge the loss of the Hamburg convoy.

During the time that the fleet was being resupplied, a number of noblemen and courtiers who arrived to serve as volunteers were dispersed around the ships of the fleet. They included the Duke of Buckingham, who was posted to Sandwich's flagship despite the fact that the two men cordially disliked each other and had come close to fighting a duel three years earlier. The Earl of Portland, whose grandfather had been ambassador to Rupert's father when he was King of Bohemia, and who had been with him at the time of the flight from Prague, is shown as having been sent to the *Royal James* (this may be a mistake for the *Old James*, whose captain, the Earl of Marlborough was

Portland's uncle). Holmes in the *Revenge* got Lord Castlemaine, husband of the King's mistress. With Holmes he would, like Uriah the Hittite, be sure to find himself in the forefront of the battle; unlike Uriah, he survived.

One day Rupert decided to go ashore with Buckingham and another volunteer called Lord Blaney to have dinner with a friend who lived near the coast. On their return in one of the ship's boats there was a strong wind and a heavy sea and Rupert remarked that he hoped they would not be drowned like his brother Maurice. Buckingham then said that his grandfather and three of his grandfather's brothers had all been drowned. Blaney's contribution to the conversation was to say that whereas he liked their company very well on shore he now wished himself out of it even if it meant taking to an Indian canoe, as he feared that the ill luck of their respective families would sink their boat. This evidently amused Rupert and Buckingham, who were still smiling when they got back to Rupert's flagship.

Although the cruise to the Texel could hardly be regarded as a success, it had given the squadrons a chance to shake down and their admirals the opportunity of getting to know their officers and the sailing quality of their ships. Rupert had in his squadron thirty-two ships capable of taking their place in the line, of which five were ships of the fifth rate and another five were converted merchantmen. In addition, he had six sixth-rate ships, a fireship and two other very small vessels. There can be little doubt that by the end of May Rupert would have been aboard all of these ships and that he would have met and talked to a large number of the commissioned officers and the warrant-officers.

Among his captains were three of his old associates. In his own division, sailing immediately ahead of him in the line, was Holmes, and three ships astern of him was William Reeves, his former page, in the *Mary Rose* (48 guns). In the rear-admiral's division was Valentine Pyne commanding the *St Andrew* (60). As they had all been with him throughout the four years of his voyage with the Royalist fleet, no one could suggest that they were short of sea experience. In the vice-admiral's division was Will Legge's nephew, Edward Spragge, commanding the *Lion* (52).

The captain of Rupert's flagship was John Kempthorne from Devon, born a few months after Rupert and apprenticed to the master of a Topsham merchantman. Later, when he himself was master of a vessel trading in the Mediterranean, he was attacked by a Spanish warship. Realising that with his few guns he would soon be forced to surrender and not wanting the coins he had on board to be taken with the ship, he fired them at the enemy, doing considerable damage to the sails and rigging. Luckily, the Spanish captain admired his courage and soon arranged for his release, thus enabling him to visit the Spaniard when he, in his turn, was captured by the English and lodged in the Tower. At the Restoration, as a reward for his father's faithful service to the Royalist cause, Kempthorne received a commission, becoming a captain in 1664. Of Rupert's other captains, some, such as Poole of the *Advice* (40), Penrose of the *Monck* (54) and Jennings of the *Ruby* (46), were from old county families, whereas others had been professional seamen all their lives.

On 31 May, with the fleet at sea off Lowestoft, there was another council of war at which Sandwich suggested that all the hired merchant ships should be extracted from the squadrons and put into a fourth squadron at the rear of the line in order to concentrate the strongest ships together. This proposal had some merit, but it was now too late to alter the plan, and in any case the idea had some disadvantages since a change of direction could result in the new squadron leading the line. Furthermore, the order of battle was made out in such a way that strong units could go rapidly to the assistance of weaker ones. In the event it was fortunate that the proposal was not adopted, the enemy being close at hand.

On the morning of 1 June some ships from the fleet intercepted a number of Newcastle colliers *en route* to London and caused them to anchor near Lowestoft to prevent them being taken by the Dutch. Most of the seamen were taken off and used to reinforce the crews of the King's ships for the forthcoming battle.

At 1.30 p.m. the fleet was at anchor when a look-out in the *Royal James* saw a large number of sail to the south-east. Rupert lowered and raised his ensign several times to draw attention to the enemy, and the fleet weighed anchor and set off towards them. At this time the wind was coming from the east-north-east so that the enemy had the weather gauge but did not take advantage of it to launch an attack. After the battle some Dutch officers, when asked why Obdam did not take advantage of the weather gauge when he had it, replied that he must either have lost his wits or never had any. A more likely explanation is that he did not want to engage the English fleet so close to its own coast because, if things went wrong, his ships would have too far to run to reach the shelter of their own ports and shoals. For the rest of 1 June the English fleet tried to gain the weather gauge and continued to do so throughout the following day, by which time the wind had dropped.

During the night of 2–3 June the wind got up again and shifted to the south-west. Early in the morning of 3 June the two fleets were about forty miles south-east of Lowestoft, but with the change of wind it was now the English who had the weather gauge. Before it even got light Obdam, who had failed to take advantage of the weather gauge when he had it, turned towards the English fleet in an attempt to get around the rear of their line in order to regain it. The English turned towards him and the two fleets closed with each other, the English heading roughly south-south-east on the starboard tack and the Dutch about north-west on the port tack (known at the time as larboard). Rupert's squadron led the English line.

It would be interesting to know how Rupert felt as the enemy drew near in the chill of dawn. The last time he had heard a shot fired in anger had been in the Mecklenburg campaign five years earlier, and most people find it hard to hazard their person after such a break, especially when they are no longer young. Furthermore, physical fitness is a great help when facing danger and Rupert had not been well for months. But he was known throughout Christendom for his exceptional bravery, and he may genuinely have been immune to fear. He would certainly have gained confidence from the fact that the flag officers had all been involved in discussions as to how the fleet should operate, and the ships and their crews had been at sea together for several weeks, unlike the Dutch. And so, despite the demoralising effect of a first-light stand to, Rupert was probably confident and excited with little concern for his safety. His performance during the day would show that he had lost nothing of his skill and daring as an operational commander.

By 3.15 a.m., when the first shots were fired by Myngs leading Rupert's squadron the sky can only just have been showing grey: sunrise was still half an hour away. By about 3.45 a.m.

most of Rupert's squadron were near enough to the enemy to open fire and the fighting became general. But the two fleets were still some distance apart and damage to Rupert's squadron in this first pass was not excessive, although the *Royal James* received a number of shots in her hull and sails and the very first cannon-ball fired at Myngs's flagship killed a seaman in the forecastle.

The English had certainly tried to get in line ahead before the battle started but had not been completely successful. Sandwich recorded that in places his ships were three or four abreast as they luffed up into the wind to try to avoid ships ahead of them, and it is likely that the other squadrons had similar trouble. The Dutch were making no attempt to fight in line ahead, their squadrons being three abreast towards the centre of their fleet.

When the Dutch saw that they could not sail close enough to the wind to get around the rear of the English line, they tacked in succession to avoid going right through it. This resulted in their leading squadrons sailing parallel to Sandwich's rear division and to leeward of it, heading in the same direction. As soon as Rupert's squadron was clear of the last of the Dutch squadrons, he, too, tacked, which meant that he was heading north-north-west towards the head of the Dutch fleet. In due course the other two English squadrons also tacked in succession and prepared to follow Rupert back for a second pass.

At this time the Duke of York noticed that some of the Dutch squadrons at the rear of their fleet might succeed in crossing Rupert's line of advance, thereby getting to windward of him before he could reach them. The Duke therefore put the Red Squadron closer to the wind in order to be upwind of any Dutch ships that might be tempted to try such a manoeuvre. This allowed Sandwich's Blue Squadron to come up in the wake of Rupert's ships. In this way the two fleets passed each other for a second time in opposite directions.

In the first two passes damage was limited by the fact that the ships were travelling in opposite directions and did not therefore have enough time to do each other as much harm as they would have done had they been going along in the same direction. None the less sails were torn and splinters from the hulls caused a number of casualties. At the end of the first pass one old forty-six gun ship of Sandwich's squadron, the *Charity*, which had been taken from the Dutch in the last war, had fallen so far to leeward that she drifted into the enemy's fleet and was captured: some of the crew took to the boats and escaped. Against this, Kortenaar, whom the Dutch regarded as their best admiral, was seriously wounded in the second pass.

As soon as both Rupert and Sandwich were back in action on the second pass, the Duke of York ordered each squadron to tack simultaneously instead of in succession. By doing so the order of the squadrons was reversed and should have been Blue in the van, Red in the centre and White in the rear. But because the Red Squadron was to windward of the line with the Blue Squadron overlapping it, the order was Blue in the van, Red to windward and overlapping it and the White in the rear. To get the fleet back in a single line, the Red Squadron put on more sail and cut in ahead of the Blue so that the order became Red, Blue, White.

The advantage of these complicated manoeuvres was that the English fleet had retained the weather gauge and was sailing in the same direction as the Dutch, who had not tacked for a second time. It was now about 10 a.m. and something close to the ideal situation envisaged in the fighting instructions had, from the English point of view, been brought about. They could now set about some uninterrupted fighting.

Although Rupert had taken part in a number of minor engagements at sea in the past, this was the first time that he had been involved in a full-scale fleet action. Stretching ahead of him for as far as he could see was the long line of the English fleet firing with slow deliberation at the enemy: the balance of his own squadron followed behind his flagship. On the right of their line were all the smaller ships waiting to play their part in the battle. To his left was a vast confusion of enemy hulls and sails and flags of all sorts, again stretching ahead and astern as far as he could see. Every now and again they would be obscured by smoke as the guns of his flagship fired. When the smoke cleared he would be able to see the flashes of the enemy guns and watch the flight of the incoming cannon-balls, some of which might pass overhead, punching holes in the sails or cutting through the rigging. Some falling short would plough into the sea, sending up a shower of spray, while others that hit the hull would propel splinters of wood across the deck, killing or wounding anyone unlucky enough to be in the way.

Compared with a battle on land it would all seem to be happening in slow motion and for the most part at a distance. When at Edgehill or Naseby Rupert had led his horsemen into

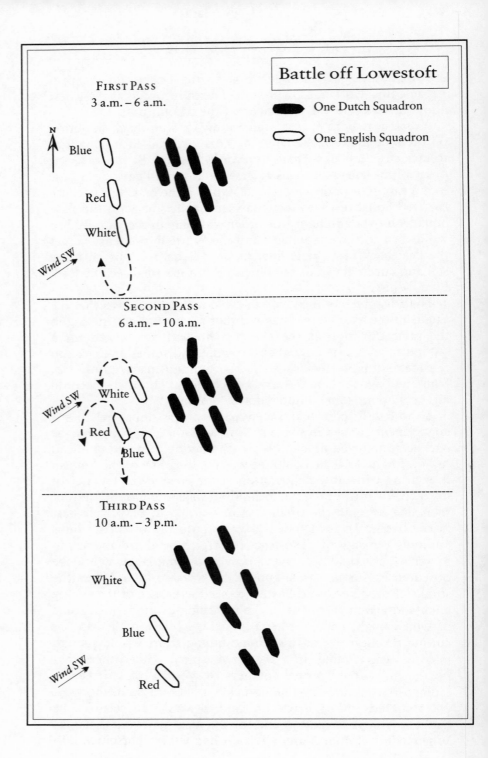

the enemy, it would have been at a canter, and when with a great crash he hit their line he would be face to face with his opponents. He would be able to see their eyes, sore from dust, and the sweat on their horses' necks. From the deck of his ship individual enemy seamen 150 to 200 yards away would seem small indeed. It would be impossible to see the expression on their faces as they manned their guns or moved around the deck. Danger there was, but it would not seem so imminent as in a land battle unless the ship were being boarded or burned. On the other hand, sea battles usually lasted much longer and always with the chance of being hit by a cannon-ball or musket shot or by a splinter torn from the ship itself. All this was accompanied by the sound of the wind in the sails and of the ship passing through the water, punctuated from time to time by the roar of a heavy gun firing close by.

In this way the battle continued for another five hours without any further tacking, the course of both fleets being south-east. For most of the time the English ships made use of the weather gauge to keep far enough from the Dutch to take advantage of their heavier guns to damage their opponents without sustaining excessive casualties themselves.

At about 2.30 p.m. the Duke of York sailed the *Royal Charles* towards Obdam's flagship, the *Eendracht*, to relieve Sandwich, who was being attacked by Obdam and a number of other Dutch ships. At one moment a chainshot killed two of the courtiers standing at the Duke's side: the Earl of Falmouth, and Mr Boyle, son of the Earl of Burlington. Boyle's head was blown off and a bit of the skull hit the Duke, causing a minor wound to his hand, his clothes and face being covered with blood and brains. The same shot killed Lord Muskerry, who was the Duke's Gentleman of the Bedchamber. Soon afterwards, it seemed likely that the *Royal Charles* would be boarded by Obdam, so close were the two ships together. And then at 3 p.m. the *Eendracht* blew up with a terrific explosion, killing Obdam himself and all but five of his 400-strong crew. Similar if less dramatic situations were taking place throughout both fleets. In the *Resolution*, sailing at the rear of Rupert's squadron, Robert Sansum, his rear-admiral, was killed.

When the *Eendracht* blew up, the head of the two fleets must have been about thirty-five miles west of the mouth of the Maas and, according to the English ambassador at The Hague, the explosion was heard clearly there, many windows being blown open by the blast. Within the Dutch fleet the effect was even more marked. Kortenaar's flagship was closest to the *Eendracht* and his flag was still flying. But by this time he was either dead or dying and could take no part in the direction of events. His lieutenant was so appalled by what he had seen that he turned away from the battle and headed for the Maas Estuary. The other ships of this squadron, not knowing that Kortenaar was dead, followed his flag.

This caused a gap to open up in the Dutch line and Sandwich led his squadron into it, cutting off from the rest of their fleet the leading Dutch squadrons that were being engaged by the English Red Squadron. At about the same time Rupert closed in on the Dutch ships opposite him, as a result of which they bore away, that is to say being on the starboard tack they moved to port so that their bows were pointing away from Rupert's squadron. There was a danger that if left to their own devices they might bear right around and get to windward of him, but he pressed them so hard that far from trying to get back into the fight they headed off north-west towards the Texel with the wind behind them. At some stage Jan Evertsen's Zealand Squadron also broke away from the battle heading for home.

By about 6 p.m., with the exception of Tromp's squadron which held together, the Dutch fleet had disintegrated. In one place three ships belonging to separate squadrons had run into each other and caught fire, all three being destroyed. In another place four ships became interlocked and were burned by an English fireship. A darkness fell at about 9 p.m., all three English squadrons, with a following wind and some miles apart, were chasing the remains of the enemy fleet. The Dutch had about ninety miles to cover before reaching the Texel and, assuming that they were sailing at about ten knots (twelve and a half miles per hour), could expect to get there by 4 a.m. next morning.

For some hours the three squadrons had been fighting virtually separate battles as they broke up resistance and put the enemy to flight. But as soon as he could do so, the Duke of York tried to regain a measure of control. He was particularly anxious that his ships should not run into a superior enemy force or become entangled with shoals as they neared the Dutch coast in the dark. He therefore gave orders that the squadrons should keep in touch with each other and not rush ahead of his own flagship.

Having issued his orders the Duke of York, who had been

on deck since the early hours of the morning, went to his cabin to get some sleep. At some stage during the night his Groom of the Bedchamber, Brouncker, went to Harman, captain of the ship, and said that the Duke wished him to reduce sail. Harman was surprised but probably thought that the Duke was still worrying about running into trouble in the dark. He accordingly did as he was told. No one has ever got to the bottom of this incident with absolute certainty, some believing that Brouncker acted on his own initiative to prevent the Duke running into further danger, others believing that the order really did come from the Duke. Either way, the result was to increase the Dutch lead over their pursuers.

Sandwich records that when it got light on 4 June, he saw Rupert's squadron some miles away on his port bow chasing about forty Dutch vessels. He, meanwhile, was following twelve more. The Red Squadron was to starboard of him trying to catch some Dutch ships heading for Camperdown (Kamperduin in Dutch). But it was now too late to complete the destruction of the enemy, and most of the survivors managed to escape, although one or two more ships were taken. At noon the fleet abandoned the pursuit and stood off to the north-west.[8]

There is no doubt that the English had won a victory. In terms of numbers, the English had lost only one ship, the *Charity*, which was captured by the Dutch at the start of the battle, whereas the Dutch had lost at least seventeen ships including their flagship. In terms of men, the English lost about 700, as opposed to the Dutch who lost at least 5,000. The Dutch were also in a state of confusion, with their squadrons broken up and their ships scattered piecemeal into any port where they could find shelter. It even took the Grand Pensionary de Witt some days to discover which admirals were still alive and which dead, since none of the survivors seems to have known what had happened to their fellows. But for all of their losses, most of their ships had survived because of the English failure to press the pursuit, so that it would only be a matter of time before another fleet under a better admiral than Obdam would be ready to renew the contest.

Despite their victory the English were not in such good shape as the figures might indicate. Although they had lost only one ship, many of the others had suffered serious damage that would

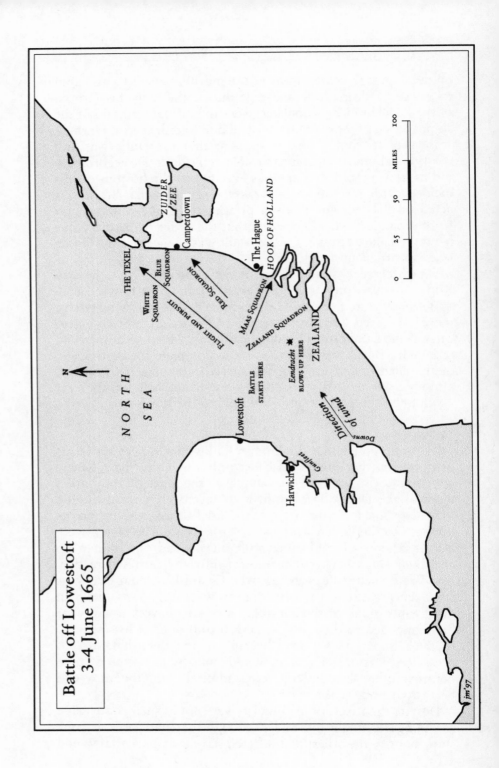

Battle off Lowestoft
3-4 June 1665

THE TEXEL

ZUIDER
ZEE

Camperdown

The Hague HOOK OF HOLLAND

WHITE SQUADRON

BLUE SQUADRON

RED SQUADRON

FLIGHT AND PURSUIT

MAAS SQUADRON

ZEALAND SQUADRON

ZEALAND

Eendracht
BLOWS UP HERE

NORTH
SEA

N

BATTLE STARTS HERE

Lowestoft

Direction of wind

Downs

Gunfleet

Harwich

MILES

0   25   50   100

jm '97

[174]

take time to put right. Also, although casualties were surprisingly light, they included a number of prominent people. In addition to the loss of Rupert's rear-admiral Robert Sansum, Sir John Lawson, vice-admiral of the Red Squadron, received a shot in the leg during the pursuit from which he subsequently died. Three captains were also dead: the Earl of Marlborough of the *Old James*, killed in the process of recapturing the *Montagu* from the Dutch, Abelson of the *Guinea* and Kirby of the *Breda*. In addition, there were the prominent members of the nobility who were killed as volunteers, the Earl of Portland being one. These casualties would certainly make an impression on the King, especially the loss of his close friend the Earl of Falmouth, who was greatly mourned by the Duke of York as well: Falmouth had accompanied the Duke as captain of his guards throughout his campaigns with the French and Spanish armies.

After the battle Rupert himself was found to have an injury to his leg, but whether it was caused by the fighting is unknown. In a letter to Bennet after the battle he ascribed it to an accident of the surgeon, but he does not say why the surgeon was treating him. In any case it is the first mention of an ailment that was to trouble him from time to time for the rest of his life.

The battle off Lowestoft must have provided the Duke of York and each of his squadron commanders with invaluable experience. All three of them had fought in large-scale land battles and both Rupert and Sandwich had taken part in smaller engagements at sea, but none of them had fought in a major sea battle before. As commander-in-chief, the Duke of York carried the major responsibility and must be awarded the credit for the victory. He also led his squadron with courage during the dogfight that culminated in the destruction of Obdam and his flagship. To Rupert goes the credit for tacking at just the right moment after the first pass, a move that won Sandwich's admiration, as recorded in his journal, and both Sandwich and Rupert deserve great credit for breaking into the enemy's defences after the destruction of the *Eendracht* and causing the breakup of the Dutch fleet. From that time on, each squadron inevitably fought its own battle, but the Duke regained control of the fleet when it got dark. In all of this it would be unfair to forget Penn, whose experience gained in many previous sea battles guided the Duke on the day as it must have influenced him when the fighting instructions were being discussed and prepared.

The one serious mistake occurred when the fleet reduced sail during the night and, regardless of whether it was the Duke's fault, he was certainly responsible for it. It is hard to imagine Rupert going below while the chase was on, however tired he was, a feeling reinforced by memories of the first Battle of Newbury. In this case, having fought from dawn to dusk after three hectic days shadowing Essex's army, he remained in the saddle all night collecting his troops together and then led a large body of horsemen to ambush Essex as he left the field of battle next morning. If he had gone to his cabin for an hour or two he would certainly have given strict orders for nothing to be changed until he came on deck to assess the situation himself.

One further lesson would have been of value to all three of the squadron commanders: the extent to which the fighting instructions had influenced the battle. On the face of it no one glancing around at the English fleet as the battle developed would have seen in the surrounding chaos much reflection of the situations envisaged in the instructions. But that would have come as no surprise to any of them. The fact is that whatever control they were able to exercise was due to them, and it was the lengthy discussions that they had engaged in when producing them that resulted in the squadrons' acting so well together for the achievement of the common aim. Doubtless, after the battle each of the admirals would have thought of some way in which the instructions could have been improved in order to rectify various things that went wrong. All three of them would at different times in the future exercise command of the fleet, and all three of them would, when that happened, issue additonal instructions to improve the chances of a future victory. But the battle off Lowestoft showed that the Duke's instructions were basically sound, and the Royal Navy made use of them consistently for the next century and a half.

The rest of 4 June and all of the next day were taken up with sorting out the ships. On 6 June the fleet chased some distant ships into Camperdown and then set sail for Sole Bay, anchoring off Dunwich on 8 June. On 13 June there was a council of war that Rupert could not attend because of the injury to his leg: he was apparently in bed in Dunwich at the time. Later in the day he went off with the Duke of York in a yacht to see the King. Before leaving, the Duke appointed the captain of the *Royal Charles*, Harman, to be rear-admiral of the White Squadron instead of Sansum. Rupert had asked that Holmes, who had won much admiration for his conduct during the battle, should be given the post. Holmes was so annoyed that he tore up his commission on the spot and went ashore.

The first official news of the victory arrived in London on 8 June in the form of a letter written from the fleet by the Duke's secretary, Coventry, on 4 June. Further information became available when the Duke and the courtiers who had been with him arrived, 'all fat and lusty and ruddy by being in the sun', as Pepys wrote in his diary that evening. A week later Sandwich complained to Pepys that in all the accounts of the battle Rupert was getting more credit than himself, although he had been more heavily engaged. He also said that privately both the Duke and Coventry held him in higher regard than Prince Rupert, whom they laughed at behind his back.[9] All of this was in marked contrast to Sandwich's repeated praise of Rupert's seamanship and courage, as recorded in his private journal. According to Pepys, Sandwich also maintained that the Duke's ship had not been heavily engaged except for the occasion of the fight with the *Eendracht*.

The King evidently did not share Sandwich's reported views regarding the extent of the danger to which the Duke had been exposed, as he decided that the Duke should not return to the fleet. The King and his advisers, backed by his mother, realised that if the heir to the throne were killed, the King himself would be in danger of being murdered by anyone wishing to destabilise the regime.

To replace the Duke of York in the fleet, the King offered the chief command jointly to Prince Rupert and Sandwich. Although Sandwich declared himself happy with this arrangement, Rupert suggested that they should each command half of the fleet. The King did not agree with this proposal and at a meeting with Rupert at Hampton Court got him to accept the joint command. Rupert immediately made the necessary arrangements, sending his staff and servants to the fleet ahead of him. According to Clarendon,[10] Coventry, who disliked Rupert for 'failing to esteem him at the same rate as he esteemed himself', persuaded the King that the combination of Rupert and Sandwich would be fatal, as a result of which the King told

Rupert that he could not do without his company during the summer, thereby cancelling his appointment. Sandwich was left in sole command of the fleet.

Coventry's poor opinion of Rupert at this time is borne out by a conversation that he had had with Pepys on 25 June in which he accused the Prince of being 'so severe in council that no ordinary man can offer any advice against him',[11] an accusation contradicted by Rupert's record of command between 1648 and 1653. It is interesting to find that Clarendon opposed Coventry in this matter: he was later to write that Rupert had done wonders during the battle.[12] At about this time Coventry was knighted and, contrary to Clarendon's advice, made a Privy Councillor.[13]

7

JOINT COMMAND 1:
THE DOGFIGHT

Rupert, having been persuaded by the King to share the
command of the fleet with Sandwich, was undoubtedly disappointed when the King changed his mind and desired him to
remain at court. But the King's decision was correct for a
number of reasons other than those mentioned by Coventry in
his discussion with Pepys. In the first place Rupert's health was
not yet restored, and it is doubtful whether he would have
withstood the autumn gales at sea. Second, despite the fact that
Rupert and Sandwich got along well together on a personal
basis, their temperaments were very different. Where Rupert
was bold, Sandwich, though physically brave, was cautious.
Where Rupert, having carefully worked out what he wanted to
do, took a lot of persuading by his flag officers and captains to
change his mind, Sandwich acted more as the chairman of his
council in determining his course of action. Finally, Sandwich's
service by land and sea had mainly been in the New Model Army
or in the Protectorate navy, where he had been accustomed to
godly and sober officers and men adequately funded, whereas
for most of his life Rupert had to make do with whatever officers
and men he could get and live from hand to mouth when it
came to resources. These differences led to a different approach
to the exercise of command. Whereas Sandwich depended on
consensus backed by discipline, Rupert relied on energetic personal leadership backed by close contact with his officers and
warrant-officers.

There was also a difference in their operational approach.
Sandwich saw the fleet primarily as an instrument to backup
diplomacy, squeezing the Dutch into submission by interfering
with their trade and overseas possessions and by bringing pressure to bear on their allies. He was particularly conscious of
the economic advantages to the country as well as to his officers

and men of taking prizes, an activity equally popular with the King. Rupert, although aware of the advantages of this approach, would at this juncture have preferred a set-piece battle designed to bludgeon the Dutch into an immediate acceptance of unfavourable terms.

The King had another reason for wanting Rupert's company. The plague was now raging in London, and it was arranged that the court should move from Hampton Court to Salisbury and then to Oxford. It was also arranged that the Duke of York should go to York, partly to organise defences there against a possible Dutch invasion but also to separate him from the King so that the plague should not strike them both down together. Albemarle would remain in London to handle Admiralty business and to keep control of the capital. In the absence of the two Dukes, the King needed a military adviser with him while he was negotiating with the Dutch for an end to the war, a task that Rupert was well suited to perform.

The negotiations in which the King was now involved had been requested by the Dutch as a result of the losses they had sustained in the battle off Lowestoft. The Dutch were also under pressure from the Prince-Bishop of Münster, who had allied himself with England and undertaken to invade the United Provinces with an army partly funded by English subsidies.

When these negotiations got under way it was found that the Dutch wanted to keep Pulo Run to offset their loss of New York and were prepared to allow the English only to maintain two forts in West Africa. By contrast, the King wanted Pulo Run returned; he also wanted to maintain three forts in west Africa, and he required the Dutch to pay a large financial indemnity.[1] Neither side was prepared to give way, both hoping that further warlike operations would cause their opponents to do so. In this respect the King was encouraged by the fact that the King of Denmark had agreed secretly to turn a blind eye on any English attempt to capture Dutch ships in his ports in return for half of the prize money.[2]

In order to put pressure on the Dutch, the fleet under Sandwich was given two tasks. The first was to intercept de Ruyter, who was known to be returning to the United Provinces with a squadron of nineteen ships from his protracted voyage to West Africa: some of these ships were prizes taken off North

America, which he had visited on his return journey. The second was to capture the Dutch East India merchantmen, also known to be heading for home. If either of these tasks could be achieved, the Dutch might well become demoralised.

In the event de Ruyter, hugging the Norwegian coast, sneaked past Sandwich's fleet while it was waiting near the Dogger Bank for the Blue Squadron to join it from England. Having evaded Sandwich, de Ruyter got his ships safely into the Ems Estuary; they arrived on 27 July. The Dutch, who looked on his return as proof that God had not forgotten their country, were greatly heartened.

Sandwich next turned his attention to the East India ships, ten of which were reliably reported as being in Bergen harbour. Sandwich put Teddiman in command of a squadron of twenty-two of his lighter vessels to which were added two fireships and some ketches. During the night of 1 August some of these ships passed through the shallow narrows and took up berths under the guns of the castle near the Dutch ships. But when Teddiman's envoy, Sir Thomas Clifford, then serving as a volunteer with the fleet, approached the governor of Bergen, he discovered that the Danish King had sent no secret orders to connive at an attack on the Dutch. Next morning, having failed to get the governor's cooperation, Teddiman opened fire on the Dutch. He was soon under fire himself, not only from the Dutch but also from the castle and a number of forts around the harbour. After three hours the English ships were forced to withdraw, having suffered much damage and the loss of around 400 men.

Teddiman's squadron met up with Sandwich at a pre-arranged rendezvous and the whole fleet returned to Southwold Bay to land casualties and repair the ships damaged at Bergen. On 28 August the fleet set off once more to look for the Dutch fleet, now at sea under the command of de Ruyter. So far Sandwich had been unlucky. Teddiman's misfortune was the result of a diplomatic mistake, but some of the blame attached itself to Sandwich until the full story became known several years later. With better reason he was also blamed for the initial failure to intercept de Ruyter. Now his luck was to change.

On 3 September, although Sandwich missed bringing de Ruyter's fleet to battle, he succeeded in capturing four warships and two East India merchantmen. Six days later his fleet fell in with fifteen Dutch ships and again captured four warships and two more East India merchantmen. While in terms of bringing pressure to bear on the Dutch this did not compare with a victory against their fleet, it brought in more prizes and prisoners than might have been taken in a full-scale battle. This in turn greatly encouraged Parliament which, in October, provided a further grant of money to the King for the prosecution of the war in 1666.

Another development designed to improve the fleet's chances in the coming year was a reorganisation of the victualling system. This system, which relied on a single private contractor to produce all the food and drink needed and get it to the ports at the right moment, was totally incapable of functioning effectively in wartime when a large number of ships were in commission. As a result, commanders were sometimes obliged to set sail inadequately supplied and then return to port just when they most wanted to remain at sea. Under the new system government surveyors, responsible to a Surveyor-General of Victualling in London, would be placed at all major ports to supervise the contractor's men. Samuel Pepys, who had designed the new system, was appointed Surveyor-General.[3] As he was still Clerk of the Acts and Treasurer of the Tangier Committee, a job he had taken over earlier in the year, he was fully committed, to say the least. Furthermore, although the new system would help in terms of planning and supervision, it could not overcome the main difficulty, which was the lack of a regular supply of money to the contractor.

Despite his ill health and injured leg, Rupert had been active since leaving the fleet. From Hampton Court he had accompanied the King on a visit to Portsmouth and the Isle of Wight to inspect the fortifications and to prepare the surrounding areas for defence. They rejoined the court at Salisbury, whereon the King became ill with an upset stomach. As soon as he recovered he went to stay with Lord Ashley in Dorset, probably accompanied by Rupert. In October the King and Rupert were with the court at Oxford, where a session of Parliament was in progress.

In the middle of September the fleet returned, and shortly afterwards a storm broke over Sandwich for his handling of the prizes. On the recommendation of his vice-admiral, Sir William Penn, he had unwisely permitted the flag officers to take their share of the goods before the proper procedures had been completed. Although the King would have been happy to smooth the matter over, Albemarle stirred up trouble. On 23 September the Duke of York returned from the north and on his behalf Coventry stoked the fire, going so far as to try to get Parliament to make the irregular breaking of bulk a felony in an attempt to get Sandwich impeached. At about this time a member of the Commons mischievously suggested that Prince Rupert should be awarded the sum of £10,000 in appreciation of his service in the early part of the year and that Sandwich should be awarded half a crown, but nothing came of this.

As soon as he could get away, Sandwich hurried to Oxford to defend himself. On arrival he found himself strongly supported by Rupert, who well understood the problems he had faced at sea and who would have resented the bureaucratic quibbling over the disposal of the prizes. Sandwich was also supported by Bennet, who had recently been raised to the peerage as Baron Arlington, and behind the scenes by Clarendon.[4] Eventually, the fuss died down and early in the following year Sandwich was appointed ambassador to Spain to get him out of the country for a while. Meanwhile, in November, the King let it be known that Rupert and Albemarle would jointly command the fleet in 1666.

The King's efforts to reach an agreement with the United Provinces were complicated by the death in September of Philip IV of Spain. This, as expected, caused Louis XIV to claim the Spanish Netherlands on behalf of his wife. Louis had for some time, in anticipation of this event, been asking King Charles to bring pressure on Spain on his behalf in return for France's neutrality in England's war against the United Provinces. At the same time he was trying to broker a peace between England and the United Provinces which, if successful, would release him from his obligations to help the Dutch and enable him to concentrate on his dispute with Spain. Although his efforts had narrowed the gap between the two sides, King Charles felt obliged to reject the revised Dutch terms because of Parliament's enthusiasm for continuing the war, and he also declined to use his influence with Spain. As a result, at the end of January 1666 Louis reluctantly declared war on England. His mother, Anne of Austria, had died a few days earlier.

Although Louis had little interest in fighting England, his intervention constituted a setback. The United Provinces now had an ally who could reinforce their fleet or threaten an invasion of England or Ireland. Furthermore, France was in a position to bring pressure on countries such as Denmark and the north German states to assist the United Provinces rather than England. By contrast, King Charles had no allies other than the Prince-Bishop of Münster. As a result of diplomatic ineptitude he had even failed to achieve an alliance with Spain.

Of the new threats posed by France, the most immediate was the danger of intervention by the French fleet. As a result of the policy originally set in motion by Richelieu, this was now large enough to swing the balance between the navies of England and the United Provinces, although still too small to be of much use by itself. In all, it amounted to twenty-three ships of the first to fourth rates plus thirty-four of the fifth and sixth rates, many of the latter having been bought in the past twelve months. At the time when France declared war it was expected that the twenty-four ships of the Toulon Squadron would pass through the Strait of Gibraltar and join forces with the Brest Squadron before sailing to join the Dutch fleet.

At the end of January the King and court returned to Whitehall. When the King nominated Rupert and Albemarle as joint commanders, Albemarle had said that if it were the King's wish he would most readily serve under Prince Rupert's command.[5] As a commander by land and sea over a long period he understood the necessity for all ranks in war to have a single clear focus for their allegiance. The well-known saying that one mediocre commander is better than two good ones may not have been coined at the time, but Albemarle would have recognised it if it had been. So, too, would Rupert, who would undoubtedly have preferred to have sole command of the fleet with Albemarle as his vice-admiral. But according to the Lord High Admiral's warrant of appointment signed on 22 February 1666, the King and the Duke of York both felt that a joint command would be safer not only because of the support that each would give the other in council but also in case one of them was killed or incapacitated during operations.

If Rupert had to share the command with anyone, no better partner could have been found for him. With regard to fundamentals the two generals, as they became known, thought along the same lines. They both understood the necessity of beating the Dutch in battle so that peace could be obtained before England ran out of money, and once battle was joined they would both fight with the utmost ferocity in order to win as complete a victory as possible. Having been professional fighters from their youth, they knew instinctively how to make the best of their subordinates without having to depend on excessive formality, either in terms of restrictive regulations or of personal behaviour. In terms of tactical doctrine Rupert accepted existing fighting instructions, moderating them only where he felt that they inhibited the achievement of the aim, and in all of this he was backed by Albemarle. In terms of administration both of them were experienced and energetic and kept constant pressure on the authorities ashore to provide what was needed for the efficiency of the fleet and the well-being of the seamen.

In other ways, too, Rupert and Albemarle complemented each other. Rupert provided the knowledge of seamanship which Albemarle, who had spent only seven months at sea, lacked. On the other hand, in those seven months he had been joint commander of the fleet in three successful battles and had been closely involved in the development of the tactics that had been accepted as the basis of the current fighting instructions. One drawback was that as a result of his victories, Albemarle had become imbued with a contempt of the Dutch which made him over-confident, a fault that Rupert with his extensive experience of command in battle was well suited to rectify: Albemarle, despite his long army service, had taken part in only one major land battle, Dunbar, and then only as a regimental commander. All of his service as a general had been taken up controlling irregulars in Ulster or Scotland.

Another advantage of the partnership was that Rupert and Albemarle liked each other. They had first met in 1637 when Rupert, as a volunteer in the Stadtholder's army besieging Breda, attached himself to the company commanded by Monck, as he then was, and with him took part in a murderous assault on the fortifications. Six years later, during the Civil War, Rupert gave Monck a commission to raise a regiment of foot after he had been sent under arrest from Ireland by Ormonde on suspicion of disloyalty. But Monck was captured before he could raise it and spent the rest of the war in the Tower. Only after the war was over did he return to Ireland in the service of Parliament. Eleven years older than Rupert, Albemarle came from a family of the lesser gentry long resident in Devon, related by marriage to the Grenvilles. Shrewd rather than brilliant, his brain did not work at great speed and he was considered dull company. But once determined on a course of action, he was decisive and powerful in achieving it. Both Rupert and Albemarle could be certain that neither of them would let the other down, either in battle or in the endless intrigues that surrounded the conduct of business in Restoration England.

On 13 February a number of captains who had served under Rupert's command in the past gave a dinner for him in London to express their delight at his return to the fleet and their confidence in the outcome of future battles. Thereafter he settled down with Albemarle to prepare for the coming campaign; for the next three months they were fully engaged in making the fleet ready for war. In general terms their activities can be looked at under two separate headings.

First was the business of collecting the ships together and seeing that they were manned and the crews paid and regulated. The ships also had to be provided with guns, ammunition, food and drink. Those coming from abroad, such as Sir Jeremy Smith's squadron returning from the Mediterranean, had to have the barnacles scraped off and shortcomings in the rigging made good. The fleet had to be divided into squadrons and divisions and concentrated at the Nore. Some of this process was conducted by the Admiralty and the Navy Board, but Rupert and Albemarle were closely involved form the start and their letter book[6] containing copies of their orders and correspondence with the Admiralty, the Navy Board and the Victualler bears witness to the mass of detail in which they were involved.

Second was the process of ensuring that all the subordinate admirals and captains thoroughly understood the concept of operations under which the fleet would fight. Broadly speaking, Rupert was satisfied with the sailing and fighting instructions that had governed the conduct of the campaign that culminated in the battle off Lowestoft and which had been discussed at such length the previous year. Shortly after being appointed to command, Rupert reissued the Duke of York's 'Encouragement for the captains and companies of fireships'. On 1 May 1666 he and Albemarle jointly issued 'Instructions for the better ordering of his Majesty's fleet', which were virtually the old Commonwealth sailing instructions together with some articles for the sternmost ships to tack first and for cutting or slipping by day or night.[7] These were the only documents issued at the start of the campaign. Rupert's principal tactical innovations, which so influenced the way in which the navy would fight over the next 150 years, were not introduced until after the first major battle.

While all this was going on the overall strategy for the coming campaign had to be worked out by the government in conjunction with the joint commanders. When fully mobilised, the English and Dutch fleets would, as in 1665, be roughly equal in terms of numbers, with an advantage to the English in terms of weight of cannon, although not in the total number of guns. But the Dutch fleet was now commanded by de Ruyter, one of the greatest admirals of all time, instead of by the inexperienced Obdam.

The main problem was to work out a way of bringing the Dutch to battle before the arrival of French ships, or alternatively of destroying the French before they could reinforce the Dutch. To achieve this it was necessary for the English fleet to be got ready before the Dutch and for reliable information to be available regarding the preparedness and movements of the Dutch and French fleets. In terms of information, the fleet commanders were responsible for getting what they could by sending ships to reconnoitre the enemy coasts and to question the crews of merchant ships on the high seas. Within the government Arlington was responsible for collecting intelligence, using embassy or commercial sources, spies and agents.

For some weeks Rupert and Albemarle exercised command from their lodgings in Whitehall, which enabled them to remain in daily touch with the Lord High Admiral, the Navy Board and the two Secretaries of State. It also enabled them to attend meetings of the Privy Council. Not until 26 April did they go on board their flagship, the *Royal Charles*, sailing three days later to join the bulk of the fleet at the Nore. At this time the provisional plan was that the fleet would bring the French to battle before the Dutch fleet was ready to put to sea.

On 3 May Rupert and Albemarle received a visit from the King and the Duke of York, and it is likely that at this time Rupert, in private conversation with the King, got him to agree that if a portion of the fleet were detached to fight the French while the rest stayed to guard against the Dutch, he should command the former. This would appear to be the first occasion when the possibility of dividing the fleet was considered.

On 11 May Rupert and Albemarle wrote to Arlington to say that they had received news from France that the Toulon squadron had passed through the Strait of Gibraltar intent on joining up with the Brest Squadron at Belle Isle, off the mouth of the Loire. They suggested that if the French fleet were to be attacked before it joined the Dutch, measures should be put in hand at once. Their letter was taken to Arlington by Sir Edward Spragge, who had obtained the information from a correspondent in France.

On receipt of the letter the King called a meeting of the Privy Council for 13 May. At the meeting Arlington maintained that the Duc de Beaufort, with the Toulon Squadron, had joined up with the ships based at Brest and was on his way to meet the Dutch, and although Morrice said that he had heard privately that the Dutch would be ready to leave port within a few days, Arlington insisted that neither the Dutch ships in the Texel anchorage nor those in the Weilings were ready for war.[8] Despite Arlington's reassurances regarding the unpreparedness of the Dutch, there seems to have been no suggestion that the whole fleet should go in search of the French. Instead, the council recommended to the King that, in view of the uncertainty of the situation, he should not take a decision there and then but send two of the councillors, Carteret and Coventry, to the fleet to discuss the matter with Rupert and Albemarle.

When next day Carteret and Coventry came aboard the *Royal Charles* they found that Rupert had gone ashore to stretch his legs. In discussing the intelligence with Albemarle it is clear that the two Privy Councillors gave him the impression that the Dutch would not be ready for sea for several weeks: in his report to Parliament after the campaign Albemarle says six weeks.[9] In Coventry's *Recollections*, written some time later, he denies that any specific period was mentioned.[10] In any case, on the strength of their briefing Albemarle said that he would be prepared to send a force to attack the French as long as sixty ships remained to guard against the Dutch. The three men then prepared a list of twenty ships to send against the French provided that Rupert agreed. Soon afterwards, Rupert appeared and approved the proposal subject to a few modifications to the list of ships selected. He also told Carteret and Coventry that the King had agreed previously that if an attack on the French were to be made, he should command it, which came as a surprise to them and possibly to Albemarle as well.

After Carteret and Coventry returned to London to make their report, there was a delay of a few days while the King decided whether or not to implement this plan. During this time the only new information received in London and passed to the fleet was that a detachment of eighteen Dutch ships had sailed from the Weilings to the Texel.

On 23 May the fleet sailed from the Nore to the Downs so that if the operation were approved Rupert's detachment would be well placed to enter the English Channel. In fact, the King had already decided to go ahead with the plan, but not until the morning of 24 May were instructions sent to Rupert, reaching him at 10 p.m. on the twenty-fifth. They ordered him to sail to Belle Isle, where it was expected that he would find the French fleet, but if he heard that it was somewhere else he was to seek it out and attack it there. If he heard that the French had already left to join the Dutch via the north of Scotland, he was not to follow them but to return to Albemarle 'so that there might be a combined fleet to encounter the forces of both Dutch and French'.

On 27 May a report was sent from The Hague saying that the Dutch were hastening out their fleet to join the Duc de Beaufort, and on 29 May Rupert took his ships into the Channel to intercept the French, sending word to Coventry that he would send a ketch to Portsmouth to pick up any further information that might become available.

When the decision was made to divide the fleet, it was also decided that the ships to go with Rupert would be drawn equally from each squadron so that in effect a fourth squadron would be formed. Rupert was to sail in the *Royal James* with Allin, who would act as his flag captain. Myngs in the *Victory* would command the van as vice-admiral, and Spragge in the *Dreadnought* would act as rear-admiral. Apart from the first-rate *Royal James* and the second-rate *Victory*, there were five ships of the third rate and thirteen of the fourth rate. Though short of large ships, Rupert had taken those deemed to be the fastest and most manoeuvrable.

Meanwhile, Albemarle had reorganised his squadrons. In the

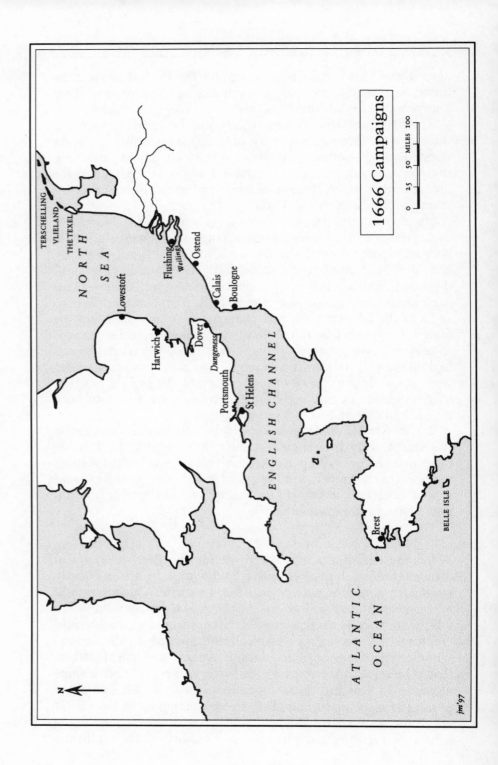

1666 Campaigns

0 25 50 MILES 100

TERSCHELLING
VLIELAND
THE TEXEL

*NORTH
SEA*

Flushing
Wellings
Ostend

Lowestoft

Calais
Boulogne

Harwich
Dover
Dungeness
Portsmouth
St Helens

ENGLISH CHANNEL

*ATLANTIC
OCEAN*

Brest

BELLE ISLE

jm '97

Red Squadron Jordan, who had been the rear-admiral, replaced Myngs as vice-admiral, and Holmes was made rear-admiral in his stead. The complete team of Ayscue, Berkeley and Harman moved from the Blue to the White squadron, replacing Allin, Smith and Teddiman. Sir Jeremy Smith became admiral of the Blue, with Teddiman and Utber as his vice- and rear-admirals. But Smith was still at Portsmouth on his way back from the Mediterranean and did not arrive in time for the impending battle.

When Rupert departed, Albemarle had with him in the Downs fifty-three ships of the line. Two more were at the Buoy off the Nore, two at Portsmouth, four, including the first-rate *Sovereign*, at Plymouth, and three together with eleven converted merchantships, were in the Thames. Without the sixteen ships at the Nore and in the Thames, Albemarle would not have the sixty he had stipulated as being necessary to take on the Dutch fleet. With them he would have sixty-nine including two out of the four existing first-rate ships and eight out of the nine existing second-rate ships. Over the coming days he emphasised the need to hurry these ships forward to him as soon as possible.

There was a strong contrary wind blowing when Rupert's squadron left the Downs early in the morning of Tuesday 29 May, and although it dropped at one point it was blowing so hard by Friday that Rupert was obliged to delay his passage down the Channel and put in to St Helens, where he arrived at 10 a.m. that morning. He was met by the ketch he had sent to Portsmouth for news, which brought a letter from the Duke of York ordering him to rejoin Albemarle with his squadron, as the Dutch fleet was at sea. Rupert's ships had to wait for the tide until 4 p.m. in order to clear the Isle of Wight, but once at sea they crammed on all sail and by Saturday evening were close to the Goodwin Sands, where they were obliged to anchor as the wind, now from the east, had dropped away completely.

By dint of taking advantage of tides and currents and of a slight shift in the wind, Rupert's squadron was off the Kentish Knock by 2 p.m. on Sunday where he saw Albemarle's fleet withdrawing towards the mouth of the Thames being pursued by the Dutch. At 4 p.m. the Dutch sent a detachment of ships towards Rupert's squadron, which prepared to attack them, but at that moment a warning arrived from Albemarle that the

Dutch were trying to lure him on to the Galloper, where some of his own ships had run aground earlier. Rupert therefore took his squadron directly towards Albemarle's fleet. Soon afterwards, Albemarle came aboard the *Royal James* to explain what had happened since Rupert's departure and to plan for the next day's battle.

When Rupert sailed from the Downs, Albemarle enquired whether he should engage the Dutch fleet should it appear while Rupert was away. The Duke of York, after discussion with the King in council, left the decision to him, but suggested that the fleet should move to the Gunfleet, where it could avoid battle if Albemarle thought it advisable and where ships from the Thames could reach him more safely than if he remained in the Downs. On 30 May Albemarle set out for the Swin which he preferred to the Gunfleet, and at the same time heard that the Dutch fleet was at sea. On that Wednesday evening the news reached London, and at a meeting of the Privy Council the King decided that Rupert's squadron should rejoin Albemarle forthwith. But the order did not reach Portsmouth until Thursday evening, and it was not until Rupert arrived at St Helens on Friday morning that he received it.

An hour or two before Rupert reached St Helens on 1 June, Albemarle, on his way to the Swin, sighted the Dutch fleet at anchor twenty-eight miles east-north-east of the North Foreland, that is to say midway between Harwich and Ostend. It was strung out, with Evertsen's squadron to the north-west, de Ruyter's in the centre and Tromp's to the south-east. The strong south-westerly wind that had blown Rupert into St Helens gave Albemarle the weather gauge. Albemarle, after consulting his council of war, decided to attack despite his numerical inferiority. He later gave the reason for this decision as being partly to take advantage of the fact that the Dutch were at anchor and that he had the weather gauge and partly because there was doubt whether the wind and currents would enable his heavy ships to get through the shoals to the safety of the Swin or Gunfleet without fighting. Another fact that must have been in his mind was that if he took refuge in the Swin, the Dutch fleet might well have headed off down-channel, thereby putting Rupert's squadron in grave danger.[11] At the time Jordan recorded a further reason as being Albemarle's concern that it

would be dishonourable to decline battle and that to do so
would undermine the confidence of the seamen.

In the initial assault the English suffered from the fact that
Albemarle attacked before the rear of his fleet had come up and
that, being to windward of the enemy, the strength of the wind
prevented many of his ships from opening their lower gun ports.
None the less at the end of the day, despite their inferior
numbers, the fleet was still intact, both sides having lost ships
and suffered casualties. Next day Albemarle renewed the attack
with forty-four ships against a Dutch fleet of nearly eighty.
Despite their great superiority in numbers, the Dutch fleet was
for a time thrown into confusion, mainly as a result of the
insubordinate behaviour of some of the flag officers. Later in
the day de Ruyter regained control, but his own ship was by then
disabled and in the evening Albemarle was able to withdraw to
the north-west.

Although the English fleet had suffered less on the second
day than on the first, the disparity of strength was beginning
to tell and Albemarle decided to withdraw towards the land
with a view to renewing the fight when Rupert reappeared. His
plan was to send the lighter and damaged ships ahead while
holding off the Dutch with a line of sixteen powerful vessels
that were still in good fighting condition. During the day this
withdrawal took place, the Dutch following at a safe distance
showing little desire to renew the battle. Unfortunately, in getting past the Galloper three of Albemarle's heaviest ships, the
Royal Charles, the *Royal Katherine* and the *Royal Prince*, ran
aground. After a short while the *Royal Charles* and the *Royal
Katherine* got off, but the *Royal Prince* surrendered to the Dutch
and was burned on de Ruyter's orders. Soon afterwards,
Rupert's squadron joined Albemarle's ships as described, just
off the southern tip of the Galloper.[12]

When Albemarle came aboard the *Royal James* he and Rupert
held a council of war attended by Allin, Myngs and Spragge.
It was decided to renew the battle next day when Rupert's fresh
squadron would lead the attack. During the night some of the
ships that had over the past three days been obliged to run into
port for repair returned to the fleet so that by the following
morning the English mustered sixty ships against sixty-four of
the Dutch. It is not certain what command arrangements were

made for the action, but it is probable that Rupert's squadron acted as the White Squadron and that the remains of the old White Squadron, which had lost both its admiral, Ayscue, and its vice-admiral, Berkeley, was split between the Red and Blue Squadrons.

During the night the English fleet pushed its way against the tide to the north end of the Galloper so that when dawn broke on 4 June it was about twelve miles north of the Dutch fleet. There was a south-westerly wind. The Dutch fleet was facing north-west with de Vries's squadron leading, followed by de Ruyter's, with Tromp's squadron bringing up the rear: de Vries had taken over from Everstsen, who had been killed on the first day of the battle.

The English line led by Myngs sailed towards the enemy on a course of south-south-east, which took them past the Dutch out of gunshot. As soon as Rupert's squadron had passed the rear of the Dutch line, Myngs with his division tacked, thus now approaching the Dutch fleet from the rear. By this time the wind had shifted to the south-south-west. But the Dutch rearguard commanded by Tromp had already borne away from the Dutch line intent on sailing into the rearmost squadrons of the English fleet, which were still heading east-south-east. Myngs followed Tromp, taking him in the rear and engaging him in a furious exchange of fire at the same time as Tromp's leading ships were approaching the English line.

Meanwhile, when the rest of the English line reached the point where Myngs had tacked, it, too, tacked. But instead of following Myngs, Rupert, now in the lead, sailed straight ahead on a course of west-north-west, that is to say eight points off the wind. Although a seventeenth-century ship of the line could in theory sail within six points of the wind, the fleet never went closer than seven. By sailing eight points off, Rupert left himself room to come a bit closer to the wind should he gain any advantage from doing so. On this occasion he caught up with and engaged de Ruyter's squadron.

It is clear that Rupert was closely engaged at this time, as the official record states that he was 'environed with as many dangers as the enemy could apply unto him: they raked him fore and aft, played him on both sides and were clapping two fireships upon him; but two of our fireships bravely burned the bold assailants, and though his Highness received very consider-able prejudice in that difficult passage in his masts and rigging,

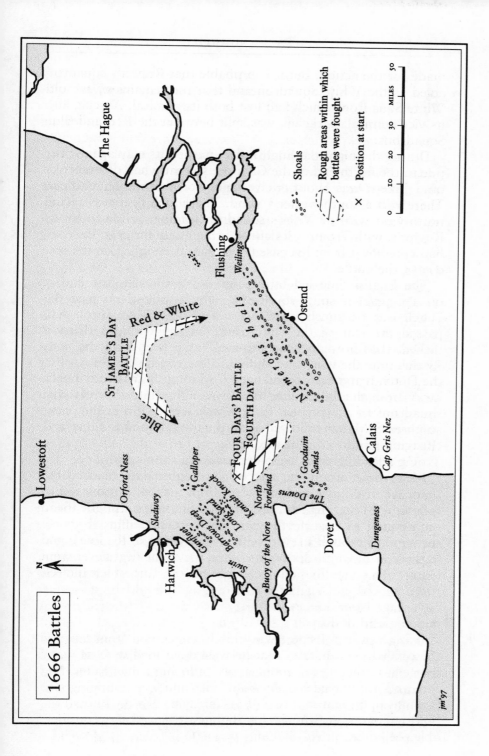

1666 Battles

N

The Hague

Flushing
Weilings
Ostend

Lowestoft

Orford Ness

Sledway

Harwich

Gunfleet
Swin

Barrows Deep
Long Sand
Kentish Knock

Galloper

North
Foreland

Buoy of the Nore

The Downs

Goodwin Sands

Dover

Dungeness

Calais
Cap Gris Nez

St James's Day
Battle

Red & White

Blue

×

Four Days' Battle
Fourth Day
×

Numerous shoals

Shoals

Rough areas within which
battles were fought

× Position at start

0   10   20   30   MILES   50

jm '97

[195]

yet he answered the shots they poured upon him with as many close returns, which the enemy felt and carried away with them'.[13]

The fighting started at 8 a.m. with both fleets heading for the Kentish Knock, which cannot have been more than about eight miles away from the head of the line. For this reason both fleets must have tacked by 10 a.m. at the latest: probably earlier, as there would have been nothing to gain by taking risks. Assuming that both fleets continued sailing eight points off the wind, they would, after tacking, have been heading for the shoals off Ostend, about thirty miles ahead of the leading ships. According to Rupert's report, the two fleets moved back and forth four times, tacking at the end of each run.

During the course of these manoeuvres Tromp's squadron rejoined de Ruyter, but part of the Dutch vanguard engaged in a dogfight with Myngs's division well downwind of the main battle. Also during the day, certain English ships drifted to leeward of the English line followed by a few Dutch ships, some of which joined in this dogfight. The remaining ships of de Vries's vanguard squadron set off to chase four English ships and subsequently rejoined de Ruyter. As the two fleets went back and forth, the English fleet was able to fire at the Dutch engaged in the dogfight to leeward as well as at the ships in de Ruyter's main line of battle.

Rupert's squadron remained in action throughout the day. Late in the afternoon de Ruyter, who after the initial encounter had been using his windward position to avoid too close an action with the English fleet, bore down on the English line in an attempt to ease the pressure on the Dutch ships that were being hard pressed in the dogfight. As he did so Rupert led his squadron through de Ruyter's line, thus gaining the weather gauge. This breaking of the enemy line from the leeward position earned much admiration from analysts of naval warfare in years to come. In Professor Lewis's words,[14] 'the fourth day saw a sight unique till then in sailing-ship warfare, the English beating upwind and breaking the enemy's line from leeward. It was magnificent, and it was of the new English kind – seek out the enemy and destroy it.' Albemarle, with his less-manoeuvrable ships, was unable to follow, but bringing his squadrons forward as fast as he could he put de Ruyter in a perilous position between himself and Rupert.

At the critical moment the *Royal James* was disabled by a

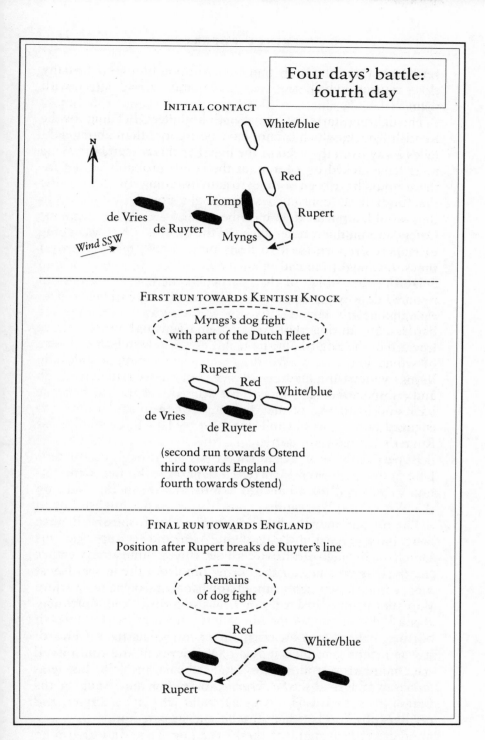

Four days' battle: fourth day

INITIAL CONTACT

White/blue

Red

Tromp

de Vries

de Ruyter

Rupert

Myngs

Wind SSW

FIRST RUN TOWARDS KENTISH KNOCK

Myngs's dog fight
with part of the Dutch Fleet

Rupert

Red

White/blue

de Vries

de Ruyter

(second run towards Ostend
third towards England
fourth towards Ostend)

FINAL RUN TOWARDS ENGLAND

Position after Rupert breaks de Ruyter's line

Remains
of dog fight

Red

White/blue

Rupert

broadside that cut through much of her rigging and brought down her main topmast and mizzenmast. Soon afterwards, Albemarle's flagship was also damaged. At about this time a thick mist descended, under cover of which the Dutch broke off the battle and headed for their ports. By the time the mist lifted it was getting dark and the exhausted English fleet, having finally seen off the enemy after four days of battle, sailed for home, the *Royal James* being towed for some of the way by the *Breda*.

Judging by the way in which the many eyewitness accounts differ, it is unlikely that anyone knew exactly what was going on at any given moment. By the same token, historians over the years have found it equally difficult to come up with an agreed version of events.[15] In particular there is a difference of opinion as to whether the two sides fought on parallel courses throughout the day, i.e. on the same tack, or on opposite courses. On the first three days, Albemarle would probably have favoured passing on opposite tacks, as this gave a better chance of survival to his weaker fleet and was more economical in terms of ammunition expenditure. On the fourth day, both Rupert and Albemarle must have wanted to fight on the same tack so as to take advantage of Rupert's fresh squadron to do as much damage as possible to the weary Dutch. Certainly, this is how the fighting started and this is how the fleets were deployed at the end, when Rupert passed through de Ruyter's line. What happened in between cannot be known with certainty, and neither Albemarle nor Rupert throw any light on the matter in their reports.

But on one matter all are agreed: notably that the English were bolder, more disciplined and performed better than the Dutch. A French observer with de Ruyter afterwards wrote: 'Nothing equals the beautiful order of the English at sea. Never was a line drawn straighter than that formed by their ships; thus they bring all their fire to bear upon those who draw near them.'[16]

During the four days of this hard-fought battle the English lost ten ships, of which six were former prizes and one a hired merchantman. Of the three English warships lost, one was Berkeley's flagship, the *Swiftsure*, captured on the first day of the battle; the second was Ayscue's flagship, the *Royal Prince*, and one was the *Essex*, which was lost when attempting to rescue another hard-pressed ship on the last day. The fleet lost around

5,000 killed and 3,000 prisoners. In addition to Berkeley, Sir Christopher Myngs was killed, as were at least nine captains. By comparison, the Dutch lost four ships and about 2,000 men, including three flag officers and a number of captains.

Although after the battle Albemarle criticised a number of his captains for failing to support him, there were innumerable acts of heroism at all levels to prove that many had done all that could possibly be expected of an English sea officer. As an example of extreme heroism the story of Rupert's former page, William Reeves, captain of the *Essex*, is worth recording. During the battle he received a musket-ball below his temple which, passing diagonally, lodged in his throat, causing much loss of blood and making him unable to speak. Most of his other officers were by this time wounded, and the junior officer left in command was obliged to heave to in order to mend some holes below the water line. While stopped, another disabled English ship ran into the *Essex*, and a Dutch ship, taking advantage of the confusion, boarded and captured her. While this was happening, Reeves dragged himself to the powder-room in an attempt to blow the ship up, but the Dutch, who had already secured it, took him on to the deck and, despite his wound, stripped him naked. Reeves then managed to throw himself overboard in an effort to escape capture, but he was fished out by the Dutch, who took him to one of their own ships where he was kept naked except for a rug and denied medical attention. Next day he was taken in a small boat towards Flushing and once more threw himself into the sea, only to be hauled out and put in irons. For the next three days he was given no food or medical attention, but he was at last seen by a doctor. Although still naked and in chains, he eventually recovered. He was repatriated at the end of the war, whereupon he received a knighthood.[17]

Despite the superior skill and heroism shown by the English, the battle could hardly be described as a victory. In the end it was the Dutch who broke off the action, but both fleets remained intact so that strategically it can best be described as a draw. In terms of damage to ships and men, the English lost more than the Dutch, but in this context the words of the Grand Pensionary, de Witt, are relevant:

> If the English were beat, then their defeat did them more honour than all their former victories; our own fleet could

never have been brought again into action after the first day's fight if they had been in the other's place; and I believe none but the English could. All that was discovered was that Englishmen might be killed and English ships burned but that English courage was invincible.[18]

Albemarle, who bore the heat and burden of the day, including a minor wound and the loss of his old friend and secretary mortally wounded at his side, was criticised for the tactics he employed initially and, with less justification, for bringing the battle on in the first place. None the less when all was done, despite their losses, the English had demonstrated clearly their superiority. At this time morale among the common seamen was high and none doubted that, had the fleet been together from the start, England would have won a great victory.

That this had not happened was no fault of Albemarle or Rupert but was directly attributable to the King's decision to divide the fleet. Clearly, this was a mistake made because intelligence about the French and the Dutch was faulty. Although the Duc de Beaufort, who commanded the French fleet, had sailed from Toulon on 19 April, he was stopped by fresh orders before he reached Brest and told to wait in the mouth of the Tagus: he was still there when Rupert left the Downs. Information about the Dutch state of readiness was equally faulty, but in this case it might still have been right to divide the fleet if the French really had been sailing up the Channel. There was certainly something to be said for trying to destroy the French before they joined the Dutch even if it meant leaving Albemarle to hold off the Dutch with an inferior force.

In the weeks and months ahead these considerations gave rise to much criticism of Albemarle and of the King's ministers, most of which was fuelled by political or personal prejudice rather than by an objective concern for the facts. In all of this no criticism was levelled at Rupert. On the contrary, his part in the proceedings was praised on all sides. As one contemporary account put it: 'During the whole day the Prince did manifest a courage and conduct answerable to the other great actions which belong to the story of his life, whereby he gave spirit to his friends and terror to his enemies.' In a letter to Arlington written on the day after the battle, Sir Thomas Clifford, who sailed in the *Royal Charles*, says of Rupert that 'he behaved himself in the whole action with such conduct that it was hard to say which was the most remarkable, either his prudence or his courage'. Rupert's own letters at this time were even briefer than usual. One to Arlington of 9 June, purporting to describe the battle, ends with a postscript nearly as long as the letter itself. It reads:

> I must needs let your Lordship know one passage of a parson who being in a ship of ours which was on fire desired to know of the boatswain the best way to be saved, who told him he should leap overboard which the parson performed accordingly and was drowned.

Rupert had the ability to get as much in to one sentence as did Cranmer in his collects.

8

JOINT COMMAND 2:
THE HARVEST

THE BATTERED FLEET arrived at Harwich in the afternoon of
5 June and the race to get it back into fighting trim began at
once. All realised that there was no time to be lost. Indeed, the
Duke of York had already dispatched Penn, with full delegated
powers, to discover what was needed and to ensure that the
joint commanders got rapid support from the Navy Board, the
Victualler and the Ordnance.

The immediate problem was to get the damaged ships
repaired, those that could not be handled at Harwich being sent
to Chatham or Sheerness. The next problem was to replace
casualties and to complete the manning of those ships, such as
the *Sovereign*, that had not joined the fleet in time for the battle.
Fifteen hundred soldiers were sent to plug the gap while further
recruitment took place supplemented by a massive and indis-
criminate use of press-gangs. Pepys complained that Navy Board
messengers were liable to disappear in this way and that even
the crews of ships taking supplies to the fleet were sometimes
taken. The same applied to the crews of colliers bringing coal
to London, despite the fact that they were supposed to be
exempt from service with the fleet. Privateers were stopped at
sea by warships and seamen removed to serve in the King's
ships. Vigorous efforts were taken to round up deserters and
prevent further abscondment.

Despite Penn's efforts, both Rupert and Albemarle were dissatisfied with the support that they received from the Navy
Board. In addition to complaining personally to the King when
he visited the fleet on 19 June, they endlessly bombarded Coventry with letters in the intervals of issuing orders to their captains. Judging from the volume of their correspondence at this
time, it is surprising that they had time for anything else.

Against this background of frantic activity, Rupert and Albemarle had to consider the lessons arising from the recent battle and to issue instructions that would enable the fleet to take advantage of them. First, Rupert issued 'Additional Instructions for Fighting' consisting of three articles. Because these came to light in Spragge's papers and were signed by Rupert alone, they were thought originally to have been written just after the battle specifically for Spragge, who had recently become a flag officer. It is now thought that they were issued to all flag officers at a council on 29 June which, considering their importance, is a more likely explanation.[1]

These 'Additional Instructions' consisted of three articles, of which the second was the most important. It was designed to ensure that excessive formality in station-keeping did not allow the enemy to slip away unscathed. It states that at a given signal from the admiral, the best sailing-ships were to move at top speed to engage the enemy and hold him until the rest of the fleet caught up, after which all ships should get into the best fighting order that they could. Of the other two articles, the first says that if a flagship were disabled or otherwise delayed, the ships of its squadron or division should keep up with the admiral of the fleet in order to further the destruction of the enemy. The third instructs any flag officer whose ship was destroyed to shift immediately into another of his ships. These three articles were, in Rupert's own words, designed to emphasise that 'the commander of every ship is to have a special regard to the common good . . . the destruction of the enemy is always to be made the chiefest care'.

On 18 July three more articles were issued to the flag officers under the heading of 'Further Instructions for Fighting', signed on this occasion by both Rupert and Albemarle.[2] A copy was sent to the King on 23 July. Like the 'Additional Instructions', they also consisted of three articles.

The first lists a series of manoeuvres designed to ensure that a battle which started with the two fleets passing each other on opposite tacks would rapidly turn into one where the two fleets sailed parallel to each other on the same tack. This article remained part of the English fleet's tactical doctrine for over a century.

The second, headed 'To Divide the Enemy's Fleet', describes how this should be done from the leeward position: there was no need to explain how it should be done from windward. The article shows how the leading squadron, sailing close to the wind, should gain the wake of a section of the enemy's ships, i.e. get behind them in their line, and then tack so that they could get a short distance to windward of them by facing in the opposite direction. The squadron was then to tack again so as to be back on the same tack as the enemy, i.e. sailing parallel with them but now comfortably to windward of them. Meanwhile, the centre squadron should run alongside the enemy from the leeward side so that the part of the enemy's fleet ahead of the divide would be caught between two fires. The rear squadron would then try to prevent the enemy's rear from intervening in the massacre of their comrades. The system described is clearly based on Rupert's famous manoeuvre in the closing stages of the four days' battle and was undoubtedly the forerunner of the doctrine of containment that became popular at the end of the eighteenth century.

The third article was an emphatic restatement of the order to fight in line, threatening with death any captain who left the line and fired over a friendly ship.

It is clear from these instructions that Rupert and Albemarle recognised that there would often be occasions when a squadron or division had to fight separately from the main line of battle, as had often happened in the past. It is equally clear that they insisted that when this occurred, the squadron or division concerned should fight in line. The fact that they accepted the need for groups to operate separately at times in the interest of destroying the enemy has led some historians to believe that they advocated a return to the general mêlée that took place before Monck's reforms of 1653, but this is patently not the case. What they wanted was to ensure that decisive action was not inhibited by excessive formality.[3]

In general, the purpose of the Additional and Further Instructions was to explain how an admiral's tactical objectives could be achieved in certain specific circumstances. Thus, Rupert, remembering how the Duke of York had struggled to get the fleet on to the same tack as the enemy during the battle off Lowestoft, outlined a series of moves that would enable it to do so automatically in the future. Similarly, having himself divided the enemy's fleet in the recent battle, he worked out and wrote down how the process could be repeated. Rupert's ability to determine how ships should be sailed in order to bring about a given tactical situation arose from his knowledge of tactics and seamanship. That he found time to put his deliberations into words and disseminate them during the busy days of June and July reflects the priority that he gave to making his subordinates understand the procedures that they might be called on to execute when next they met the enemy.

By 27 June most of the fleet was assembled once more at the Buoy of the Nore. This time the White Squadron was commanded by Allin in the *Royal James*, with Teddiman as his vice-admiral and Utber as rear-admiral. The Red was commanded by Rupert and Albemarle in the *Royal Charles*, with Jordan as vice-admiral and Holmes as rear-admiral. The Blue was commanded by Smith in the *Loyal London*, a new ship of ninety guns, with Spragge as vice-admiral and Kempthorne as rear-admiral. Although Spragge and Holmes were made rear-admirals simultaneously when the fleet was divided, Holmes was the more experienced commander and, having been highly commended by Albemarle for his part in the recent battle, resented Spragge's appointment as vice-admiral of the Blue. Both were protégés of Rupert, but Spragge's greater popularity with the Duke of York probably accounted for his preferment.

During the last week of June a number of letters reached London from sources in the United Provinces giving forecasts of Dutch intentions. They gave the impression that the Dutch were undecided as to whether their fleet should sail into the English Channel to join the French or sail into the mouth of the Thames to catch the English fleet unawares at the Nore. One mentioned that the Dutch had 5,000 soldiers embarked for a possible landing in England, but warned against building up a force to oppose such a landing at the expense of manning the fleet. Another said that the Dutch would put to sea before the English if for no other reason than to prove that they and not the English had won the four days' battle. This letter also states that although the King of France was pressing the Dutch for a junction of their two fleets, he was likely to hold back until he saw what happened in the next battle.

The fleet remained at the Nore for the next three weeks while the crews were brought up to strength. During this period no fewer than fifteen ships were laid up so that their men could be transferred to those ships in service: six fourth-rates, six fifth-rates and three sixth-rates.

While this was going on, a number of fifth- and sixth-rates

were sent out to get information about the Dutch. One went to watch movement off the Weilings and another had orders to cut away the buoy marking the channel to the north-west of the Swin should the Dutch appear. One had the task of watching the Long Sand and Gunfleet and another was detailed to do the same off the North Foreland. In order to relay signals from these ships to the fleet, another was stationed some fifteen miles east of the Nore.

Early in July Rupert and Albemarle sent pilots to take soundings along the Barrows Deep so that if necessary they would be able to get the fleet out through this channel. Ketches were used to mark the channel instead of buoys so as to mislead the enemy. By this time Rupert and Albemarle had heard that the Dutch were at sea and later that they had anchored near Long Sand Head. They later moved to the Gunfleet and Sledway, where they still were on 17 July: they had been unable to find sufficiently well-qualified pilots for an attack on the Nore.

The Dutch fleet consisted of eighty-eight ships of the line, together with many smaller craft, and was again commanded by de Ruyter with Jan Evertsen commanding the van and Tromp the rear. By 17 July, when the English fleet was ready for battle, it was almost exactly the same size, consisting of eighty-nine ships of the line, including the massive *Sovereign* and twenty fireships.

On 17 July Rupert and Albemarle sent word to the King that they intended to dislodge the enemy from the Gunfleet and then sail towards the Dutch coast. Their reason for doing this was to thwart what they believed to be a Dutch plan of sailing towards the shallows off the French coast where the English would be at a disadvantage. On 19 July the fleet sailed from the Nore but, owing to lack of wind during the next two days, it was not until 22 July that it reached the Gunfleet, having passed through the narrows with great difficulty. It is reported that Rupert and Albemarle spent the whole day on deck and were none too gentle with the pilots in their determination to get the fleet through in time. Meanwhile, the Dutch set sail and by the evening were fifteen miles off towards the Galloper.

On the morning of 23 July there was little wind, but during the day it rose and by the evening was blowing hard from the north-north-east, bringing with it high seas, thunder and periods of limited visibility. On 23 and 24 July the English tried to get ahead of the Dutch with a view to gaining the wind but succeeded in doing so only late on 24 July. For most of this time the Dutch could not take advantage of their windward position for fear of bringing on a battle among the coastal shoals. In the evening of 24 July the English anchored thirty-three miles east of Orford Ness: a smack sent to watch the Dutch reported that they had anchored twelve miles to the south-east.[4] If the wind held, the English would next morning be in a favourable position.

On 25 July, St James's Day, the English fleet weighed at 2 a.m. and set an easterly course. Two hours later it sighted the Dutch fleet twelve miles to the south-east, on the same tack, heading south-east, his van and rear squadrons being to windward of and separated from the centre. Rupert and Albemarle immediately gave the order to bear away so as to intercept the enemy. De Ruyter, meanwhile, brought his fleet closer to the wind in order to converge with the English. The result of this was to bend the Dutch line slightly so that it looked to the English as if their opponents were in a crescent formation with gaps between the squadrons.

At about 10 a.m. Teddiman's division of the White Squadron opened fire as it closed with the Dutch van. By this time the Dutch had been firing at them ineffectually for about half an hour. Soon afterwards, the rest of Allin's ships were hotly engaged. By 11 a.m. the Red Squadron had closed with de Ruyter's centre squadron and was also in action. The two forward squadrons of each fleet were now fully engaged, sailing on the port tack on a course a point or two south of east.

If Tromp had been prepared to follow de Ruyter into battle as he should have done, both fleets would have fought in a continuous line. But Tromp, whom Rupert sometimes referred to as his spitz-broder, was always ready to take the initiative if he felt that he could gain an advantage by doing so. In this case the fact that there was a gap between his own squadron and de Ruyter's squadron meant that by putting on more sail he was able to get ahead of Smith's Blue Squadron and cut across its bows. He then tacked, thereby gaining the wind, and started to pass down the line of the Blue Squadron. The battle between these two squadrons had started at about midday but, owing to the wind dropping, Tromp's manoeuvre took some hours to complete.

Tromp now found himself sailing in the opposite direction to the rest of the Dutch fleet. Rightly or wrongly, Smith also tacked to stay with Tromp, so that both the rear squadrons eventually were heading west towards England and away from the main battle, while the rest of the two fleets fought their way towards the coast of the United Provinces. As Tromp's squadron was the strongest in the Dutch fleet and superior to Smith's, the Blue Squadron was in a dangerous position. On the other hand, Tromp's departure meant that the rest of the Dutch fleet was weaker than the two English squadrons now assailing it.

Fighting between the forward and centre squadrons was now intense. An observer aboard the *Royal Charles* described how she bore down on de Ruyter's flagship, the newly built *Seven Provinces* which, though thirty feet longer than the *Royal Charles*, drew less water and carried the same number of guns. The *Royal Charles* held her fire until she was within musketshot, whereon Rupert ordered a broadside. This was followed by a period of heavy firing, during which the two ships got closer and closer together. De Ruyter launched his fireship on the *Royal Charles*, but the *Royal Charles*'s fireship fended her off. The exchange between the *Royal Charles* and the *Seven Provinces* continued for around three and a half hours before de Ruyter bore away, at which time Rupert called on the *Triumph* to board her, saying that he would give close support. But because the wind had dropped, this proved impossible to accomplish. Soon afterwards, the *Royal Charles* had to spend half an hour repairing damage to her sails and rigging. By this time about twenty-five of the crew had been killed and the same number wounded.

No sooner was the *Royal Charles* back in action that she was assailed by another large Dutch ship, but after a short time the *Sovereign* came up and, with the assistance of several more English ships, quickly put the Dutchman out of action. An English fireship that tried to burn her was foiled by a Dutch fireship until this in turn was sunk by the *Sovereign*. And so the battle raged for some hours.

During this time an observer described Albemarle standing like a rock on the deck of the *Royal Charles*, chewing tobacco. The eighteen-year-old Earl of Mulgrave, then serving as a volunteer aboard the flagship, later recorded that Albemarle left all things to the conduct and skill of Prince Rupert, declaring modestly on all occasions that he was no seaman. But Mulgrave also mentions that there were sometimes disagreements between them because Albemarle always wanted instant attack, which was not necessarily part of Rupert's plan. But, says Mulgrave, Rupert usually obliged the good old man to yield at the last, but with a great deal of reluctance. At the end of the campaign Rupert's efforts at restraining Albemarle became well known and were celebrated with glee by a writer of doggerel who made much of the fire-eating Rupert holding back the usually stolid Albemarle.

By 3 p.m. what little wind there was had backed to the north-west, and the Dutch van was in dire straits, its admiral, Evertsen, mortally wounded. Soon afterwards, it broke and ran before the wind towards the Dutch coast. Within the hour the centre was also obliged to turn away and follow suit. Both the White and the Red Squadrons sailed in pursuit. During the chase the White captured a new Dutch ship of sixty-six guns, and later Allin himself boarded and captured the flagship of the Dutch vice-admiral Banckert; the flagship was burned to avoid any delay in the pursuit. De Ruyter's squadron fared slightly better because de Ruyter himself on several occasions put his flagship about in order to rescue hard-pressed ships of his squadron. None the less by the time darkness fell the van and centre of the Dutch fleet were routed.

The last that Rupert and Albemarle saw of Tromp and the Blue Squadron was at about 6.30 p.m. At this time they were still battling it out far to the west. Some distance from them could be seen Sir Robert Holmes's flagship, which had fallen away from the Red Squadron, having been heavily damaged in the fighting.

During the night the Red and White Squadrons followed the retreating Dutch behind a screen of smaller vessels commanded by Jordan, whose task was to keep in touch with the enemy. He did this to such good effect that when it got light he found himself within 200 yards of de Ruyter's flagship.

By this time the wind had gone round to the south-west, which meant that the Dutch had the weather gauge and it was almost impossible for the English to close with them. The Dutch held their course towards the coast while the English fired their bow chasers at them; they returned fire with their stern chasers. On one occasion Allin managed to exchange a broadside with de Ruyter, as a result of which Allin was wounded by flying splinters. Some of the fifth- and sixth-rates also managed to cross behind the rearmost Dutch ships, firing broadsides into their sterns. Later it looked for a moment as if the *Seven*

Provinces might be burned by a fireship, but at the last moment de Ruyter managed to have her towed away by his ship's boats.

During this period when there was still little wind, a sloop called the *Fan Fan*, which had just been built for Prince Rupert by Deane at Harwich, made use of her oars to close up to the *Seven Provinces* and open fire with her four small guns. The *Seven Provinces* was unable to depress her main armament sufficiently to return the fire so that de Ruyter was obliged to suffer the indignity and discomfort of being attacked in this way for nearly an hour. The incident provoked much merriment in the English fleet. Eventually, the *Fan Fan* received two shots below the water-line from a light gun which killed one of her crew and she withdrew behind the *Royal Charles*. Some writers have described the *Fan Fan* as Rupert's yacht, but unlike the yachts of that period she was square rigged and had three masts as well as her oars. At forty-four feet long and displacing thirty-three tons she was smaller than most yachts and ketches, but was none the less listed as a sixth-rate. After the fleet came home at the end of the year Rupert employed her as a privateer.

The two fleets made their way towards the coast until there were no more than six fathoms of water, whereon the English abandoned the chase for fear of running aground. De Ruyter ushered the battered remnants of his two squadrons into Flushing, and after a short time the English sailed off to the north-west to discover what had become of the Blue Squadron and Tromp.

During the afternoon the wind veered round to the north-east, and before dark the fleet spotted Tromp's squadron followed at some distance by the Blue Squadron. It transpired subsequently that after the previous day's battle, in which Smith had lured Tromp further and further from de Ruyter, these two squadrons had spent the night in the neighbourhood of the Galloper. During the night Smith was met by Holmes who, having repaired his flagship, joined the Blue Squadron as being the nearest body of ships in touch with the enemy.

The change of wind to the south-west during the night had put Smith to windward of Tromp, but, weakened by the loss of the *Resolution* on the previous day, he felt disinclined to renew the fight. As the Blue Squadron would not fight him, Tromp, not knowing what had happened to the rest of the Dutch fleet, headed for home.

As soon as Rupert and Albemarle saw Tromp's squadron,

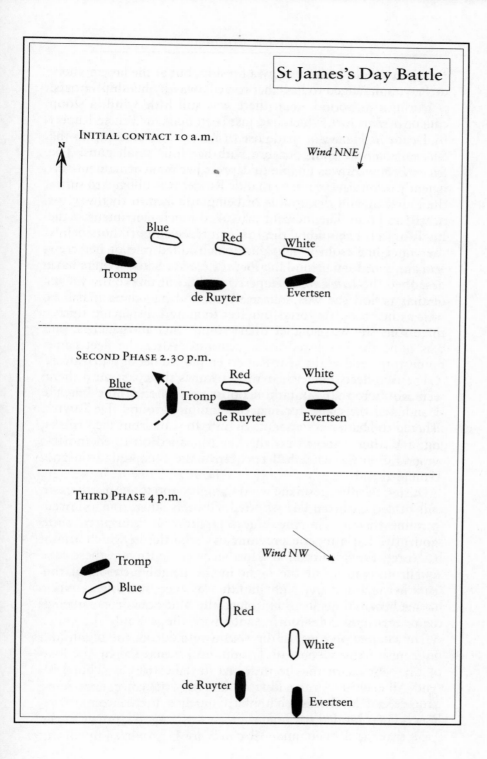

St James's Day Battle

Initial contact 10 a.m.

N

Wind NNE

Blue   Red   White

Tromp

de Ruyter   Evertsen

Second Phase 2.30 p.m.

Blue   Tromp   Red   White

de Ruyter   Evertsen

Third Phase 4 p.m.

Wind NW

Tromp

Blue

Red

White

de Ruyter   Evertsen

they put about in order to get between it and Flushing. Pressing on through the darkness, the *Royal Charles* anchored at midnight in a position where tide and wind should bring Tromp the next morning. But the rest of the Red and White Squadrons failed to hear the gun signal ordering them to anchor, so that the next morning the *Royal Charles* found herself alone save for the *Fan Fan*, a ketch and a fireship. The rest of the two squadrons were some six miles away, downwind, which meant that it would take them several hours to return to the *Royal Charles*. Meanwhile, Smith, who was nervous of shoals, failed to keep in touch with Tromp. The following morning, 27 July, Tromp sailed past the *Royal Charles* and rejoined de Ruyter at Flushing. In a letter to Arlington, Clifford, who was still aboard the *Royal Charles*, says that it was lucky that Tromp did not attack as he went past, because Rupert and Albemarle had no intention of retiring and would certainly have been torn to pieces before the rest of the fleet could come to their rescue.[5]

Looked at from any angle the St James's Day battle was an English victory. Excluding support vessels and fireships, the Dutch lost two ships compared with one lost by the English. They also lost 4,000 killed, including four of their flag officers, and a further 3,000 wounded, as opposed to 300 killed and 900 wounded in the English fleet. Many Dutch ships were heavily damaged and the morale of their officers and men badly shaken. A series of disputes broke out among their commanders in which de Ruyter and Tromp blamed each other, and Evertsen, for the disaster. De Ruyter and Tromp both vowed never to go to sea again together: Tromp, a supporter of the House of Orange, was dismissed.

The outcome of the battle did more than reverse the situation that existed at the end of the four days' fight. It is interesting to see how this came about, especially as the two fleets were of equal strength. As recently as the beginning of July the Dutch were forecasting that the English would be destroyed without even being able to deploy outside the Thames Estuary.

The first factor that contributed to the victory was Rupert's and Albemarle's insistence that the flag officers commanding squadrons and divisions should be ready to exploit opportunities as they developed rather than stick rigidly to a pre-arranged plan that the fleet commander could not be expected to control because of the distances involved. The fighting instructions that Rupert and Albemarle had so effectively supplemented explained to the flag officers how they should execute the manoeuvres needed to take advantage of such opportunities.

Rupert and Albemarle's next contribution to the victory was the careful preparation that they made to collect information and reconnoitre and mark channels. This enabled them to wrest the initiative from de Ruyter by dislodging him from the Gunfleet and forcing him over into the deep water of the North Sea where the heavier English ships had the advantage. Had they been obliged to follow de Ruyter into the shallow waters off France, the Dutch ships, drawing less water, would have been favoured. Thus, an unfavourable opening situation with the English boxed up in the Thames was transformed into one where the Dutch would be brought to battle in deep water from the windward position.

Once battle was joined, the determination of the flag officers to fight with their heavier gunned and stronger ships at close quarters and on the same tack as the enemy soon overcame the Dutch van and centre. During the dogfight the Dutch as usual concentrated on destroying masts and rigging in order to put English ships out of action, while the English fired at Dutch hulls to slow down and sink their ships and kill their men.

Although Tromp skilfully divided the English fleet using a manoeuvre not unlike that described in Rupert's and Albemarle's Further Instructions, he took the action contrary to de Ruyter's wishes when still in close contact with him. Furthermore, instead of preventing an English squadron superior to his own from attacking de Ruyter, he drew off an inferior enemy force, leaving de Ruyter deprived of the support of his own superior squadron. And having done so, he did not even manage to neutralise the Blue Squadron, thanks largely to Kempthorne's division, which kept tacking back to bring off damaged English ships before Tromp could finish them off in the same way as de Ruyter had saved some of his own ships during his retreat to Flushing. Meanwhile, Smith, who had more men killed in his flagship than were killed in any other ship in the English fleet, led Tromp further and further away from de Ruyter.

Unfortunately, Smith then failed to hold Tromp until the rest of the English fleet could finish him off after it had driven de Ruyter into port. This was due to his reluctance to renew the contest on the second day and in particular to his failure to take risks in the evening when close to shallow water. But the failure of the Red and Blue Squadrons to anchor in the right place during the night of the twenty-seventh also contributed to Tromp's escape.

In the short term the escape of Tromp's squadron made little difference, as the Dutch were too shattered to interfere with the English. Two weeks later Albemarle bet Rupert five pieces (around £500 in today's money) that the Dutch would not come out to fight again in 1666. The ever-realistic Rupert won the bet. None the less Holmes was so incensed with Smith for letting Tromp escape that he accused him of cowardice before Rupert and Albemarle, thereby giving rise to a delicate situation as Holmes was a protégé of Rupert and Smith of Albemarle. The matter was eventually brought before the King in council who acquitted Smith of cowardice but declared him guilty of an error of judgement.

From Friday 27 July until Tuesday 31 July the fleet lay at anchor off Goree. A council of war held in the afternoon of 27 July decided to send the wounded men and badly damaged ships back to England and then head up towards the Texel.

For the next four days Rupert and Albemarle issued a stream of instructions to the flag officers concerning the repair of ships and the handling and replacement of the wounded. They also sent two long letters to Coventry outlining their requirements of ships, ammunition, water and other supplies in which there is no suggestion that the Dutch fleet was unlikely to reappear.

On 30 July Rupert and Albemarle shifted into the *Royal James* because the *Royal Charles* was one of the ships that would have to return to England for repairs. Allin moved into the *Royal Sovereign*, which became the flagship of the White Squadron. On the same day four ships were sent out to the north with orders to take or destroy all Dutch, French and Danish vessels, including fishing boats, that they could find and to rejoin the fleet off the Texel within five days. The *Fan Fan* and another sixth-rate, the *Little Mary*, had already been dispatched with a Dutch deserter called Laurens van Heemskirck to reconnoitre.

On 1 August the fleet sailed slowly north along the coast, passing Scheveningen and The Hague on 3 August before anchoring for the night. For the next few days the fleet continued in like fashion, taking prizes and destroying small boats as they went. The master of one such vessel reported that three days earlier seventy merchantmen from Hamburg had passed into the Texel under the impression that the English fleet had been defeated and was confined to the Thames. On 7 August the fleet anchored off the Texel.

A year and a quarter earlier, just before the battle off Lowestoft, Rupert and Sandwich had recommended an attack on the shipping in the anchorage behind the Texel. At that time they had been overruled by the Duke of York. Now Rupert and Albemarle decided to see what could be done in this respect. Early in the morning of 7 August, taking advantage of the recent victory that gave them a free hand along the Dutch coast, they gave out orders for a major raid. Sir Robert Holmes, who had shown himself to be as resourceful and skilful as he was aggressive, was to be in command.

The task given to Holmes was to land 900 men on the two islands between which ran the main channel giving access to the anchorage. Five hundred men were to land on Vlieland and 400 on Terschelling, where there were a number of warehouses and stores, for the purpose of taking as much property as possible and burning the rest. Holmes himself would command the men landed on Vlieland, while Sir William Jennings, operating under him, would command on the Terschelling. Holmes was also instructed to seize all vessels in the harbour and use them to carry off material captured by the landing parties. Any ships that could not be captured were to be burned. No harm was to come to women, children or workmen unless they tried to resist. The better sort of inhabitants were to be brought back to the fleet to be disposed of as the joint commanders thought fit.

Each of the nine divisions of the fleet were to provide 100 men, of whom two-thirds should be soldiers, some pikemen and some musketeers. The ships allocated to Holmes were five fourth-rates, three fifth-rates, five fireships, seven ketches and enough ships' boats to land and take off the soldiers. In the event two extra companies of volunteers were formed from the fleet as a whole.

On 8 August the task force left the main fleet heading for the channel between Vlieland and Terschelling. No more was seen of them that day, but on the following day Rupert and Albemarle saw great clouds of smoke and flame belching up into the sky. In the evening, supposing that everything on the two islands had been destroyed and fearing that the smoke might cause the Dutch to launch a superior land force against Holmes, they ordered him to embark his force and return to the fleet.

In fact, events had followed a different course. Having left the fleet, Holmes took his force to a point three miles off the entrance to the channel but a contrary wind prevented him from entering it that day. While waiting for the wind to change he was joined by the *Fan Fan* with news that at least fifty large merchantmen were in the anchorage. Next morning Holmes's ships entered the channel in order to land the men as originally intended, but Holmes himself, now in the *Fan Fan*, pushed right through to a position where he could see the anchorage. As the mist cleared he saw that it was thick with ships – possibly as many as 170. Holmes realised immediately that he could do far more damage to the Dutch by destroying this array of shipping than by raiding Vlieland and Terschelling so he amended the plan accordingly.

The many merchant ships in the anchorage were guarded by two Dutch warships and a few small craft. Holmes, leaving most of his warships in the channel, took one fifth-rate, some ketches and his five fireships into the anchorage. The fireships soon disposed of the Dutch warships, whereon Holmes sent the ketches and ships' boats, meant to be landing the men on the two islands, into the anchorage to burn as many ships as possible. By evening these ships were nearly all in flames; and it was this bonfire that Rupert and Albemarle saw from their position out to sea.

By the time he had recovered his boats and ketches, some of which had run aground, it was too late to carry out the raid on Vlieland and Terschelling. Next morning wind and rain prevented the landing on Vlieland, but the operation on Terschelling went as arranged, the main town being burned together with most of the villages. Holmes re-embarked the men in the evening when, according to the official account, he received the order to withdraw. He may well have got the order earlier and delayed implementing it on the grounds that Rupert and Albemarle would not have known the true situation when they sent it.

Holmes's Bonfire, as it became known, caused immense damage to the Dutch economy and therefore to their war effort. The cost of the destruction was estimated at the huge sum of

£1,000,000, more than half the amount needed to maintain the English navy at war strength for a year. It was achieved with the loss of fewer than a dozen men.

The success of the enterprise was due first and foremost to the leadership of Holmes himself, who had seen the opportunity provided by the concentration of enemy shipping and who had the boldness and professional skill to take advantage of it. Equally important was his preparedness to take responsibility. That he felt able to do so arose partly from the fact that he had worked for so long under a commander of Rupert's calibre and partly from his own experience of independent command. Even if his contribution to the great battles of the summer is discounted, this one action would entitle him to be regarded as one of the great commanders of his day.[6]

By 11 August, when Holmes's force had rejoined Rupert and Albemarle, the fleet was running short of provisions. It was also necessary to replace the fireships that had been expended. The fleet therefore sailed for England, anchoring in Sole Bay on 15 August.

For the next two weeks the fleet remained at Sole Bay, during which time it was inadequately supplied with food and drink. In four letters – to the Duke of York on 17 and 22 August, to Coventry on 22 August and to the King on 29 August – Rupert and Albemarle poured out their frustration at getting accounts instead of supplies, making particular representation about the state of the beer sent in defective casks. Only the Ordnance department was congratulated on the speed with which it provided powder and shot. Unfortunately for Coventry and the Navy Board, Rupert was an expert on fleet logistics, and Albemarle, having stood in for the Duke of York at the Admiralty during the Lowestoft campaign, knew all too well how the business was conducted.

Another cause for discontent was the failure to provide an adequate number of fireships, although a new fourth-rate joined the fleet at this time together with some of the ships sent back for repair after the battle. One of these was the *Royal Charles*, which Rupert and Albemarle reclaimed as their flagship, Allin moving back to the *Royal James*.

*   *   *

Despite Albemarle's prediction, de Ruyter got his fleet to sea on 26 August and headed for the Strait of Dover in search of the French fleet. On 30 August the English fleet moved south from Sole Bay, by which time de Ruyter was at anchor fifteen miles off the North Foreland. Hearing that the English were at sea, de Ruyter temporarily abandoned his search for the French and headed north-west to find the English. At midday on 31 August the two fleets came in sight of each other, but with a north-east wind de Ruyter had no desire to fight with the Thames Estuary shoals under his lee. He therefore tacked and headed out to sea followed by the English, but in the course of doing so the *Royal Charles* and the *Royal Katherine* grounded once more on the Galloper. They were soon got off, but by now the Dutch had made good their escape.

During the ensuing night the Blue Squadron made contact with part of the Dutch fleet and there was an exchange of fire, but the weather worsened and several ships on both sides suffered storm damage. Next morning the Dutch were sighted heading for Boulogne and by mid-afternoon had gained the shelter of Cap Gris Nez. The English fleet, much battered by the gale, made for St Helens on the Isle of Wight, where most of the ships arrived on 2 September: five ships, together with some fireships and ketches, rejoined the fleet later, but the *St Andrew* and the *Charles Merchant* were wrecked. On the following day those ships that could not be repaired in the anchorage were sent into Portsmouth.

It took ten days to repair the damage caused by the storm, during which time Rupert paid two visits to Portsmouth Dock to hurry on the work. On the second occasion he took Smith, Holmes and Utber with him, but such was the violence of the storm that they were unable to get back to their respective divisions. Rupert managed to reach Teddiman's ship where he spent the night; the others were obliged to return to Portsmouth. While confined to St Helens, Rupert fired off a series of letters to Coventry, the Duke of York and the King pointing out that shortages of food and drink would preclude him from following the Dutch into northern waters should he need to do so.

At about this time the Great Fire broke out in London and the King sent for Albemarle to take charge of the troops involved in securing the capital. He left the fleet on 6 September, thereby terminating his highly profitable joint command with Rupert.

According to Albemarle's chaplain and later biographer, Dr Thomas Gumble, who accompanied Albemarle throughout the campaign, 'the two generals governed with that unity and agreement as if they had been activated by one soul and in all that service there never was the least appearance of so much as a strangeness between them, which was a certain pressage [*sic*] of glory and victory'.

By this time, at long last, Beaufort had made a move, reaching Dieppe on 14 September with forty ships. But de Ruyter had meanwhile retired through the Strait of Dover in order to await the French in a more sheltered anchorage, a move that had been misinterpreted by the French King as being designed to leave the French to fight the English alone. Beaufort was therefore ordered to withdraw to Brest, where he arrived on 20 September. The English fleet, having heard that the French fleet was in the Channel looking for de Ruyter, left St Helens on 13 September and headed back towards Calais in the hope of finding it. But Rupert narrowly missed the French, who were by this time sailing for Brest.

On 18 September the Red and Blue Squadrons were at anchor in the Downs while the White Squadron remained at the fleet's previous anchorage off Dungeness. Suddenly Allin saw six French ships under vice-admiral de Roche sailing directly towards him. It seems that de Roche, who had become separated from the French fleet, mistook Allin's white flag for the French standard and thought that he was closing with his friends. By the time that he realised his mistake, he was too close to retreat. In a briskly fought action de Roche and his flagship were captured. The remainder escaped. De Roche had made the same mistake in the *Tagus* sixteen years earlier when he approached Blake thinking he was Rupert. Next day Allin sent him aboard the *Royal Charles*, where Rupert entertained his old ally to the best of his ability, afterwards ensuring that his sojourn as a prisoner of war in the Tower of London was as pleasant as possible.

On 23 September, when the Dutch fleet was at Ostend, its famous commander, now sixty years old and ill, had to go ashore. He was replaced by van Ness. Two days later Rupert, who was off Dover, heard that the Dutch were again at sea, and soon after midday the two fleets were in sight of each other. The English had the weather gauge, and both fleets prepared for battle. But once more the wind rose to such an extent that the English had to tack and anchor. The Dutch failed to do so and were blown far to the north and scattered.

On 28 September the Dutch finally put into port for the winter. On 3 October Rupert brought his fleet to the Nore and on the following day sent Holmes to the King with a full report on its condition. On 5 October, having arranged for Penn to organise the dispersal of the ships to the different anchorages in and around the Thames Estuary, he headed for London in accordance with the King's instructions.

The campaign was over. Although the fleet had failed to bring either the Dutch or the French fleet to battle after the victory in July, it had taken a large number of prizes in addition to the damage done by Holmes. Furthermore, it did so at little cost to itself beyond damage caused by the storms. Professor Callender's assessment that the St James's Day battle was the greatest victory ever won by the British over the Dutch may not be sustainable in terms of ships sunk or captured at the time, but it most certainly was in terms of its aftermath. Sir Julian Corbett summed up an important aspect of Rupert's contribution to this situation when he wrote: 'his genius for war and his scientific and well-drilled spirit revealed to him in the traditional minor tactics of the seamen, the germs of a true tactical system and caused him to urge its reduction into a definite set of fighting instructions.'

Two days later Rupert was with the King, the Duke of York, Albemarle, Clarendon and some other members of the council, including Coventry, when the Navy Board was called in for a discussion of their requirements for getting the fleet ready for future operations. Their most pressing need being money, Pepys, as spokesman, started by representing the present ill state of the fleet. In doing so he was foolish enough to say that the greatest fleet the King had ever put to sea had returned in as bad a condition as the enemy and weather could put it in. This infuriated Rupert, who got really angry and said that he had brought home the fleet in as good a condition as any fleet was brought home. All that was lost were twenty ships' boats and the anchors, which had been cut away when the ships were forced off Dungeness in a storm and these could easily be recovered. Pepys was terrified and blamed Penn for telling him that the surveyors' reports would confirm his assessment. After the meeting Coventry told Rupert that what Pepys meant was that, although the fleet was in splendid condition and well capable of putting to sea at once should the need arise, it would need much spent on it during the winter if it were to be ready for a further campaign.[7]

Clearly, Rupert failed to realise that Pepys was trying to get urgently needed money rather than to discredit him. But Rupert was still angry with the Admiralty and the Navy Board for their failure to keep the fleet properly supplied during the past campaign and particularly with their attempts to justify their actions. On this occasion he misinterpreted Pepys's statement as a continuation of this dispute, which was still smouldering away a year later when Parliament started its investigation into the mismanagement of the war.

The incident is also indicative of Rupert's frame of mind at this time. He had just spent six months cooped up in a warship, shot at by the enemy, buffeted by the wind and the sea and carrying all the while the responsibility for the conduct of a war that, for all its set backs, had been a colossal success. He was bound to be on edge, which, added to the violence of his temper, made it certain that there would be an explosion sooner or later. Nothing could be more sure to spark it off than criticism from a Civil Servant, even if it had not been meant as personal criticism. It was the classic confrontation between the commander and the bureaucrat: it was Pepys's bad luck that he happened to be sitting over the mine when it exploded.

There was a sequel to this confrontation when Batten as Surveyor, accompanied by Pepys, took the reports of each ship's condition to the Duke of York. When they arrived they found that Rupert was with the Duke, as a result of which Batten said nothing, although the meeting was called solely to consider the reports. After the meeting Pepys asked him why he had kept silent, to which Batten replied that he knew the Prince too well to anger him and that he was frightened to do it. Batten, though less effective at his job than Pepys, was wiser in his handling of Rupert. After all, he, too, had been a commander in his day.[8]

Another command matter that attracted comment in London was that of appointments in the fleet. Rupert and Albemarle had been given a free hand to promote flag offices and captains, and the criticism was that they filled the fleet with their friends at the expense of better men previously appointed by the Duke of York on the advice of Coventry and Penn. In particular, it was suggested that the old professional seamen of Commonwealth days were disadvantaged for the benefit of gentlemen officers.

In Dr Davies's excellent study of the Restoration navy[9] he shows that between 14 May and 21 September 1666 Rupert and Albemarle issued eighty-four commissions to captains. Of these, fourteen went to interregnum officers, six to supporters of the King during his exile, nineteen to gentlemen and thirty-six to professional seamen, usually referred to as tarpaulins. These figures hardly support the contention that the joint commanders were discriminating against the professionals at this level. On the other hand, after the four days' battle they got rid of five captains, three of whom were old professionals, the other two being closely connected with the Duke of York.

In terms of flag officers, six of the eight inherited from the previous year were Commonwealth men, i.e. Myngs, Jordan, Smith, Teddiman, Ayscue and Harman. Only Allin and Berkeley were original supporters of the King. When the fleet was divided, three new flag officers were needed, and three of the King's supporters from the days of his exile were promoted to fill the vacancies, i.e. Holmes from Rupert's old fleet, Spragge, who had commanded a privateer during the exile period, and Utber, who had also served in privateers at that time and who was Allin's brother-in-law. After the four days' battle the fourth squadron was reabsorbed into the fleet, but there had been four casualties: Myngs and Berkeley killed, Ayscue captured and Harman wounded. This meant that one more flag officer was needed, who was found by promoting Kempthorne, a former royalist. Thus, by August only three of the old Commonwealth men remained, which could have given the impression that they were being discriminated against.

But it is much more likely that the new appointments were made on merit and that the reason for the change of emphasis had more to do with age than with former associations. In this respect it is interesting to compare the ages of those appointed by Rupert and Albemarle with those in place at the start of the campaign. Those appointed were Holmes at forty-three, Spragge at thirty-seven (the same age as Tromp), and Kempthorn at forty-six. Utber was a man in his fifties; his exact age is unknown, but he had a son killed as captain of a ship in 1665, so it is unlikely that he was younger. Of those in place at the start of the campaign, Jordan, Albemarle's flag captain in 1653, was sixty-two. Allin was fifty-three, Ayscue fifty, and Smith fifty-one. Only Myngs, at forty-one, well known as the Prince's favourite, and Berkeley, at twenty-seven, who owed his position to his close ties with the court, were younger than Rupert.

In considering the accusation of favouritism, two more points are relevant. First, both Rupert and Albemarle were professional fighters to their fingertips and would be most unlikely to risk losing a battle for the sake of gratifying their friends. Second, the criticism emanated from certain disappointed captains in the fleet and was relayed and magnified by Penn who, having been branded a cowardly rogue by Albemarle, could never hope for a place in the fleet while Albemarle maintained his influence. Pepys also disliked Albemarle at this time because of his hostility to Sandwich, so he was happy to listen to Penn and embellish his stories despite the fact that he repeatedly described him as a false rascal and a coxcomb.

On balance, it seems that the appointments made by Rupert and Albemarle were sensible in the context of the campaign itself and, by bringing on younger men, beneficial for the future. But in the last resort it is the voice of Pepys, speaking through his astonishing diary, that tends to be remembered while more responsible opinions are forgotten.

9

THE YEARS BETWEEN

DURING THE SUMMER, before the St James's Day battle when Rupert was struggling to get the fleet ready for sea, Frances Bard bore him a son. Where she was living at the time is not recorded, but it is known that she had a strong aversion to the court and would not have lodged in Whitehall. Rupert owned Drury House, just to the north of the city wall near the site now occupied by the Barbican Arts Centre, and she may well have lived there. On his return from sea Rupert acknowledged the boy, took a close interest in him and directed his upbringing. He was christened Dudley and was known during Rupert's lifetime as Dudley Bard. Later, he was sometimes referred to as Dudley Rupert, the Prince's son.

In January of 1667, the old wound in Rupert's head started to cause trouble. It rapidly got worse, and on the sixteenth of the month Pepys, visiting Whitehall, heard that he was very ill. On 28 January Pepys was told by Rupert's secretary, Hayes, that he was still bad and had at last agreed to be trepanned. Pepys could not resist recording the discreditable suggestion put forward by a Dr Clerke that it was 'a clap of the pox' that had eaten to his head and come through his skull and that there was great fear for his life. On 3 February Pepys, Batten and Penn were with Coventry in Whitehall Palace when they heard that the trepanning was going on at that moment in Rupert's lodgings. They enquired at the door and expressed their wishes for the good success of the operation, though in his diary Pepys comments that few of them were really concerned in their hearts. On 4 February, and again on the sixth, Pepys recorded that Rupert was improving, but he added that Dr Clerke and Mr Pierce both said that they did not think that he would recover because 'his whole head within was eaten by this corruption . . .'.

Fortunately, things were not as bad as Pepys was led to believe. The operation was conducted by Sir James Mullins, the King's surgeon, who was obliged to repeat it on 21 February, when he managed to get deeper into the skull and release a great quantity of corrupt matter. In doing so he evidently did a better job than Choqueux had managed on previous occasions, because after the second operation Rupert started to mend and ultimately made a full recovery, his old wound giving him no further trouble. During his convalescence he amused himself by designing surgical instruments to help the doctors treat him more easily.

At the end of 1666 the King was in urgent need of a Parliamentary grant to enable him to balance his books. Parliament had been in session since October but was in conflict with the King over Ireland. Members were also concerned that if they made him a large enough grant he would make peace with the Dutch and use the money to govern without Parliament for a considerable time, during which he would be able to push through various measures of which Parliament disapproved. By giving in to Parliament on Ireland and by persuading it that he was not negotiating for peace with the Dutch, the King managed to get a vote of £1,800,000 to continue the war. Early in February he prorogued Parliament.

Despite his assurances, the King had been sounding out both the French and the Dutch in an attempt to make peace with each of them separately. With Parliament out of the way he set about formal negotiations. Although the Parliamentary vote was on paper adequate, the money would be slow to come in, and in any case much of it would be needed to pay off past debts. On 23 February, according to figures provided by the Navy Board to the Duke of York,[1] only £1,315 out of the £150,000 owing to suppliers had been paid, so that few of them were prepared to enter into new contracts. Of the £930,000 due to the seamen, only £140,000 had been paid, as a result of which half-starved men and their families hung around London and the ports, stealing and rioting.

The King was in a difficult position. Despite the damage caused to their economy and shipping in the previous year's fighting, the Dutch showed no inclination to accept the English peace proposals. The safety of the realm demanded that the fleet be set out once more. But the measures needed to fund this would be highly unpopular, so that there was a temptation to gamble on the success of the negotiations and keep the ships laid up. After discussion, the King decided on a compromise. The larger ships would not be put into commission, but a number of the smaller vessels would be set out to keep the ports and estuaries safe from French and Dutch privateers, which were already causing significant loss of revenue to the Customs and Excise to say nothing of the adverse effects they were having on trade. These ships would also do as much damage as possible to Dutch trade when the opportunity occurred. In addition, the fortification of Sheerness, which Rupert had urged on the King in 1666, and further work at Portsmouth would be pushed ahead.

The King made this decision against his better judgement but with the agreement of the majority of the council, although both Rupert and the Duke of York, together with the Archbishop of Canterbury and a few others, opposed it. As the business was conducted when Rupert was ill, it must be assumed that his opinions were not pressed as forcibly as might otherwise have been the case.

Initially, the arrangement worked well. Flag officers were stationed ashore in the most sensitive areas: Allin at Plymouth, Holmes at Portsmouth, Spragge in the Medway, Teddiman at Dover, with Smith and Harman made responsible for those areas of the north-east and south coasts not otherwise covered. Ships were allocated to the flag officers as required, as a result of which the depredations of the privateers were quickly got under control. In addition, work started on the fortifications supervised by de Gomme but proceeded slowly.

By early April Rupert was well enough to be seen about within Whitehall, although it was noticeable that he still had a dressing on the top of his head underneath his wig. It was also noticeable that the Dutch were still some way from a peace settlement. Despite specific reports reaching Arlington from the United Provinces at the end of May which spoke of soldiers joining the fleet, both he and the King were of the opinion that the Dutch were merely putting pressure on the English to conclude a peace. It would seem that they were basing their assumptions on an undertaking given by King Louis that he would use his influence on the Dutch to end the war. This would be in France's interest, as Louis had embarked recently on a campaign in the Spanish Netherlands and had nothing to gain from supporting further Dutch operations against England. So unconcerned was King Charles that he told the Duke of York to make further savings in naval expenditure, which caused Coventry on 29 May to tell the Navy Board to reduce the number of men manning the fireships.

On 7 June a Dutch fleet of about eighty sail with 4,000 soldiers embarked, arrived in the King's Channel, just north-east of the Swin. Next day the Dutch decided to send a squadron of light vessels into the Thames to capture or destroy some merchantmen known to be lying in the Hope. The rest of the fleet would ensure that the squadron was not taken in the rear by any of the small English squadrons that might be put together in Portsmouth, Plymouth or Dover.

On 9 June the squadron of light vessels commanded by van Ghent and accompanied by a political representative of the States General called Cornelis de Witt, brother of the Grand Pensionary, entered the river. Fortunately, an unfavourable combination of wind and tide delayed the Dutch, thus enabling the English to move the merchantmen upstream and out of danger. After pursuing them for a short distance the Dutch dropped back towards Sheerness. By this time alarm bells were ringing vigorously from Whitehall to the Medway, where Spragge was collecting together whatever forces he could lay his hands on and where Pett in the dockyard at Chatham was doing the same. On 10 June the King ordered Albemarle to Chatham to coordinate the defence of the area.

The fortification of Sheerness, ordered some months earlier, had scarcely been started, and the garrison consisted of a few untrained militia. In the afternoon of 10 June the Dutch landed 800 soldiers who, with support from some of their ships, rapidly captured the fort, which left the entrance to the Medway unprotected. By this time the acting Lord-Lieutenant of Kent commanding the militia had joined Spragge and Pett at Chatham, where Albemarle arrived the next morning. These men now put in hand what measures they could to defend the valuable ships laid up in the Medway and the dockyard itself.

On 11 June the Dutch sent a reconnaissance force of sloops, yachts and ships' boats up the Medway followed closely by three larger ships and some fireships. The hastily deployed English defences included two ships sunk in the channel, below which was a chain covered by the fire from other ships. The great warships, unmanned except for skeleton crews, lay at anchor above the chain.

On 12 June the Dutch sailed past the two ships sunk in the channel, which they had towed out of the way on the previous day, and engaged the ships covering the chain, one of which was destroyed and another, the fourth-rate *Unity*, captured. They then sailed two fireships at the chain, the second of which broke it. Passing through, they captured the *Royal Charles*, after which their action was halted by the ebbing tide. Upstream, the rest of the English ships were covered by the guns of Upnor Castle.

By this time Albemarle had been able to move some heavy guns into the castle, and Spragge had raised another battery on the opposite side of the river. Albemarle had also arranged for the *Royal James*, the *Loyal London* and the *Royal Oak* to be sunk on the mud to prevent them being towed away; only their upper works remained above water. During the evening de Ruyter arrived in person to take command of the Dutch for the next day's fighting.

On 13 June, soon after midday when the tide was right, the Dutch moved upriver. While their warships engaged Upnor Castle, their fireships tried to set fire to the three English ships sunk on the mud. But this time they met fierce resistance and suffered casualties. They eventually succeeded in burning the upper works of the three great ships but had to abandon any thought of attacking the dockyard at Chatham or of getting at the rest of the English ships further up the river. On the day that this battle was in progress, the King told Rupert to go to Woolwich and put in hand measures to prevent the Dutch passing up the Thames to London.

On 14 June the Dutch withdrew from the Medway into the Thames at Sheerness, taking the *Royal Charles* and *Unity* with them. Soon afterwards, these two ships were towed across the sea to the United Provinces, where their arrival was greeted with intense jubilation. De Ruyter then sent two detachments from his fleet to attack shipping on the south and east coasts and withdrew with the remainder to the mouth of the Thames, having taken what stores of food he could find on Canvey Island. All these measures were designed to put pressure on the English with a view to getting rapid agreement to Dutch terms for peace, and it was abundantly clear that they meant to do as much damage as they could while the war lasted. This might well lead to another major operation.

By now Rupert had raised effective fortifications around Woolwich and had sunk ships in the main channel so that it would be difficult for the Dutch to pass. The greatest danger therefore lay in a further assault up the Medway designed to damage the dockyard at Chatham and capture or destroy more of the fleet laid up there. On 6 July the King instructed Rupert to go to the Medway and ensure that the defences there and at Sheerness were as impregnable as possible.

Within a month Rupert had fully fortified Sheerness and raised an emplacement of thirty heavy guns there. In addition, he erected two batteries, of eighteen and ten guns, downstream of Upnor Castle and two smaller batteries together with a number of single guns, in commanding positions in and around Chatham Dockyard. To make assurance doubly sure, he installed an unbreakable boom consisting of a double raft of masts, together with the old chain, just below Upnor Castle.[2] Any further Dutch incursion up the Medway would certainly have met with disaster.

Meanwhile, two more skirmishes with the Dutch had taken place in the Thames. On 24 July some Dutch ships under van Ness, pushing up into the Hope, were encountered by Spragge and repulsed. On 26 July, when falling back to the sea, they were again attacked, this time by Jordan from Harwich, who was able to get into the river because de Ruyter with the majority of the Dutch fleet was cruising along the south coast, where he caused alarm but did little damage. On 31 July a treaty ending the war was signed at Breda; it was ratified on 14 August.

The disasters that afflicted England during the summer were the result of the overall plan that Rupert, among others, had opposed. The catastrophe in the Medway was directly attributable to the King's failure to see that the fortification of Sheerness, recommended by Rupert during the previous year, was properly completed. Rupert, with his strong sense of military honour, must have felt intensely the disgrace of letting enemy ships roam at will to within a few miles of the capital. The loss of the great ships, particularly the two in which he had lived and fought, would have hurt him personally in a way that only a seaman can fully understand. Above all he must have minded that the successes of 1666, which had put England into such a strong bargaining position, were now lost.

Because of his illness Rupert had not been involved in the early stages of the campaign. When he was brought in, he acted with speed and vigour, first in the area of Woolwich and then in the Medway. As Spragge said later in his evidence to Parliament, if the Ordnance Board had done as much in ten weeks as Rupert achieved in ten days, the disasters would not have occurred. Anyone doubting the extent of Rupert's recovery would have been reassured had they watched a tennis match on 2 September, when the four best players in the land performed in front of the King and court. Rupert, aged forty-seven, was one of them.

Quite apart from the war, 1667 was notable for a considerable shift in the administration of the country in general and of the navy in particular. The first major change took place in May when the Earl of Southampton died at the age of sixty leaving the important post of Lord Treasurer vacant. He had throughout his life been a devoted Royalist but as treasurer he had been incapable of getting hold of the money needed to run the country. At his death the King decided to put the Treasury into a commission consisting of Albemarle, Ashley and Coventry to whom were added Sir Thomas Clifford, who had spent so much time with the fleet, and Sir John Duncombe. This move further increased the influence of Coventry and brought Clifford forward into the front row of the government.

At the end of June Carteret, an old Cavalier, resigned as Treasurer of the Navy and was replaced by the Earl of Anglesey, a former president of the council of state during the Protectorate. He was an honest and competent man in his fifties, but he found himself unable to cope with the task and was replaced the following year by two men acting jointly, Sir Thomas Osborne, later Earl of Danby, and Sir Thomas Littleton, a protégé of Arlington.

In the last days of August the King got rid of Clarendon himself, who was becoming the focus of government unpopularity in the wake of the summer's disasters. He had coordinated the King's administration throughout the exile period and since the Restoration, but the King, who was getting increasingly annoyed by Clarendon's nagging criticism of his behaviour, hoped that if Clarendon resigned before Parliament reassembled he would be able to spare him from their fury. In the event,

Clarendon made such a fuss about going that the King turned against him. Clarendon was not replaced as Lord Chancellor, a Lord Keeper being appointed to carry out the legal part of his duties. No one person took over as the director of government business.

A week later Coventry, who had for some time been opposed to Clarendon, handed over his appointment as the Lord High Admiral's secretary to Matthew Wren, a former secretary of Clarendon. The Duke of York, although aware that it was time that his father-in-law retired, was shocked at the manner of his dismissal and was unwilling to continue employing one of his opponents. As Secretary of the Admiralty and latterly as a Navy Board commissioner, Coventry had been the linchpin of the navy's administration since the Restoration. Wren was an able man, but it would take time before he could fill Coventry's shoes. Early in October a further change was made necessary by the death of the Surveyor, Sir William Batten. He was replaced by Colonel Middleton, a former Parliamentary officer who had been the commissioner at Portsmouth.

On 10 October Parliament was recalled and within the week set up a committee to inquire into the miscarriages of the war. A few days later Parliament sent a deputation of six men to Rupert and to Albemarle to convey their thanks for their service in the war and to ask them to write a report to the House of Commons regarding the way in which it had been conducted. Both men sent in reports dated 31 October.[3] Nearly all of Albemarle's report dealt with events leading up to the division of the fleet at the end of May 1666, although he also complained about delays in refitting the fleet after the four days' battle and of the inadequacy of the victualling which led to the fleet having to return prematurely to port after the St James's Day fight. In this connection he specifically stated that had the fleet been able to spend longer off Vlieland and Terschelling after Holmes's Bonfire, they would have been able to capture fifty merchant ships that arrived there three days after the fleet departed.

Rupert's report ranged wider. He first pointed out that had the Duke of York's order for the pursuit after the battle off Lowestoft been complied with, the victory would have been greater and in all probability the whole of the Dutch fleet would have been destroyed. He then ran over the events leading up to the division of the fleet, adding that when his squadron departed he supposed 'there to be no probable danger from the enemy in case they should come out, because the same wind which would bring them into the Channel would also serve to bring down our fleet to a conjunction with the squadron under my command'. (In his evidence to Parliament given on the day after Rupert's report was written, Spragge confirmed that this was what Rupert expected, saying that Rupert had told him so at the time.)

Most of the rest of Rupert's report dealt with the neglect of the authorities ashore to support the fleet properly. It starts:

> The next miscarriage I shall mention was the intolerable neglect in supplying provisions during the whole summer's expedition, notwithstanding the extraordinary and frequent importunity of our letters, which were for the most part directed to Sir William Coventry as being the fittest person to represent our desire to His Royal Highness, and to the Commissioners of the Navy, of which number he was also one.

Rupert went on to point out that because of this shortage he and Albemarle were obliged to put the fleet on short rations on three occasions. Rupert's report then goes into detail as to the specific shortages, after which he stated that

> this want of provisions did manifestly tend to the extraordinary prejudice of His Majesty's service in that whole summer, but most especially after the victory obtained in July fight, when we had carried the fleet to the enemies coast, and lay there before Vly in the way of all their merchant ships, we were enforced, merely for want of provisions, to quit out to Sole Bay.

Rupert then went on to criticise the Blue Squadron for letting Tromp escape after the St James's Day fight before harping back to the slowness of the Navy Board in getting new ships to the fleet after the four days' battle. He also criticised the slowness with which the King's commands to fortify Harwich and Sheerness were carried out, to which he ascribed the disaster in the Medway. His final shot was to deplore the fact that some at least of the ships that were set out in 1667 and which employed

18,000 men were not kept together in the mouth of the Thames, since that would probably have been enough to prevent the mischief that ensued.

Rupert's report represented a sharp criticism of the administration and, by implication, of the Duke of York. The Parliamentary Committee on Miscarriages drew up a list of fourteen points for their inquiry,[4] including the failure to follow up the Dutch after the battle off Lowestoft, the breaking bulk of the prizes taken by Sandwich, the division of the fleet before the four days' battle, the causes of the Medway disaster, the payment of the seamen by ticket and the shortcomings of the victualling system.

In parallel with the inquiry was Parliament's determination to destroy Clarendon in order to ensure that he could never regain his influence in the government. In an attempt to get urgently needed money, the King now allowed Clarendon to be impeached. With difficulty, a bill was passed through the Commons and sent to the Lords, where it was supported by Albemarle, Buckingham, Bristol and Arlington but opposed by the Duke of York and most of the bishops and peers of the Privy Council; the opposition carried the day. This divided the government and put the King in a difficult position. He therefore put it about that he was prepared to send Clarendon for trial by a tribunal of peers specially selected to sentence him to death; a distasteful expedient that was none the less legal. On hearing this, Clarendon fled abroad at the end of November.

Rupert's part in these manoeuvres is unclear. Since the Restoration he and Clarendon had got along comfortably together, and in the summer of 1665 Clarendon had even supported Rupert, though probably to annoy Coventry. There is some faint evidence that Rupert played a minor part in Clarendon's destruction,[5] but although he was present in the House of Lords when the charges against him were heard and again when Clarendon's defence, written in the ship that was carrying him to France, was read, he did not vote in favour of impeachment nor was he a member of the committee that subsequently drew up the bill to banish him.

The deliberations of the Committee on Miscarriages continued on and off for some time, to the considerable discomfort of those who felt themselves vulnerable, such as the members of the Navy Board. A second committee, known as the Brooke House Committee, was by now also at work inquiring into the

accounts in an attempt to discover the extent to which pecu-
lation, bribery and corruption were the cause of the neglect
from which the fleet had suffered. Rupert was not prepared to
accept either inefficiency or dishonesty and was only too happy
to see the Parliamentary committees do as much as they could
to bring the guilty to book. Not only did he regret the fact
that the fleet could have achieved more, had it been properly
supported, but he also felt strongly for the officers and men
who had fought under his command. Having shared the perils
and hardships of the campaign with them, he was glad to see
brought to account those who had starved and cheated them
while enjoying the shelter and plenty of their homes and amuse-
ments. Rupert's anger and indignation were often apparent at
meetings of the various councils that he attended, as he spoke
up for operational efficiency and fair dealing.

Rupert's recorded views at this time highlight an increasing
difference of approach between himself and the Duke of York.
Pepys records two examples. On 2 January 1668, at a meeting
when the King and the Duke were present, the Duke complained
that in the summer of 1666 Rupert and Albemarle had sacked
one of his captains and replaced him with someone who had
been turned out earlier for being drunk. In an aside to Pepys,
Rupert said: 'If they turn out every man that will be drunk,
they must turn out all the commanders in the fleet. What is the
matter if he be drunk, so that when he comes to fight he does
his work? At least let him be punished for his drunkenness and
not be put out of his command.'[6] Three weeks later the Duke,
talking privately to Anglesey, Penn and Pepys, told them that
he had warned Rupert and Albemarle that discipline would
suffer if they brought in drunken men just because they were
good fighters, adding that it was a reproach to the nation to
suggest that there were insufficient sober men who would fight
equally well.[7]

Throughout the first half of 1668 tension existed between the
Duke of York and Rupert regarding arrangements for setting
out a fleet for the summer. The Duke, having no wish to see
Rupert in command, put forward Penn, saying that Rupert
could not in honour command so small a fleet. Parliament,
possibly prompted by Rupert, pursued Penn in the Committee
on Miscarriages for his share in the prize goods scandal and
ultimately impeached him. In April the Duke considered going
to sea himself, although there was still no agreement on the size

of the fleet needed. In a council held in May Rupert maintained that the international situation did not warrant the setting out of a sizeable fleet. In the end Allin took a squadron to the Mediterranean in August and normal peacetime arrangements prevailed, so that no fleet commander was required. Gradually, the ill feeling engendered by the war faded and Rupert's interests became focused elsewhere.

In February 1668 the mechanics of handling government business were somewhat improved by the formalising of the four standing committees of the Privy Council. Of these the Foreign Affairs Committee, which also dealt with links between the Privy Council and local leaders within the country, such as Lord-Lieutenants and Justices of the Peace, was limited to nine specified persons, namely the Duke of York, Prince Rupert, the Lord Keeper (Bridgeman), the Lord Privy Seal (Robartes), the two Secretaries of State (Arlington and Morrice, soon to be replaced by Trevor), together with the Dukes of Albemarle, Buckingham and Ormonde. Likewise, the Admiralty Committee was extended to cover all military affairs and fortifications and was to consist of fifteen members, including the Duke of York, Rupert, Albemarle, Arlington, Ashley and Coventry; later the membership rose to nineteen.[8]

For the next four years Rupert's main public interest was focused on foreign affairs, although he continued to play a full part in the activities of the Admiralty Committee, which in its reconstituted form was sometimes used by the King to carry out functions that the Duke of York considered to be part of the duties of the Lord High Admiral. But before turning to foreign affairs, it is worth looking at a number of developments that were occurring in Rupert's private life.

The first of these happened in June 1668 when the King gave him a large house in Spring Gardens. At that time Spring Gardens spread from the area now occupied by Carlton House Terrace in a curve via the site of Admiralty Arch to that of the Admiralty itself: thus at one end it bordered the garden of St James's Palace and at the other Horse Guards Parade. The house given to Rupert must have been a few yards to the north-east of where the Duke of York's Column now stands. It became his main London residence, although he retained his lodgings in Whitehall.

The next thing that happened was that Rupert fell deeply in love with an actress. In July or August he accompanied the King and Queen to Tunbridge Wells, where each of the courtiers took a country cottage in which they lived simply, all formality abandoned. In the morning they would take the waters and later turn to bowling on the green or dancing under the stars. At some stage the Queen sent for the King's company of actors to provide some extra entertainment; one of them was Margaret Hughes. Pepys met her in May, when he kissed her. He described her as 'seeming modest, but not so'. She was young and beautiful, with long well-shaped legs, and had recently been the mistress of Sir Charles Sedley. She did not immediately surrender to Rupert but waited until he was ready to take her fully under his protection. He then set her up in a large house at Hammersmith which had formerly belonged to an old Royalist called Sir Nicholas Crisp. She remained with Rupert for the rest of his life.

A description of Rupert at Tunbridge Wells written by a twenty-two-year-old nephew of the Duke of Ormonde is worth recording, as it gives an idea of how he appeared to the younger members of King Charles's dissolute court. This account describes him as

> brave and courageous even to rashness; but crossgrained and incorrigibly obstinate: his genius was fertile in mathematical experiments, and he possessed some knowledge of chemistry: he was polite even to excess, unseasonably; but haughty and even brutal, when he ought to have been gentle and courteous: he was tall and his manners were ungracious: he had a dry hard-favoured visage, and a stern look, even when he wished to please; but when he was out of humour, he was the true picture of reproof.

The account continues: 'The Prince Rupert found charms in the person of a player called Hughes who brought down and greatly subdued his natural fierceness . . . Nobody was bold enough to make it the subject of satire though the same constraint was not observed with other ridiculous persons.'[9] The picture of Rupert given here is hardly flattering, but to someone in his early twenties, the idea of falling love when nearing fifty is difficult to take seriously.

In September, after the court's visit to Tunbridge Wells,

Rupert accompanied the King and the Dukes of York and Buckingham for ten days' hunting at Windsor and in the New Forest. Soon after their return, the King made Rupert Constable of Windsor Castle. The constable was governor and keeper of the castle and had command of the garrison. He could make use of any of the rooms that the King did not want, was judge of the castle court and keeper of the forest, which extended to 120 square miles. He had the right to let the lodges to whom he pleased. During the time that Rupert was constable a major programme of restoration, supervised by Hugh May, took place. Rupert himself lived in the Round Tower.[10]

Another event that took place in 1668 had far-reaching consequences. Rupert and Ashley merged two companies to form the Mines Royal[11] and thereby started a commercial partnership that developed into a firm if somewhat surprising friendship. Three years later, when Rupert was granted a patent by the King to exploit his invention of a metallurgical process that could be used to produce high-quality cannon, he was joined by Ashley and Sir John Chichely, Master of the Ordnance, who together agreed to finance the project in return for half of the profits.[12]

Ashley was also involved in another of Prince Rupert's projects at this time. When the court was at Oxford in the autumn of 1665, two Frenchmen named Groseilliers and Radisson, who had been trading with the Indians around Hudson Bay in Canada, arrived in England. They had been poorly supported by the French governor of Quebec and, knowing of Rupert's concern for trade and exploration, gained an introduction to him. Rupert was interested both in the trading prospects and in the possibility of finding the elusive north-west passage to Asia. He brought the two Frenchmen to the King, who handed them over to Sir Peter Colleton to examine their suggestions. Nothing could be done while the war lasted, but Rupert, Ashley, Craven and others raised enough money to fit out an expedition. In 1667 this expedition left for Canada in two ketches, one, the *Eaglet*, provided by the King and another, the *Nonsuch*, provided by an Englishman named Gillam, who had already been trading around Hudson Bay. In the spring of 1669 the *Nonsuch* returned with a cargo of fur and with news of an agreement reached with the natives to trade over a large area. Rupert applied for a charter for a Company of Adventurers Trading with Hudson Bay which was granted by the King in

1671. It gave the company powers of possession, succession and full legal rights over a very large area to be known as Prince Rupert's Land. It could enlist soldiers, erect forts, make laws and had exclusive trading rights. Rupert was the first governor of the company, and two years later Ashley became deputy governor.[13]

By 1670 the Company of the Royal Adventurers Trading into Africa, which Rupert had been influential in setting up, was in financial difficulties despite having sublet some of its business to the Gambia Merchants' Company. It was therefore decided to raise extra capital with which to form a new company that would take over the assets of the other two, with considerably extended powers. Two years later, when £111,600 had been raised, the Royal African Company came into being with a new charter presented by the King. This authorised the company to set up forts and factories, to make war and peace with local chieftains, to raise troops and declare martial law if necessary. These powers were granted to twenty-four named individuals, the first three being the Duke of York, Prince Rupert and Ashley, who had by now become the Earl of Shaftesbury. Trade was the purpose for which the company was set up, particularly in 'gold, silver and negroes'.

The treaty that brought the second Dutch War to an end was naturally unfavourable. England kept New York but lost Pulo Run in Surinam (South America), Nova Scotia and the African forts taken by de Ruyter in 1664: no compensation was paid to English merchants in the African forts and certainly no reparations to the English government. It was very disappointing considering the favourable conditions that had existed in October 1666. Meanwhile, King Louis, who had done little enough to help the Dutch, had made considerable inroads in the Spanish Netherlands. King Charles and Arlington therefore wondered whether Louis might be persuaded to give Ostend and Newport to England, together with an alliance against the Dutch, in return for English recognition of his conquests. Louis refused unless England was prepared to go to war with Spain.[14]

Faced with this refusal, Charles persuaded the Dutch, who were becoming nervous of France's incursions into the Spanish Netherlands, to sign a treaty. While recognising Louis's existing gains, both parties undertook to oppose any further incursion and agreed to use force against France or Spain if either of them tried to alter the status quo. Soon afterwards, Sweden joined the pact, which was henceforth known as the Triple Alliance. Some months earlier Sandwich had persuaded Spain to end her long war with Portugal so as to be in a better position to oppose further advances by Louis into the Spanish Netherlands. It is in this context that the decision not to set out the fleet in 1668 must be seen: Rupert's opposition to doing so, mentioned above, was based on his assessment that operations against France would not take place in the current year.

Within the first few months of 1668, Charles had detached the Dutch and Portuguese from their alliance with France and made King Louis understand that England's friendship was worth buying. Arlington was mainly responsible for this success. France had undoubtedly received a setback.

These manoeuvres set the scene for the events of the coming three years. On the one hand the King tried openly to get support around Europe for the Triple Alliance in order to contain the expansionist ambitions of Catholic France. On the other he secretly worked for a treaty with France.

In August 1668 Colbert de Croissy arrived in London as French Ambassador Extraordinary with a brief from King Louis to break up the Triple Alliance and negotiate an Anglo-French treaty. In January 1669 King Charles sent a cipher to his sister Minette that would enable him to communicate through her to Louis in absolute secrecy. Later in the month, on the feast of the conversion of St Paul, the King held a meeting with the Duke of York, Arlington, Clifford and Lord Arundell of Wardour at which he told them, with tears in his eyes, that he intended to be received into the Roman Catholic Church when the time was ripe. Only Arundell, Master of the Horse to Henrietta Maria, who had been living in France since 1665, was a Roman Catholic at the time, although the Duke of York secretly became one soon afterwards during a visit to the Spanish Netherlands and Clifford acknowledged his own adherence to the faith in 1673. Arlington was a sympathiser. The meeting was probably staged to make those present realise that the King was serious about the negotiations. No one else in England was to know. During 1669 negotiations continued, partly through Minette and partly under cover of negotiations for a maritime trade treaty. There was at one time concern that the English ambassador in France, Sir Ralph Mountagu, had guessed that something was in the wind, but Charles was adamant that neither he nor the Duke of Buckingham, who was in France at the time, must be told. In August Henrietta Maria died.

In May 1670 King Louis visited Dunkirk and while there Minette took the opportunity of sailing across to Dover to spend a few days with her brother. Everyone knew of the great love these two had for each other, so that there was nothing suspicious about the meeting. She was met by Charles, accompanied by the Duke of York and Rupert, amid great scenes of rejoicing. Three days later, having ironed out the few points that had not previously been agreed by correspondence, Arlington and Colbert quietly signed the Secret Treaty of Dover. None of those taking part in the festivities knew what had happened, other than those who had been in the know from the start.

Under the treaty Charles undertook to declare himself a Roman Catholic when he felt the time to be right in return for which he was to receive immediately and secretly £150,000 from Louis. Louis also undertook to send and pay for 6,000 troops to help him maintain order should his conversion cause trouble in England. Charles and Louis agreed jointly to attack the United Provinces, England to be responsible for the war at sea and to provide a fleet of about fifty ships, with France putting a squadron of thirty ships under English command. France would also provide extra money to fund the campaign at sea. France would be responsible for attacking the United Provinces by land. When the war was won, England would be given three islands in the Schelde Estuary, which would enable her to command access to the river. France's gains were not specified.

Within a month of her return to France, Minette died from a sudden and acute stomach disorder. Her husband, who was on bad terms with her, was suspected of poisoning her, but an autopsy performed by a panel of French and English doctors found no sign of it. A few days before she died she told Montagu of the secret treaty in strictest confidence.

Meanwhile, Rupert, who knew nothing of these negotiations despite his presence at Dover, was working hard for the Triple Alliance. Indeed, from 1668 onwards, whenever the possibility of moving closer to France was raised, he opposed it so vigorously that Colbert de Croissy described him as an enemy to France.[15] In 1669 he was in charge of negotiations with Denmark[16] designed to gain commercial benefits for England at the expense of France. The result was a treaty signed in July 1670. In 1670 Rupert was involved in negotiations with the Elector of Brandenburg[17] designed to ensure that he favoured the Triple Alliance over France. Initially nothing came of this, but the following year the Elector negotiated a treaty with the Dutch.

In order to implement the agreement with France, Charles had to prepare Parliament and the country for another war against the Dutch. Clearly Parliament would become totally alienated from the King if any hint of the so-called Catholic clauses of the treaty became known. On the other hand there was a strong body of opinion in both Parliament and the country which would support a further war with the Dutch in order to gain the trade advantages that had been denied them in the last one. To renew the war, with France as an ally rather than an enemy, might prove popular, especially if it could be shown that France was paying some of the cost.

For some time the Duke of Buckingham, who since the departure of Clarendon had become influential in the government and in Parliament, had favoured another war with the Dutch. Without telling him of the secret treaty, Charles put him and Ashley in charge of negotiating a second treaty with France that would cover the same points as the secret one, but with no mention of Charles's conversion or of the money that he was to receive for it. This treaty could therefore be disclosed to members of the government, and eventually even to Parliament, as suitable opportunities for breaking with the Dutch presented themselves. Not surprisingly, the negotiations progressed swiftly, and on 21 December 1670 the Treaty of London was signed by Clifford, Arlington, Buckingham, Ashley and Lauderdale, sometimes known as the Cabal. Somewhat to King Louis's annoyance, the negotiators pressed for and got two further islands included in the spoils that were to be handed to England at the end of the war. The money to be paid to Charles for his agreement to joining the Roman Catholic Church was included in the subsidy for setting out the fleet, so this was passed to him without attracting attention.

Rupert and Ormonde were told of the Treaty of London in May 1671, and in the following month a definite decision was taken by the government to go to war with the Dutch when a suitable pretext could be found. In the latter part of the year pressure was put on the government of the United Provinces to return Pulo Run, and a quarrel was picked over the failure of a Dutch squadron to salute a small English warship that had passed through it on its way to pick up the English ambassador. Meanwhile, Charles had become popular with Parliament by seeming to give up his proposals for religious toleration and also for the pressure he was putting on the Dutch in the interest of gaining trading advantages. In 1671 Parliament voted him enough money, when taken together with the French contribution, to enable him to go to war. In February 1672 Charles prorogued Parliament and then, in its absence, issued a Declaration of Indulgence designed particularly to distract the attention of dissenters from his abandonment of the Dutch. He declared war shortly afterwards.

It can easily be imagined that Rupert had grave misgivings about abandoning the Dutch in favour of the French. He could of course see the trade advantages of the war which had caused men such as Ashley and Buckingham to support it, but with his much greater understanding of the European scene he could also see the long-term danger to England that would result from the gains that France was likely to make. If the United Provinces were to become truncated as a result of the fighting, Louis would become the undisputed master of north-west Europe. Nothing could then deter him from expanding further into the Spanish Netherlands and along the Rhine at the expense of the Empire. Spain at least saw the danger and, as soon as the break-up of the Triple Alliance became apparent, entered into an alliance with the United Provinces. Ashley, who knew Rupert well, realised how he would react and warned the King not to disclose the existence of the treaty to him too soon.

But Charles knew him even better and was confident that in the last resort he would do whatever was required of him. In any case Rupert was too valuable to be left out. His answer to Rupert's opposition was not to leave him on one side but to give him more to do. In 1670 he had already made him Lord-Lieutenant of Berkshire which, together with his duties at Windsor, would keep him fully occupied. Early in 1671 the King also put him in charge of discussions with Colbert de Croissy designed to reduce trade tariffs between England and France and later in the year he made him head of a commission set up to settle Irish affairs.

* * *

Before describing Rupert's activities in the third Dutch War, it is worth taking a closer look at the sort of life he was leading at the end of the 1660s and the early 1670s. Some of his biographers have suggested that he was settling down to a quiet life of country pursuits and leisurely scientific studies in his laboratory at Windsor with occasional visits to London to attend court functions. In fact, the reality was very different and must have caused him to expend a great deal of physical and mental energy.

To take his routine work first, he was a member of the Privy Council and its two main sub-committees, all three of which met frequently. He was also a member of the Tangier Committee. Naturally, Rupert could not attend all the meetings of all these committees any more than any of the other members did, but in 1669 he attended no fewer than thirty meetings of the highly important Foreign Affairs Committee. In addition to these government committees, he was intimately concerned with the affairs of the Royal African Company and the Hudson Bay Company. On top of this again were the specific government tasks given him from time to time, such as introducing negotiations with Denmark and Brandenburg and the two jobs that he was given in 1671. On top of all this were his duties at Windsor and his attendance on the King in his pleasures, as at Tunbridge Wells, Newmarket and when he went hunting in the New Forest. He was also present with the King on many other occasions, such as the visit of the Grand Duke of Tuscany in 1669 and of Minette to Dover in 1670.

The positioning of Peg Hughes at Hammersmith must have been very convenient, being about seventeen miles from Windsor and six from Whitehall. Thus, if Rupert were at Windsor and wished to attend a meeting at Whitehall the next day, he had only about a two-hour ride to Peg Hughes where he could spend the night. The next day he could be in the Palace of Whitehall within the hour. He could then spend the next night at Spring Gardens or visit Frances Bard at Drury House or return to Peg Hughes if he preferred.

It is difficult to know how Frances Bard fitted into the picture, since no mention of her appears during this period. At some stage, judging by correspondence between Rupert and his sister Sophie, he quarrelled with Frances and she left England, but when this happened is not known. Perhaps she looked on Rupert as her unofficial husband and resented his having a mistress in the form of Peg Hughes. In this case she may have tolerated the situation for some years while Dudley grew up in the hope that Rupert would tire of Hughes and return to her. During this period she could have stayed at Windsor from time to time when the court was elsewhere.

A first-hand description of Rupert's lodgings at Windsor is given by Evelyn when he visited the court there in 1670. He records:

> Windsor was now going to be repaired being exceedingly ragged and ruinous. Prince Rupert the Constable had begun to trim up the keepe or high round tower, and handsomely adorned his hall with furniture of arms, which were very singular, by so disposing the pikes, muskets, pistols, bandeliers, holsters, drums, back, breast, and head pieces, as was very extraordinary. Thus those huge steepe stayres ascending to it had the walls invested with martial furniture all new and bright, so disposing the bandeliers, holsters and drums, as to represent festoons, and that without any confusion, trophy like. From the hall we went into his bedchamber, and ample roomes hung with tapisserie, curious and effeminate pictures; so extreamely different from the other, which presented nothing but war and horror.[18]

The Round Tower has twice been altered since Rupert's time, first in the reign of George IV when it was heightened and again more recently when adapted to take the Royal Archives. As a result none of Rupert's rooms would now be recognisable to him.[19]

Although the King had not frequented Windsor much in the early part of his reign, he was doing so more and more by the end of the 1660s. Part of the attraction was the planning of the restoration work, but he also enjoyed hunting and walking in the park as well as swimming, rowing and fishing. Fishing was an unusual sport for a King at this time, but there is ample evidence that Charles became increasingly addicted to it. Although fly-fishing was just beginning to become popular, it is almost certain that the King would have been fishing with bait. Rupert frequently accompanied him hunting and on his walks, but there is no reference to him fishing. When the court came to Windsor, Peg Hughes joined Rupert in his apartments.

Some weeks before Evelyn's visit, a serious incident had occurred. At this time the King and court were in residence and had brought with them the King's players, among whom was one of his more recent mistresses, Nell Gwyn. One evening a dispute broke out between Peg's brother, a follower of Prince Rupert, and one of the King's followers as to whether Nell Gwyn or Peg Hughes was the more beautiful. So strongly was the matter contested that Hughes was killed. Brawling around the court was not unusual, but fatalities other than in duels were mercifully rare.

At the end of 1671, when Rupert reached the age of fifty-two, he was living a full and enjoyable life. If he were annoyed about the Treaty of London he did not show it. He was frequently in the company of the King, who liked and trusted him and who had rewarded him so well. The irritations of the second Dutch War had doubtless faded from his mind to some extent as the remembrance of the noises and carnage of the battles also faded. But during the last few years death had not only taken his aunt Henrietta Maria and his cousin Minette, but also, in 1670, his companion in arms, Albemarle, and his greatest friend, Will Legge. For someone who had few close personal friends, the loss of Legge must have been hard to bear.

10

THE THIRD DUTCH WAR

As in 1665, it was Holmes, now senior officer at Portsmouth, who sparked off the war. As a result of English provocation, the Dutch fleet had mobilised at the end of January 1672. Taking this as a warlike act, orders were sent on 18 February to English ships in the Mediterranean to take and destroy all Dutch ships; on 5 March the order was extended to home waters. Holmes immediately took out nine ships and started to take prizes. On 13 March, acting on instructions from the Foreign Affairs Committee, he fell in with a large Dutch convoy consisting of six warships and fifty-four merchantmen, most of which were armed, some heavily. Although Holmes's squadron greatly outgunned the Dutch warships, the Dutch fleet as a whole greatly outnumbered Holmes's squadron. Holmes went into the attack and over two days inflicted much damage on the Dutch, killing their commander, de Haes. He also suffered a considerable number of casualties and managed to capture only one Dutch warship, which subsequently sank, and three merchant ships. A story that Holmes failed to coordinate his attack with Spragge, who happened to pass up the Channel on his return from the Mediterranean several days before the arrival of the Dutch, has been exaggerated,[1] as has one that Spragge could have done more to help Holmes. All that can be said is that these two did not get along well together.

On 17 March England declared war on the United Provinces. France followed suit a few days later, as did Cologne and Münster in early April. For King Charles the war gave him the opportunity to become Louis's ally, which he hoped would ultimately enable him to become independent of Parliament. Those of his subjects with trading interests and those who would benefit from warlike activities looked forward to the dismemberment of the United Provinces to provide them with rich pickings. Those wanting war were encouraged by the fact that the French intended to put 120,000 men into the field and augment the English fleet with thirty-six ships, so that a cheap victory seemed certain. The King was anxious that the cost might be met without further recourse to Parliament, but this would depend on hostilities being concluded in 1672.

But the war, when it started, was above all King Louis's war; England was very much the junior partner. Louis's reasons for wanting it were complex. First, he wanted to conquer the rest of the Spanish Netherlands, which the United Provinces was certain to oppose. Second, like the English, the French were in competition with the Dutch for trade. Third, he found objectionable the very existence of a Dutch Republic so close to France. Before mounting his attack on the United Provinces, Louis had embarked on intense diplomatic activity. Lorraine was occupied by Louis in 1670 without excessive protest, and Bavaria, frightened by Lorraine's fate, struck up an alliance with France. Louis then entered into a non-aggression pact with the Empire, a condition of which was that he would not attack Spain. When Louis tried to recruit Brandenburg into the alliance he was rebuffed; instead, Brandenburg became an ally of the Dutch. Finally, on 7 May Sweden signed a treaty with France under which she agreed to attack states in northern Germany to tie down their armies and to prevent them from going to the assistance of the United Provinces.

April 1672 was spent by both the English and the French in mobilising men and ships. In England the King prepared for war by promoting some of his principle advisers. The Earl of Lauderdale became a duke, while Arlington and Ashley both became earls, the latter taking the title of Earl of Shaftesbury. The energetic Clifford was made a baron.

At sea it was decided that the French should form the White Squadron of a combined fleet, with the English providing the Red and Blue Squadrons. By this time the losses inflicted by the Dutch in 1666 and 1667 had been made good by the building of a number of new ships, including a new *Prince* of 100 guns and three new first-rates of ninety-six guns: the *Royal James*, *London* and *St Andrew*. A further first-rate of 100 guns with the name of Rupert's former flagship, the *Royal Charles*, would be ready within the year. In addition, there was one new second-, third- and fourth-rate ship, together with four of the fifth-rate and three of the sixth.

The King of France could only be expected to put his squadron under an admiral who combined seagoing fighting experience with the ear of the King of England. Two people measured up to these requirements: the Duke of York and Prince Rupert. Rupert had made no secret of his opposition to the French alliance, as a result of which the Duke was more acceptable to France. For this reason concern about his personal safety was put aside and he was charged with commanding the fleet. Rupert was given the task of handling the work of the Admiralty in London.

Command of the Blue Squadron was given to Sandwich, who had returned from Spain some years earlier. He was by now heavy and gouty and could barely stand without assistance. In the Red Squadron Spragge became vice-admiral and Harman rear-admiral. In the Blue Squadron Jordan, now sixty-eight years old, became vice-admiral with Kempthorne as rear-admiral. Holmes, a far more effective flag officer than any of these, with the possible exception of Spragge, was left out to avoid dissension.

On 18 April the campaign at sea was discussed at a meeting of the Foreign Affairs Committee and the minutes shed an interesting light on the way in which such business was conducted. Members present were the King, the Duke of York, Prince Rupert, Arlington, Shaftesbury and Lauderdale. The members of the Navy Board, together with Sandwich and Holmes, were in attendance. The meeting started with a statement that if the English ships were ready before the Dutch, they should go into the Downs. The question was then raised as to whether, once there, they should immediately go west to meet the French or whether they should do so only if the Dutch approached. Sandwich maintained that they should stay unless pressed by the Dutch, so that if the Dutch went into the Thames the English could close in behind them. The King said that if they stayed in the Downs, fast Dutch frigates would get up with the rear of our fleet and force a battle. Rupert said that, providing we got between the frigates and the Dutch fleet, it would not attack us, the Duke of York adding that any Dutch frigates thus taken could be put into Rye Harbour. Rupert resumed by saying that in any case the Dutch would not close with us in such circumstances if we had fifty ships. Lauderdale said that if they got as far west as Beachy Head, the English could fall on them and destroy them. The King stated that the Dutch would not push us into the Channel for fear of the French. It was decided to stay in the Downs until the French arrived, remaining ready to act as the situation required. Rupert then raised the question of what should be done if the Dutch occupied the Gunfleet before we were ready to leave the river. In this case should we wait for the French or attack? The Duke's feelings were that in this case the Dutch should be attacked as soon as it was known that the French were off the Isle of Wight, because the Dutch would not fight in the sands but would edge out to sea, at which we could get past them into the Downs and on to the French. Rupert cautioned against allowing the Dutch into the river.[2]

Later it was decided that the two English squadrons should sail to meet the French squadron off the Isle of Wight. The Dutch wanted to block the Thames before the English were ready to sail, but they themselves were not ready in time and the English left the Buoy of the Nore on 2 May, the same day as de Ruyter left the Texel.

The next discussion in the Foreign Affairs Committee also took place on 2 May, when the conduct of operations after joining the French was considered. This time the proposal was not to occupy the Downs but to lie off Dungeness and not to fight the Dutch in a position where, if beaten, they could slip back into their own ports and 'bolt out on us again'. Rupert started the discussion by saying that if we went to Dungeness, the Dutch would go north to Tynemouth to stop the colliers, and then it would be necessary to find them out wherever they were to prevent the seamen becoming disheartened. The King said that Dungeness was dangerous for the great ships when the wind was in the south, but Rupert contradicted him by saying that a south wind carries you directly into the Downs. Shaftesbury's view was that the Downs was the right place to be until all the ships were together, after which the best move was to go to the Dogger Bank to intercept returning Dutch merchantmen. If the Dutch fleet interfered, it could be fought in an advantageous place. Again Rupert interrupted to say that if our fleet fought between the enemy and Holland, and then lost the battle, the whole fleet would be lost.[3] The minutes of both meetings demonstrate the vigour with which Rupert contradicted those who spoke with an imperfect understanding of the technicalities of the matter; not even the King was spared.

On 2 May the Duke of York, as Lord High Admiral, issued a letter appointing Rupert to 'take care of the affairs of H.M.

Navy at London', adding that 'the great zeal and affection which
you have always had for the service and your large experience
and ability in these affairs having assured me that I could not
make a choice more advantageous for H.M. Service . . .'. On 3
May Rupert received his warrant of appointment from the King
which specifically mentioned the main tasks that he was
expected to carry out. These included, first, the issue of orders
to the officers of the Navy Board and to the dockyards. Second,
to decide where ships should be fitted out and repaired and to
issue the necessary orders for this to be done. Third, to deploy
and dispose of all ships not with the main fleet, with power to
dismiss and appoint officers in these ships as required.

Rupert now had to familiarise himself with the details of the
Navy Board's business so that he could carry out the first two
tasks given him by the King. At the same time he had to give
directions to those ships that were not with the main fleet
according to the operational situation which included the imminent arrival of the Dutch fleet off the mouth of the Thames. In
this connection it is worth pointing out that the machinery that
existed to help him exercise his responsibilities was unsophisticated to say the least.

As mentioned earlier, the Admiralty itself consisted of nothing
but the Lord High Admiral, his secretary and a few clerks.
When Rupert took over, the Lord High Admiral had taken his
secretary, Wren, with him to the fleet. Rupert's secretary, Sir
James Hayes, therefore took over the running of the office and
had the task of transmitting Rupert's instructions to the Navy
Board, to the ships and to the shore bases, except when Rupert
was acting on behalf of the Privy Council or of one of its
sub-committees, in which case Joseph Williamson, clerk of the
council and Arlington's right-hand man, transmitted his instructions. It is from the correspondence of Hayes and Williamson
that Rupert's activities over the next four months can best be
discovered.

The principal agency at Rupert's disposal was the Navy
Board, the composition of which had changed for the better
since the end of the previous war. Of the officers, Sir Thomas
Allin, who had become Comptroller on the death of Mennes,
was far more effective than his predecessor. Middleton, who
had succeeded Batten as Surveyor, had not proved a success

and had been replaced by the competent Tippetts: Middleton went as resident commissioner to Chatham. The senior commissioner was Lord Brouncker, who had been in office since 1664 and was a man of considerable ability. Although Sir Jeremiah Smith, who had replaced Penn when he died in 1670, did not have such varied experience of naval matters as his predecessor, he had, with Allin, the advantage of having commanded a squadron in Rupert's fleet. Samuel Pepys, perhaps a little sore at not being promoted into the place of the Comptroller or Surveyor, remained as Clerk of the Acts and secretary to the board. His encyclopaedic knowledge, long experience and administrative ability were priceless assets. Another asset was that money was more plentiful at the start of the third Dutch War than it had been in 1666, a situation that would not prevail for long.

Rupert's first move on the day he was appointed was to order the Navy Board to report to him in three days' time to brief him on the details of its business. This has been represented as an unnecessary diversion of the board's efforts at a busy time, but from the point of view of Rupert it was essential since, unlike the Duke of York, he had not been living with the problems for years, acquiring knowledge as he went. But there was one matter that was even more urgent than getting properly briefed, and this was to take precautions against the Dutch fleet appearing in the mouth of the Thames while the English fleet was far away down the Channel.

On 4 May Rupert ordered 100 soldiers from the garrison at Rochester to move to Sheerness and on the same day sent word to the Master General of the Ordnance to move some extra guns into the defences there. He also asked the Lord-Lieutenant of Kent, Lord Winchelsea, to be ready to defend the coast while the fleet was away and to arrange for the resupply of some ketches that had taken refuge in Ramsgate.

In these matters Rupert acted none too soon. On 7 May the English fleet met up with the French off St Helens, the Dutch fleet being at anchor off Dover. The allied fleet then tried to sail back in search of de Ruyter but was delayed by a strong headwind. Meanwhile, de Ruyter had moved first to Zealand and then to a position in the King's Channel south of Harwich, where he arrived on 13 May, at which time the allies were still to the west of Dungeness. A detachment of six English ships under the command of Captain Coleman in the *Gloucester* (62 guns), together with three fireships and a hospital ship originally intended for the main fleet, were in the mouth of the Thames.

On 14 May the King, greatly concerned that the Dutch were about to sail up the river, told Rupert to go in person to the threatened area and take under his direct command all ships, seamen, troops and civilians with a view to repulsing the enemy.

On the same day de Ruyter sent van Ghent with a squadron of twelve ships, of which seven carried fifty guns or more, into the Thames. There they met Coleman's detachment, which retreated before them as far as Sheerness. Luckily, the reinforcements sent by Rupert had arrived and van Ghent realised that he was up against much stiffer opposition than had been the case in 1667 and could go no further.

On 15 May Rupert moved from Gravesend to Chatham and then on to Sheerness, where he met Allin and Smith. Next day he embarked on a yacht and was in time to see van Ghent turn around and head off to rejoin de Ruyter. As the Dutch ships departed, Rupert moved the ships that had been in the river downstream to where they could keep in touch with the Dutch and join the main fleet when it came within reach. On 17 May the allied fleet, which had at last passed through the Strait of Dover, was able to move north on a southerly wind. De Ruyter, who was in the Gunfleet, moved out to sea as they approached. Two days later the two fleets were in sight of one another, but first the shoals and then some thick weather prevented an engagement taking place. On 21 May the allied fleet anchored in Sole Bay.

The danger to the Thames was over, but now Rupert was faced with getting the fleet replenished as soon as possible. Despite the proximity of the main battlefleet, Dutch privateers were operating so that the victualling ships had to be protected as they moved from the river to Sole Bay. Another problem was that as far as anyone knew the Dutch were to the south of the Thames in a position to capture shipping coming in from the Channel. Rupert therefore sent word to have all ships stopped and held at Portsmouth until further notice.

While these events were happening around the British coast, Louis XIV was advancing at the head of his 120,000 men down the line of the Meuse. Approaching Maastricht and not wanting to be held up by a lengthy siege, he bypassed it and marched to the Rhine at Cologne. Then, with his army astride the river, he moved downstream, Condé in command on one bank and

Turenne on the other. On 26 May they reached the four Cleves fortresses belonging to the Elector of Brandenburg, which acted as the gateway to the United Provinces.

On the Dutch side, although at the declaration of war the States General had appointed the young William of Orange as Captain General of the Army, he was not made Stadtholder, which meant that he had virtually no political power. John de Witt, the Grand Pensionary, who had done so much over the years to undermine the position of the House of Orange, remained in overall charge. In the earlier Dutch Wars the fleet had suffered severely from the complications of republican government, under which five separate admiralties controlled the provision and manning of the ships. Now, faced with an invasion by land, each province and even each major town expected to have its say. The Captain General, without the powers of the Stadtholder, had to submit his plans from day to day to various delegates and representatives who knew nothing whatsoever of the business but who were accustomed to taking part in interminable discussions which seldom ended in decisions. The result was total chaos.

Realising that the United Provinces were soon going to be heavily pressed from the land and not wanting to be subjected to attack from the sea at the same time, John de Witt urged de Ruyter to attack the allied fleet and disable it, if only for a time, before the invasion took place. On 28 May, when Louis was attacking the Rhine forts, de Ruyter, accompanied by Cornelius de Witt, surprised the allies in Sole Bay. The allied fleet of seventy-four ships of the line was lying about two miles offshore taking in victuals and water. The French squadron was anchored to the south, the Red Squadron in the centre and the Blue in the north. De Ruyter, with sixty-two ships of the line, sailed in from the north-east on a light east wind.

At the start there was a muddle. When the Duke of York gave the order to set sail, the French, being the van squadron, thought that he meant them to lead and, having no instructions beyond being told to stick close to the wind, set off in a southerly direction on the port tack. The Blue and the Red Squadrons, however, set off to the north on the starboard tack. De Ruyter, who had approached in line abreast with an advance guard of lighter vessels and fireships, turned into line with van Ghent opposite the Blue Squadron and himself opposite the Red. Banckert's squadron on the opposite tack pursued the French. Thus, two separate battles took place.

Fighting between the English and the Dutch started at about 7 a.m. and was intense throughout the day. On the Dutch side van Ghent was killed. On the other hand, after a long and bitter fight Sandwich's flagship, the *Royal James*, was burned by a fireship and he too was killed as he tried to move his flag. Fighting between de Ruyter and the Red Squadron was equally severe, and the Duke of York was obliged to shift into the *St Michael*.

In the south the fighting was less severe as Banckert did not manage to close with the French to the same extent. None the less both sides suffered a considerable number of casualties. In the evening the squadrons in the north and those in the south tacked and in consequence moved towards each other again. By the time that night fell both the Dutch and the allied fleets were reunited and were sailing south-east with the Dutch in the lead. Next day the two fleets were in sight of each other, and by noon the allies were closing with the Dutch. But a heavy mist came down and, when some hours later it dispersed, the wind was too strong for an engagement. At the end of the day the allies anchored off the Galloper, and the next morning the Dutch anchored under cover of their shoals.

In terms of casualties the allies had come off worse to the tune of about 900 killed as opposed to 600. In terms of ships the Dutch lost three compared with one of the allies. The English, the French and the Dutch each lost a flag officer. Another significant casualty was the Duke's secretary, Wren, who was wounded and died soon afterwards, being replaced by Henry Saville, brother of Lord Halifax. The Duke's flag captain, Sir John Cox, was also killed, and the deaths of these two revived misgivings about the safety of the heir to the throne, although for the time being he remained in command of the fleet. Spragge replaced Sandwich as admiral of the Blue.

In a strategic sense Sole Bay was a Dutch victory because the allied fleet was prevented from harming the United Provinces during the critical days of the French invasion. By the time the allied fleet was again ready for sea, the opportunity for using it decisively in 1672 had passed.

*   *   *

As soon as news of the battle reached London, Rupert set to work to restore and resupply the fleet. On 29 May he sent orders to Harwich that all disabled ships were to be repaired in the Thames. Next day he ordered twelve more fireships to be fitted out and thirty new ships' boats to be provided. On the same day he ordered 300 loads of timber to be sent to Sheerness. Topmasts were to be prepared for each rate of ship, Chatham Dockyard to provide masts. All available hemp and tar were to be bought up. Hayes ordered the Navy Board to meet Rupert on the following day to report how these orders were being carried out. On 31 May Rupert sent orders to fill up the vic-tualling stores at Portsmouth.

On 6 June the allied fleet arrived at the Buoy of the Nore and for the next three weeks Rupert spared no efforts to get it ready for sea. During this time he was ordered by the King to dispatch small squadrons to Tangier and Barbados. Soon afterwards, Sandwich's decomposed body was found floating in the sea off Harwich, identified by the star of the garter still pinned to his coat. Rupert's sloop, the *Fan Fan*, brought the body to Deptford from where, in due course, it was taken in a procession of barges to Westminster for burial in the Abbey.

While the battle of Sole Bay was being fought, Louis was investing the frontier forts on the Rhine. Within a matter of days Rheinberg, Orsoy, Wesel and Emmerich were in his hands and he was pushing down the right, or north, bank of the river. At the junction with the Waal he stayed with the Rhine, but before arriving at the junction with the Yssel he crossed the river and by 6 June was established between the Rhine and the Waal. William, meanwhile, was to the north manning positions behind the Yssel.

There was nothing for the Dutch army to do but to retreat as fast as possible, which William did, leaving sizeable detach-ments in fortresses such as Arnheim. Fortunately for him, Louis wasted time occupying various towns that he had conquered, which enabled William to retreat to Utrecht. At first the Dutch intended to hold Utrecht, but owing to the contradictory views expressed by the town and provincial authorities it was aban-doned. William then split the remains of his army between five fortresses which covered the approaches to Holland from

Muyden outside Amsterdam in the north to Gorinchem on the Waal in the south. With the exception of some major fortresses such as Maastricht and Nijmegen and some outlying areas not worth occupying, Louis or his allies were now in control of all the United Provinces except for Holland and Zealand. Furthermore, few Dutch soldiers stood between Louis's vast victorious army and the remaining two provinces. Louis thought that he had won a famous victory.

But then, between the fifteenth and twentieth of June, the Dutch, arguing and even fighting each other on occasions, opened the sluices and breached the dykes. Water flooded in, submerging the livelihood of thousands, and Holland was surrounded by a moat many miles across and up to four feet deep. William with his army guarded the crossing-points.

A few days before the first sluices were opened, John de Witt was wounded in an assassination attempt and on 24 June William was given the full powers of the Stadtholder and made Captain General for life. At the end of the month a French detachment from the Spanish Netherlands attacked Aardenburg in the extreme south of Zealand but was driven off. On 27 June the allied fleet was again ready for sea.

Nine days earlier the King had visited the ships at the Nore to discuss with the Duke of York and the flag officers the best way to use the fleet in the light of the overall situation. Some, including the Duke, were in favour of sailing to the Zealand coast in an attempt to force de Ruyter into giving battle, but the King was persuaded that more harm would be done to the Dutch by intercepting the East India ships that would be trying to return to Amsterdam in the near future. In coming to this conclusion he may have been influenced by the fact that the Dutch had sent out peace feelers and that Arlington and Buckingham were about to visit The Hague before going on to meet King Louis near Utrecht.

The fleet was at sea from 27 June to 6 August, when it returned to Bridlington Bay to replenish. Although two of its scouts met up with the East Indiamen on 22 July, the fleet itself was too far off and the Dutch ships got past into the Ems Estuary. From Bridlington Bay the allies made their way slowly back to the Nore, where they arrived on 23 August. Meanwhile, de Ruyter had collected the East India ships from the Ems

Estuary, delivered them to the Texel and returned to his anchorage off Zealand.

On 10 August John de Witt and his brother Cornelis were murdered by a furious mob in The Hague. William, with a new Grand Pensionary who was one of his own supporters, then turned down King Louis's humiliating peace demands offered in place of the reasonable proposals already put forward by the Dutch. Safe for the time being behind his flooded fields, William set out to build up his army and develop the alliances that would eventually save his country from the invader.

If King Louis was now held in check, the same could be said for King Charles. Even if de Ruyter could be brought to battle and destroyed, the English had no army large enough to fight the Dutch which could be landed from the sea. In any case it would soon be too late in the year to embark on such an operation.

Throughout August Rupert had been busy providing for the fleet and organising convoys to protect merchant ships from Hamburg and colliers from Newcastle which were being harassed by enemy privateers. He was also involved with Deane, the commissioner at Portsmouth, who was trying out Rupert's idea of building a wooden frame around a warship, designed to reduce the kinetic energy of cannon-balls before they hit the hull. In a sense it was the precursor of the torpedo net and the torpedo bulge fitted to battleships in the First World War. Rupert felt that it would be particularly valuable for guard-ships.

At the end of August and again in early September Rupert accompanied the King on visits to the fleet at which operations for 1673 were discussed. The main contribution was to be the landing of a sizeable force in Zealand once the Dutch fleet was defeated. This meant that the small regular army would need to be built up, and it was decided that three extra regiments of foot should be raised at once and that the remnants of a regiment of dragoons which had returned from Barbados five years earlier should be brought up to strength; six more regiments of foot were to be raised in 1673. All of this was in addition to eight regiments raised between 1671 and 1673 for service with the French army.[3] The Duke of York was given a commission as generalissimo of all forces engaged in the Zealand expedition and Rupert was made general under the Duke.

On 15 August Rupert had also been made Vice-Admiral of

England in place of Sandwich at a salary of £365 per annum, and on 29 August he was given a commission as colonel of a maritime regiment designed to sail with the fleet as opposed to following on in transports. From correspondence regarding the selection of officers for the dragoons, it appears that he had been colonel of this regiment since early June, if not before. When he inspected the regiment in late October it was already 800 strong, that is to say only about 200 under strength.

Another subject raised at the council of war held in early September was the possibility of the Duke of York taking the fleet to the Dutch coast, before it was laid up for the winter, to try to bring de Ruyter to battle. A successful engagement at this time when the Dutch were in so perilous a position would encourage them to accept the peace proposals put forward by Charles and Louis. The King, backed by Rupert and Shaftesbury, was in favour, but the Duke of York and the flag officers disagreed on the grounds that it was too late in the year. The proposal was dropped, and on 19 September the Duke of York returned from the fleet and took back the direction of affairs in London. Soon afterwards the French squadron returned to France.

The next problem to be faced by the King was financial. For a number of reasons the position was not as critical as usual and the King had enough money to pay off the fleet for the winter. Having done so, he would still have about half what he needed to set it out again in 1673. If, by some miracle, Louis managed to bring the war to an end within the next few months, King Charles would be able to avoid calling Parliament, but if the fleet were needed in 1673 Parliament would have to vote the money in November for it to be raised in time. The problem about calling Parliament was that members were bound to demand that the King withdraw the Declaration of Indulgence before voting the money. When the matter came before the council those who would have to handle Parliament – notably Arlington, Clifford, Shaftesbury and Lauderdale – recommended that the King should take a chance and postpone calling it, whereas Rupert, who would be intimately concerned with setting out the fleet, wanted it recalled and in this he was backed by Ormonde. The King took the gamble and postponed the recall of Parliament until February.[5]

In November the King got rid of the Lord Keeper and promoted Shaftesbury to the post of Lord Chancellor. At the same time the post of Lord Treasurer was restored and given to Clifford, while Duncombe, a former Treasury commissioner, replaced Shaftesbury at the Exchequer. Arlington remained Secretary of State, the second one being Henry Coventry, who had taken over in the summer on the death of Trevor. He was a brother of Sir William Coventry, who had been deprived of all his offices in 1668 ostensibly for challenging Buckingham to a duel.

During the winter, peace negotiations with the Dutch continued but no agreement was reached. At one moment when the floods in the United Provinces froze over, it looked as though the French would be able to mount a successful attack in the area of Amsterdam, but just as the attack was about to be launched an unseasonable thaw made the waters impassable once more. Early in February Parliament reassembled.

When it did so, events followed the course predicted. There was no shortage of enthusiasm for the war, but the House of Commons insisted that the King should renounce the right to suspend laws designed to weaken the influence of Roman Catholics and Dissenters. There would be no money for the war unless he did so. Shaftesbury, Clifford and Lauderdale, backed by the Duke of York, insisted that, as a matter of principle, the King's right to legislate on religious matters must be upheld, even at the expense of the war, but Rupert, Arlington, Ormonde and Henry Coventry argued that the war must come first. This time the King, encouraged by Louis, backed the war. He revoked the Declaration of Indulgence with apparent enthusiasm and ordered the expulsion of Roman Catholic priests. He even approved the passing of a Test Act which obliged all those holding public office to take the sacrament according to the usage of the Church of England. In return he got a grant of £1,250,000.

At some stage during the winter the King decided that the Duke of York should not command the fleet in 1673, mainly because of the risk to his life. Rupert naturally supposed that if the Duke was not to command, he would do so as being the only person of the necessary standing with previous experience of commanding a fleet, and this is certainly what the King intended. But

Spragge, who had held a number of responsible posts between the wars and who had taken a squadron to sea for a short time after the Duke had left the fleet in the previous September, may have felt that he had a chance, especially as he knew of Rupert's unpopularity with the French. In February, without telling Rupert, the King sent Spragge, together with the Earl of Sunderland, on a mission to the French court to settle arrangements for the coming year. They were warmly received by King Louis and were back in England by 6 March, but Rupert was upset that the King should have sent Spragge without letting him know.

It is not known when Rupert's appointment was announced, but as early as 2 March Louis wrote to d'Estrées to say that Rupert would get the fleet and on 19 March he told him that Rupert was already in command. By 7 March the fact was taken for granted in England, and arrangements were being made to fit out the *Swan* to attend Rupert's flagship and carry the extra provisions and stores that the flagship would need. Spragge was nominated as admiral of the Blue. Rupert was keen to have Sir Robert Holmes as one of his vice-admirals, but his wishes were disregarded on the grounds that Holmes and Spragge did not get on with each other and had failed to cooperate over the attack on the Smyrna convoy the previous year. The fact that Holmes was considered to have mishandled that affair and that he had caused trouble after the campaign of 1666 must also have weighed with the King and the Duke of York. Unfortunately, the fact that Spragge was the reason for Holmes not being allowed in the fleet and that he had been sent to France without Rupert's knowledge produced a coolness between Rupert and Spragge which was not helped by Spragge's own disappointment at not getting the command.

In due course Rupert received a commission from King Louis to command the French squadron, and on 17 April he wrote warmly to d'Estrées saying that he was sure that they would work together in perfect harmony and trust. But it seems that Rupert had trouble getting his commission from King Charles, because as late as the end of April he was writing to Arlington saying that he had not yet received it. He added: 'In the meantime I could send many sad complaints of our disorder and wants ... but according to my wonted practice I shall very patiently desist.' It would be interesting to know how Arlington took this reference to Rupert's patience: he could have hardly forgotten how, in 1668, Rupert had struck him during a row over the deferment of pay due to his captains, knocking off his hat and wig in the process.

During the period when Rupert was getting the fleet ready for sea there were two major problems. In the previous year there had been plenty of money, so few insurmountable difficulties had presented themselves in terms of victuals and supplies. The big problem then had been getting enough seamen, even though the press had been at work since November 1671. In 1673 the press only started to operate in March, and the position over manpower, aggravated by the recruiting of the new regiments, was critical. The provision of pilots was another cause of complaint. Furthermore, money was extremely tight because the supply voted in March had not come in. Letter after letter testifies to the obstacles that the Navy Board were having to overcome in order to buy what was necessary with particular relation to victuals, while the pursers of some of the ships were notifying the board that they could not make ends meet unless they were sent the money due to them.

Rupert went aboard the *St Michael* on 23 April. The new *Royal Charles* was to be his flagship but was still at Portsmouth, together with a number of other ships. The *St Michael* was designated as the flagship of Narborough, who was to be the rear-admiral of the Blue, but he had not yet returned from the Strait of Gibraltar. The other flag officers were Harman, vice-admiral of the Red with his flag in the *London*, and Kempthorne, vice-admiral of the Blue with his flag in the *St Andrew*. The rear-admiral of the Red was John Chichely.

Although the flag officers were chosen by the King and the Duke of York, Rupert's wishes were clearly considered. Harman was a fine seaman and a good fighter whom Rupert would have been happy to have had it not been for the fact that he was very ill and so crippled by gout that he could hardly leave his cabin: he died soon after the end of the campaign. Kempthorne, Rupert's former flag captain, was someone he knew and trusted. Narborough, a seaman from his youth, had been promoted by Rupert and Albemarle to captain immediately after the four days' fight: in the event he did not get back in time to become rear-admiral of the Blue. The Earl of Ossory, son of the Duke of Ormonde, became rear-admiral of the Blue in his place. He was a good commander but his seagoing experience was limited. Chichely, a relatively young man of thirty-seven from a good family, had commanded ships in 1665 and 1666 and at the battle of Sole Bay. The weakness of the team was Harman's condition and the inexperience of Ossory and Chichely, but, when after the first two battles Rupert was empowered to make his own appointments within the fleet, he made no changes among the flag officers. He was still not permitted to bring in Holmes from outside.

Rupert had particularly asked for Haddock, who had been captain of Sandwich's flagship at Sole Bay, to be first captain of the *Royal Charles*; at the end of April Haddock was at Portsmouth, having taken over the ship from the builders. With him were five more ships of the line which had wintered in Portsmouth together with a number of small ships, all of which were destined to join the fleet.

The original plan had been for the fleet to join the French off the Isle of Wight, but, as the main body of the French did not leave Brest for their rendezvous with other French ships in Camaret Bay until 24 April, it was unlikely that they would get to the Isle of Wight before de Ruyter put to sea. De Ruyter himself was straining every nerve to start the campaign before the English were ready, with a view to bottling them up in the Thames. His plan was to block the Swin, the main exit from the river, by sinking ships full of rocks there and then to deal with the French squadron and the ships collected at Portsmouth before the English fleet could intervene.

By 30 April de Ruyter had collected a total of eighty ships in the Schooneveld Channel off Flushing, of which about half were ships of the line organised in two squadrons. On 2 May he was in the King's Channel between the Swin and the Gunfleet, and he detached some frigates and fireships to escort the ships he was intending to sink in the Swin. But at the critical moment a thick fog descended and the detachment got held up among the shoals. Rupert was fully aware of the danger and wanted to sail for the Downs on 30 April, but with the wind coming from the north-east he could not get out. On 2 May the wind changed to north-north-west and Rupert got his two squadrons into the Swin, although much to his annoyance he was obliged to leave four of his best ships behind because they were still not ready to sail. Next day these squadrons moved further forward, and on 4 May Rupert pushed some light vessels covered by a few fourth-rate ships ahead of the main body. On that day the Dutch, who could not afford to become involved in a full-

scale battle among the shoals, withdrew back to the Schooneveld where they awaited the arrival of the remainder of their
ships.

Two days later, in a remarkable display of seamanship and
in contravention of Trinity House standing instructions, Rupert
sent ketches forward to mark the shoals and then took the
whole fleet through the narrows on an ebb tide. Spragge greatly
admired this manoeuvre, stating that it had never before been
done by the King's ships. By 10 May Rupert was anchored off
Dungeness, where he intended to wait for the French.

On 11 May Haddock arrived in the *Royal Charles* with the
other ships from Portsmouth; two days later Rupert moved
into the *Royal Charles*. The French squadron arrived on the
sixteenth, but d'Estrées was still short of his second-in-
command, Martel, who failed to reach the fleet in time for the
first two engagements. Rupert's fleet now consisted of seventy-
two ships of the line, that is to say of the first four rates: no
ships of the fifth rate were now in the line. By the time de
Ruyter's fleet was assembled, it consisted of sixty-two ships of
the line.

At the start of the 1672 campaign the Duke of York had issued
a new set of Fighting Instructions containing twenty-six articles.
With a bit of reordering these consisted of the articles issued
by him on 10 April and 18 April 1665 before the battle off
Lowestoft, plus the three issued by Rupert and Albemarle
between the four days' fight and the St James's Day fight. Rupert
was satisfied that the 1672 edition contained all that was necessary for the conduct of the coming campaign and made no
further amendment or addition. He had, however, sent what
he described as a book of instructions and a scroll to the French,
so that they could translate them before joining the fleet. He
was evidently anxious that there should be no misunderstanding
such as occurred at the start of the battle of Sole Bay. Possibly
for the same reason he had decided to alter the usual position
of the three squadrons by changing the Red and the White
around. Thus, the Red would lead; the White (French) would
be in the centre and the Blue in the rear. He notified the French
of these arrangements when he sent the book of instructions.

On the same evening that d'Estrées's ships joined Prince
Rupert, the King and the Duke of York came out from Rye in

their yachts and stayed with Rupert for about one and a half hours. Next day they returned and a council of war was held aboard the *Royal Charles*. The main issue was whether to attack de Ruyter if he stayed within the anchorage of the Schooneveld, since with inferior strength and in the light of the general state of the war it was unlikely that he could be induced to give battle in the open sea. An inshore battle would be hazardous in the extreme because the Schooneveld Channel was surrounded by shoals that were inadequately charted and which would be better known to the Dutch than to the English. When the possibility of making such an attack was discussed in September 1672, it had been discounted on the grounds that it was too late in the year; nor was there an army to land if the battle was won. Now the situation was different. Troops had been raised but could not be landed while de Ruyter's fleet lay unharmed in the anchorage. Despite the risk it was determined that the attempt should be made. It was also decided that to prevent de Ruyter escaping into Flushing as the English approached, a detachment of lighter vessels and fireships which could pursue him through the shallows should move ahead of the main fleet to hold him until the main fleet could bring him to battle.

Next day, 18 May, the King had dinner with d'Estrées and then moved to the *Royal Charles* for supper before returning to Rye. During the King's visit Rupert had again tackled him about Holmes but without success. All he got was an undertaking that Holmes would be made governor of Cork. In a letter to Sir R. Carr, who was looking after Arlington's business while he was away for a few days, Rupert told him of this appointment and also asked that the *Royal Sovereign* and the other ships waiting in the river for men should be hastened out to Dungeness.

For the next few days contrary winds prevailed, but on 22 May the fleet anchored in the afternoon about fifteen miles north-west of Ostend. Scouts reported that on its arrival the Dutch fleet, which had been anchored in the Schooneveld about twenty-five miles to the north-east, weighed anchor and edged down towards the mouth of the Weilings, that is to say the channel leading into Flushing. By this time three of the four ships that Rupert had been obliged to leave behind in the Thames, including the massive *Sovereign*, had rejoined the fleet, and it was determined that the attack should take place on 24 May.

But a south-westerly gale blew up, and it was not until 27 May that the lighter ships forming the advanced guard could be separated out from their squadrons and moved into position. By this time the allies had closed up towards the Dutch so that the two fleets were no more than twelve miles apart.

At this point it is necessary to try to describe the intricate combination of deep water and shoals over which the ensuing two battles were fought. The coast between Ostend and the mouth of the southern branch of the Schelde Estuary runs from south-east by east to north-west by west. Immediately across the mouth of this estuary, on the island of Walcheren, lies Flushing. Out from the coast from Ostend and parallel to it all the way up to and beyond the island of Walcheren lies an area of very shallow water between three and four fathoms deep which varies in width from around four and a half miles opposite Ostend to thirteen miles off Flushing. Further out to sea adjoining it is a shelf from six to eight fathoms deep known as the Schooneveld Bank or Anchorage. This belt is about four miles across in the south-west, getting narrower towards the north-east. Beyond this bank the water becomes much deeper, but this deeper water is peppered by a number of shoals running parallel to the shore, some being very long and thin whereas others are much smaller. The depth of water over these shoals also varies considerably, some being as deep as the Schooneveld Bank but a few being much shallower. Extending almost due west from Flushing is the Weilings Channel, which connects the port with the Schooneveld Bank and which is therefore the entrance to the southern branch of the Schelde Estuary.

Clearly the direction of the wind and the state of the tide would greatly affect the way in which a battle in such a place was fought. By the evening of 27 May the fleets were deployed in two lines, each stretching roughly north and south, the allies being to the south-west of the Dutch. In the allied fleet the Red Squadron was on the north or seaward side, the French in the middle and the Blue Squadron to the south, lying some of the way across the Schooneveld Bank. In the Dutch fleet Tromp's squadron was in the north, de Ruyter in the centre and Banckert in the south, lying right across the Schooneveld Bank about four miles north-east of the mouth of the Weilings Channel.

At around 10 a.m. on the morning of 28 May, with the wind at north-west, the allied fleet set off towards the Dutch, the detachments of light ships leading. Each squadron's detachment

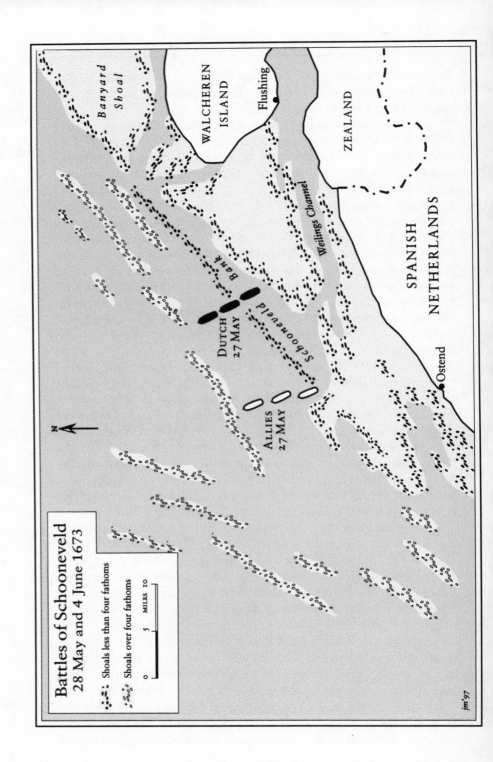

Battles of Schooneveld
28 May and 4 June 1673

Shoals less than four fathoms

Shoals over four fathoms

0   5   MILES   10

Banyard Shoal

WALCHEREN ISLAND

Flushing

ZEALAND

Weilings Channel

SPANISH NETHERLANDS

Ostend

DUTCH 27 MAY

Bank

Schooneveld

ALLIES 27 MAY

N

jm '97

was commanded by its senior captain and it is possible that Captain Wetwang of the *Henry* had some coordinating function for the three of them. Their purpose was to prevent the Dutch from withdrawing into the Weilings, but soon it became apparent that they intended to stay and fight so the detached ships fell back on the main allied line. In doing so they caused some confusion, as the three detachments were concentrated towards the north and could not easily return to their parent squadrons.

As the allies approached, the Dutch turned into line on the port tack, that is to say they headed out to sea on a course of north-east by north. As the allies came up with them they, too, turned into line on the port tack so that the Red Squadron should have been opposite Tromp, the French opposite de Ruyter and the Blue opposite Banckert. But because the Red and Blue were sailing better than the French, the squadrons did not exactly hit off their opposite numbers. In the north Tromp, who was already engaged with the bulk of the retreating light detachments, found himself engaged by the whole of the Red Squadron and was therefore considerably outnumbered. In the south Banckert found himself opposed not only by the Blue Squadron but also by the rear division of the French squadron. Action was joined in the north at 1 p.m. and in the south around an hour later.

As Rupert turned into line he could see ahead of him Harman's division closing up on the Dutch van. Harman in the *London* was soon exchanging fire with Tromp's vice-admiral Schram in the *Pacificate*. Within a short time Schram was killed.

Rupert himself closed with Tromp in the *Gouden Leeuw*, a ship of eighty-two guns. Ahead of him was George Legge in the *Royal Katherine*; astern was Reeves in the *Edgar*. Soon after the action was joined, Colonel Hamilton, who was standing with Rupert, was hit. As he fell, some seamen standing nearby mistakenly thought that it was Rupert who was down and the cry went up that the Prince was slain. Hamilton, the elder brother of Anthony Hamilton, who had written the rather unflattering description of Rupert at Tunbridge Wells, died a few days later from his wound, but Rupert was unscathed.

From the start of the battle Rupert was concerned by the fact that the *Royal Charles* was hopelessly unmanoeuvrable, heeling over so far in the wind that the lower-deck guns to windward were unusable. This put her at a disadvantage compared with the *Gouden Leeuw*, but luckily the *Conquérant*, a French ship that had been with the advanced detachment, gallantly engaged Tromp and so disabled his ship that he had to move into the *Prins te Paard*.

Subsequent events are hard to follow. At about 3 p.m. de Ruyter, taking advantage of the fact that he was not heavily engaged, tacked and headed off south-south-east in an attempt to get to windward of the Blue Squadron and in doing so broke through d'Estrées line, thereby getting to windward of his last few ships. D'Estrées, with the rest of his squadron, tacked at this time, thereby remaining to windward of de Ruyter, whom he followed south-south-east. When Spragge saw what had happened he, too, tacked, as did Banckert, and they headed south by east, Spragge remaining to windward of Banckert. Not long afterwards Spragge tacked again to the north in an attempt to make contact with Rupert, and in doing so had to sail first past Banckert and then past de Ruyter, both of whom were still heading roughly south by east.

Some time earlier Rupert, realising that de Ruyter and the French were not following him, had put about and was therefore heading back towards Spragge, followed by Tromp. As soon as he saw Spragge's ships he tacked again in an attempt to draw the Dutch out into deep water. Soon afterwards Spragge came up on the leeward side of Tromp's squadron, Rupert still being to windward of it. Thus, at the north end of the line Tromp was sandwiched between Rupert and Spragge, all three sailing north by west. In fact, they must have been sailing or drifting further to the east than most accounts indicate, as Legge describes in his journal that at one point he came within half a cable's length of the Banjard Sands, which lie due north of Walcheren, something like fifteen miles east of where the Dutch fleet lay at the start of the battle. While Tromp was engaged in this way he was twice more obliged to move his flag when the ships he was in were dismasted. Meanwhile, de Ruyter and Banckert followed along behind, with most of the French to windward of them. It was by now around 6 p.m.

Soon, de Ruyter caught up with the leading squadrons and when he did so he tacked to the south-west, followed by Tromp and the English. Shortly after, the whole battle was moving once more in this direction. And so it continued until it started to get dark. By this time the Dutch were not far from the place where they had started the battle, and here they anchored. The allies stayed under sail for some time and anchored early the next morning about twelve miles to the west of the Dutch, that is to say a bit to the west of where they had started and probably rather further out to sea.

During the battle no major ships were lost by the allies or the Dutch, although each side had to send three back to port for repair. Losses of men were also comparatively light, possibly of the order of 200 to 300 on each side, excluding those killed when a Dutch ship trying to get into port foundered. Only in terms of senior officers were losses significant. The Dutch lost two flag officers and four captains, the English three captains and the French one, the captain of the *Conquérant* who had come to Rupert's assistance early in the battle. These figures exclude commanders of fireships. But at the end of the day the allies had not destroyed de Ruyter's fleet nor had they bottled it up in port, so that no strategic advantage had been gained. A further battle would be needed before any troops could be landed.

Rupert was clearly disappointed that more had not been achieved in what came to be known as the first battle of Schooneveld. He certainly had the advantage of numbers to the tune of seventy-six ships of the line compared with fifty-two of the Dutch, but against that he was obliged to fight in a confined area of shoals with inadequate charts. The fact that the French had little experience of fighting a fleet action and none of operating in shoals was also a disadvantage, although for the most part they fought well. Rupert has been accused of undue caution, but only a bold commander would have attacked at all under such conditions. Several French and English commanders later testified that they were more frightened of the shoals than the enemy.

The detachment of light ships, which could have played an important part in the battle if the Dutch had tried to withdraw, turned out to be a liability when de Ruyter stood his ground. Another difficulty resulted from Rupert's being with the leading squadron, which made it more difficult than usual for him to control the battle, but this was the inevitable consequence of avoiding a misunderstanding with the French.

As usual, Rupert blamed nobody. In his official dispatch to Arlington after the battle he stated that Count d'Estrées and the French behaved very bravely. He was also lavish in his praise of Spragge, whom he described as 'maintaining the fight with so much courage and resolution that had it not been for fear of the shoals we had driven them into their harbours and the King would have a better account of them'. But Spragge recorded in his journal that the battle was badly fought by the English and the French, and he referred to the ill conduct and notorious cowardice of many who took part. In a personal letter to the King Rupert goes some way towards supporting this assessment, saying that if the French fireships had more skill and the English more bravery, both the Dutch flagships would have been burned. For the rest there may have been occasions when ships failed to close up to the enemy despite having the wind, but the Dutch, whose interest was to avoid damage and casualties, had the advantage of knowing the shoals better and were therefore more capable of taking advantage of them.[6]

During the six days that followed the battle the fleet lay at anchor trying to repair the damage and bewailing the shortages with which it had started the campaign. Rupert is reported as saying that the ships were in so great want of men that captains came to him with tears in their eyes to tell him how few seamen they had aboard. They complained that when they wanted to mend their sails they found themselves in want of needles and thread and in addition there were almost no spare topmasts. The boatswain of Spragge's flagship told Rupert that he had no small stores but what he had stolen from the dockyards, that is to say what he had persuaded friends to give him. Rupert's view was that the fleet was 'merely whoddled out and maintained by fortune'.

On 1 June the allied fleet redeployed within its existing anchorage so that the Red Squadron was to the south nearest the shore, the French in the middle and the Blue to the north out to sea. Also, the divisions anchored in a series of nine parallel lines, each running north-west to south-east with its divisional flagship in the centre. The intention was that each of the divisions would be just under half a mile from its neighbour, but it appears that in taking up their positions they became more dispersed so that instead of being spread over around four miles from north to south they covered almost twice that distance.

Rupert, who was dissatisfied with the sailing qualities of the *Royal Charles*, decided to take the *Royal Sovereign* as his flagship, contrary to Haddock's advice. The move was made on 3

June, Rupert bringing with him both his captains and 250 men from the *Royal Charles*. During the evening of 3 June, while the move was still in progress, the wind changed into the north-east. Rupert was alert immediately in case de Ruyter should take advantage of this fact to close up to the allies during the night and remained up and fully dressed throughout the hours of darkness.

Next morning Spragge, who had evidently felt no concern at the change in the direction of the wind, set off in a ship's boat to visit Rupert; some say that he was accompanied by Ossory. At 11 a.m. the Dutch fleet, which was ten miles to the east, weighed anchor and set off towards the allies on the starboard tack, a fact that could be observed from Rupert's flagship. Whether Spragge could see it from his boat is uncertain, but at any rate he did not return to his squadron which, with a north-east wind, would clearly have to take the lead. It was noon by the time he met Rupert, whose topsail was loose, the signal that the enemy were approaching. Rupert wasted no time in telling Spragge to return to his squadron and lead the fleet out to sea, something that he could hardly do in less than two hours.

After a short time Rupert became worried that the Dutch would reach his fleet before it was under way, and he decided that the Red Squadron would have to sail through the French and take the lead. This he proceeded to do, but he was unsuccessful in explaining the situation to d'Estrées, as a result of which the Red and White Squadrons became intermingled. In the event Spragge reached his flagship in time and the Blue Squadron set off in the lead on a course of north-north-west close-hauled on the starboard tack, the other two squadrons following.

Firing started at about 4 p.m. when Tromp's squadron, which led the Dutch line, came in range of the Blue Squadron. The other two squadrons came into action at around 5 p.m. but, although de Ruyter originally looked as if he would come to close quarters with Rupert, he backed off and thereafter all three of the Dutch squadrons contented themselves with firing at a great distance in an attempt to preserve their fleet while causing the allies to use up their ammunition to little purpose.

And so the battle continued throughout the evening and the early part of the night. At some stage, probably at around midnight, de Ruyter tacked and made for home, although some of Tromp's squadron lost touch and continued on the original course for an hour or more. Sunrise was at 3.45 a.m. and soon afterwards the allies tacked, but it quickly became apparent that the Dutch were too far ahead to be overtaken. Rupert called a council of war at 5 a.m. at which time the allies were about thirty miles off Sole Bay, very short of powder and shot and with a number of damaged ships. It was therefore decided to bring the fleet back to the Nore for repair and replenishment.

This engagement, known as the second battle of Schooneveld, was little more than a skirmish. No ships were lost on either side; casualties are not recorded but are thought to have been light. Spragge afterwards maintained that, had Rupert tacked earlier and turned on de Ruyter and Banckert while he kept Tromp engaged, a victory would have been achieved. The difficulty about this is that such a manoeuvre would not have been successful until both fleets were well clear of the shoals, by which time it was getting dark. In a letter to Louis XIV, d'Estrées criticized Spragge for leaving his squadron to visit Rupert in the morning, thus delaying his squadron's move and causing Rupert to lead off through the White Squadron. He further criticised Spragge for crowding on sail when he did get back, despite seeing that the Red was trying to take the lead, as a result of which the whole fleet was thrown into confusion at the start. In the same letter he quotes Rupert as telling him that Spragge should have tacked and divided the Dutch fleet, but that he was so taken up with his personal duel with Tromp that he did not want to do so. As the Blue Squadron was leading and therefore furthest from the shoals, it was undoubtedly best placed to carry out this manoeuvre.

Confirmation of Spragge's obsession with Tromp is provided by Sir Charles Littleton, who was at sea with Spragge at this time. He states that Spragge used to drink Tromp's health at each meal until the second battle, after which he stopped because he considered that Tromp had not fought with sufficient bravery.[7]

The allied fleet spent the next night at anchor in the Gunfleet before returning to the Nore. Rupert cannot have been particularly happy at this time. From his point of view matters had gone consistently wrong from the start. The fleet had been short of seamen, because the press had not started early enough, and was poorly equipped because of a shortage of money which was the result of Parliament not being called in 1672. Rupert's commission, which had not been signed until 26 April, did not give him the power he needed to appoint officers. When he finally got to sea he had been obliged to fight the Dutch in circumstances that prevented him from making use of his superiority in ships, and although the fleet had acquitted itself well in the first battle it had not been able to achieve its strategic purpose. When he got a second chance, confusion had been caused by his attempt to rectify Spragge's original misjudgement in leaving his squadron, followed by failure to take advantage of the Dutch leaving the shelter of their shoals, so that once more the strategic aim was not achieved. Although he was not to blame for most of these shortcomings, Rupert knew that what mattered was success, not the reasons for failing to deliver it.

On the credit side Rupert and d'Estrées were still on speaking terms despite fears that his dislike of French policies would make it difficult for him to work with the French squadron. Rupert had not openly complained about its performance, nor had d'Estrées criticised Rupert, even in his letters to the French authorities. Indeed, King Louis wrote to Rupert while the fleet was in the Thames 'to testify to the gratitude I owe you for the manner in which you have used the Comte d'Estrées and those in his charge'. In view of what was to follow, this is worth recording.

The King was keenly aware of the fact that Rupert would be in a bad temper when he reached the Nore, the more so as there would be delays in providing the equipment needed to refit and resupply the fleet. He said jokingly that he must expect a chiding when he met his cousin and that he would do his best to sweeten him up beforehand. On 12 June the King visited the ships at the Nore and the next day went on to see those at Sheerness. Although Rupert was polite to the King, it was said that he was furious with certain members of the Navy Board even to the extent of threatening them with his cane.[8]

At this time important events were taking place which would affect the future direction of the war. For 1673 the French had divided their army into three. The first part, under Condé, was to the north of the United Provinces, the second, under Turenne, was operating against Imperial forces in Alsace and the third and largest part, under the King himself, was besieging Maastricht. When on 22 June much of the outer defences of

Maastricht were breached, Louis moved to join his forces in Alsace, assuring Charles that French troops would support any landing that the English might make in Zealand. In fact, he had ordered his general in the Netherlands to stand fast and leave the English to face the full force of the Dutch as he had no desire for them to gain possession of territory there.[9] But regardless of allied military operations, Louis was still hoping for peace by negotiation, and a congress sat at Cologne where Dutch delegates negotiated with representatives of France, England, Sweden, Münster and Cologne.

All of this was highly relevant to Rupert's task, but of more immediate importance was the resignation on 15 June of the Duke of York from the posts of Lord High Admiral and generalissimo of the expedition against Zealand. This resulted from his refusal to take the sacrament according to the usage of the Church of England, as required by the Test Act. The Duke was followed a few days later by Clifford, who resigned as Lord Treasurer for the same reason.

In order to take part in discussions on these important matters, Rupert left the fleet on 14 June to spend a week in London. On 16 June he was issued with a new commission that supplemented the one of 26 April and gave him power to appoint and discharge officers in the fleet as necessary. This removed one of his major grievances.

The replacement of the Lord High Admiral was more complicated. Rupert would probably have liked to be appointed in his place but the King decided to put the office into commission, Rupert being made the first commissioner. The others were the two Secretaries of State, the new Lord Treasurer Sir Thomas Osborne, soon to be made Lord Danby, his replacement as joint Treasurer of the Navy Board, Edward Seymour (who was also Speaker of the House of Commons), Ormonde, Buckingham, Lauderdale, Monmouth, Anglesey and Carteret. Samuel Pepys was moved from the Navy Board to become the Secretary of the Admiralty.

But the new commissioners were not to have the full powers of the Lord High Admiral: the King reserved to himself the appointment of commissioned officers, together with the formulation of major policy. In effect he made himself his own Lord High Admiral and over the coming years handled much business directly with the Secretary of the Admiralty in the same way as his brother had formerly done with his secretary. By doing this the Duke of York was able to retain a lot of his influence, acting as the King's unofficial adviser. Although the first meeting of the new commission did not take place until 9 July, the arrangements were worked out by the time that Rupert returned to the fleet on 21 June.

Soon after his return, the two English squadrons started to assemble at the Buoy of the Nore. Manpower shortages had been largely made up by taking crews from Narborough's ships that had returned from the Mediterranean and by a draconian press. By this time the Marquis de Martel, who became d'Estrées's second-in-command, had arrived with three more ships of the line. Only the French squadron remained in the river, complaining of sickness and manpower shortages.

On 1 July the flag captain Haddock, having forfeited Rupert's confidence during the two Schooneveld battles, left the fleet to become a Navy Board commissioner. In his place came Sir William Reeves from the *Edgar*, who was replaced in that ship by Young, formerly second captain of the *Sovereign*. This post was now given to Captain Wetwang, who had excited Rupert's admiration during the first Schooneveld battle.

It is during this period, when Rupert was again very annoyed with the victuallers, that friction between him and d'Estrées seems to have built up. In a letter to the King of 28 June he says that d'Estrées is still not out of the Swale and suggests that the King should send someone down to the fleet to sort out a thousand things necessary before the enemy can be engaged. On 4 July he sent to Arlington in his own hand a list of demands for the attention of the King. They are written in a peremptory manner and indicate a degree of exasperation which is of interest as an indication of his state of mind:

That I may have my commission as soon as may be.

That His Majesty and His Royal Highness be pleased to name the ships designed for this fleet, and that none be diverted for convoys, guard of coast etc.

That I may have power to command all the yards, victuals, stores and what shall be necessary to set out the fleet.

That I may have power from His Majesty to punish all misdemeanours according to the custom of war and the Seas.

And a power to sink, burn, destroy or take any ships, men or country in possession of the Dutch.

On 4 July Rupert received another new commission, made necessary by the resignation of the Duke of York as generalissimo, which gave him immense power over all the seamen and soldiers committed to the expedition and over the yards and stores supporting it and over any land taken from the Dutch and the population found therein.

Meanwhile, the army intended for the invasion of Zealand was assembling on Blackheath. The men would ultimately number around 10,000, but many of the regiments were untrained. The Count of Schomberg, a soldier of wide experience, was appointed to command it. Like Rupert, he was a Protestant whose father came from the Palatinate and whose mother, daughter of Lord Dudley, came from England. Fifty-seven years old, he had started in the service of the United Provinces and had later served as a company commander of a Scottish regiment in the French army. In 1661 he moved to Portugal and was soon in command of the Portuguese forces fighting the Spanish, which included the English contingent paid for by the French under the terms of the treaty arising out of King Charles's marriage negotiations. He remained in Portugal until the end of the war in 1668. As an English speaker with experience of English and Scottish troops, he was well suited to commanding the army in Rupert's expeditionary force, but on arrival in England he showed some reluctance at taking the command for fear of provoking jealousy among the English. Indeed, the Duke of Buckingham, who had no military experience but who had hoped to command the army himself, declined to serve under him.

By this time de Ruyter's fleet had been ready for sea for some days. In fact, during the last week of June it had crossed the North Sea and anchored briefly off Harwich, but three days later, with sickness rife among the crews, it returned to the mouth of the Maas. By 6 July it was anchored off Walcheren.

On this day the King came down to the fleet accompanied by the Duke of York and Schomberg, together with a number of councillors such as Arlington and the Dukes of Buckingham and Ormonde, to hold a council of war with Rupert, d'Estrées and Spragge. The main points discussed were, first, how to get de Ruyter to fight in deep water where he could be defeated and, second, whether it was safe to land the troops before de Ruyter's fleet was sufficiently damaged to ensure that it could no longer interfere.

The King returned to London on the following day and for the next nine days preparations continued for getting the fleet and the army ready for sea. Rupert was clearly worried that some doubt existed regarding the decisions taken at the council of war, particularly regarding the landing of troops. On 15 July the fleet was ready and the soldiers were embarking at Gravesend. The King and the Duke of York tried to get to the fleet to see it off but were delayed by contrary winds. They arrived on 16 July when another council of war was held, by the end of which firm decisions had been reached. The text of the resolutions passed is as follows:

Resolved that his Highness Prince Rupert do immediately, wind and weather permitting sail away with his Majesty's fleet under his command out of the river of Thames, taking with him several ships and vessels in which the land-forces with their ammunition, provision and baggage etc, are embarked.

That being at sea, his Highness do in the first place take care to send under sufficient convoy the said land-forces with their ammunition, provision, baggage etc, to Yarmouth; there to be disposed of according to such directions as his Majesty has on that behalf given to the Count de Schomberg.

That this being done, His Highness with the fleet shall sail to the coast of Flanders, and there show himself (nearer or farther off) to the enemy's fleet lying within the Schooneveld, as upon consideration had of the posture of the enemy, condition of the weather, and other circumstances, shall be by him judged most advisable. But that he do not for any consideration whatever adventure upon attacking the enemy within the Schooneveld – until upon further knowledge of the condition of the Treaty and his Majesty's other affairs he shall receive directions from his Majesty for his so doing.

That his Highness having thus shown himself to the Dutch fleet shall make the best of his way to the Texel, whither it is to be hoped the enemy will be drawn (and give the opportunity of fighting them where there is sea-room) for the preventing a descent upon their coast and securing their East India ships – now expected home – and his Highness being

[277]

arrived there, shall proceed in the further employing and disposing of the fleet as he shall from time to time judge to be the best for his Majesty's service.

CR[10]

On 17 July the fleet sailed, accompanied for some distance by the King and the Duke of York until they returned in their yacht to London. Next day, while the fleet was passing through the shoals at the mouth of the Thames, a vexatious incident occurred which caused offence to Schomberg, who was sailing in a small ship called the *Greyhound*.

In order that his position should be known to the troop transports, Schomberg ordered that one of Lord Mulgrave's company colours should be flown from the masthead, much to the surprise of the fleet. Regulations covering the use of standards and ensigns were a matter of importance because of the prestige attached to them and because they were used for signalling. Accordingly, Rupert sent a lieutenant in a boat to order the colour to be removed, but Schomberg declined to remove it and the lieutenant started back to the flagship. Rupert then fired a shot across the *Greyhound*'s bows. This had the desired effect and Rupert sent for the ship's captain, who was put in irons pending an inquiry by the judge advocate which took place on the following day. The captain's defence was that the King had ordered him to follow Schomberg's instructions and when told to hoist the colour he had done so only under protest. Rupert pardoned him but asked the King's pardon for having done so, it being an affront to the sovereign. On 19 July Schomberg and the transports moved to Yarmouth according to plan, but Schomberg held a grudge against Rupert and at the conclusion of the campaign challenged him to a duel which the King prevented.

Even without the transports it was a mighty fleet that headed off towards the coast of Zealand. According to Spragge's journal, the allies had eighty-nine men-of-war besides ships of the fifth and sixth rates, fireships, ketches, sloops, yachts and other small vessels. As before, the Red Squadron led, followed by the French, followed by the Blue. Spragge recorded that the line was so long that he could not see any signal made by the flagship. He also wrote that sailing with the admiral in the van was contrary to any custom ever used at sea before, and might prove of ill consequence. On 21 July the fleet anchored in sight of the enemy, who were away to the south-west in the Schooneveld.

Next day there was almost a battle. In accordance with the plan to draw the enemy out of the Schooneveld, Rupert set off on a course of north-north-east with the wind west-north-west, the Blue Squadron now being in the van with the White in the centre and the Red in the rear. The Dutch, who would have the weather gauge if they could come up with the English, followed. At midday, when the Dutch were closing up on the Red Squadron's weather quarter, Rupert sent word to Spragge to tack in order to get to windward of the Dutch. Unfortunately, as he did so the wind backed to the south-west and then to the south. This meant that the Dutch were able to keep to windward of Spragge. It also meant that the White Squadron and then the Red had to fall away to the north-east to avoid becoming entangled with the Blue. Seeing that the fleet was in a dangerous position, Spragge tacked again and later rejoined the rest of the fleet. A few hours later de Ruyter realised that he would not be able to engage the allies at an advantage and returned to the Schooneveld.

Dutch propagandists made much of the fact that the allies had refused battle with a greatly inferior Dutch fleet, and it must be accepted that an opportunity was lost. Again Spragge felt that more might have been achieved had the Red Squadron been where it belonged – in the middle – and this time Rupert was convinced of the advantage of deploying the fleet in the traditional manner.

After this encounter the allied fleet sailed north-east along the coast of Holland until the afternoon of 25 July, when it anchored well out to sea from the Texel. For some days the Dutch did not follow. On 27 July Rupert wrote to the King, and in more detail to Arlington, to ask whether he should send for the land forces or whether he should go after the Dutch East Indiamen now expected to be returning to port and, if so, whether he should pursue them into port. He also asked whether he should now attack the Dutch fleet in the Schooneveld if it refused to come out as, the season being well advanced, whatever was to be done needed doing soon. As if to prove his point, the weather became very wild over the next ten days so that little manoeuvring was possible.

On 2 August William of Orange visited the Dutch fleet to

brief de Ruyter on the general state of the war, in the course of which he gave his opinion that the English were close to breaking with the French. Although William had been stirring up anti-French feeling in England and although his efforts had met with some success, especially in Parliamentary circles and among the common people, his assessment was premature. At any rate a decision was made that de Ruyter should make every effort to fight the allies and drive them off the Dutch coast so as to enable the returning East Indiamen to enter port in safety. Next day, despite heavy seas, de Ruyter managed to sail up the Dutch coast and anchored fifteen miles south of the Texel, the allies being thirty miles away to the north-west of the Texel. Thereafter both fleets were immobilised by deteriorating weather.

On 9 July Rupert got answers to his request for directions. In his covering letter the King said that it was a time for caution as 'if we have no ill luck and keep masters at sea, I am confident that we shall have a good conclusion of our treaty at Cologne. And if any accident should happen to our fleet though but small, it would so puff up that party in Holland who do not desire a peace, as we should have no good conclusion of the treaty for a long time'. No clearer indication of the framework within which he wished Rupert to operate could have been given.[11]

The detailed answers to Rupert's points sent by Arlington were, first, he was not to send for the army until the enemy was worsted at sea and in any case the landing was now considered 'a less good idea'. Second, he was not to attack the Dutch in the Schooneveld. Third, in searching for the East Indiamen he was to stick to the area between the Dogger Bank and the Texel except for sending a few ships to pursue them into the Elbe if necessary. The King's concern was that Rupert should not leave the Thames and the rest of the English coast open to the enemy. As it happened, a French ship captured one of the East Indiamen on the day that these instructions arrived. On the same day Spragge came aboard the *Sovereign* to see Rupert. Before he returned to his ship, Rupert, aware of his intense desire to fight it out with Tromp, got an assurance from him that he would not allow himself to become separated from the main battle.[12]

The battle of the Texel, which took place on 11 August, is one of the most difficult to unravel and therefore to describe because, in

addition to the usual divergence of opinion among the partici-
pants as to what actually happened, the wind veered round
steadily throughout the day, so that efforts to gain and hold
the windward position involved more changes of direction than
would normally have been the case. But before describing the
battle itself it is necessary to explain the manoeuvring that took
place on 10 August as this determined the position of the two
fleets at the start of the contest.

When it got light that morning the allied fleet was about
twenty-one miles west and a bit north of the Texel. The Dutch
fleet was twelve miles west of Camperdown and therefore about
twenty miles south of the allies. The wind was from the north-
east. By sailing south-east Rupert hoped to get the allied fleet
inshore of the Dutch. This would not only give him the advantage of the wind but also prevent the Dutch taking advantage
of the shallow water near the coast. The allies were under way at
8 a.m. with the French leading, followed by the Red Squadron,
followed by the Blue. By the afternoon the fleet was still sailing
south-east while the Dutch were moving north on the opposite
tack. At 4 p.m., by which time the wind had veered round to
the east, the two fleets were passing each other with the Dutch
out to sea. The Dutch, realising that they were in danger of
being cut off from their ports, tacked and headed off to the
south, cramming on sail in the hope of passing in front of the
allies and gaining the wind. Rupert, thinking it too late to bear
down on them and start a battle, decided to keep with them
until morning.

But the French were worried that they might get too close to
the shore and run aground. Twice in the night they hove to
altogether, and it took Rupert time to get them on the move
again. As a result the Dutch got ahead of the allies and tacked,
thereby gaining the wind. As Rupert had no wish to run into
the enemy's fleet in the dark, he, too, tacked. When it got light
the following morning both fleets were sailing east-north-east,
the Dutch inshore of the allies. When the Dutch, taking advantage of their windward position, started to close, Rupert decided
to tack so that the battle could be fought well clear of the shore.
The Dutch followed suit so that both fleets, now back off the
mouth of the Texel channel, were heading just south of south-
west. The wind, which had continued to veer during the night,
was south-east by south.

At this time, as Rupert looked across the sea towards the

Dutch ships he must have felt some satisfaction despite the loss
of the wind. His whole fleet was in a good line and the wind,
blowing offshore, would help to draw the Dutch into deep
water. The French had gained considerable operational experience since the start of the campaign, and the two English squadrons were by now well drilled and accustomed to working
together. Although he would doubtless have preferred Holmes
to be commanding the Blue Squadron, he knew that Spragge
was a good seaman, a good fighter and one who had formerly
been his friend. Beside him as his flag captain was Reeves, as
gallant as Holmes and a man whom he had trained and trusted
for years. Ahead in the battleline was the *Royal Katherine*,
commanded by George Legge, son of his greatest friend and an
officer whom he had promoted into his first command at an
early age. Altogether Rupert must have started the battle full
of confidence.

In his plan for the battle de Ruyter had made a bold decision
designed to offset the fact that he had only sixty ships of the
line with which to confront the eighty-six ships of the allies. As
the Dutch fleet closed up, the forward division of Banckert's
squadron, commanded by Cornelis Evertsen, which was in the
lead, moved in on the leading French division as expected, but
Banckhert himself ignored d'Estrées division and ranged himself
against the rear French division. This meant that Banckert's
own rear division of seven ships was free to join de Ruyter's
own squadron of eighteen ships in attacking the thirty ships of
the Red Squadron.

In the rear, Tromp closed on the Blue Squadron as Spragge
had hoped. Spragge, who had dropped back when the fleet
tacked in order to let Ossory's division get in front of him and
Kempthorne's division to close on him, reversed his sails and
waited for Tromp, who was well astern of de Ruyter. In terms
of strength Spragge and Tromp were evenly matched, Spragge
having twenty-seven ships to Tromp's twenty-six, although five
of Tromp's ships were of less than forty guns. Soon, these two
squadrons, which were stationary apart from drifting downwind, were engaged in a slogging match at an ever-increasing
distance from the main body of their respective fleets, which
was contrary to the undertaking that Spragge had given Rupert
to stay close by him.

This, then, was the general shape of the battle from its start
at about 8 a.m., when Evertsen's division came within range of

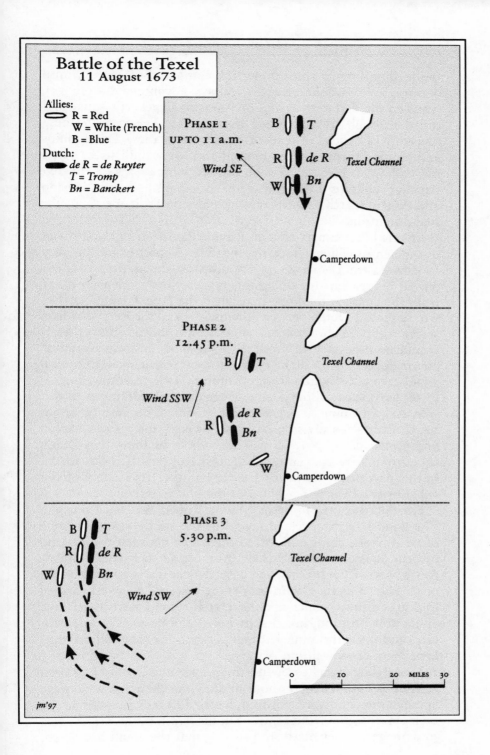

Battle of the Texel
11 August 1673

Allies:
R = Red
W = White (French)
B = Blue

Dutch:
de R = de Ruyter
T = Tromp
Bn = Banckert

PHASE 1
UP TO 11 a.m.

B   T
R   de R
W   Bn

Texel Channel

Wind SE

Camperdown

PHASE 2
12.45 p.m.

B   T

Texel Channel

Wind SSW

R   de R
     Bn

W

Camperdown

PHASE 3
5.30 p.m.

B   T
R   de R
     Bn
W

Texel Channel

Wind SW

Camperdown

0   10   20   MILES   30

jm'97

the leading French ships under the command of Martel, until about 11.30, when d'Estrées, taking advantage of the gap between the first and second divisions of Banckert's squadron, sailed through it and gained the wind of Evertsen's leading division. But then, instead of closing with these Dutch ships and pinning them between himself and Martel, d'Estrées stood off, calling on his rear division to follow him. This meant that Banckert with his division was free to join his own rear division and de Ruyter, thereby increasing pressure on Rupert and the Red Squadron.

Meanwhile, Rupert and de Ruyter had been fighting it out in the centre. Throughout the morning Rupert edged his way to leeward, that is to say in a south-west direction. No doubt one of his reasons for doing this was to draw de Ruyter away from the coast in the hope that when the French came up they would pin the Dutch between themselves and the Red Squadron so far from the shore that they could not escape. Until then it would be necessary to preserve his own ships from too close an encounter in the light of the King's recent instructions to avoid giving the Dutch an opportunity for representing English losses as a defeat in the course of the peace negotiations. If this were his reasoning, it was certainly justified, because by about 12.30 Evertsen's division had also broken away from Martel and joined de Ruyter, so that the whole of these two Dutch squadrons were concentrated against Rupert's Red Squadron. In this part of the battle, de Ruyter had therefore established a superiority of thirty-five ships of the line to thirty.

For the next one and a half hours Rupert was hard pressed. The wind had now veered round to the south-west and some of de Ruyter's ships had forced their way between Rupert and his rear division under Chichely. At this time de Ruyter's squadron was on Rupert's quarter with Banckert's squadron ahead of it. Had d'Estrées, who was some distance to windward of this mêlée, now come up, the Dutch would have been in a vulnerable position, but despite being able to see the opportunity, and notwithstanding Rupert's signal for close action, they kept themselves well out of range.

Meanwhile, away to the north Spragge and Tromp had been fighting it out. When at about midday the changing wind gave Spragge the windward position, he tried to tack in order to get even closer to the Dutch ships. But his flagship, the *Prince*, was so damaged in her masts and rigging that she could not do so.

He then tried to wear around instead, but this brought his mainmast down, so he shifted into the *St George* while Ossory's division tried to save the *Prince*. Soon afterwards, the *St George* was crippled and Spragge tried to move to the *Royal Charles*, but in doing so he was drowned. Tromp was also obliged to shift his flag but did so without losing his life. Thereafter Kempthorne, who had been wounded, and Ossory kept the Blue Squadron in action, giving as good as it got for the next three hours.

Soon after 2 p.m. Rupert, furious with the French for their lack of support and concerned for the safety of the Blue Squadron, which was by now nearly nine miles away, decided that he would have to regain contact with it. First, he edged down on his rear-admiral's division, dispersing the Dutch ships that had got between them and him. Then, with the Red Squadron reunited, he tacked and headed north towards the Blue Squadron. In doing so he crossed ahead of the two Dutch squadrons, thereby gaining their wind. As he sailed north, the two Dutch squadrons came up to leeward intent on joining Tromp in the same way as Rupert was intending to rejoin the Blue. Although just in range, neither side fired in order to preserve some ammunition for the last phase of the battle.

By 5 p.m. Rupert had reached the Blue Squadron, at which time many of its ships were disabled in their masts and rigging: the same could be said of Tromp's ships. As he came up with the Blue Squadron he gave the order for the whole fleet to form line on the flagship, but only about seven of the Blue Squadron were in a fit condition to do so. The French failed to respond, continuing to follow out of shot to windward. Meanwhile, de Ruyter picked up the remains of Tromp's squadron and renewed the action with the English. All could see that, had the undamaged French squadron joined the battle at his stage, the allies must have won a complete victory. The Dutch, like the English, had many ships disabled and were in no condition to face the full force of the French squadron. As Rupert later wrote, it was the greatest and plainest opportunity ever lost at sea.

The battle continued for a further two hours until it started to get dark, at which time the Dutch bore away towards their coast while the allies continued on to the north-west. Despite the damage, no ships of the line were lost on either side.

In addition to Spragge, the allies lost five captains and the French one. The Dutch lost two flag officers and four captains.

As usual, no reliable figures for casualties among the seamen are available. As with the two Schooneveld battles, the Dutch were more interested in their strategic aim of staying in being and forcing the English off their coast than they were in sinking and capturing allied ships. They therefore kept their distance, firing at their opponents' masts and sails. In doing so, they avoided the heavy casualties of the second Dutch War. In the first two battles Rupert had tried for a decisive result but was foiled by de Ruyter's use of the Schooneveld shoals. On this occasion, when the King had explained the need for caution and when Rupert was virtually abandoned by his ally after the initial stages of the battle, he felt obliged to keep his distance to some extent. None the less casualties were high in some of the ships. In the *Sovereign* itself around sixty men are known to have been killed or severely wounded. Among those who died of their wounds was Reeves, the last of many friends to have fallen at Rupert's side over the last forty years. There would be no more. Rupert had fought his last battle.[13]

On the day after the battle Rupert dispatched five of his ships back to England for repair, including the *Prince*. He moved Harman to command the Blue Squadron, giving his place as vice-admiral of the Red to Ossory. John Holmes, brother of Sir Robert, was made rear-admiral of the Blue in place of Ossory. In the afternoon the fleet anchored about sixty miles west of Vlieland. At this time the Dutch fleet was also at anchor some twelve miles off Vlieland.

Next day Rupert called a council of war, at which it was decided that the fleet should sail to the Dutch coast off Scheveningen to show the flag and to give the lie to any Dutch claim that they had won the battle. But in the event a great storm blew up, followed by strong contrary winds, so the plan had to be abandoned. Eventually, storm damage combined with sickness and a shortage of provisions caused the fleet to return to the Gunfleet, where it arrived ten days later. At the end of the month it moved to the Buoy of the Nore.

Bad weather also affected the Dutch. Not until 29 August was de Ruyter able to beat his way back from his anchorage off Vlieland to a point south of the Texel, at which time he heard that the allies were back in the Thames. He was then ordered to take his fleet to the English coast to show that it had not been defeated, but high winds and heavy seas prevented him from getting more than half-way across the North Sea, after which his squadrons dispersed to their own ports. To all intents and purposes the campaign was over.

Although the naval campaign was over, a political one designed to disentangle England from the French alliance was well under way. In a sense it had been going on for some months, but it was the battle of the Texel which gave it its impetus. On the surface the battle was similar to the two fought in the Schooneveld: the allies, though suffering no significant loss, had failed to dispose of de Ruyter to the extent necessary for them to land troops in the United Provinces. But unlike the earlier two battles, it was felt throughout the fleet that failure to defeat de Ruyter on this occasion was due to a deliberate decision on the part of d'Estrées not to support the English. This feeling was not restricted to the officers but was strongly felt by the ordinary seamen who had seen with their own eyes how the French ships hung back at the critical moment when their intervention would have resulted in victory. On the day after the battle, when d'Estrées came aboard the *Sovereign*, the officers had their work cut out to prevent the seamen from being rude to him. When the fleet reached the Thames, their roughly expressed indignation reverberated outwards from the inns and bawdy-houses along the banks of the river to the furthest corners of the kingdom.

It may be that Rupert himself initially did not feel that all the blame should be put on d'Estrées. For one thing he felt that Spragge's decision to fight a separate battle with Tromp was partly responsible for the fleet's lack of success, since if the Red and Blue Squadrons had fought together he would have had more flexibility to deal with the lack of French support even though de Ruyter would also have had more ships at his disposal. But Spragge may have done Rupert a favour, since by keeping an equal number of a smaller enemy fleet away from the action he was removing a higher proportion of de Ruyter's total resources.

There were three other reasons why Rupert was at first reluctant to put the blame on the French. First, on meeting Rupert the next day d'Estrées said that he had not understood what Rupert had wanted him to do and in particular claimed that he had not known what one particular and critical signal meant. Second, Rupert was not exactly sure whether the wind would have enabled d'Estrées to do what everyone was saying he ought to have done at a particular time, and until he could get precise confirmation on this matter he was not prepared to condemn him. Third, Rupert knew only too well how damaging it could be to fall out with an ally. The King put it well in a letter to him of 20 August, when he asked him to suppress criticism of the French as much as possible 'lest the enemy come to gain a greater advantage upon us than they can possibly have by fighting'.

By 17 August Rupert was sure of the facts. In a letter that he wrote to the King on that day he made the point that it was not just the English who were dissatisfied with the French. 'I must as my duty binds me acquaint you that both officers and mariners of the French are extremely unsatisfied with their generals not bearing in . . . more than your Majesty can imagine'. Later in the same letter he reports having a Dutch prisoner aboard who saw the whole fight and who said that the French were condemned by the Dutch for damned cowards. In another letter to the King a week later he attempts to allay the King's concern about differences between the English and French by saying that both are in entire agreement in laying all the fault on the commander of the French.

To remove all possible doubt about the responsibility of d'Estrées for the way in which the battle turned out, it is necessary only to quote from a letter sent on 27 August by his second-in-command, Martel, to Louis's most influential minister, Colbert. At the end of a long account in which he detailed every move of the French squadron from the beginning to the end of the action and in which he said that each of the French divisions had had its hands tied by an order not to attack without direct instructions in writing or by word of mouth from d'Estrées, he says: 'd'Estrées has dishonoured the nation having done everything as badly as possible. The English have good reason not to be satisfied with him . . .' Soon afterwards, he published a shorter version of his complaint, which resulted in his being imprisoned in the Bastille on his return to France.

On 27 August, at the King's direction, Rupert left the fleet temporarily for a visit to London. It seems that initially the King may have been dissatisfied with Rupert's conduct of the battle and also that he may have held him responsible for the extent to which the French were being blamed. It was reported that the King told the French ambassador that he would never again trust Rupert with the fleet. But by the time

Rupert reached London, the King had heard enough to dispel any such thoughts. He warmly welcomed Rupert, but his welcome was as nothing compared with that of the common people, who regarded him not only as a hero in his own right but also as one who hated the French as much as they did themselves. At the King's request, in order to limit the damage done to the alliance, he later issued a statement praising d'Estrées's bravery, but by then it was well known that he was thoroughly disaffected with the French as allies.

Rupert returned to the fleet on 4 September, but the bad weather persisted and it was soon evident that no more could be attempted in 1673. On 11 September he received a warrant from the King to bring the first and second rates into Chatham to be laid up for the winter, and on the same day d'Estrées took his leave prior to taking his squadron back to France. Soon afterwards, Rupert struck his flag for the last time and the troops under Schomberg's command were disbanded.

11

FINAL YEARS

Soon after Rupert returned from the fleet a pamphlet appeared in London entitled 'An Exact Relation of the several Engagements and Actions of His Majesty's Fleet under the command of His Highness Prince Rupert. And of all circumstances concerning this summer's expedition, Anno 1673. Written by a person in command in the fleet. London: Printed for J.B. Anno Dom. 1673.'[1]

From the way in which the pamphlet is written it is evident that J.B. was an eyewitness to the events recorded. It is also apparent that he was with the Blue Squadron at the Schooneveld battles and in the Red Squadron at the battle of the Texel. Whoever J.B. was,[2] it is clear that he was a strong supporter of Rupert and was indignant at the way in which the fleet was set out at the start of the campaign and outraged by the behaviour of the French at the Texel. His views undoubtedly reflected those of many officers in the fleet, and it is worth taking account of them since they played a part in influencing public opinion.

In the opening paragraphs of the pamphlet, J.B. set out his reasons for writing, which was to contradict, for the benefit of King, Parliament and people, false accounts of the events of the summer put about by enemies of the Protestant cause. He claimed that, although the staunchly Protestant Rupert was hailed widely as the best possible man to put in charge of the fleet, 'a generation of men of another mind, having found all their arts and endeavours of diverting His Majesty from his choice to be in vain, tacked about to the old trick of State, of devising how underhand to take off the chariot wheels of the Prince's expedition and to clap on dead weight to retard him ... so as to render the whole enterprise of no more effect than might just suit with their own ends and if possible bring back the Prince with no more victory than might please them and

their accomplices'. He goes on to describe how this was managed on behalf of these people by some members of the Navy
Board and a few of the sea officers. In particular, he highlighted
the ill effect of keeping Holmes from the fleet and implied that
Spragge was employed by the malcontents to spy on Rupert's
management of affairs. He summarised the effect of all these
measures as being to 'clog the wheels, to sicken the officers and
deflate the morale of the seamen'.

When it came to describing operations, he consistently praised
Rupert for his skill and courage and was initially complimentary
about the French. Spragge got the blame for the confusion at
the start of the second Schooneveld battle. His description of
the Texel battle is probably the best of the eyewitness accounts.
He condemned Spragge for his failure to stay with the Red
Squadron and was eloquent in his indignation of d'Estrées.

J.B.'s account ends with a great blast which, despite some
misunderstanding of the circumstances, stands as a memorial
to Rupert's ability to overcome adversity:

In the midst of so many intrigues of opposition at home, so
many delays of his commission, so few powers contained in
it, such scanty numbers of seamen, so little assurance of divers
Chief Commanders, such failure of provisions, such want of
ammunition and all other necessaries, such deceit of Navy-
Officers [Navy Board], such non-observance of orders at sea
amongst his own English, and so manifest defections of the
French, not to be staggered in his resolution, nor to be put
out of all patience and prudence in action, nor to abate of
his affection and zeal for the honour and service of His Majesty, the safeguard and interest of Religion and the Kingdom,
in a season when so many Popish projectors played a game
under board, and above too, will be an everlasting argument
of His Highness's valour and renown; and must needs be a
strong obligation on the King, the Parliament, and the people
of England; who are now left to judge whether it was not a
wonderful good Providence of God, and one of the most
memorable pieces of service ever done at sea, to surmount
all those difficulties, and even envy itself; and after all to
bring home the Fleet Royal of England without the loss of
one man-of-war to her own shore in safety, in despite of all
enemies that designed otherwise by sea and land.

In fact, Rupert knew perfectly well that most of his problems in getting the fleet to sea and in maintaining it there were not the result of a popish conspiracy to take the wheels from his chariot. Far from wanting to undermine him, it was in the interests of Roman Catholics and their sympathisers that he should succeed, since their aspirations rested on the success of the French alliance. As previously explained, most of his troubles in these respects arose from the late recall of Parliament and failure to get the press going early enough. Only the weakness of his original commission was avoidable, and this was almost certainly due to the Duke of York's desire to limit Rupert's power to select commanders who might sacrifice the long-term good order and discipline of the fleet for short-term operational advantage: it had nothing to do with clapping on dead weight to retard him.

When Rupert finally came ashore in mid-September he must have been disappointed that the campaign had not been more successful, and in particular that he had not reaped the reward of his manoeuvring before and during the battle of the Texel. Twice at least he got the Dutch positioned so that they must have sustained substantial damage had the French played their part. But he was restricted by the King's instruction not to risk losses that the Dutch could publicise to strengthen their negotiating position. He was therefore obliged to be less aggressive than he might have been, which prevented him from going for a victory such as he and Albemarle had achieved in the previous war.

In all three of the battles fought during the campaign, Rupert appears to have made few mistakes. Despite being opposed by one of the greatest of all admirals who clearly intended to avoid becoming too closely engaged with Rupert's superior fleet, he missed only one good opportunity, which occurred at the end of the second Schooneveld battle. Then it should at least have been possible to have surrounded and destroyed those ships of Tromp's squadron which had become separated from the rest of the Dutch fleet during the night.

But despite the skill with which Rupert manoeuvred and fought, there seems to have been something missing in the way in which he went about his business. He was not quite his old self. When J.B. wrote that malcontents had managed to 'clog the wheels, to sicken the officers and deflate the morale of the seamen', he was in effect pointing out that Rupert had failed to inspire his officers and men in the way that he had managed to do in the past regardless of comparable or worse difficulties. From his earliest days as a soldier, through the victories of the first two years of the Civil War and even during the time when the Royalist cause was flagging, men competed to join his units and fought like demons under his banner. When he alone of the Royalist commanders remained in arms at the end of the second Civil War, the men in his rotten leaky ships worked wonders on his behalf over four long years. As late as the second Dutch War, he was still radiating a degree of light-hearted confidence that belied his advancing age. By 1673 some of this was lost. Despite his periodic rages he had formerly been relaxed with his subordinates, but now he seemed less approachable and even tense. There was no Will Legge or Maurice or Albemarle with whom to discuss his problems: probably no one even to enjoy his dark humour.

Rupert's handling of Schomberg serves as an example of his shortcomings in this respect. Although Schomberg was unwittingly to blame for the incident of the flag described in the last chapter, Rupert's response, though ostensibly directed at the captain of the *Greyhound*, was hardly tactful. Schomberg was not only Rupert's lieutenant-general; he was also a very old acquaintance. Rupert's father was his godfather, and he and Rupert had been at Leyden university together for three years. Together they had shared a first campaign at the siege of Rheinburg. Subsequently, both had gained renown in the various wars in which they had taken part. Above all, both were too old and distinguished to become involved in such a ridiculous quarrel in the middle of a war in which they were leading players. In this connection it is only fair to point out that, although Rupert precipitated the row, Schomberg pursued it in an unnecessarily vigorous manner.

On the face of it the campaign of 1673 had not been a success. The superior allied fleet had not gained command of the sea, and in consequence the English army had not been landed behind the Dutch lines in accordance with the plan of campaign agreed on at the end of 1672. In retrospect it can be seen that this was fortunate because, as is now known, Louis XIV had no intention of supporting an English landing, and the hastily raised and ill-trained English army would have stood little chance against the more numerous Dutch veterans. Having decided not to support the landing, it made sense for Louis to give orders that his ships should not become too closely engaged with the Dutch. Judging by the creditable performance of the French squadron in the Schooneveld battles, instructions to this effect probably reached d'Estrées while the fleet was in the Thames in the second half of June, which was at the same time as Louis gave orders that an English landing was not to be supported. As Sir William Coventry put it, France would gain nothing from the total destruction of the Dutch fleet, which would merely give complete control of the oceans to England. Better that the Dutch and English fleets should weaken each other to the benefit of French influence at sea.

Soon after Rupert left the fleet, King Louis's position worsened when both Spain and the Empire declared war on him, thanks to William of Orange's careful diplomacy.

It is ironic that Rupert, who had been so strongly opposed to the French alliance, had been the person most directly concerned with making it work. And the fact that it did not work was not through any lack of effort on his part. Once appointed to command the fleet, he tried his utmost to follow to the letter the various instructions given to him by the King. Now that he no longer held an operational command, he was free to exercise his responsibilities as a member of the Privy Council and of the Foreign Affairs Committee as he thought best fitted the interests, though not always the desires, of his sovereign. To this end he devoted his efforts towards getting clear of the French alliance. Later he used his influence to foster an alliance with William of Orange against Louis. These were the aims that he pursued during the next six years.

With regard to the first of these aims, Rupert was pushing at an open door. News of the Duke of York's marriage to the Roman Catholic Mary of Modena in October accentuated a hostility among the people towards France which had been growing ever since his conversion to Rome became public knowledge at the end of May. When Parliament assembled in October, the King asked for money to continue the war. What he got was a demand that he should force his brother to annul his recent marriage; this was out of the question. Instead, as tempers flared in Parliament and as his ministers became increasingly harassed, the King prorogued it until January.

It is clear that for some months the King had suspected Shaftesbury of stirring up trouble against the alliance despite the vigour with which he had been conducting government business. He had no evidence, but it was well known that Shaftesbury disliked the Duke of York and was strongly opposed to his marriage to a Roman Catholic. On 9 November the King dismissed him from his post of Lord Chancellor, appointing Sir Heneage Finch Lord Keeper in his place.

It is claimed that Rupert was also busy forming an anti-French party.[3] Although little evidence substantiates this assertion, Colbert had in September complained to Louis XIV of the bad effects that Rupert was having on the alliance. Indeed, the French considered that it was he and not Shaftesbury who was at the root of the trouble.[4] From October onwards Rupert and Shaftesbury were in close contact with each other, both being equally anxious that England should withdraw from its alliance with France. After Shaftesbury's dismissal, when he was confined to his house by gout, Rupert's carriage was often seen at his door.

When Parliament reassembled in January 1674 it was determined to bring about an end to the war. At the critical moment the Dutch made assurance doubly sure by putting forward peace terms that were particularly favourable to the English. On 9 February a peace treaty was signed and the third Dutch War came to an end. Within a few weeks the King prorogued Parliament to November. In September, finding that his financial position was better than he had hoped thanks to Danby's careful stewardship, he extended the date to April of the following year. Also in September, Arlington handed over as Secretary of State to Williamson, taking up the post of Lord Chamberlain instead.

Although Rupert was doubtless happy that England was no longer formally allied to France, he still wanted to go further and provide help to France's enemies in an attempt to control Louis's aggressive ambitions. For the King to adopt such a policy, which ran contrary to his personal feelings, would require pressure from Parliament. Rupert was therefore annoyed that Parliament should have been prorogued for such a long time and, according to the King, made no secret of the fact when the King announced his decision to the Privy Council. On the other hand, a spell of political calm during which he could revive his domestic life and get to grips with his responsibilities as First Lord of the newly constituted Admiralty Commission was welcome.

The main event in his domestic life which had taken place while he was away at sea during the summer of 1673 was the birth of a daughter to Peg Hughes. The baby was christened Ruperta and soon became the apple of Rupert's eye. It may have been this event that prompted the final departure of Frances Bard. Dudley Bard was now based at Windsor and was soon sent to be educated at Eton.

At about this time Rupert received a letter from his brother Charles Louis, whose only son was so delicate that it was thought unlikely that he would survive for long, begging him to return to the Palatinate, marry and produce an heir to become Elector in due course. But Rupert, mindful of his oath never to set foot in Heidelberg again and being in any case well settled in England, refused.[5]

From 1674 onwards the King, now well into his forties, took to spending most of the summer at Windsor, where Rupert was frequently in his company. The King knew perfectly well that Rupert's ideas on foreign policy did not coincide with his own and that he maintained contact with men such as Shaftesbury who not only opposed the King's foreign policy but who were also intriguing to displace the Duke of York from the succession. Their views varied as to how this might be achieved. One suggestion was that the King should divorce his faithful but barren wife and marry a Protestant. Another was that somehow the Duke of Monmouth should be made legitimate and thereby become heir to the throne. The King was opposed to both these ideas. From his point of view Rupert, as a highly respected and popular Protestant prince, would be a source of danger if he gave his full backing to Shaftesbury and his friends. On the other hand, if Rupert merely used these people to forward his ideas on foreign policy, which he could do only when Parliament was sitting, but backed the King on other matters particularly those regarding the succession, Rupert would be a source of strength to the King. It was therefore in the King's interest to stay on good terms with him for the time being, and relations between the cousins at Windsor remained friendly.

*   *   *

The Admiralty Commission was another area where Rupert and the King frequently met. In the five years and three months between January 1674 and April 1679, the committee sat on 308 occasions. Some of these meetings were very brief and were attended by no more than two of the commissioners, whose purpose was to give formal backing to a routine measure. For example, the two Secretaries of State sat together on 28 July 1674 to authorise an extra year's pay to one of the yachts off the coast of Ireland and to instruct the Navy Board to submit a letter to the King at the next meeting of the commission; there were numerous other meetings of this sort that neither the King nor Rupert attended. Of the rest, Rupert attended 164 meetings, taking the chair when the King was absent. The most frequent attender was the King himself, who, to his credit, sat through no fewer than 195 meetings, many of which dealt with relatively trivial matters.[6] The average attendance of the twelve men who remained members of the commission throughout the whole period was 130 meetings.

When the Duke of York was Lord High Admiral he carried out his duties from his lodgings in Whitehall. With the advent of the commission it was necessary to establish an Admiralty office. This was set up in Derby House in January 1674, conveniently situated between the Palace of Whitehall and Westminster.

The main purpose of the Admiralty Commission was to lay down the policy for shipbuilding and manning, both of which the Navy Board was responsible for carrying out, and to make orders regarding provisioning, discipline and finance; its other functions were to control Admiralty Courts and to order the deployment of ships.

During Rupert's time as a commissioner the most pressing matter was trying to ensure that enough ships were available to handle the threat posed by enemies or potential enemies. But during the period other measures, fundamental to the long-term future of the Royal Navy, were brought into effect. The first of these was a closer regulation of matters concerning manning, gunning and the selection of commissioned officers. The second was the development of priorities for the deployment of naval forces between the English Channel, the Mediterranean and the Atlantic, together with an understanding of the relative merits of convoy or patrol, or a combination of both, for the protection of merchant ships in dangerous waters.

At the beginning of 1675 there was no immediate prospect of war with a major European power. Narborough was sent to the Mediterranean with thirty ships to defend English traders from attack by Algerian vessels; he was later reinforced by eight more ships and diverted to a blockade of Tripolitania. Meanwhile, the fleet as a whole had been run down because of lack of funds, so that it consisted of no more than seven ships of the first rate, five of the second, eighteen of the third and thirty-six of the fourth at a time when both France and the United Provinces were building up their strength.

During the session of Parliament that started in April 1675, members agreed that one extra ship of the first rate, five of the second and fourteen of the third ought to be built, but they declined to provide the necessary money for fear that the King would prorogue Parliament and use the money to govern without it.

During this time Shaftesbury's friends and Rupert were still trying to shift the country from neutrality into support for the coalition against France. But the King was still against the idea and was secretly negotiating with Louis for a subsidy that would enable him to prorogue Parliament again. By the autumn Danby had lobbied the House of Commons sufficiently to ensure that the King would not be forced into support for the coalition against Louis, but the House of Lords then became troublesome over an unrelated issue. After making efforts to resolve the dispute, the King prorogued Parliament from November 1675 until February 1677 and accepted a subsidy from his French cousin. By this time Louis, who had been hard pressed by the coalition against him, recovered some ground when he persuaded Sweden to become his ally.

In the absence of Parliament, 1676 was a relatively peaceful year. For a time the King tried to mediate between Louis and the coalition, as there did seem to be a general feeling that the war had gone on long enough. But Louis, sensing an upturn in his fortunes, pitched his demands too high. In England King Charles was hoping that further French subsidies would enable him to prorogue Parliament again when it reassembled in the following February. This might have been possible but for a revolt in the colony of Virginia which made it necessary to send soldiers and a fleet across the Atlantic to restore the situation.

The resulting expense meant that Parliament would have to vote money to keep the country going.

Sixteen seventy-six was also a quiet year for Rupert, who was able to spend more time at Windsor pursuing his scientific interests. It was in 1676 that the Royal Society took notice of his system for painting colours on marble which, when polished, became permanent. Other inventions that he brought to fruition at Windsor included his production of 'Prince's Metal', a mixture of copper and zinc with a higher zinc content than brass; a self-loading automatic pistol; an airgun for firing a dart or pin; and a smokeless, noiseless musket. He also perfected a system for blowing up rocks in mining by fixing wedges into a ten-inch hole in order to concentrate the effect of an explosive charge. In 1671 he had taken out a patent for a large cannon made of improved iron which the government later bought but failed to develop for economic reasons. Rupert eventually got a licence to sell them in France. Also in connection with weapons, he developed a method of tempering gun barrels in a glasshouse and a new method of boring them by hydraulic power. He even experimented with an embryo torpedo.[7]

Windsor was not always a haven of peace and quiet. One night in January 1677 Rupert's scientific activities received a set-back when some drunks broke in to his apartments and smashed a number of his stills. So wild were the courtiers that evening that one stabbed another to death in the room next to where the King was sleeping. The King was roused by the Duke of York asking him whether he intended to lie in bed while his throat was cut, after which they both returned through the night to London.

Parliament reassembled on 15 February 1677. In his opening speech the King drew attention to the dangerous weakness of the navy as a result of French and Dutch shipbuilding and asked for thirty new ships to be constructed without delay. On this occasion Shaftesbury, backed by Buckingham, pressed for the election of a new Parliament in a bid to ensure that the King got no more money before agreeing to redress grievances. But this was too much for the House of Lords to stomach, and Buckingham and Shaftesbury were both sent to the Tower. By this time, too, the majority of the Commons was becoming genuinely frightened of the growing strength of the French navy and was in a more receptive frame of mind.

It now fell to Pepys, who had become a Member of Parliament three years earlier, to put the detailed case for the new ships to the Commons, which he did in a memorable speech on 21 February. After much discussion, Parliament agreed to build one new ship of the first rate, nine of the second rate and twenty of the third rate. In view of the increasing size of French ships, fourth-rates were no longer considered suitable for use in the line of battle. Six hundred thousand pounds was voted for the building programme, to be paid over the following two years. It is worth recording that the King later provided some money of his own to enable the dimensions of the ships to be extended.[8]

This moment of sanity was succeeded by a bewildering series of events, spread over the next eighteen months, ostensibly designed to secure England from its enemies abroad but distorted by the attempts of Shaftesbury's friends, known as the Country Party, to weaken the power of the King and his supporters. These circumstances were exacerbated by the King's attempts to preserve his prerogative with the assistance of secret subsidies from Louis.

In March 1677 Louis captured Valenciennes and Cambrai from the Spanish and defeated William of Orange at Cassel. Charles hoped that this would force William into a peace with Louis, but Parliament, under the influence of the Country Party, pressed the King to help secure the Spanish Netherlands. Then, when the King agreed to do so, Parliament offered a hopelessly inadequate amount of money, thus fanning the flames of the King's anger at its interference in his conduct of foreign policy which traditionally was his business.

In June William of Orange asked his uncle to approach Louis with new and generous peace proposals. This greatly pleased Charles, as it would produce a situation that would enable him to achieve what Parliament wanted without having to go to war with France. But Louis refused William's offer. Charles was now in a fix. Either he had to offer unacceptable concessions to Parliament in return for the money that would enable him to go to war, or he would have to prorogue Parliament in the autumn, which he could afford to do only if he could get a subsidy from Louis. Charles chose the second alternative.

At the end of August Charles started negotiations for a treaty

with William of Orange to be combined with William's marriage to the Duke of York's eldest daughter, Mary. Rupert, who
was Mary's godfather, was delighted: apart from the King and
the Duke of York, only he, Danby and the ambassador, Temple,
were in on the secret. In October William came to England, a
treaty was signed and the marriage took place. The King then
prorogued Parliament in accordance with his agreement with
Louis. But Louis was so furious about William's marriage and
the accompanying treaty that he refused to send the subsidy.

It was now King Charles's turn to get angry, and he started
to prepare for war with France. But this meant that Parliament
would have to be recalled to provide the necessary funds. Parliament, despite pressure from the Country Party to withhold
money from the King, agreed to find £1,000,000 for the war,
and by the spring of 1678 the King had eighty-nine warships
in commission. He also raised a considerable number of troops
for the defence of the Spanish Netherlands, including a regiment
of dragoons of which Rupert was the colonel. The Country
Party, strengthened by the recent release of Shaftesbury, accused
the King of preparing to use these troops against Parliament.
At the Country Party's instigation, Parliament voted the King
enough money to disband them, but the King merely used the
money to maintain them. Meanwhile, Louis set about bribing
the States General in The Hague to put pressure on William.
As a result, a peace favourable to France was reached at the
end of July 1678.

From Rupert's point of view the events of the past eighteen
months had not only given him a lot of work; they had also
caused him to take a different view of the Country Party's
activities. As mentioned, he had given his support to Shaftesbury
in the first place because of his long-held belief that his cousin's
interests would not prosper while he remained tied to Louis
XIV. Not only would Louis's ambitions lead to conquests in
Europe and overseas which would harm England's position, but
a close tie with such a strongly Roman Catholic and absolutist
monarch would inevitably alienate a Parliament that was always
on the look-out for Roman Catholic or absolutist tendencies in
the King. Rupert's support for the Country Party had been
based on his assessment that they were the most likely people
to save the King from alienating his people in this specific way,

but he naturally disapproved of their efforts to withhold the money that the King needed to make war with France.

He also failed to share Shaftesbury's obsession with excluding the Duke of York from the succession. While appreciating the danger of having a Roman Catholic on the throne, there was no immediate danger. The King was only two years older than his brother and might well outlive him. Both of the Duke's children were Protestants, the eldest married to the Prince of Orange. Rather than exclude the legitimate heir, who was also his frequent companion, Rupert would have preferred an arrangement that enabled the King himself to produce a legitimate Protestant heir. Failing that, he probably hoped that the Duke of York could have ruled without making any more concessions to the Roman Catholics than Parliament would allow. Only if the Duke produced a male heir from Mary of Modena would the danger become severe enough to warrant drastic action.

Rupert certainly opposed anything designed to reduce the Royal prerogative. The events of 1677 and the first half of 1678 showed that Shaftesbury and some of his followers were more interested in shifting power from the King to Parliament than they were in fighting the French, and as this understanding dawned on Rupert his support for the Country Party became weaker. In April 1677 he opposed Parliament's plan to ask the King to appoint him Lord High Admiral on the ground that the appointment was part of the Royal prerogative: at the same time he told the King that he would of course take the post if the King wished him to do so.[9] By the end of the year he was so dismayed at the way the Country Party first urged action against France and then tried to sell its support for political concessions that he told the Imperial ambassador that he would no longer support the party. In future he would restrict himself to using his influence with the King to promote those of its policies with which he agreed.[10] None the less he maintained a close personal friendship with Shaftesbury.

Needless to say, the work of the Admiralty Commission increased greatly during 1677 and 1678, when war with France became a possibility. The first matter that took up much time was the building of the thirty ships agreed in the spring of 1677. During May and June there were seventeen meetings of the commission, of which thirteen were attended by Rupert. A series of routine meetings followed until another burst of activity occurred from November 1677 to April 1678, during which time Rupert attended twenty-two of the twenty-five meetings held.

Quite apart from the emergency measures needed to get the fleet to sea, two major reforms were finally approved by the commission at this time. The first of these, which concerned future policy regarding the manning and gunning of warships, was taken by the commission on 3 November 1677.

The second arose from a suggestion made by the Duke of York, who was sitting in at a meeting in September, that men seeking commissions as lieutenants should have certain specific qualifications.[11] The commission ordered Pepys as the secretary to prepare a paper on the subject; this was presented at a meeting on 1 December chaired by Rupert. In all probability Pepys persuaded the Duke to raise the matter because he had for some time wanted promotion to lieutenant to be properly regulated. His paper proposed that every candidate must have served three years at sea, one of which was to be as a midshipman, and that he should be examined in seamanship by Navy Board and Trinity House officers. He would also have to have a certificate of fitness from his captain. When the commissioners considered the paper they agreed that it would be 'a diminution to the honour of lieutenants to be submitted to the examination of any but the King's own commanders' so that it should be conducted by flag officers or captains of first- or second-rate ships on halfpay. The question of service as a midshipman was also 'judged by some to be a service beneath the quality of a gentleman'.[12] There is no reference in the minutes as to which of the commissioners adopted this view, but Rupert, as chairman, ordered the matter to be considered by the Navy Board together with a number of commanders from the fleet. A written report was prepared by George Legge, as spokesman for this group, which confirmed the desirability of the proposal. It was adopted at a meeting on 8 December chaired by the King at which Rupert was present.

In this context it is worth recording that the midshipman of the day was a seaman, not always young, who rated somewhere between the men in the forecastle and the officers, volunteers and warrant-officers, who were accommodated aft, hence the term midship(s)man. The effect of the new rule was to split midshipmen into a number of different categories, e.g. midshipman (old rating), midshipman (ordinary), midshipman (extraordinary), etc. Only after about a century and a half did they all become young apprentice officers, as we know them today.[13]

Ever since 1674 the navy had continued its activities in the Mediterranean where, despite the growth of trade in West Africa, America and the Caribbean, the majority of England's merchant fleet still operated. Narborough had returned to England at the end of 1674 but went back to the Mediterranean the following year with fourteen ships. Between this time and the end of 1678 his squadron rose gradually to a strength of thirty-five ships.[14] By deploying some of his ships as convoy escorts and some as uncommitted detachments he at length provided such good protection from the depredations of corsairs from Algiers and Tripolitania that other countries took to shipping their goods in English vessels. Also during this period England moved away from its reliance on Tangier as a base, where the mole was incapable of handling the bigger ships, and increased its use of the Tuscan port of Leghorn. From 1679, after Narborough was relieved by Herbert, the Spanish port of Gibraltar was developed as another alternative to Tangier,[15] after which small detachments of English ships operated against corsairs from Sallee based outside the Strait.[16] These developments, supervised by the Admiralty Commissioners, had a considerable influence on the way in which the Royal Navy operated in the eighteenth century.

It is difficult from reading the minutes of the meetings to know who was the prime instigator of the measures discussed, because the secretary, Pepys, seldom attributed views to individuals. But it is worth recording that between the Admiralty Commission and the Navy Board, which was normally in attendance at their meetings, there was an unprecedented weight of experience of all matters relating to the provision of ships and seamen and the way in which they should be deployed and fought at sea. For example, in the administrative and financial sphere there were, as Admiralty Commissioners, two former Navy Board treasurers, Carteret and Danby, and a Navy Board Commissioner, Anglesey. Ossory, who took his father's place on the commission when Ormonde returned to Ireland, also had battle experience as a flag officer. The Navy Board included an experienced flag officer in the form of Allin, who had twice commanded in the Mediterranean. It also included Sir Anthony Deane, whose shipbuilding skills equalled those of the Pett dynasty, and Sir John Tippetts, the Surveyor, who was the one member of the Navy Board to be officially commended by Rupert for his good work during the 1673 campaign.

There were therefore many individuals capable of raising matters for discussion and of bringing much knowledge and experience to bear when the discussion took place. Pepys himself had a detailed knowledge of naval affairs going back to the Restoration and was skilled at getting the chairman, who was usually the King, to pursue long-term aims. It is not surprising, therefore, that the period between 1674 and 1679 saw the adoption of many measures that were important for the future development of the Royal Navy. During this time Rupert, who had wide experience across the whole field of naval operations and administration, together with an understanding of the political and foreign policy background to events, contributed fully, but the King, manipulated by Pepys and advised unofficially by the Duke of York, exercised more influence than any other single person.

No sooner was the threat of war lifted than a serious crisis erupted in England when informers produced evidence purporting to show that there was a 'popish plot' to kill the King. The plot raised its head in August 1678 and became serious in October, when a magistrate who had been taking evidence from witnesses was found dead. Shaftesbury and his friends in Parliament naturally tried to take advantage of the passions aroused to promote their opposition to the Duke of York's succession to the throne. The King, who at this stage was suspicious that the whole business was a put-up job, told Parliament to leave the plot to the due processes of law. But this accentuated Parliament's determination to use it for its own purposes. In early November attempts were made to discredit the Duke of York and later in the month the Queen's entourage was subjected to hostile scrutiny.

In December matters got worse when the King dismissed Ralph Montagu, his ambassador in Paris, for irregularities not connected with the plot. Montagu then disclosed in Parliament the negotiations that Danby had secretly conducted with the French in the autumn of 1677 at the very time that the King was trying to get money from Parliament for fighting the French. Parliament threatened to impeach Danby, whereupon the King prorogued Parliament despite Rupert's attempts to dissuade him from doing so.

At the end of January the King dissolved Parliament and called an election. A month later the King sent the Duke of York abroad in an attempt to placate the new Parliament as it was about to assemble. On 6 March the new Parliament met and showed itself even less amenable than its predecessor. Shortly afterwards, Danby resigned. A month later he was sent to the Tower. In order to show Parliament that he was getting rid of his 'bad advisers', the King dismissed the Privy Council and the Foreign Affairs Committee on 20 April 1679. The Privy Council was re-formed with thirty members instead of forty-six and Shaftesbury, together with some of his Country Party friends, was brought into it. Shaftesbury himself was made Lord President of the Council. The Foreign Affairs Committee was not re-formed as such, but a Committee of Intelligence was established to prepare matters for the council as a whole. Rupert retained his position as a Privy Councillor and, although not specifically a member of the Intelligence Committee, was told that he could attend whenever he wished to do so.

At the same time the Admiralty Commissioners were also dismissed and replaced by seven new ones agreeable to the Country Party. Sir Henry Capel, brother of the Earl of Essex, was made first commissioner. In the following month Pepys was packed off to the Tower, from where he was soon released, although not re-employed at the Admiralty until 1684. Rupert's direct links with the navy came to an end at this time.

From the middle of 1679 affairs started to improve from the King's point of view. First, the King was able to exploit a rift that had appeared in the Country Party between on the one hand Shaftesbury, who was determined to exclude the Duke of York from the succession in favour of the Duke of Monmouth, and on the other Essex, Halifax and Sunderland, later known as the triumvirate, who were not. Also from about this time the popish plot was losing some of its impetus. Deep down, the tide of Protestant fanaticism had started to turn.

In August the King, while staying at Windsor, became dangerously ill and the Duke of York returned without waiting to be recalled: he was probably tipped off by the triumvirate, who were frightened that if the King died in his absence Monmouth would seize the Crown. The King's illness caused Rupert to stay at Windsor instead of visiting his ailing sister Elizabeth in Germany. At the King's request he persuaded Monmouth to leave the country on the grounds that the Duke of York would not do so unless he did. Rupert arranged for Monmouth to stay in his house at Rhenen.

After a few weeks the King recovered his health. A surge of affection greeted him as relief swept through the country: the people had no wish for a dispute over the succession leading to a period of prolonged strife. For his part the King dispatched the Duke of York to Scotland to settle the differences that had recently beset that country. By doing so he hoped to gain favour with Parliament. Soon afterwards, as Shaftesbury was so clearly continuing to act against the King's interests, he was expelled from his position as Lord President of the Council. At the end of November Monmouth returned to England uninvited. The King stripped him of all his appointments and forbade him the court. In December the King prorogued Parliament until October 1680.

During this period Rupert's position was somewhat ambiguous. He still wanted England to exercise its influence to oppose French expansion, although in December 1679 he told the Imperial ambassador that England was balanced on the fulcrum of a see-saw and must move to the right or the left to keep the see-saw from tipping too far in one direction, meaning as between Louis XIV on the one hand and the Habsburgs of Madrid and Vienna on the other.[17]

At the same time he was opposed to the idea of substituting the Duke of Monmouth for the Duke of York as heir to the throne despite the fact that it was the Duke of York who so strongly supported the policies of Louis XIV. He therefore found himself opposing both the basic logic of the Country Party, which wanted to be rid of the Duke, and the fundamental position of the King, which was to stay close to Louis XIV. An example of how this affected him in practice is afforded by the fact that he presented a petition to the King on behalf of Shaftesbury and his friends as Charles left church on 7 December, requesting that Parliament should not be prorogued, but he did not himself sign it. As the Imperial ambassador reported to Vienna in January 1680, Rupert stood alone, holding a unique position in the English political scene.[18]

In January 1680 Rupert, in an attempt to reinforce the

likelihood of a Protestant succession, wrote to his sister Sophie suggesting that she consider a match between her son George Louis and the Duke of York's second daughter Anne, a match which, according to him, would be popular throughout the country.

Soon afterwards, much to Rupert's sorrow, his sister Elizabeth died. At almost the same time Rupert received a visit from Charles Louis's son, with whom he got along well according to a letter that he wrote soon afterwards to Sophie. Rupert kept up a friendly correspondence with him after his return to the Palatinate. Charles Louis himself died in August to the great sorrow of his people, for whom he had laboured unceasingly during his time as Elector. His son succeeded him but died in 1685.

In the absence of Parliament, the first nine months of 1680 were comparatively quiet, although Shaftesbury continued his subversive activity against the King's interests. For his part the King formally denied that he had ever been married to Monmouth's mother, in order to scotch attempts to declare his bastard son legitimate. From October 1680, when Parliament reassembled, there was a burst of acrimonious political activity which culminated in January 1681 when the King again dissolved Parliament, calling for a new one to assemble at Oxford in March.

It was during this period of bitter political strife that the visit of Prince George Louis took place. Aged twenty, he had gained a reputation as a soldier but was rough and lacking in courtly graces. Furthermore, unlike his tall and handsome younger brother whom people likened to Rupert, he was distinctly plain. He certainly did not get on well with Princess Anne, who liked him as little as he liked her. When after the dissolution of Parliament the Duke of York returned from Scotland, he also took a dislike to his daughter's suitor. George Louis stayed in England for some weeks, lodged in the Palace of Whitehall. For much of this time Rupert was unwell and on some occasions confined to bed or a wheelchair. The main trouble was apparently an ulcerated leg, possibly a recurrence of the hurt received at sea in 1665. He may also have been unwell in other ways, as George Louis wrote to his mother that Rupert had to take good care of himself. None the less George Louis saw him nearly every day, and the two of them got along well together.

Whether because of his illness or for other reasons, Rupert

appears to have taken less part in public life during 1681. The Parliament that met in Oxford in March was no more cooperative than its predecessors had been. At this time the King briefly considered the idea that his brother should succeed him as King but that Princess Mary and her husband William should be appointed Regents and act for him.[19] But although the Commons knew that the King was considering a compromise proposal of this sort, they immediately introduced another seclusion bill. The King, fortified by a further subsidy from Louis, dissolved Parliament at the end of the month.

A further period of calm ensued, but this time it was the King who was making ground. By July the King felt strong enough to arrest Shaftesbury. At a meeting of the Privy Council Rupert, Radnor and Fauconberg, a former Parliamentary supporter who had married Cromwell's daughter Mary, were permitted to withdraw and the rest ordered to sign Shaftesbury's committal to prison. Unfortunately, on 9 December Shaftesbury was acquitted by a grand jury rigged by his followers in the city. Next day Rupert ostensibly dined with him to show that he remained his personal friend even though he disapproved of some of his activities.

The licence that Rupert had taken out for selling the cannon that he had patented in 1671 was due to expire in November 1681. On 5 October, at a Privy Council meeting, Lord Fauconberg objected to Rupert's proposed sale of the cannon to King Louis. Rupert, who was present, maintained that the guns were undervalued in England and that in accordance with the terms of the patent he was entitled to seek his own market. Fortunately, the English Ordnance Board agreed to buy them soon afterwards.[20]

The second half of 1681 and the early months of 1682 were again taken up by preparation for war with France as Louis threatened Luxemburg. But faced by the concerted opposition of the United Provinces, Spain, England and the Empire, Louis withdrew. Meanwhile, the King had strengthened his position in London to such an extent that another trial of Shaftesbury looked sure to succeed. In view of this, Shaftesbury fled abroad. At last it seemed that the worst of King Charles's troubles were over.

By the late summer of 1682 Rupert 's physical condition had

evidently improved, as in a letter to Sophie he said that he no longer had much need of his invalid chair. He also thanked her for writing complimentary things about Peg Hughes, adding that he owed much to her for the great care she had taken of him during his illness. Speaking of Ruperta, he said that 'she is turning into the prettiest creature. She already rules the whole house and sometimes argues with her mother, which makes us all laugh.'[21] This is the last recorded glimpse of Rupert as a private person.

Rupert still attended meetings of the Privy Council when his health permitted. He was also involved with the affairs of the Royal African Company, which started to make sizeable profits from 1676. As governor, he was much more closely involved in the Hudson Bay Company, of which his former secretary, Sir James Hayes, was now deputy governor and, in modern parlance, chief executive. This company made its first large profit in 1681, which must have caused Rupert considerable satisfaction.

On 25 November 1682 the Hudson Bay Company, as was customary, held its annual meeting in Rupert's house in Spring Gardens. Unfortunately, Rupert was unable to leave his bed, having been taken ill that morning. He had a fever and a bad cough that turned to pleurisy. Four days later he died.

Rupert's state funeral took place in Westminster Abbey on 6 December. He lies in the crypt. In his will Rupert left Dudley Bard his house at Rhenen and all money owed him by the Elector Palatine and the Emperor. The rest of his estate went in equal parts to Peg Hughes and Ruperta.

It is said that Rupert wanted his daughter to marry Lord Burford, the King's son by Nell Gwyn, but at his death she was only nine years old and by the time she was ready to marry, Charles was dead and nothing came of the idea. Later she married General Howe, who was King William III's and then Queen Anne's envoy at the court of Hanover. There she must have had contact with Frances Bard, who until she died in 1708 was a close friend and confidante of the Electress Sophie. Dudley Bard became a soldier and was killed in 1686 fighting for the Emperor against the Turks. Had Sophie lived another six weeks she would have become Queen of England on the death of Queen Anne. As it was the Crown went to her son, George Louis, who reigned as George I.

There can be no doubting the sincere regret of the English

people at Rupert's death, which was reflected in a number of poems and articles produced at the time. Nor is it difficult to understand why this should be so. In the first place it was known that he was Protestant to the core and, as one writer put it, 'for old England'. His reputation as a general and as an admiral was as yet unchallenged. He was also considered to be honest beyond the possibility of intrigue. His extreme gallantry by land and sea was greatly admired, and the care he took of his old soldiers and seamen was widely appreciated. Only months before his death he was still trying to get compensation for men who had ruined themselves for Charles I forty years earlier. John Campbell, the author of *Lives of the Admirals*, who was born and lived in Windsor not many years after Rupert died, wrote 'in respect of his private life he was so just, so beneficent, so courteous, that his memory remained dear to all who knew him. This I say of my own knowledge, having often heard old people in Berkshire speak in raptures of Prince Rupert.'[22]

Of course, this was not the whole picture. Some of the great men at court resented Rupert's temper and his pride, which tended to keep him at a distance from all but a few close friends. Undoubtedly some were in awe of him as a result of his legendary past and many were wary of him, not without cause. The firmness with which he held his opinions and his abstemious behaviour in surroundings where extreme self-indulgence was the order of the day were not designed to make him popular.

In some ways the most difficult relationship to pin down is that which existed between Rupert and the other two members of the royal family with whom he spent so much time, the Duke of York and the King himself. Like Rupert, James was honest, brave and industrious, but he lacked Rupert's common sense and intellect. He was also considered to be rigid and lacking humour, characteristics that became more marked as the years went by. The famous historian A. L. Rowse, writing of him as he was in 1665, said: 'James had two passions, hunting and women – which he was apt to combine; in course of time he added a third – religion, which was more disastrous.'[23] So far as religion was concerned, James's Roman Catholicism was at the heart of the political difficulties that bedevilled the second half of the King's reign and which pushed Rupert into the company of those who opposed the King. An important part of James's make-up omitted by Rowse in this quote was his genuine interest in the Royal Navy. When Rupert was serving as vice-admiral of James's fleet during the first half of 1665, they got along well together in council and in battle. But after James became a Roman Catholic he must have been aware that Rupert was capable of replacing him as Lord High Admiral at sea or ashore and also that Rupert was more popular with the populace than he was, so there may have been an element of jealousy in their relationship. On Rupert's part, although he did not intrigue against James, he may have felt irritation and even contempt at the problems James heaped on his brother by his uncompromising attitude towards religion.

The relationship between the King and Rupert was quite different. It is clear that Charles hero-worshipped his cousin during the early stages of the Civil War, a feeling that turned to friendship later in the conflict and during the first part of the exile. Charles relied heavily on Rupert during the second Civil War and its aftermath when Rupert was getting the fleet ready for its long voyage. When Rupert returned, the relationship changed because the King had grown up and had no intention of being under the influence of anyone. The disagreement of 1654 put further distance between them, but after the Restoration their long-standing friendship and shared interests, both intellectual and sporting, made them comfortable in each other's company. From the middle of the 1660s Rupert's popularity in the country and his capability as a commander at sea were useful assets. Rupert's opposition to the King's attachment to France and his close relations with some of the King's political opponents must have caused irritation, but the King rightly had confidence in Rupert's loyalty. There is no evidence to suggest that the King objected to Rupert's asceticism, although he may have joked about it behind Rupert's back, nor that Rupert was annoyed by the King's self-indulgence. That the King was physically strong enough to spend the evening and night with his women and still be ready early the following day to conduct business in a series of council meetings before setting off to take exercise would have been enough for Rupert. The fact that the King got into political scrapes through misjudgement or carelessness would not have bothered Rupert any more than his sexual adventures would have done.

In assessing Rupert's performance as an admiral it is necessary to realise that in the first half of the seventeenth century sea warfare was not a separate profession but merely an aspect of 'the profession of arms'. Commanders-at-sea were mainly army officers who were put in charge of ships or groups of ships. The sailing of the ship was a technical matter that could be left to seamen, although the commander as a soldier was expected to know about the ship's weapons and would be responsible for the way in which the ship was used. Naturally, a seaman who had been employed for years in a warship would learn about the weapons and could pick up the business of using ships for warlike purposes. Some, such as Drake in the previous century, had become famous admirals, but for the most part fleets and squadrons were commanded by men of rank with military experience.

Rupert became an admiral in this way, as did the great Commonwealth admirals such as Warwick, Blake, Deane and Monck. But at the same time a number of the subordinate commanders in the Commonwealth navy, such as Batten, Penn, Ayscue and Lawson, were trained to the sea from their youth and had picked up the profession of arms as they went along. There were also Royalist exiles who had served in Rupert's fleet or in privateers who had come to the profession of arms in this way.

At the Restoration these two groups joined forces to command the ships and provide the flag officers in the fleet, and as the century progressed the division between them became increasingly blurred. Pepys described as gentlemen those who started as army officers or who were given commands as an act of patronage. Those who started as seamen he described as tarpaulins. In this he has been followed by many historians. But the terminology is misleading because it confuses an activity, such as seafaring or soldiering, with a distinction based on the differences between a gentleman and someone from a lower social class. The fact is that some professional seamen, such as Ayscue, the son of a courtier, and Batten, whose father was a knight, were from the gentry and some, such as Lawson, were from the lower orders of society. The same applied to those who started as officers in the army: for example, Monck came from the gentry and Blake from a family of merchants. The Royalist Allin and the Parliamentarian Penn were also from merchant families.

None the less a distinction did exist, but it was – between those who knew the whole job of a sea officer – that is to say seamanship and fighting – as opposed to those who knew only one part of the business. In both the second and third Dutch Wars the fleet suffered from some seamen who did not want to fight and from some fighters who did not know enough seamanship to do so effectively. Of the two it was the first group who were the more dangerous as the second could at least be advised by their sailing masters.

Rupert bridged these divisions. A member of the royal family, he was a famous commander of troops in the field, experienced in council and an effective organiser. As a result of his service with the Royalist fleet between 1648 and 1653, he had become a fine seaman with a knowledge of the Mediterranean, the coast of Africa and the Atlantic. He had also learned the nuts and bolts of naval logistics under testing conditions. His energy and courage were well known. At the outbreak of the second Dutch War he combined a knowledge of his job, leadership qualities and a formidable reputation as a fighter so that he inspired confidence among the officers and men of the fleet. What has to be established is the extent to which he was able to use these assets to achieve the various aims given to him.

In each of his campaigns, Rupert had to undertake a number of tasks before meeting the enemy. First, he had to collect together the ships allocated to him and ensure that as far as possible they were properly armed, manned and supplied. Then he had to gather what information was available about the enemy. Then he had to ensure that his flag officers and captains understood the procedures governing the way in which the ships of the fleet were supposed to work together in pursuit of a tactical aim. He also had to be confident that they knew the various signals that would activate each particular movement. Finally, he had to make a plan to carry out the task given to the fleet.

Although this programme was in many ways similar to the procedures that Rupert had followed when commanding land forces in the Civil War, there were significant differences, the most important being the lack of continuity. Unlike his armies, the fleet was paid off at the end of each summer and a new one put in commission in the following spring. Not only was the commander-in-chief reappointed each year but also all the flag officers, captains and lieutenants, except for those in the few ships kept in commission over the winter. The majority of the seamen would also be newly acquired each spring, and some of those picked up by the press often knew nothing of the sea. Furthermore, because of the expense of keeping a large fleet in commission, everything was left to the last moment so that there was likely to be a scramble to get it to sea ahead of the enemy. This meant that the commander-in-chief would have little time to carry out the necessary preliminaries. Another difference was that the arrangements for assembling resources and maintaining the fleet logistically were not directed by its commander but were handled by the Lord High Admiral through the Navy Board and Victualler and by the Master General of the Ordnance through the Ordnance Board. The complexity of setting out the fleet and supplying it made this inevitable, but it reduced the commander-in-chief's influence on its preparation for war. The degree to which it was reduced depended on the way in which his commission was worded, with particular reference to his authority over the dockyards and the extent to which he was empowered to make appointments in the fleet.

It is with these points in mind that Rupert's success in carrying out the necessary preliminaries must be assessed. With regard to collecting his resources, he was most directly involved between 1648 and 1653. That this fleet got to sea at all was almost entirely due to his colossal energy and resourcefulness, as was recognised at the time by Hyde. That he kept it in being for four and a half years provided further evidence of his determination, skill and persistence in this field. The knowledge he gained at this time stood him in good stead after the Restoration, during both Dutch Wars, particularly during 1672 when he was carrying out the Lord High Admiral's role while the Duke of York commanded the fleet at sea. It is fair to say that during 1672 the fleet was better supported than it had been in the previous war or in the following year, but this was not entirely due to Rupert.

The next question relates to Rupert's success at getting the information that he needed during his campaigns, an area in which he had excelled as a land-force commander. Here his record as an admiral is less impressive, although from the start of his voyage in 1649 he repeatedly dispatched ships to gain information. None the less he was badly caught out by Blake off the coast of Spain in 1650. Again, in May 1666 he failed to get accurate information about the Dutch state of preparedness despite dispatching various small ships to watch their harbours. He also failed to get accurate information of the whereabouts of the French fleet. But in both these cases the responsibility lay mainly with the government rather than with the fleet commanders. Apart from these two failures, Rupert took a lot of trouble over reconnaissance and was usually successful at keeping one jump ahead of his opponents.

The next point to consider is the matter of keeping flag officers and captains aware of the way in which Rupert wanted them to sail and fight. It is clear that he gave priority to this aspect of his work in the two Dutch Wars. In 1665 he took part in the long conferences held by the Duke of York before the start of the campaign, designed to review and disseminate the lessons of the previous war. On taking over the chief command with Albemarle in the following year, he reissued these instructions and took trouble to see that they were understood. Between the four days' fight and the St James's Day battle, Rupert issued two further sets of instructions of great importance to the way in which future naval tactics developed. Partly these were designed to ensure that too strict an adherence to standing orders should not prevent the exploitation of opportunities, but if such exploitation resulted in the temporary breakup of squadrons or divisions, ships in contact with the enemy were, on pain of death, to fight in line and not in a disorganised mêlée. Other parts of the new instructions were designed to reduce to a series of set movements, complete with signals, the procedure needed to get a fleet passing the enemy on an opposite course on to the same course, so that it would be sailing parallel to its target; the manoeuvre that was completed with great difficulty in the battle of Lowestoft. Another part laid down the drill for breaking the enemy's line from leeward, as Rupert broke it on the fourth day of the four days' battle. At the start of the 1673 campaign Rupert was content with the fighting and sailing instructions as they had been reissued by the Duke of York the previous year, but he took trouble to send copies to his French squadron well in advance of their joining him so that they could be translated and explained to all captains in advance. In this whole field Rupert showed care, good sense and originality.

When it came to planning, Rupert assembled the information available to him and reached certain conclusions before assembling his council. Mostly the options were limited by logistics, tides and wind conditions as much as by tactical considerations, but he certainly listened to the views of his subordinates before making up his mind. Sometimes he allowed himself to be dissuaded from his favoured option, as happened during his voyage to the West Indies when he was strongly opposed by his captains. But he usually got his way and was occasionally criticised for being too forceful. None the less it was his inspired planning of the moves leading up to the St James's Day battle that was largely responsible for the victory. Similarly, at the start of the 1673 campaign it was his early planning, together with his confident seamanship, that enabled him to reverse the advantage de Ruyter had gained by getting his fleet to sea before the English.

It only remains to attempt an analysis of his conduct once battle was joined. In this he favoured a simple but bold approach. At the same time he related his actions to the overall situation, taking great risks if necessary but showing caution when required. During the fighting he often successfully manoeuvred his opponents into unfavourable positions, but his arrangements for keeping control once battle was joined did not always work: indeed, signalling systems related to the size of fleets made it impossible to retain tight control. This enabled admirals such as Spragge on the English side and Tromp on the Dutch to behave as they did. Rupert's nerve and courage never failed him, and he was invariably in the thick of the fighting.

As a commander Rupert always inspired confidence in the seamen, but by 1673 he had lost some of his sparkle. He also seemed more distant from his flag officers and captains, so that some at least failed to respond as they would have done in earlier years. Although he handled the fleet with skill in 1673, despite his problems with the French, it is likely that he was at his best in 1666. That was when he used his seamanship to develop original tactical concepts at a time when his powers of leadership and drive were still at their peak. As a result, in combination with the equally brave and honest Albemarle, he won his most decisive victory over de Ruyter, on a level playing field, at the St James's Day battle, exploiting it afterwards to devastating effect.

Between the time that Rupert took to the sea in 1648 and his death, a number of men exercised great influence on the future of the Royal Navy. The first of these was Blake, who pioneered the business of keeping a fleet at sea over a long period. An elderly and puritanical bachelor, his single-minded persistence, unfettered by worldly affection or outside interests, led him to make his ship his home and the men of the fleet his family. From Blake the navy learned discipline and how to maintain a blockade. Although he commanded the fleet in a number of set-piece battles in the first Dutch War and was as brave and dogged a fighter at sea as he had been when defending Lyme and Taunton in the Civil War, naval tactics were in their infancy and he was not notably successful. His strength lay in his ability to use the fleet to put pressure on enemy powers by interfering with their trade and blocking their ports. With his intense though limited vision, Blake achieved great things and was the father of the modern navy.

It was the soldier Monck who, in his first brief period at sea as joint commander with Blake and Deane, inserted some order into the field of naval tactics and then proceeded to beat the Dutch in two battles. But he cannot be described as a great admiral as he had no idea of seamanship, being dependent on his subordinates for this aspect of command. In 1666 his contempt for the Dutch was also a weakness.

Penn, though a good seaman and organiser with a considerable grasp of tactics, was not at heart a great fighter and did not have the leadership qualities of a commander-in-chief. Although Cromwell employed him as a general-at-sea, he finished up in the Tower after the premature return of his expedition to the West Indies. After the Restoration, like many other able admirals such as Holmes, Allin, Myngs, Spragge, Jordan and Harman, he was too distant from the centre of government to command the main battle fleet, but like them he contributed to building the navy into a professional fighting service.

Sandwich followed Blake, with whom he shared the chief command after the first Dutch War, in his understanding of the way in which the fleet should be used as an instrument of diplomacy. He was not commander-in-chief in any major battle, but he twice took part as an able and fearless squadron commander under the Duke of York. As commander-in-chief for the second half of 1665 he took some valuable prizes but failed to bring the Dutch fleet to battle. As a person he was totally different from Blake, being broad-minded and tolerant and a devoted family man of wide interests. He was an important figure in the history of the navy whose opinion was insufficiently regarded by the Duke of York in the five years following the Restoration.

The Duke of York himself was a considerable figure in the development of the Royal Navy, over the whole field of organisation and the development of tactical doctrine. His time as a commander-in-chief at sea was limited, but his first battle, against the inexperienced Obdam, led to the breakup of the Dutch fleet, victory being thrown away by his failure to exploit it. His second battle, against de Ruyter, was not a success as he was taken by surprise. He then saw his French squadron set a course diametrically opposed to that of the rest of the fleet because he had not ensured that they understood the sailing and fighting instructions. The Duke of York does not merit a place as a great fighting admiral, but he presided over the Admiralty at an important period in its development.

Rupert was an all-rounder. The breadth of his personal experience, spanning high command at sea, logistics and a thorough knowledge of seamen, ships and weapons, was greater than that of any of his contemporaries, and his influence on the future of the Royal Navy was considerable. In this respect, if one factor has to be singled out it would be the offensive spirit that he inserted into the fighting and sailing instructions. He had contributed to the collection of past experience that made up the Duke of York's instructions of 1665 but later spotted the weakness of them, which was to cramp the exploitation of opportunity by the insistence on too great an adherence to detail. It was the supplementary instructions that he inserted in 1666, retained by the Duke of York in 1672, which paved the way for admirals of the future, such as Howe, St Vincent and Nelson, to win their great victories. In this way Rupert's unquenchable fighting spirit lived on in better-regulated and better-equipped fleets than those of the seventeenth century, commanded on occasions by greater admirals than himself.

In his lifetime Rupert was grandson of one King of England, nephew of another and first cousin of a third. He was commander-in-chief of the King's army in the Civil War and of his son's fleet, first against the Commonwealth and then against the Dutch. He was influential in laying the foundations of empire in Africa and Canada. He was a conscientious contributor to the Privy Council in both reigns and during much of the interregnum. He never wavered in his loyalty to either King even when he disagreed with them. Of all his achievements there can be little doubt that the greatest was the way in which he built up the King's army during the early stages of the Civil

War, establishing temporarily a complete superiority over Parliament's army. But it was his contribution to the development of the Royal Navy which has had the most lasting effect in the ways described in this chapter. In both fields his courage, energy, integrity and sheer brilliance will be remembered as long as there are people interested in the conduct of war.

BIBLIOGRAPHY

ALLIN, Thomas, ed. Anderson, *Journals*, Navy Records Society, 1939.

ANDERSON, R. C., *The Royalists at Sea*, vols 9 (1923), 14 (1928), 17 (1931), 21 (1935), Mariner's Mirror.

ANDERSON, R. C., ed., *Journals and Narratives of the Third Dutch War*, vol. 86, Navy Records Society, 1946.

BARLOW, *Journal of His Life at Sea*, Hurst and Blackett, 1934.

BAUMBER, M., *General-at-Sea: Robert Blake*, John Murray, 1989.

BENTLEY DUNCAN, T., *Atlantic Islands in Seventeenth-Century Commerce and Navigation*, University of Chicago Press, 1972.

British Naval Documents 1204–1960, vol. 131, Navy Records Society, 1993.

BRYANT, Arthur, *Samuel Pepys: The Years of Peril*, Collins, 1967.

BRYANT, Arthur, ed., *Letters of King Charles II*, Cassell, 1968.

CAMPBELL, John, *Lives of the Admirals and Other Eminent Seamen*, Pemberton, 1742.

CAPP, Bernard, *Cromwell's Navy*, Clarendon Press, 1989.

CARTE, T., *Life of James, Duke of Ormonde, 1610–1688*, Oxford, 1851.

CHARNOCK, *Biographia Navalis*, Faulder, 1794.

CHILDS, John, *The Army of Charles II*, Routledge & Kegan Paul, 1976.

CLOWES, William Laird, *The Royal Navy: A History*, Sampson Low and Marston, 1898.

CORBETT, Sir Julian, ed., *Fighting Instructions 1530–1816*, vol. 29, Navy Records Society, 1905.

DAVIES, J. D., *Gentlemen and Tarpaulins*, Clarendon Press, 1991.

DEWHURST, Kenneth, 'Prince Rupert as a Scientist', *British Journal of the History of Science*, vol. 1, parts i–iv, British Society for the History of Science, 1962–1963.

ERSKINE, Mrs Steuart, *A Royal Cavalier*, Eveleigh Nash, 1910.

ESSON, D. M. R., *The Curse of Cromwell*, Leo Cooper, 1971.

GARDINER, Robert, ed., *The Line of Battle*, Conway Maritime Press, 1992.

GARDNER, Samuel, ed., *Prince Rupert at Lisbon*, Royal Historical Society, 1902.

HALEY, K. D. H., *The First Earl of Shaftesbury*, Clarendon Press, 1968.

HALEY, K. D. H., *The British and the Dutch*, George Philip, 1988.

HANNAY, David, *A Short History of the Royal Navy*, Methuen, 1898.

HAMILTON, Anthony, ed. Sir Walter Scott, *Memoirs of the Count Grammont*, George Routledge, 1905.

HARRIS, F. R., *Edward Mountagu, First Earl of Sandwich*, John Murray, 1912.

HASWELL, Jock, *James II, Soldier and Sailor*, Redwood Press, 1972.

HORNSTEIN, Sari, *The Restoration Navy and English Foreign Trade 1674–1688*, Scolar Press, 1991.

HUTTON, Ronald, *Charles the Second*, Clarendon Press, 1989.

LATHAM, R. C., and MATHEWS, W., eds, *Diary of Samuel Pepys*, vol 1–11, Bell and Son, 1970–1983.

LAVERY, Brian, *The Arming and Fitting of English Ships of War, 1600–1815*, Conway Maritime Press, 1987.

LEWIS, Michael, *England's Sea Officers*, Allen and Unwin, 1939.

MAHAN, A. T., *The Influence of Seapower on History*, Sampson Low Martin, 1918.

MORRAH, Patrick, *Prince Rupert of the Rhine*, Constable, 1976.

OLLARD, Richard, *Clarendon and his Friends*, Hamish Hamilton, 1987.

OLLARD, Richard, *Man of War*, Hodder and Stoughton, 1969.

OLLARD, Richard, *Pepys*, Hodder and Stoughton, 1974.

OLLARD, Richard, *Cromwell's Earl*, Harper Collins, 1994.

O'MALLEY, Leslie Chree, 'The Whig Prince: Prince Rupert and the Court vs Country Factions During the Reign of Charles II', *Albion*, vol. 8, 1976.

POWELL, The Rev. J. R., *Robert Blake*, Collins, 1972.

POWELL, J. R., and TIMINGS, E. K., eds, *The Rupert and Monck Letter Book 1666*, vol. 112, Navy Records Society, 1969.

ROGERS, H. C. B., *Generals-at-Sea*, Galago, 1992.

ROWSE, A. L., *The Early and the Later Churchills*, Reprint Society, 1959.

SCOTT, Eva, *Rupert, Prince Palatine*, Constable, 1904.

TANNER, J. R., ed., *The Naval Manuscripts in the Pepysian Library at Magdalene College, Cambridge*, Naval Records Society, 1923.

TAYLOR, Rear-Admiral A. H., 'The Four Days' Fight and the St James's Day Fight', *Naval Review*, 1953.

TUNSTALL, Brian, ed. TRACY, Nicholas, *Naval Warfare in the Age of Sail*, Conway Maritime Press, 1990.

TURNER, E. R., *The Privy Council of England 1603–1784*, John Hopkins Press, 1927.

WARBURTON, Eliot, *Memoirs of Prince Rupert and the Cavaliers*, Richard Bentley, 1849.

WARWICK, Sir Philip, *Memoirs of the Reign of King Charles I*, James Ballantyne and Co., 1813.

WILSON, Charles, *Profit and Power*, Longman, 1957.

NOTES

Full references to abbreviated entries are given in the Bibliography.

CHAPTER 1 1648

1. Mahan, p. 93.
2. Wilson, pp. 3–6.
3. Haley, *The British and the Dutch*, p. 63.
4. Baumber, p. 112.
5. Ibid., p. 116.
6. Rogers, pp. 6–7.
7. Lavery, p. 114.
8. Rogers, pp. 7–8.
9. Warwick, p. 343.
10. For a detailed account of the revolt of the Parliamentary fleet, see Capp, pp. 15–29.

CHAPTER 2 FROM GENERAL TO ADMIRAL

1. Rogers, p. 28.
2. Scott, p. 230.
3. Capp, p. 38.
4. Timings of events following the arrival of Warwick's ships on 19 September up to the time of their departure on 21 November are confused because of contradictory accounts given in Warburton, vol. 3, pp. 253–4, and in Anderson, *The Royalists at Sea*, vol. 9, pp. 34–46, which itself provides two alternative versions of events. The version given here is an attempt to reconcile these sources together with accounts given in more recent works.
5. Capp, p. 39.
6. Scott, pp. 226–7, quoting a letter from Hyde to Sir Richard Fanshaw.
7. Ibid., p. 234.
8. Ibid., p. 233.
9. Warburton, vol. 3, p. 266.
10. Carte, vol. 3, p. 439.
11. Ibid., p. 440.
12. Gardner, pp. 8–10.
13. Carte, p. 441.
14. Capp, pp. 45–7.
15. Warburton, vol. 3, p. 290.
16. Anderson, *The Royalists at Sea*, vol. 14, p. 327.
17. Esson, p. 84.
18. Scott, p. 234.
19. Warburton, vol. 3, p. 294.
20. Powell, pp. 84–5.
21. This assessment is based on lists given in Baumber, pp. 75–6, and Anderson, *The Royalists at Sea*, vol. 14, pp. 330–3.
22. Powell, pp. 84–5.
23. Warburton, vol. 3, p. 294.
24. Morah, vol. 3, p. 241.
25. Carte, p. 464.
26. Warburton, vol. 3, pp. 294–5, quoting *Prince Rupert's Voyage to the West Indies*.

CHAPTER 3 FROM PORTUGAL TO THE WEST INDIES

1. Gardner, letters B, C and D, pp. 12–17.
2. Powell, p. 93.
3. Baumber, p. 85.
4. Ibid., p. 86.
5. Powell, p. 98.

6. Ibid., p. 98.
7. For a careful balancing of these accounts the reader is referred to Anderson, whose conclusions have been accepted by Powell in his biography of Blake. Anderson, *The Royalists at Sea*, vol. 17, pp. 150–7, and Powell, p. 101.
8. Allin, vol. 1, p. xii.
9. Ollard, *Man of War*, pp. 35–6, discusses the question of likely strengths and opts for a slightly lower figure.
10. Warburton, vol. 3, p. 313.
11. There is some doubt about Blake's movements after he reached Cadiz, one theory being that he returned to Toulon to dissuade the French from assisting Rupert, but this seems unlikely. See Anderson, *The Royalists at Sea*, p. 167.

12. Baumber, p. 90.
13. Anderson, *The Royalists at Sea*, vol. 21, p. 65, quoting Sir Julian Corbett.
14. Details of this council and of the written opinions submitted by the captains are included in a letter written by Rupert's secretary, Captain Pitts, and included in Warburton, vol. 3, pp. 531–8.
15. Bentley Duncan, p. 113.
16. Morrah, p. 260, quoting from *Prince Rupert's Voyage to the West Indies* and from Captain Fearnes's report.
17. Warburton, vol. 3, pp. 348–50.
18. Ibid., pp. 361–2.
19. Morrah, p. 268, and Ollard, *Man of War*, pp. 45–6.
20. Morrah, p. 269, quoting CSPD 1651–1652, p. 309.
21. Capp, p. 117.

CHAPTER 4 LENGTHY INTERLUDE

1. Dewhurst, p. 32.
2. Hutton, pp. 74–5.
3. Ollard, *Man of War*, p. 53.
4. Scott, p. 270.
5. Morrah, p. 282.
6. Ibid., p. 284, based on the Nicholas papers, vol. 11, p. 9.
7. Scott, p. 272, quoting a letter from Hatton to Nicholas of 9 December 1653 and three from Hyde to Nicholas dated 27 February, 13 March and 10 April 1654.

8. Hutton, pp. 81–2.
9. Ollard, *Clarendon and His friends*, p. 158.
10. Morrah, p. 289.
11. Scott, p. 279.
12. Ibid., p. 281.
13. Bryant, *Letters of King Charles II*, p. 51.
14. For an overview of Rupert's activities in this field, see Dewhurst.
15. Morrah, pp. 393–9.

CHAPTER 5 ENGLAND ONCE MORE

1. Turner, vol. 1, p. 377.
2. Ibid., vol. 1, pp. 390 and 405, and vol. 2, pp. 263–4.
3. Morrah, p. 404.
4. Hutton, pp. 157–9.
5. Warburton, vol. 3, pp. 446–58.
6. Hutton, p. 217.
7. Ollard, *Cromwell's Earl*, p. 94.
8. Campbell, vol. 2, p. 416.
9. Davies, p. 10.
10. Ibid., p. 12.
11. Latham and Matthews, vol. 1, p. 55.
12. Mahan, p. 107.
13. Ollard, *Cromwell's Earl*, p. 91.
14. Wilson, p. 111.

15. Haley, *The English and the Dutch*, p. 95.
16. For a more detailed account, see Hutton, pp. 214–18.
17. Ollard, *Man of War*, p. 86.
18. Ibid., p. 125.
19. Morrah, pp. 409–11.
20. British Naval Documents 1204–1960, p. 145.
21. Tunstall, p. 22.
22. Ollard, *Cromwell's Earl*, p. 124.
23. Hutton, pp. 219–20.
24. Ibid., p. 221.

CHAPTER 6 ADMIRAL OF THE WHITE

1. Haswell, p. 158.
2. Tunstall, pp. 8–9.
3. Corbett, p. 96.
4. Morrah, pp. 109–11.
5. For a fuller treatment of the weather gauge, see Gardner, p. 186.
6. Morrah, p. 322, based on Calendar of State Papers, Domestic, 1664–1665, p. 240.
7. Clowes, vol. 2, pp. 256–8.
8. The account of the battle given here is based on a number of different sources, notably Allin, Barlow and Clowes. Also an unpublished manuscript by C. Frewer based largely on Sandwich's journal.
9. Latham and Mathews, vol. 6, pp. 134–5.
10. Scott, p. 310, quoting from Clarendon's *Life*, vol. 2, pp. 402–3.
11. Latham and Mathews, vol. 6, p. 139.
12. Morrah, p. 327.
13. Turner, vol. 1, p. 377.

CHAPTER 7 JOINT COMMAND 1: THE DOGFIGHT

1. Hutton, pp. 223–4.
2. Harris, vol. 1, p. 318.
3. Latham and Mathews, vol. 10, p. 416.
4. For a full account of this business, see Ollard, *Cromwell's Earl*, pp. 140–5.
5. Morrah, p. 230, quoting from Clarendon's *Life*, vol. 2, p. 591.
6. Powell and Timings.
7. Tunstall, p. 26.
8. Powell and Timings, supporting doc. 7, p. 203 (Clarendon Continuation).
9. Ibid., supporting doc. 88, p. 283 (Albemarle to Commons, October 1667).
10. Ibid., supporting docs. 7 and 8 (Coventry, *Recollections*), pp. 203–4. Also Latham and Mathews, vol. 7, p. 514, and fn. 1 and 2.
11. Allin, vol. 2, p. xxii.
12. Taylor, p. 287 et seq.
13. Powell and Timings, supporting doc. 54, p. 246 (Anon. Narrative).
14. Ibid., p. 192, quoting Lewis, *History of the British Navy*, Pelican Books, p. 100.
15. See, for example, accounts written in the 1890s in Mahan, pp. 124–5, Clowes, pp. 275–6, and Hannay, pp. 359–60. Later accounts, such as Anderson's introduction to Allin's *Journals*, vol. 2, 1940, and Powell's and Timing's in the introduction to Part 2 of *The Rupert and Monck Letter Book*, also vary in several particulars. The version given by Taylor, p. 287, recognising the difficulties, gives a good general impression of the battle without going into too much detail.
16. Mahan, p. 126, quoting de Guiche's *Memoires*.
17. Charnock, vol. 1, pp. 122–3.
18. Campbell, vol. 2, p. 257, quoting Wicquefort's *History of the United Provinces*.

CHAPTER 8 JOINT COMMAND 2: THE HARVEST

1. Tunstall, p. 26, fn. 45.
2. Powell and Timings, p. 104. Taylor's statement that the articles were given out at a council held that day in the Sledway in the presence of the King and the Duke of York must be discounted because according to Pepys the Duke of York presided at a meeting in St James's Palace on that day. Furthermore, the fleet was still at the Nore, and the Gunfleet and Sledway were occupied by the Dutch.
3. The paragraphs dealing with the Additional and Further Fighting Instructions are based on Corbett, pp. 129–30, and Tunstall, pp. 26–9. It is important to realise that Corbett mistakenly attributed the Further Instructions to the Duke of York in the run up to the third Dutch War because when he was writing, documentary evidence that they belonged to the earlier period was not available.

4. Allin, vol. 2, pp. xxvii–iii, reconciles conflicting opinions regarding the position of the two fleets.
5. The account of the St James's Day battle given here is based on a number of contemporary accounts, notably that given in Allin's *Journal*, vol. 1; *Naval Operations in the Latter Part of 1666*, probably written by Sir Thomas Mostyn and edited by R. C. Anderson, in the Navy Records Society's *Naval Miscellany III*; and in the supporting documents to *The Rupert and Monck Letter Book* Nos 75 (Rupert and Albemarle Dispatch), 78 (*London Gazette*, 28 July 1666), 79 (Anon. Narrative) and 81 (Clifford to Arlington, 27 July 1666). It also draws on the account given by Taylor and that given by Anderson in the introduction to vol. 2 of Allin's *Journal*.
6. For a full account of this raid, see Ollard, *Man of War*, pp. 148–61.
7. Latham and Mathews, vol. 7, p. 312.
8. Ibid., p. 316.
9. Davies, pp. 146–7.

CHAPTER 9 THE YEARS BETWEEN

1. Hutton, p. 242.
2. P. G. Rogers, *The Dutch in the Medway*, Oxford University Press, 1970, p. 142.
3. Copies of both reports can be found in the British Museum's Additional Manuscripts 32094 ff 197 and 202. They are also included as supporting documents 88 and 93 in *The Rupert and Monck Letter Book* ed. Powell and Timings.
4. Davies, pp. 149–50.
5. O'Malley, p. 336, referring to a letter written by Marvell, MP for Hull, to the mayor and aldermen.
6. Latham and Mathews, vol. 9, p. 5.
7. Ibid., p. 39.
8. Turner, vol. 2, pp. 267–8.
9. Hamilton, pp. 323–4. The 1965 Deakin edition and translation of these memoirs – they originally appeared in French – is less vivid although better attuned to modern thinking.
10. Christopher Hibbert, *The Court at Windsor*, Allen Lane, 1977, p. 66.
11. Haley, p. 228.
12. Ibid., p. 229.
13. Ibid., p. 231. Mrs Erskine, *A Royal Cavalier*, Eveleigh Nash, 1910, pp. 364–5. Also Morrah, pp. 384–5.
14. Hutton, pp. 249 and 256.
15. O'Malley, p. 337.
16. Ibid.
17. Ibid.
18. Evelyn, diary for 28 August 1670, p. 349.
19. Morrah, p. 419.

CHAPTER 10 THE THIRD DUTCH WAR

1. Anderson, *Journals and Narratives of the Third Dutch War*, pp. 6–7.
2. British Naval Documents 1204–1960, doc. 118.
3. Ibid., doc. 119.
4. Childs, pp. 181 and 234.
5. Hutton, p. 295.
6. Anderson, *Journals and Narratives of the Third Dutch War*, introduction, pp. 32–6, together with relevant parts of the journals of Spragge, Haddock and Legge have been the main source for this account of the First Battle of Schooneveld, which was even more confused and complicated than described.
7. W. D. Christie, ed., *Letters Addressed from London to Sir Joseph Williamson while Plenipotentiary at the Congress of Cologne, 1673–1674*, 2 vols, 1965. Yard to Williamson, 13 June 1673. This was one of a number of letters dealing with the conduct of the war, the veracity of which varies according to the writers' sources of information.
8. Ibid., Ball to Williamson, 13 June.
9. Hutton, p. 304, quoting the authority

of Ekberg, *Louis XIV's Dutch War*, pp. 24 and 157.

10. Bryant, *Letters of King Charles II*, p. 267. NB The original of this document in Pepys's handwriting is correctly dated 16 July, but when it was included in a collection of papers the covering note gave the date as 26 July, which was erroneously attributed to the document itself in the book edited by Bryant.

11. Ibid., p. 268.

12. Anderson, *Journals and Narratives of the Third Dutch War*, p. 382. See also the Introduction to the Calendar of State Papers 1673.

13. This account of the battle is largely drawn from the *Journals and Narratives of the Third Dutch War*, ed. Anderson.

CHAPTER 11 THE FINAL YEARS

1. A contemporary manuscript copy is in the library of the Royal Naval College formerly at Greenwich. A printed copy is included in *Journals and Narratives of the Third Dutch War*, ed. Anderson.

2. It is likely that J.B. was John Brookes who, as captain of the *Greenwich*, had fought in Holmes's division of Rupert's squadron at the St James's Day battle in 1666. According to *Biographia Navalis* he was captain of the *Mary* in 1672 and may have been with this ship in the early stages of the 1673 campaign. Furthermore, the *Mary* was one of only two ships of the line that changed from the Blue Squadron to the Red between the Schooneveld battles and the Texel. But at the Texel, according to J.B.'s own account, she was commanded by Roger Strickland, which raises a problem.

3. Leopold von Ranke, *History of England Principally in the Seventeenth Century*, Clarendon Press, 1875, vol. 3, p. 547.

4. O'Malley, p. 341.

5. Morrah, p. 422.

6. Tanner, vol. 4, contains the minutes

of all these meetings together with their locations.

7. Dewhurst, pp. 368–9, gives details of these inventions and experiments.

8. Arthur Bryant, *Samuel Pepys, the Years of Peril*, pp. 161–9.

9. O'Malley, p. 344, quoting the 'Diary of the Duke of York', Original Papers, ed. J. Macpherson, 1776.

10. O'Malley, p. 343.

11. Tanner, vol. 4, p. 494.

12. Ibid., pp. 535–6.

13. For a more detailed understanding of the role and various categories of midshipman at this time, see Lewis, pp. 82–7 and 216–21.

14. Hornstein, p. 265. This study includes a valuable account of naval events in the Mediterranean at this time.

15. Ibid., p. 184–94.

16. Ibid., p. 138.

17. O'Malley, p. 346.

18. Ibid., p. 349.

19. Hutton, p. 400.

20. Morrah, p. 425, and Dewhurst, p. 369.

21. Morrah, p. 425.

22. Campbell, pp. 421–2.

23. Rowse, p. 123.

INDEX